To Faith and Vicki,

To our mirror-couple — a good
Midwesterner and a not-so-good Jew,
or maybe I'm just projecting.

CLARA
MONDSCHEIN'S
MELANCHOLIA

A Novel by Anne Raeff

MacAdam/Cage Publishing
155 Sansome Street, Suite 550
San Francisco, CA 94104
www.macadamcage.com
Copyright © 2002 by Anne Raeff
ALL RIGHTS RESERVED.

Library of Congress Cataloging-in-Publication Data

Raeff, Anne, 1959 —
    Clara Mondschein's melancholia / by Anne Raeff.
        p. cm.
    ISBN 1-931561-16-8 (hardback: alk. paper)
    1. Children of Holocaust survivors–Fiction.
    2. Mothers and daughters–Fiction. 3. Holocaust survivors–Fiction. I.
    4. New York (N.Y.)–Fiction. 5. Teenage girls–Fiction. 6. Suburban
    life–Fiction. 7. Jewish women–Fiction. 8. New Jersey–Fiction. I.Title.

PS3618.A36 C53 2002
813'.6–dc21

                                                    2002005120

Manufactured in the United States of America.
10 9 8 7 6 5 4 3 2 1

Book and jacket design by Dorothy Carico Smith.

Grateful acknowledgment is made to New Directions Publishing Corp for permission to reprint three lines from "Dreamwork Three" by Jerome Rothenberg
from Khurbn & Other Poems, Copyright © 1989 by Jerome Rothenberg.
Reprinted by permission of New Directions Publishing Corp.

CLARA MONDSCHEIN'S MELANCHOLIA

A Novel by Anne Raeff

MacAdam/Cage

To Lori Ostlund, my harshest critic:
For her honesty, her friendship, and her love.
Enough said.

Author's Note

Pribor is a small village in the former Czechoslovakia about fifty miles (or approximately eighty kilometers) from Auschwitz (the Polish town of Oswiecim). I have chosen this village as the site of my fictional concentration camp so I could pull together the events and circumstances of various camps without tampering with historical facts.

The man with a fish between his teeth dreams of famine for
Forty-five days
The man dressed in white dreams of a potato

—From "Dreamwork Three"
Khurbn & Other Poems
Jerome Rothenberg

PART I

THE SONATA
OF THE
BROKEN-FOOTED
SOLDIERS

MRS. MONDSCHEIN AND TOMMY
AT THE CHRISTOPHER STREET
AIDS HOSPICE

February 1996

One sloppy step, one tiny obstacle like a used syringe or a cigarette butt (people have fallen over even smaller objects) and it could be the end. One more flight and I'll be safe. Safe until tomorrow. My daughter Clara thinks I'm crazy for insisting on making this journey—the six flights of stairs down and up everyday, no matter what the weather. She tells me she'll bring me groceries and the newspaper, but I don't take on the stairs for the groceries or the newspaper. Why do people climb Mount Everest or jump out of airplanes during peacetime? It's not because they have nothing better to do. I like my stairs. I like the worn-out marble covered with years of soot and urine and spilled beer. I like the cracks and chips, and the wobbly banister makes the climb particularly thrilling, for it could never be counted on to break a fall or reestablish balance. Ironic, isn't it, that I spent a good ten years in court trying to get us an elevator, and now I'm happy I failed? My stairs are a familiar reminder—life should never be too easy.

Last year on my eighty-fifth birthday, Clara took me to visit what she calls a *very nice retirement community* just five minutes from her house in New Jersey. Everyone had his own studio apartment and there was a music room, and gardens, and a library, and apparently all sorts of educated people too although I didn't see anyone reading a book or even having a conversation. But I have an apartment, the same one we've had since my husband, daughter, and I came to this country in 1947—a large two-bedroom with a view of the Hudson. Why would I trade this for a little box in New Jersey? If I ended up breaking my hip or losing my mind in the Colonial Manor, I would be stuck. Here, a fall would be fatal, so I won't have to worry about sitting in a wheelchair, a wool blanket covering my legs, with nothing to do but stare out the window.

Luckily for me, Clara hasn't been trying to convince me of the Colonial Manor's virtues too much lately. She is in one of her depressions again, so she has been doing a lot of staring out of the window herself. She just watches the cars go by their house. She says she likes the sound of cars on wet asphalt. But when I hear them—*swish, swish*—all I can think of are women in fancy dresses waltzing. Waltzes never intrigued me much, not even when I was a young girl in Vienna, and my sisters and their friends dreamed of going to the *Opernball*. They would have died for an opportunity to go even though none of us from the hunched, kosher Second District would have ever been allowed in the door. It's funny that I was the one who ended up learning to waltz and wear fancy dresses while they stayed, unmarried and drab, in our almost windowless apartment, nursing my father through his long, debilitating illness. And when he was finally dead, my two sisters had run out of time. It was 1938, so in fact we all had run out of time.

So how can my daughter sit there day after day, not even dressed for life in an old robe and slippers, watching the cars go by? She does not know what it is like to wait. Yesterday on the phone she told me that she wished she were an old woman so she wouldn't have to worry about doing meaningful things. I hung up on her and she didn't call back. Does she think my life has no meaning? Who spends Mondays, Wednesdays, and Fridays at the Christopher Street AIDS Hospice? Who is heading for the hospice at this very moment after having braved the stairs? Who is sitting on the IRT squooshed between two sullen businessmen, probably from New Jersey, with their legs wide apart so there's hardly any room for me to sit? Who reads the *New York Times* every day and keeps lists upon lists of new words and idioms? (English is such a rich and mind-confounding language.)

I started coming to the hospice about a year ago, just after Karl died. He had set aside some money for AIDS causes and asked me to find the best place for it. It wasn't much, but it wasn't just a little either. It gave me something to do in those first months after he died. Every day I went to a different place, asked them about their services, spoke to people. I decided on the hospice because they needed the money the most. It seems people would rather donate money to research or education. There is something about hopeless cases that does not attract large donations. It surprised me, actually. I thought our human sense of pity would be most moved by those who were so visibly sick, so on the edge of death.

You get to know people fast here at the hospice, I suppose since there's not much time. The dying tell me their life stories in a few hours and then in a week they're dead. It's as if they haven't ever told anyone anything about themselves, so eager are they to tell me—a stranger. Of course there are some patients who always have a lot of visitors. I rarely talk to them, but since I am a nurse by training, I help the nurses attend to their medical needs. I'm glad I didn't have to give up working. All those years of working from dawn to dusk and it's hard to get used to being idle. I wonder if some of the patients, some of whom are only a quarter my age, resent being ministered to by an eighty-five-year-old woman. But I don't think so. Why would they tell me so much if they resented me?

There's a new patient, Tommy, who doesn't talk much and doesn't get any visitors as far as I can tell. He has three suitcases full of CDs, which he listens to morning, afternoon, and night on a CD Walkman. Today I've brought him a new CD—some late Haydn symphonies played by the Vienna Philharmonic. The only things I know about Tommy are that he likes music and he's not demented; I can tell by his eyes.

Tommy was very happy with the Haydn CD, and before I could say anything else, he insisted on plugging us both into his Walkman—me into one side and him into the other—so by the time the CD was finished, it was time for lunch. I fed him very carefully and slowly. He only ate twenty bites. I counted.

After lunch, I thought Tommy would want some sleep, but he said he was not at all tired—"feeling kind of chipper" was how he put it. Then he asked me if I had any good stories to tell him. "I'm in the mood for a good story," he said. "But I want it to be something moving and true."

"How are you going to know if I'm telling you the truth?" I asked.

"I won't," and then he got a sly grin on his face, "but you wouldn't want to fool a dying man, would you?"

"No, of course not, though I'm afraid I don't have any interesting stories that I feel like telling right now."

"So you do have interesting stories, but you just don't feel like telling me them?"

"Not exactly." He was right; it's almost impossible to lie to an AIDS patient. "I only have one story really, but it's very long and melodramatic,

3

I'm afraid."

"Aren't all good stories long and melodramatic? I mean, just look at Dickens. What a bunch of long and melodramatic swill, but I love it. Do you like Dickens?" he asked me.

"Yes, of course, but sentimentality was cultivated in the nineteenth century. Our own century is so intolerant by comparison."

"Well," he said, "I'm a faggot, remember, and faggots love a good tearjerker, so please, Mrs. Mondschein, without further ado, I'm all ears." And I pulled my chair up close to the bed so that only Tommy would be able to hear my words.

I realize now that there were plenty of stories to tell: about my neighbors, about the children of the Korean fruit-stand owners, about the old woman I met the other day who was trying to carry a door, which I helped her do without questioning her purpose. We carried the door up four flights of stairs. No one asked whether we needed help. We left the door in the middle of her apartment amidst heaps of red milk cartons, doorknobs, half a dozen mangled shopping carts. But I didn't mention any of that, since every true New Yorker has dozens of similar stories. I had no choice but to tell Tommy the only real story I knew. Perhaps I thought my story would have a kind of cathartic effect on Tommy, like a good play or novel, but it would be dishonest and arrogant to insist that my main purpose for speaking was to help him, for, in fact, as soon as I began to speak, I felt a calm that I have not felt since Karl's death. Tommy's company made me think of sitting in the living room with Karl at dusk, talking quietly about the day's events or not talking at all, just sitting next to each other at the end of a day. And thinking of Karl made me think of Clara and how she could never appreciate such a simple thing as sitting in a room at dusk. I guess Clara and her depressions were on my mind because she had been going through a particularly bad phase since her return from Spain at the end of the summer. In any case, it was with Clara that I found myself beginning.

"Karl used to say it was our fault that Clara has these bouts with depression."

"Hold on a minute now. Who's Karl?" Tommy said, putting his hand gently on mine. It was freezing. I guess that's why they always keep the heat turned up.

"I'm sorry. How silly of me. My husband. Karl's my husband, was my husband. He died about a year ago."

"And who's Clara?"

"My daughter."

"Okay, now you can continue."

"Thank you," I said rather formally. "'We never should have told her,' he would say, and sometimes we would argue about it. But what could we have done after the fact? We had both agreed; we believed in telling the truth. And we both thought it would make her strong, give her a sense of pride, of hope."

"What would make her strong?"

"I'm sorry," I said. "Since Karl's death, I haven't spoken much. It has been a very private tale, one I know so well that I forget I have to explain. You see, my daughter Clara was born in a concentration camp—Pribor. Karl, my husband . . ."

"Yes, I remember."

"Karl and I were hiding for most of the war, at a sanatorium. His friend was the director. But I'm getting ahead of things. I don't want to get ahead of things."

"I can understand. Sorry I interrupted."

"No, I wasn't being clear. I'll try to be clearer," I said and paused for a moment, trying to think where to start. "Okay, when Clara was old enough, eight or nine, we told her, 'Your birth was a symbol of our rebirth,' and, at first, we thought she understood. She started reading the Old Testament; she insisted on Hebrew lessons, and later she begged us for a bat mitzvah. If it had been up to us, we would have abandoned religion altogether, but rituals seemed to give Clara a sense of purpose, so we joined a synagogue, let her have the bat mitzvah. It wasn't difficult, really.

"For a while Clara tried to get us to move to Israel. She left little notes all around the apartment—in our underwear drawers, in the sugar bowl, in the coffeepot. Everywhere we turned, there was a note about Israel. If it had not been for New York, we would have gone. If we had settled in Cleveland or even Philadelphia, we might have given in, but Karl and I could not leave New York—not the concerts and our favorite hall at the Metropolitan Museum. The room with Bruegel's *Winter Scene* was as close as we could get to the old Vienna, to those few years we had between my dreary childhood in the Second District and the War. In New York there was the Eclair, where you still can get the only good *Wienerschnitzel* in town, even if it is cooked by Hungarians. Have you ever been there?"

"No, I'm afraid not."

"Well, I will just have to take you one day."

"Please, Mrs. Mondschein. I can only stand listening to the truth."

"I'm sorry, Tommy. I was trying to be polite, which, I realize, is a great insult. Please forgive me."

"Forgiven," Tommy said. "Please continue."

"So we waited out Clara's Israel campaign. By the time she was in high school, she hardly spoke of it at all, and by the time she started City College, she had apparently forgotten about Israel completely. She studied to be an English teacher at City College, but she also had quite a bit of promise as a poet. When she was still a very young child, maybe seven or eight, she started her first poetry notebook and every evening she would read her latest creation to us. She was best when she wrote about the city and the people in our neighborhood, whom she knew but not well, like the super and the man and woman who owned the stationery store. She made up little lives for them. Once when she had the flu, she wrote a series of poems from the points of view of various parts of her body—the aching those parts felt and what they would do when they were better and could return to running in the park and eating chocolate. But when she was thirteen, right after her bat mitzvah, she stopped showing us her poetry, and we thought that she had lost interest in writing even though she always had a book of poetry by her desk.

"At about that time, when we thought she had stopped writing poetry, she asked whether she could help us at our clinic. Karl was a general practitioner in the Bronx. Every week, it seemed, he got ten new patients. They loved him. He was gentle and didn't charge much if there was no insurance. Karl was pleased that she was interested in our work and he agreed that, after school, she would take the subway to our clinic, where she would help us until we left, which was often not until eight or nine at night. Karl often let her observe when he was attending patients. He taught her to listen to the heart and look into ears and eyes and noses and to take blood pressure and even draw blood, which she did so naturally, finding the vein and slipping the needle in before the patient even knew she had done so. She was very proud of her blood-drawing abilities and we were amazed at how quickly she learned to do it, and Karl started dropping hints about how she would make a good surgeon, but she would never acknowledge his compliments. Then one night I caught her practicing on herself. I had been up late reading and, on my way to the bedroom, I noticed that her light was still on, so I knocked and entered without waiting for her to respond, which is what I should have done. She was sitting on the edge of her bed with the needle in her arm. On the night table a candle was burning and in front of the candle was a glass filled with blood.

"'What are you doing?' I asked her.

"'Nothing,' she answered, pulling the needle out of her arm and applying pressure to the vein with a tissue as we had taught her.

"'Do you have any idea how dangerous this is?' I asked.

"'I know the limit. I looked it up.'

"'I don't want you to do this again. Is that clear?' I spoke sternly but did not raise my voice because I never raised my voice with Clara. Since infancy, she has been sensitive to noise. And then I left her alone because I was afraid to ask her about the glass and the candle.

"I did not tell Karl what I had seen because I knew how much he enjoyed her help at the clinic, so Clara helped us until she finished high school and went to City College. I think Karl was somewhat surprised when she announced that she was going to be a teacher, but he never pressured her about studying medicine. That was not in his nature.

"Clara's depressions began soon after I found her drawing her own blood—on her fourteenth birthday—and they continued to fall each year around her birthday. She would lock herself in her room around the ninth or tenth of February and not emerge until the day after her birthday, which is the twelfth. She wouldn't eat or wash. She kept a bedpan under the bed, which I discovered once while cleaning her room about a week after one of her bouts. She had forgotten to wash it out, so her urine and feces were still in it, encrusted and stinking. I cleaned it thoroughly and returned it to its place underneath the bed without saying a word to her about it. I wonder whether she noticed that it had been cleaned or whether she had forgotten that she had left it there. I can't imagine, though, why she wouldn't have noticed the smell. Maybe the smell was part of what she was trying to create. During these rituals, she also turned the radiator off and kept the windows wide open, so you could see your breath in the room. Otherwise, we never knew what she did in there all those days. We put our ears up against the wall to listen for clues, but it was always silent. No crying.

"We decided not to harp on these yearly observances. Perhaps that was a mistake too. Was it that she wanted us to knock the door down with our bare fists? Did she want us to cry and scream, to plead with her? Yet she always emerged from her room rejuvenated, full of energy, eager to get back to her books. She would go shopping then, birthday shopping, I suppose, bringing back an expensive suit from Bergdorf Goodman's. We always bought her books for her birthday—German literature, mostly. She read them all, all the classics—Goethe, Schiller, Heine. Do you know German literature, Tommy?"

"When I was a young man, I read Rilke, but that was a long time ago," Tommy said without a hint of nostalgia.

"Yes, Rilke, a poet for one's youth. I would be afraid to read Rilke today."

"If you are afraid to read Rilke, Mrs. Mondschein, then that is precisely what you should do," Tommy said. "Look at me, afraid of dying, and that is what I will have to do. But I'm being self-indulgent. Now it is your turn to forgive me. Please, continue," he said, propping himself higher up on his pillows.

"We wanted to be sure she had nothing against the German language and those who had died long before the insanity of the twentieth century. So many of our compatriots refuse to utter a word in German—still, to this day, not even a word. It is as if they believe the language itself were to blame. But we were not able to convince Clara about German. On the contrary, the more we insisted, the more she resisted until we gave up, left her to her British poets and Italian composers. She became, at a very young age, like those poor old people who, in their youths, braved all their adolescent fears and anxieties accompanied by Mozart or Beethoven or Mahler or Bach, yet, in their lonely old age, wait out their last days in drafty apartments, reading mystery novels and listening to

Puccini. Can you imagine dying to Puccini?"

"I can imagine it, Mrs. Mondschein, very vividly in fact, although I agree with you—the German masters are better for pain."

"I'm sorry, Tommy. I hope you don't feel I'm being insensitive, but if I am going to continue, I have to be perfectly frank."

"I wouldn't want anything short of frankness, Mrs. Mondschein." Tommy laughed.

"Good, because that's what you're going to get," I said, laughing along with him. "I've tried to talk to Clara about the music, especially since my granddaughter is a cellist. Karl and I were never like that. Once a month we would make a special trip to Bremen Haus in Yorkville to stock up on German chocolates and marzipan. I think we loved Mozart, especially Mozart, even more in exile. But where was I? The depressions. Yes, the depressions. Perhaps you would prefer to listen to another CD?"

"I can listen to a CD when you're gone. Please continue."

"Are you sure? Well, if you insist. Shall I continue?" I asked eagerly.

"Please do, Mrs. Mondschein. Please do," Tommy said, bowing in his bed.

"It was only after Clara's marriage that the long bouts of depression began, the long bouts that lasted for an entire year—an entire year of lying in bed. Her marriage surprised us. We did not even know that she and Simon were . . . what is the term they use today? Involved? He seemed to us more like a brother or friend for Clara. They studied together and he taught her Hebrew and Talmud, two subjects that Kar l and I knew very little about. We all called him the Tutor, even Clara. In those days he still wore a yarmulke, which made him look like both a boy and an old man.

"Then one evening when we were all eating dinner together, Clara announced that they had gotten married that afternoon, and Simon shyly told us that they had rented a small apartment farther uptown. After dinner they sat next to each other on the sofa holding hands and we drank a toast to their life together. It was about half a year afterwards that Simon came to tell us about Clara's depression. She had stopped going to her classes, stopped bathing, stopped talking. He looked like he hadn't slept in days and he needed a bath as well. We sat him down at the kitchen table and gave him some tea, but when he lifted the cup to his lips, his hand shook so much that he spilled it all over the table. This made him even more distraught. Though I assured him that it was not important, he kept apologizing for spilling the tea and interrupting our 'quiet evening.' Then he put his hands over his eyes and started weeping. After a few minutes, Karl and I both got up and stood near him, one on each side, and this seemed to calm him down. Then he stood up and put his hands on the table and addressed us. I remember thinking that he looked like a professor about to begin a lecture. He told us about the bedpan and about how he emptied it every morning and about how she refused to let him change the sheets and how he slept on the floor next to the bed and about the smell that came from her mouth and from other places. We should have stopped him because the details were not the point, but we listened like students until he was finished. And then he looked at his watch and jumped up, frantic—it was late and Clara would be worried—and then he thanked us for the tea and he was gone. That was the only time that Simon ever came to us for help. I suppose he realized that he was better suited for Clara than we were, and we did not want to interfere because Simon was so very patient.

"Still, years later, when Deborah was born, we thought that Clara might change and we tried to impress upon her that a child was a great responsibility. 'Think of Deborah,' Karl and I used to say, but she would always say that she *was* thinking of her. She didn't want her daughter to grow up with a false impression of life. 'Then move to the city,' I would argue. 'No, the schools are better in the suburbs,' she would reply, but that's an excuse they all use out there. They really do want to give their children and themselves the wrong impression of life—clipped lawns with Japanese shrubbery, Formica countertops, driveways, computerized alarm systems to keep the city at bay.

"Clara is always trying to get me to move out of my apartment, especially now that Karl is gone, and I haven't even told her that just last month someone followed me up the stairs, pushed into the apartment with me, stole my television and cash, and locked me in the closet. It took me three hours to bash the door down, and my shoulder was bruised for weeks afterwards. It seems they're selling crack up on the roof now, so there are all sorts of unsavory people tramping in and out of the building at all hours of the day and night. I didn't bother reporting it to the police since I know it doesn't do any good. The only person who knows about it is Mr. Claromundo, my friend next door. He's been living here almost as long as I have, and we're the only ones who appear at court about the lack of heat and the holes in the ceiling and the cracks on the stairs. Mr. Claromundo loves to tell me about his son who lives in New Jersey too, and about his grandchildren and his little village in the Dominican Republic. Every Christmas he goes back. He often talks about building a little house in the Dominican Republic and staying there for good, but I think he knows he has come to need New York as so many of us immigrants do.

"Of course, Clara will never know that my television was stolen since she never comes here anymore. And I don't mind—it's better if I go there. I like the trip—a nice walk to the George Washington Bridge Bus Station and then the half an hour on the bus. Sometimes I make a bet at the OTB office even though I have no idea what I'm doing. I just like waiting on line with all the men analyzing the racing section of the newspaper, smoking cigarettes and cigars. I like the smell of smoke every once in a while; it reminds me of Vienna, the cafés, the wine cellars. Karl and I used to smoke in those days, which scandalized my father and sisters; in their eyes, it was almost worse than eating pork, which we did too, though I never told my family that. And would Clara's life have been so different if we hadn't told her about her beginnings? Would she instead have run off to Israel to live on a Kibbutz and marry a Sephardi with whom she would have had loads of children? Would one of my grandchildren have been killed by a suicide bomber? Would she have had the strength to go without us? Or perhaps the depressions are just genetic, a legacy of the Second District, of my father and my two sisters. Though sometimes I think my sisters were the prophets, and I the fool who could not knit calmly in the dark sitting room where my father lay for over a year, dying of an incomprehensible illness that Karl called *melancholia*, for lack of a better word.

"That's how Karl and I met. He was my father's doctor and he came to check up on him religiously though he always said there was nothing wrong with him except for the *melancholia*. In those days, Karl was extremely interested in psychology. He knew Freud. Can you imagine? But my father's death discouraged him terribly, particularly because Karl had even tried hypnosis and begged my father to see Dr. Freud. Karl insisted that he could make the appointments himself, pay for everything, but my father simply shook his head. He already had lost his desire to speak. Of course, it was not only my father's death that changed Karl. That was just the beginning.

"In the months before his death, my father would lie on the couch staring at the clock, crying quietly, always shivering, while my sisters knitted numerous blankets and piled them high on top of him. Still, the shivering never stopped. Sometimes my father would mutter something about how *our time* was coming soon. My sisters refused to leave the house, refused to leave his bedside. 'When he dies, we will no longer be able to live,' they said, and it sounded almost biblical to me. When I entered the apartment, trying to stifle the sound of my heels on the floor, they would shake their heads sadly. They muttered about the smell of cigarette smoke in my hair and the books they found by my bedside. 'You should spend more time with your father,' they said as if he weren't their father, too. 'There is so little time left.'

"It seemed they never slept, neither Sarah, the middle one, nor Clara, the youngest, nor my father. They did not leave the sitting room, and they did not sleep either. The day my father died, the blankets had reached almost to the dusty chandelier.

"We never told Clara about my father and my sisters, not exactly, just that they all died, but not that my father had actually died just before the *Anschluss*. You know what the *Anschluss* is, of course? When the Germans annexed Austria in 1938?"

Tommy nods.

"She knows my sisters died in the camps. What if we had told her all the yellowed details of their lives instead? Would that have made it better? Was there a part of us that could predict how she would take our gift to her, a part of us that hoped it would *not* give her hope, a part of us that was sick of hope, that watched the enslavement of the Palestinians with disgust, that believed that hope was the scourge of humanity? And perhaps it is. Do you think so?"

When he didn't answer, I looked over at Tommy. "Finally you're sleeping," I said, dropping my voice to a whisper. "I'm sorry. I know I talk too much, and you, don't you have anything to say ever? Tomorrow, no

Wednesday, on Wednesday when I visit, you will tell me things. I didn't mean to make you so tired. I should not be talking to you of such things."

"Mrs. Mondschein, I'm not sleeping, just closing my eyes," Tommy said dreamily.

"Are you sure you were just relaxing, not sleeping?"

"Absolutely positive. Please continue."

"Very well," I said, beginning slowly, making sure Tommy really was listening. "Karl did come to believe that it was a mistake to have told Clara about the circumstances of her birth. The night before he died, he even said that we should have known she would take it the wrong way. Was that why he worked eleven or twelve, sometimes even fifteen or sixteen, hours a day, seven days a week? Was he trying to convince himself that his work made a difference, that prolonging life made a difference? But there are so many things we never allowed ourselves to discuss, not even at the end. It was as if Clara's birth in that cold bunker in Pribor had been enough to keep us together all those years. It was as if the miracle of her birth—and we always saw it as a miracle, had to see it that way or it would have torn everything apart, ripped it all to shreds until there was nothing left—it was as if the simple fact that I had given birth in a concentration camp, and that neither I nor Clara had died, was enough. It was as if the fact that Clara never cried, despite the cold and my dried-up breasts, the fact that she took the bread I chewed for her in my own mouth without a complaint, without even a twitch, despite the fact that she lived practically soaked in excrement the first week of her life because we could not risk cleaning the blankets in which she lay, the fact that they did not discover her, that she was not taken away, the fact that they believed we had murdered her as the prisoners had murdered all the other babies born in that terrible place, as if all that was enough. But I am tired now, and this time you are surely sleeping."

I stayed with Tommy a little longer, watching him sleep, listening to his tired breathing, rubbing his hand to warm him up, softly so as not to wake him.

DEBORAH GELB IN NEW JERSEY

February 1996

When I was younger, I wished I had been born in a concentration camp like my mother, instead of in boring Englewood Hospital. I used to imagine all the prisoners crying mutely with joy while my grandmother lay swallowing her screams so the guards wouldn't hear. But that was before we spent this past summer in Madrid, before I befriended George Liddy, whom I still consider my best friend even though I haven't seen or heard from him in half a year and even if he is about three times my age and can't go for more than one or two hours without a drink.

"Deborah," he said when I told him about my mother's miraculous birth. "When I was a child, I wanted to be Jesus Christ. That was before I discovered Yeats and my next-door neighbor Frankie Farley, of course." George Liddy is a poet, a prose poet who has published what he describes as "a few slim volumes."

"During Maths class while the other children daydreamed of riding their bicycles, I longed to be hanging from the cross, my hands and feet bleeding, my lips parched, wallowing in the taste of vinegar."

"There's a girl in my school who mutilates herself. She has scars on her arms and legs and on the back of her neck like some Africans have," I said.

"Ah, Deborah, suffering is ultimately so unimaginative. Poor Jesus. He thought his suffering could save the world, when, in fact, it has nearly destroyed it."

The circumstances of my own birth were, in comparison to my mother's, completely uneventful except that my father could not be present because he was giving a lecture at NYU about the importance of Abraham and Isaac in both Jewish and Islamic theology. My father has devoted his life to studying the intrinsic similarities between Judaism and Islam and thinks that pointing out these similarities to others contributes to what he calls the *Peace Process*. If you ask me, all religions are intrinsically the same, and we would all be much better off without any of them. My father says most people have a need for religion and that it is unrealistic to try to convince them to give up on religion altogether, but I think that's because he envies people who can believe. I think he thinks that if he devotes his whole life to studying religion, something might happen, he might make that leap of faith, have an epiphany or whatever you call it. I guess all I can do is hope that it never happens.

Anyway, to continue the story of my birth, my mother wasn't even conscious because they had to do a Caesarean section since I was breached. "Doing everything upside down right from the beginning," my grandmother likes to say. When I was little, maybe until I was in middle school, I used to believe my mother when she told me about how she remembered the first week of her life—the cold, the smell, the hunger pangs. And when I was in the fourth and fifth grades, at least two or three times a week, I would sit on the bare floor in the bathroom with my legs crossed and my palms upward like the Buddhas in the Metropolitan Museum, trying to remember the first week of my own life. I had read that meditation could help bring back the most distant memories, even memories of past lives. That was when I believed in reincarnation because my fourth-grade teacher told us that she had been a Navajo weaver in her past life. Apparently this had been revealed to her in a dream. She had gone to New Mexico during Christmas vacation that year, which is where she had the dream, and, when we returned from break, we started a unit on the Navajos. She had us make little looms out of sticks and she pushed all the desks and chairs up against the wall and made us do all our work sitting on the floor. Every morning after the National Anthem and the Pledge of Allegiance, we played little mournful tunes on our recorders. In any case, I tried meditating, but I could never recall anything before the day the raccoon fell down our chimney and was running loose and scared in the house until my father finally lured it out into the garage. I had wanted to keep it as a pet, but my parents said that it might have rabies, which made me scared of raccoons for years. I was three when that happened.

Because of the circumstances of my mother's birth, Yom Hashoah, which is Holocaust Memorial Day, and my mother's birthday are the only two holidays we celebrate in our house. It wasn't until the second grade, when I met Amy, who is my oldest and only friend except for George Liddy (and maybe Mercedes, though that's a whole other story), that I realized the Holocaust and Yom Hashoah are not really the focal points of Judaism. I didn't even know that Judaism was a religion until I met Amy, and her parents invited me to temple. We never go to temple. We don't celebrate Pesach or Yom Kippur or light the Sabbath candles, except on Yom Hashoah and on my mother's birthday. I never knew about that stuff until I met Amy, but I can't remember a time when I didn't know about Pribor and about the Six Million. I swear I knew about the Six Million before I could count. It was like the name of a familiar food—the Six Million.

Both Yom Hashoah and my mother's birthday are celebrated in the same way: We turn off all the heat in the house and open all the windows, and we have to wear shorts so that we're really cold. Then we decorate the house with photographs of dead relatives and pictures that I drew of concentration camp life—black crayon on white typing paper. We still use the same pictures every year although it's been about three years since I've drawn anything new. For twenty-four hours, we don't eat anything except stale bread, which my mother chews first and then spits into our mouths. During my mother's birthday celebration, just a week ago, I nearly vomited during that part, but I closed my eyes, swallowed quickly, and pretended I was eating my favorite dessert—these couscous biscuits topped with honey and nuts that my father makes on special occasions.

For the feeding part of the ceremony, my father and I lie on the floor and close our eyes while my mother chews the bread and puts it into our mouths—first one piece for me, then one for my father, then one for me, then one for him, until we have each consumed one thin slice of stale bread. When I was young, I thought of the rituals as a kind of theater and wondered why my father and I always played the role of the newborn baby in our family drama. Finally, when I was in third grade, I asked my father why we didn't feed my mother instead of the other way around. "It is a way for us to get closer to your mother" was his answer. "It is almost a way for us to become her." After he told me that, I was afraid my father and I would actually turn into my mother. When it was my turn to be fed, I repeated my name in my head over and over again, to convince my own brain that I was not my mother and did not want to become her. I really thought that if I let it happen, I would actually be her—look like her, talk like her, that there would be two of her and none of me. I was worried about my father too, so I started watching my mother feeding my father when it was his turn. I thought that if something happened and my father started transforming before my eyes, I would be able to do something to stop it. By the time I got to middle school, it started making me feel weird to watch my mother feed my father, so I started keeping my eyes closed again.

After this year's feeding ceremony, I made the mistake of telling my mother that the whole bread thing was some sick version of taking the Eucharist, and that put my mother back into the depression she had already been in, off and on, since we came back from Madrid in August. I think my father thought the onset of our *holiday* would get her out of bed and back on track, but I ruined that hope. I'm not saying I don't feel bad about what I said. I know it was cruel, but eating the prechewed bread is sick, and I don't think I should have to deal with that kind of stuff anymore. If my father still wants to go along with it, then he can do it without me. He can lie there and become my mother or whatever it is he does. They can sit in their freezing cold bedroom stark naked for days for all I care, and they will have to do it all without music because I am not going to play for the ceremonies anymore.

Since I started playing the cello in kindergarten, I've been in charge of the music for the ceremonies. Last year on Yom Hashoah, I refused to play the same Kaddish set to music by some obscure Israeli composer that I've been playing since I was seven. I decided to play the Adagietto from Mahler's Fifth Symphony instead because I think it's probably the most melancholy piece of classical music ever written. My mother doesn't allow anything German or Austrian in the house, so she stormed upstairs and locked herself in her room, and my father had to spend most of the afternoon talking to her through the closed door before she would let him in, and neither of them emerged until the next morning, which was fine with me. Imagine how difficult it is to become an accomplished musician if you're not allowed to play Mozart, or Bach, or Schubert, or Beethoven. Imagine explaining that to an Armenian cello teacher. Mrs. Abadjian had the strictest instructions from my mother to eliminate the German and Austrian composers from my musical education, and it took me until I was nine to convince her to go behind my mother's back and teach me some Bach. Of course I had been playing all the illegal composers on the sly way before that, but I needed feedback, especially for Bach; it's so hard to strike that balance between emotion and intellect with Bach. As soon as I saved up enough of my allowance, I would ride to the music store in Englewood to buy a new forbidden piece. Then I would ride my bicycle, with my cello strapped to my back, all the way up Clinton Avenue—about three miles uphill—to the Nature Center. I would carry my cello into the woods and off the trails (even though there were signs every few feet warning you not to leave the trails) and there, as far away from people as I could get, I would practice the forbidden masters. My mother used to get on my case about riding my bike with my cello, but my father always stuck up for me about that kind of thing. He never does any exercise himself except walk down to the post office to mail his letters. (My father still writes letters to his colleagues every day. Every morning from seven to nine, he works on his correspondence, and he has files and files of letters from his friends and colleagues, all neatly labeled and packed away for posterity in the basement.) Still, my father is a great admirer of the Greek practice of exercising the body as well as the mind and is always saying that he wishes he had made more of an effort to study Greek when he was in graduate school.

All of this clandestine activity made me appreciate the genius of the great German composers even more. It used to make me feel like Mozart himself, freezing cold, pumping up the hill, carrying the burden of my passion. I used to dream of being buried in a pauper's cemetery just like Mozart was. Of course, now I play whatever and wherever I want, and my mother just ignores it. I started openly disobeying my mother's rules about music on my fifteenth birthday. My mother shook her head sadly to make me feel guilty and went to her room crying, but I didn't let it get to me. Then she got on an anti-rock 'n' roll kick and tried to convince me not to listen to it anymore. She used to sit with me in my room and listen to CDs, pointing out all the repetitious chord progressions in rock music, and I would try to explain that a lot of great music, like salsa and Middle Eastern, is repetitious, that repetition gives music a hypnotic quality. I made her listen to all my CDs until she just gave up on me. I guess she figured I was the musician of the family and now she doesn't bother me anymore about what music I play or listen to. But, to this day, when I'm feeling especially introverted, I still go to the Nature Center to play my cello.

There are other times, though, especially when I've been working really hard on a piece of music and I feel like I've made a breakthrough, and I can play it over and over again without making a single mistake, that I need to get out of the house, distract myself a little. That's when I like hanging out with Amy and her boyfriend, Josh. We go to the movies or drive around listening to the Cranberries. Amy and Josh like to smoke a little dope, which doesn't bother me because then we can all space out and not talk. I don't like to smoke because it gives me a stomachache. Sometimes we all take the bus into the city and walk around the Village. They're really into weird clothes, so they go to all the secondhand places while I either browse through bookstores or sit in Washington Square Park and watch people. No one pays too much attention to me because I'm not that interesting looking—no pierced nose or lip, no spiked hair.

When I was younger, in middle school especially, I used to wish Amy's parents were mine. Her father is a big joker and they have really noisy dinners with Bruce Springsteen playing in the background. Amy's parents are huge Bruce Springsteen fans and go to all his concerts when he plays at the Meadowlands. Sometimes they even drive all the way to Boston or Albany to see him play, and they take Amy and her brother with them. They invited me to go with them once when I was in seventh grade, but my parents didn't let me. They said we wouldn't get home until way after midnight and that people get trampled at *rock and roll* concerts. My parents always refer to rock music as *rock and roll music*.

Back in middle school Amy and I would lie on the floor in her room for hours, listening to Bruce Springsteen CDs, and she had a big signed poster of him in her room. Her parents had one the size of a picture window over the couch in the living room, plus they had all his records, which they actually still listen to. Amy's father won't even buy CDs because he says the music sounds too far away on them, that records sound live, like you're actually in the room with Bruce. He always calls Bruce Springsteen *Bruce*. Then a couple years ago, Amy took down her Bruce Springsteen poster and replaced Bruce with a life-size print of Monet's *Water Lilies*, which she bought on one of our trips to the Metropolitan Museum. I tried to convince her to get something more interesting, Van Gogh at least, but she loved the Monet. "It's just so pretty and peaceful," she told me, and I said I wouldn't be able to sleep with Monet's pretty flowers in my room, and she told me I was weird. I wonder what it's like to have parents who go to rock concerts and smoke pot. I guess it's kind of like sleeping with Monet's lovely *Water Lilies*.

Even though Amy and I don't have that much in common anymore and we haven't seen that much of each other since I came back from Madrid, I know I am always welcome at her house. Amy's mother even told me once that if things *got rough*, I could live with them. We've never actually talked about my mother's illness, but Amy has told her mother some things over the years. When I first met Amy in the second grade, she used to come over to my house to play as often as I went to her house, but it was a long time before she ever got to even glimpse my mother because my mother was going through a particularly bad time the year I met Amy. When we played at my house, we usually did a lot of quiet things like drawing because my mother was in her room and I knew not to disturb her with loud games. One day while we were drawing pictures of sailboats on the patio with colored chalk, Amy asked, "Where's your mother?"

"In her room," I said.

"You know what I think?" she asked.

"What?"

"I think you don't really have a mother. I think your mother's dead." She didn't say it in a mean or taunting way. It was just that she really wanted to know.

"She's not dead. She's tired. Do you want to see her?" My father was in the middle of putting the screens back on the windows and had left the ladder right at my mother's window.

"Sure," Amy said.

"Go up and see for yourself." I pointed to the ladder.

"You go first," she said.

I didn't say anything because I knew that if I waited without saying a thing, she would do it. She climbed up really slowly. When she was halfway up, she looked down at me, as if asking for my encouragement, and I nodded, so she kept going. When she got to the top of the ladder, she looked down again, and I nodded again, and then she got up really close to the window and looked in. After what seemed to be a very long time, I started getting nervous because she was so high up on the ladder and because my father might come out at any minute to check on us.

"You'd better come down now," I called up to her.

"Just a minute," she said.

"I think I hear my father," I said even though I didn't.

So she scrambled down the ladder as fast as she could and jumped to the ground from about the fourth rung, but she landed on her feet triumphantly.

"Now you believe me?" I asked.

"Yeah," she said. "She wasn't wearing anything, not even underwear," Amy whispered as if it were a big secret.

"So?" I said.

"So nothing," Amy said, grabbing the chalk from my hand and taking off with it. I chased her around the yard a few times, letting her keep ahead of me even though I could have caught her easily if I had wanted to. Then I just stopped running, but she kept running around the yard, not aware that I wasn't chasing her anymore. It took her a long time to notice that I had gone back to our drawing and, when she finally realized that she wasn't being pursued, she yelled, "I won!" putting her arms up in the air like an Olympic champion. "I won!" she said as she handed the chalk back to me, but I didn't look at her. I took the chalk and started drawing and then she started drawing again too. Her mouth was loosely open and her tongue was sticking out the way it always did when she concentrated really hard.

After that Amy didn't want to play at our house anymore. She said it was boring, that all we could do was draw or play checkers and that there were never any snacks. So we just moved our activities over to Amy's house. We would go there directly after school and her mother always had snacks ready for us—little boxes of raisins, an Oreo cookie each, and orange juice. At Amy's house we could make as much noise as we wanted and watch television, which was always a treat for me since we didn't have one, and, in the summer, Amy's mother took us to the swim club.

I can't imagine moving in with Amy now even though I would have loved it at one time. She wouldn't want me around all the time anyway because she has Josh and she would feel like she had to invite me to come along all the time and her mother would always be trying to cheer me up. At least here I get ignored most of the time whether my mother is going through a good or bad phase. When she's up in her room all day like she is now, my father spends most of his free time in there trying to talk her through things, coax her back into the world, and when she's feeling okay, my father spends all his free time working on his articles and my mother works as many hours as she can at the store.

She works at a rug store called the Magic Carpet, which I think is a totally unoriginal name, but it seems to work. She's a really good salesperson even though you wouldn't think she would be. I've seen her, pointing out the *richness in color and texture* and the *tight weave* and assuring even the most skeptical that no enslaved children sweated for eighteen hours a day, eating only scraps from their masters' tables like dogs, to make the rug that would fit so perfectly under the glass coffee table in their sunken living room.

She got into Middle Eastern rugs while accompanying my father on his research trips to Egypt, Morocco, Algeria, Lebanon, Syria, and even Iran. In fact, he's one of the few Western scholars even allowed in Iran. He meets with renowned Mullahs and sifts through brittle manuscripts in ancient libraries while my mother bargains her way through the *medinas*, buying up rugs. She knows how to spend hours sitting on the floor in a rug shop, drinking tea, showing only a cursory interest in the carpets until the sun starts to set and the rug dealer wants to go home with a nice sale under his belt. Our whole house is filled with rugs. There are at least twenty rugs in the living room so that not an inch of floor is showing. My mother calls it the *tent effect*. At first she would just bring rugs back and sell them to Mrs. Kornfeld, the woman who owns the Magic Carpet, but a few years ago Mrs. Kornfeld got breast cancer and had to have a mastectomy, so my mother started helping her out at the store and she's been there ever since even though Mrs. Kornfeld seems to be fully recovered. She is very understanding about my mother's condition. Sometimes my mother has me call her to tell her that my mother will not be coming in for a while, and Mrs. Kornfeld has told me at least ten times that, as a cancer survivor, she "knows what my mother is going through," although if I were a cancer survivor, someone like my mother, who wasted half her precious life in bed, would make me angry. But I am not a cancer survivor, so it's not really fair of me to say that. I guess my mother and what Mrs. Kornfeld calls my mother's *perfect eye* have brought in quite a bit of business, so she is happy to have her. As for my mother, the job amuses her, gets her out of the house, and, as she is always reminding me, her earnings go to my college fund, so I can go to "the college of my choice."

Actually, I'm thinking about not going to college at all. With my cello, I can earn my own living. I could go to Europe when I finish high school and play my way around—spend a year in Budapest, maybe. I've always had this thing about Hungary. The summer before last I spent about three or four days a week playing my cello in front of Lincoln Center. Once a policeman told me that *technically* he should give me a ticket for soliciting without a license, but that was all the trouble I ever had. At first I was scared of the police all the time because these two Jamaican guys who play the steel drum told me to always be ready to pick up and beat it. I even practiced getting my cello and music into my case as fast as I could so I would be prepared, but then I realized that a cello-playing white girl doesn't have to worry about being chased away by the police. On my last day I had planned to tell the police they were racist idiots, but I didn't because I felt hypocritical enough as it was, and then I really felt like shit when one of the Jamaican drummers gave me fifty dollars because he knew it was my last day. "You keep playing that cello," he said. My cello made me about a hundred dollars in five hours on average, and by the end of the summer, I was able to open up my own savings account, which no one knows about. If things get really bad, I figure I can use the money to get out of here. I could buy a plane ticket to Budapest, or I could buy a used car and move to someplace that is the total opposite of here—like Oklahoma.

Actually, I'm thinking of moving to New York when I graduate from high school next year. I haven't told anyone, not even my grandmother, who would probably be thrilled. She hates New Jersey about as much as I do. "How can you sleep with all this clean silence?" she always asks me. But she lives on 148th Street and Broadway where, if you don't like *merengue*, you could lose your mind, especially in the summer.

I asked my mother once why my grandparents didn't celebrate my mother's birthday and Yom Hashoah with us, and she said disdainfully,

"Because they don't like to be reminded. They'd rather forget." But I don't think it's that they want to forget, but that they somehow think of my mother's depressions as a kind of weakness, as a way that the Nazis had beaten them.

Usually, when my grandparents came to visit with their pastries and chocolates, everyone made an effort to get along. My grandmother was careful not to overly criticize the suburbs, and my mother would rouse herself from her bed for the visit. Sometimes, though, things didn't go so smoothly. I remember one Sunday when my father had spent the whole morning telling her that she "had to make an effort" for her parents, and my mother had said that they didn't make an effort for her, which I don't think is true. Anyway, she had managed to get up and dressed and was sitting in the living room when they arrived. Right away my grandmother knew that my mother was in one of her moods, and instead of just ignoring it like she usually did, she said something about how they came all the way from New York to visit and about how it was a beautiful spring day out and we should all sit in the garden and have coffee and eat the pastries they brought. My mother sat there staring at the rug and when my grandmother finished speaking, my mother looked up and said, very slowly, that she despised the spring. My grandmother got really tense and looked straight into my mother's eyes. Then my mother started crying and crying and my grandmother just sat there without saying anything. Finally, my grandfather and my father brought in the coffee and pastries and my father put on Vivaldi and my mother stopped crying, and my father and grandfather talked and my grandmother sat really close to the CD player with her ear right up to the speakers as if she were waiting for a special part and didn't want to miss it.

I think my grandmother believes that if my mother really wanted to, she could be happy and productive. What she doesn't understand is that everyone has a different definition of happiness. I guess she also thinks that she and my grandfather should have been able to do something to make my mother happy and that somehow they failed because they were the ones who brought her up and they were the ones who should have been able to give her the same strength to carry on that they had. I don't really think of things in terms of strength and weakness, though, because it depends on how you look at it. Some people would say that it was only the fear of death that keeps people from killing themselves and that the ultimate act of courage is suicide. Anyway, one thing I know is that parents always have an inflated idea of their power over their children and always feel like it's their fault if things go wrong, just like it's all their doing if their child does something great like win a prize at school or become a lawyer, which I don't think is so amazing anyway. They won't accept that there are so many things that parents don't have anything to do with at all.

I guess I ended up apologizing about my Eucharist comment because I really did feel that I had been harsh and just like children don't want their parents to be cruel, parents don't deserve cruelty from their children. My mother didn't accept my apology. She just looked at me sadly and went back to flipping through her magazine. A year ago I would have kept trying. I would have played pieces by her favorite composers— Vivaldi, Boccherini—even though I knew it wouldn't work. She loves the Italians. I guess she doesn't think of them as having been fascists, too. Once I asked her about it, and she said the Italians weren't *real* fascists, but she got angry when I pushed her to explain what wasn't *real* about Italian fascism.

Music is sometimes the only thing that will get my mother out of a depressed state. When I was little, as young as eight or nine, my father used to wake me up in the middle of the night and have me come into their bedroom to play for her. She would usually start crying after about half an hour and then I would want to stop, but my father would make me continue playing while she cried and cried. Then finally she would fall back asleep, and the next day she would be better. There she would be in the morning, greeting me with freshly squeezed orange juice and bagels, lox, and cream cheese, which we usually ate only on weekends. She would give me a kiss and send me off with chocolate in my lunch bag. It's always been like that; I seem to have a great effect on mother's moods, though now I am only able to get her depressed, having lost the ability to cure her. Maybe that's because I have stopped trying to experience what it is she feels when she has us do the rituals and when she lies in her bed for days on end. I have never told her that I have stopped trying, but she can tell.

Before we went to Madrid last summer, the only person with whom

I could spend hours and hours at a time without getting bored was my mother. Now I guess the only person I can spend hours and hours with is myself. My mother and I never did the usual mother-daughter things. We didn't go shopping or to the movies or even go into the city. A lot of times we just sat in the living room and listened to music while my mother sipped bourbon. She's not an alcoholic although I bet some people would say she is. She just likes a bourbon or two at the end of the day. At other times, we drank strong coffee with heavy cream and sat at the kitchen table while she read me her favorite poems by Yeats, Auden, T. S. Eliot, Emily Dickinson, Dylan Thomas, Keats, Blake, and, of course, Sylvia Plath. She would give me assignments to memorize her favorite poems, and then she'd test me the next day. When I was younger, I didn't really understand what I was memorizing, but I memorized them all perfectly and proudly. I think I was eight when she first read me "Daddy," and it was easy to memorize because it contained so many familiar words like "Auschwitz" and "Vienna" and "swastika." It was only much later that I came to hate that poem and Sylvia Plath, and I never could understand why my mother liked that poem so much because my grandfather was so kind and quiet and his patients lined up outside his office at dawn. Sometimes I would try to get my mother to show me her own poetry because my father told me she had written some "very promising poems" when she was in college, but she said she had burned them all. Maybe she did, but I'm sure she knows them by heart. I know all the music I've composed by heart.

I suppose other children wouldn't find any of this very amusing, but sometimes I would lie awake all night practicing a poem so I could say it perfectly for her the next day. I still know them all by heart, too. They come in handy—when I can't sleep or when I'm waiting for a bus or suffering through a boring class at school, I start reciting poems to myself. I even remember the poems I don't like, and when I'm just spacing out or walking, one will suddenly pop into my head like that stupid one by Wordsworth:

> I wandered lonely as a cloud
> > That floats on high o'er vales and hills,
> When all at once I saw a crowd,
> > A host, of golden daffodils,

Beside the lake, beneath the trees,
Fluttering and dancing in the breeze.

Three years ago, when I was in eighth grade, my mother and I went on a really long walk. She asked me to bring my cello because she wanted me to play for her when we got tired. Of course, she never offered to help me carry it, but my mother never thinks of stuff like that. My arm was so numb by the time we got to the park and sat down that it was really difficult to play properly. But I played anyway. Mendelssohn. Then she said that she wished she could play an instrument the way I did, and I told her I would give her lessons, and then she started crying, so I just kept playing because that always made her feel better. After a while, she stopped crying, and I packed up my cello and we walked back home.

It was around that time that she started bugging me about my clothes. She said I was getting to be a young woman and I should take more interest in my looks, and I would always tell her that she shouldn't be judging people by how they look, and she would say she wasn't judging, but that I looked like a chimney sweep. I've never even seen a chimney sweep except in *Mary Poppins* and she probably hasn't either, which is what I told her, but she said it was just a manner of speaking. She also started bugging me about the way I sat and every time she caught me with my hands in my pockets she would tell me to stand up straight and get my hands out of my pockets. Then she wanted me to take dancing lessons, but I refused. It's not like I've ever seen her and my father dance. Even at bar mitzvahs, they just sit there and watch.

My mother has always insisted on getting dressed up even for occasions that most people don't get dressed up for. Whenever we go out to eat at the Chinese restaurant in Tenafly, she always makes me put on a dress, and my father always wears a tie and jacket. Even when he is at home working on his articles or preparing his lectures, he wears a tie and jacket, except in the summer when it's too hot. I always feel really stupid going to the Chinese restaurant with my parents because no one else dresses up to go there and, since we usually go on Sundays, we always look like we've just come from church. I've explained this to my mother plenty of times, but she just tells me I'm conventional because I worry about what people think, and then we get into an argument about which one of us is more conventional.

Last spring, before we went to Madrid, was the last time my mother and I did anything fun together, and now, after all that happened there, she is in the worst depression I can remember although my father says that the worst period ever was when I was a baby. It was so bad he had to ask his mother to come stay with us to help him take care of me. I don't remember too much about that grandmother since she died when I was five. All I do remember is that she scared me because she was always talking really loudly and wore a heavy fur coat that smelled of mothballs and made her look like a bear. I could never understand, either, why moths were such a problem that she had to keep her drawers and closets full of mothballs and why the moths never ate any of the clothes in our house even though we didn't use mothballs. I asked my father about it once, and he just laughed and said that old people have an irrational fear of moths. I would always picture my father's mother sitting up late in the middle of the night (she had insomnia) watching for moths by the glow from the television. Of course, I don't remember her taking care of me those first few weeks when I was a baby, and I don't remember that even after my grandmother went back home, my mother wouldn't leave her room for almost half a year. I suppose I should be angry at her about that, especially since they say those first months in a baby's life are so important.

I'm embarrassed to say that I went through a period in middle school when I was into reading pop psychology books. I especially liked the ones about mothers and daughters. That's when I got freaked out that my earliest memories are all about my father and that's when my father told me about my mother's great depression after my birth. I wonder if they ever thought of having more children or if they were too afraid to risk my mother's falling completely into the abyss and never being able to crawl out again. As far as I'm concerned, I'm glad they didn't take that chance. Most people tend to believe that it borders on child abuse to have only one child, but I don't think that's fair. On the contrary, being alone a lot at a young age can be very edifying, and I don't think I would have become so dedicated to the cello if I had had the distractions of a brother or sister.

A HUSBAND AND A DOCTOR

"I should be in New Jersey. Simon, my son-in-law, says Clara hasn't left her room in days. I know I should rush out there, sit with Simon on her bed, explain to her that it makes no sense to waste the day lying around. As if it were so simple. But instead of making a rescue mission to New Jersey, I headed for the Village, even treated myself to a cappuccino at the Peacock Cafe."

"The Peacock. I wouldn't mind going there one more time before I die," Tommy agreed.

"Maybe we could go together. It's not far, not like the Eclair, you know."

"I can't go like this." Tommy ran his fingers through his hair and along his face.

"You need to get out. That's exactly what you need."

"And you need to go visit your daughter, but instead you're here with a dying fag."

"So you think I should go to New Jersey?"

"What I think is irrelevant, although I admit I prefer company to being alone these days. Strange, isn't it? I used to prefer my own company."

"Then you want me to stay?"

"I can't make it that easy for you, Mrs. Mondschein."

"That is exactly what Karl would have said."

"Was Karl handsome?"

"Handsome? Yes, he was, very handsome."

"What did he look like?"

"When he was old or young?"

"When he was young. Why should we think about age?"

"He had small, strong, hairless hands that were always very clean. Doctors' hands have to be very clean. He was dark and had almost black eyes, thin, aristocratic eyebrows, strong legs and arms. He wore glasses. He always wore good Italian suits. He always walked slowly, looking around as if he were watching for people who were admiring him. We were the exact same height. For a while he wore a mustache. That was before the war."

"He sounds terribly sexy."

"Tommy, I'm an old woman."

"I'm sorry. I didn't mean to upset you."

"I'm not upset."

"Please, Mrs. Mondschein, tell me more about Karl. It takes my mind off the pain."

"Do you feel a lot of pain?"

"Sometimes."

"Perhaps you would prefer to rest."

"Why does everyone always think rest is what we want?"

"I'm sorry."

"No apologies, Mrs. Mondschein. I can't bear apologies. Tell me a story. Please."

"You want to hear about Karl, but I cannot begin with Karl. I must start much farther back with my mother, who first pushed me out of the dull safety of the Second District. If she had not escaped and if I had not tried to find her, well . . . my life would have been much different. For one year, I looked for my mother. You see, she simply disappeared one night. She kissed us all before she left—my father, my sisters, me—and when we woke up in the morning, we all had bright red lipstick smudges on our cheeks. She kissed us all in the same place, even my father. There was no warning. I didn't even know she was unhappy.

"I searched for her in the fancy cafés of the First District, snuck out of the house and waited for her in front of the opera and the theater, walked up and down the Kärtnerstrasse, looking past window displays of fur hats and French pocketbooks, but I never dared walk through the gilded doorways framed by Art Deco Greek goddesses, or talk to any of the tall, glittering participants in this world I was sure my mother had entered.

"I met him on the streetcar coming back from another unsuccessful day spent searching for my mother in the park, absentmindedly observing laughing couples, watching them perform waltzes under the gazebo. I was sitting and he was standing—a tall man in a linen suit with a clean, clipped mustache. He smiled at me, and I smiled back. I got off the trolley at my stop and he followed, caught up with me and asked if there was a florist's nearby because he wanted to buy me flowers. That's when I noticed a tiny stain, coffee maybe, on the lapel of his suit. A momentary surge of repulsion welled up in me, and I wanted to run away, but instead I said, 'No, there is no florist in the whole district.' And he said, 'What a pity. Come, we will go where there are flowers.'

"I went with him, and he was my first husband although we were never married. That was something I never told my father and my two sisters, but they probably would have said nothing anyway, so stunned were they by my mother's sudden disappearance. It was as if she had taken their senses with her, along with her constrained laughter and the faint smell of cheap perfume. After only a week of outings in the park and coffee and pastries at the most elegant cafés in Vienna, my husband took me to his big apartment in the First District, and I began taking piano lessons, but I found that my fingers were too short and big, and I could only bang out a few chords without feeling like a complete stranger to that instrument. My granddaughter Deborah, now there's a musician. She only has to touch her cello and music flows out of it.

"My first husband insisted on inviting my father and sisters to dinner. He thought he was being charitable; it made him feel that all his fine suits and his apartment and the maids in black dresses and white aprons could do some good in the world. He even bought a special set of dishes for their visits and ordered his maids to go all the way to the Second District to buy kosher meat.

"We didn't talk much because he was rarely home. He left me in his large apartment with the shy maids from the countryside and would return only in the evenings and often not until long after dinner. He said he frequented communist meetings, but he never took me with him, and I never asked to be taken. Instead, he brought me fancy clothes in which I waited for his return. Every once in a while, he took me to the opera or the theater and out to an expensive dinner. He always requested a dark, private table in the back.

"When he came home, he often had those same tiny stains on his shirt or jacket or pants, just like on the first day. When he was gone, I would dream about tearing him apart like a wild beast and leaving him to bleed to death on the carpet, but then he would take my hands and kiss me, move me to the bed, untie my nightgown and cup his hands over my breasts and leave them there patiently. Excuse me, Tommy. I shouldn't be so self-indulgent, but look! My hands are trembling. How can I still be angry after all these years?"

"It's good to be angry, Mrs. Mondschein, and I am a big believer in self-indulgence. Please continue."

So I continued although my hands did not stop trembling. "He knew he would not have to wait long before my breasts began rising up to be tighter in his hands, and he would sit there quietly, and I would have to pull him down to me and force my tongue into his mouth and press myself against him. Often, he would not take off his clothes. It seemed that he preferred the cigarette and cognac that came afterwards. He was like that about everything—didn't really enjoy his dinner but liked the silver cutlery and the maids who fussed over him saying *mein Herr* this and *mein Herr* that. He treated them very well—gave them long holidays and gifts to take to their families. They were very grateful.

"If something was disturbed or imperfect, if the food was slightly salty or he found a bit of cork in his wine, he would grow more and more restless and then the only thing that would calm him would be to knock billiard balls around until dawn. Yet he never noticed those tiny dots on his clothing. The stains were what finally did it. The stains on his suits, the stains in the bed—little accidents that you can't avoid. In a way, I liked the stains—they made him human—but I knew that if I ever pointed them out, he would clench his fists and stiffen his back, and I would have to listen to the sound of billiard balls cracking against each other all night. I would have preferred him to smell and come home every night tired with dirty fingernails. I missed the odor of onions hanging in the air, the grease stains on the wall over the stove, and my sisters' silly chatter while they knitted.

"*This is my punishment for going with a gentile, for thinking that I could escape the darkness of our little apartment,* I thought to myself as I waited all afternoon in my fancy bed. I started spending more and more time in bed. I grew thin and bony, and my husband stopped coming to me. He left me to myself. I refused to see my family, though I knew they must be worried. Gertrude, the youngest, prettiest maid, brought me eggs and apples every morning without ever looking me in the eyes. At night, I heard her laughter coming from the next room where my husband lay.

"I started smelling my own stink. It filled the room, but I would let no one open the windows. I would wake up and almost vomit from my own smell, but after a few minutes, that would pass, and I would concentrate on the odor and the sheets that were a pale yellow from my sweat. All this was my only comfort. I could have stayed like that for a long time, but one day he came to me and said he had had enough, that I was contaminating his house, that he smelled me when he was trying to eat his dinner and in the mornings when he was shaving. I said nothing because there was nothing to say. His jaw muscles twitched in anger, his manicured nails dug into his palms, and then he dragged me out of bed, threw my coat over my shoulders, held my head up so as not to bang it as he dragged me down the stairs. In the taxi, I knew he was taking me to my father's house, and I felt neither regret nor relief, but part of me was laughing. I had managed to upset him after all. Now he would know not to take the daughters of crouched, dingy families into his almost odorless house with brass doorknobs and tea cakes.

"He left me at the door without an explanation. I waited until he had driven off in the taxi and only then rang the bell. My father and sisters did not dare look at me, so I went directly to my old room and my old bed where I used to dream of my mother kissing army officers. All through the night, I heard the regular noise of billiard balls cracking against each other in my head. I pitied my husband because he missed the easiest shots and because he could not stop himself from finding solace in the earthy-smelling arms of Gertrude. And I laughed thinking about all those handsome gentlemen at their Communist Party meetings sipping wine and underlining important passages in *Das Kapital*. My father and sisters must have trembled all night listening to my hysterical laughter.

"In the morning, however, there was a new smell in the air that made me think of school excursions. Someone had come into my room and opened the window after I had finally fallen asleep. I was enraged by that fresh smell of wind and spring-around-the-corner, but at the same time couldn't help breathing in deeply. And then I realized I was hungry. It wasn't a stirring morning hunger but rather one that grabbed at my guts and spread all over my body. I felt it in my arms and legs; my throat called out for food. I tried not to surrender to the whiff of air that brought the message of spring. I battled against it, but I couldn't push the thought of noodles and chicken and thick rye bread out of my mind. I called to my sisters and they brought me food, mountains of food—potatoes, noodles, stringy meat and boiled carrots with dill, and a whole box of cookies. And still I was hungry. I ate more and my sisters called for the midwife Mrs. Blumstein, a short woman with skinny legs and big breasts, who felt my forehead, looked at my empty plate, examined the brown area around my nipples, and smiled. Within an hour, the entire district was informed that the oldest Feinberg girl had returned home and was with child. So I, the oldest Feinberg daughter, had once again justified their dark, righteous homes, with their fat mothers, arthritic before fifty, and their quiet fathers who scurried through the streets selling rolls of cheap fabric. 'The bad blood in that girl comes from her mother,' they would say, feeling sorry for my father, who carried his burdens so quietly, so heroically, although his eyes were always fixed on the ground."

"I knew so many men like your first husband." Tommy spoke as if from a dream. "Beautiful men in business suits, but they never took me home. I waited for them behind the bleachers at the baseball field near the train station. They seemed to have passed the word among themselves—there's a scrawny guy with hair covering his eyes who's willing to suck cock or take it up the ass for free. I'm sorry, I shouldn't talk like that, but there's no other way to say it. Not that I know of. Sometimes their suits were brushed lightly with cigarette ashes; sometimes they smelled of martinis; sometimes they were fat, sometimes they weren't. That was a very long time ago before I learned to take refuge in the warmth of the baths. The funny thing is I never liked the baths half as much as my little spot behind the bleachers. Only now have I stopped despising myself for it. Why should I despise myself when, if it hadn't been for me, all those suited men with the *Wall Street Journal* in their briefcases would never have been able to keep themselves from falling off the edge and into the abyss of Long Island loneliness? We kept each other from that abyss just like your first husband saved you."

"Saved me? Saved me from what?"

"Only you can know that. Only you."

"Did you ever have a . . . longer relationship?"

"Ah, Mrs. Mondschein. Didn't you say you were bringing me some Mozart?"

"Of course, I almost forgot. Good thing you reminded me."

"Yes, a day without Mozart is like a day without . . . Please, Mrs. Mondschein, don't leave just yet. Stay and listen with me. Your story is making me so very emotional."

"Perhaps it is too much for both of us."

"No, but we have to pace ourselves, don't you think?"

So we listened to Mozart until Tommy fell asleep, and then I headed home, tired. It was a good tired, though, like after a long walk in the winter.

The next morning I was the first volunteer to arrive and Tommy was the first patient to wake up, so there was a strange peacefulness in the hospice that I had never experienced before and the usual smells and noises were muffled and almost friendly. Tommy wondered why I had come so early.

"I was up before dawn and sometimes I cannot bear being in the apartment. I actually thought I might make the trip to New Jersey to visit Clara, but when I called, Deborah answered the phone and told me that Clara would not speak to anyone, not even to Simon, so I happily got myself ready to visit you. You see, I prefer talking to you because you can really appreciate my story."

"Why?" Tommy asked.

"No reason, really," I said.

"You know very well, Mrs. Mondschein, that there is a reason for everything. Is it because I won't tell anyone since I have no one to tell, no one who cares?"

"No, I'm just afraid that others would misinterpret everything."

"And it doesn't matter if I misinterpret things since I'll be dead soon."

"Tommy, that might work with some people but I'm beyond guilt," I told him.

"Why? Do you have so much to feel guilty about?"

"Didn't you want to hear about Karl?"

"Of course I do. I dreamt about him last night."

"What did you dream?"

"I dreamt that he was my doctor and he was examining me very gently, caressing me more than examining, and then all of a sudden he saw the lesion on my stomach and he recoiled. Then I woke up."

"How can you be sure it was Karl?"

"I just know. When I woke up, I felt as if I had betrayed you. Isn't that ridiculous?"

"Perhaps not. But I don't want to get ahead of my story."

"And I, Mrs. Mondschein, don't want your story ever to end. It gives me something to fantasize about besides my death."

"You remember that I was pregnant. The life I was carrying inside me was like spring. My whole life I have hated spring when it first arrives, bringing life and hope that something new will happen. I always tried to hold onto winter—dark, cold, familiar winter when a warm bed makes you feel like the luckiest person in the world. Yet the more I tried not to let hope into my darkened room, the more I felt an uncontrollable urge to open up the windows and let it in. So I got out of my bed and announced I was going to visit the sea. My father, in his usual baffled and acquiescent way, pressed money into my hand at the station.

"At the sea, it was windy and cold. I took a small room facing the water with neat wooden furniture and a warm goose-feather quilt, and I fell asleep to the sound of waves, feeling so wonderfully alone—as if nothing, no one, could ever bother me again because I was protected by crashing waves and a plump matron who kept watch downstairs with pink cheeks and uninquisitive eyes. I brought books with me because I had always loved to read before I met my first husband and became a slave to lethargy and bitterness."

"Where did you go, Mrs. Mondschein? I have to know the country for an exact picture." Tommy's eyes were closed very tightly as if he were trying to conjure up my seaside escape.

"Italy, a little town. I don't remember the name, near Venice."

"Thank you. I have always wanted to go to Venice. Perhaps you could rent Death in Venice and we could watch it here together. Have you seen it?"

"No, I know the book, of course."

"We must watch it together. How could I have forgotten to watch Death in Venice again? Yes, I must see it one more time."

"I would like that, too. Yes, the little hotel in Italy. I had never been to another country before, so I was happy to listen to Italians chattering in the bar downstairs without being able to understand them. Not understanding made my solitude more complete, more perfect, while the cheerfulness kept me from sinking into a depression and worrying about my condition—'husbandless and with child,' as my neighbors would say.

"On the fourth morning, I arose with that same all-embracing hunger. I took a table near the window and ordered a whole basket of warm rolls, butter, and jam. Yet I could feel something disturbing in the room, something that didn't belong in my little paradise. Far away in a corner, far away from the windows and the view of the sea was a table that should have been unoccupied because there were so many free tables in the restaurant from which you could see the water and feel the warm sun on your face while you dined. A solemn couple had chosen the darkest spot and they were sitting opposite each other not talking. It was their silence in all that gaiety that disturbed me, that made it obvious they were neither Italians nor happy vacationers. I noticed the woman first—her large eyes, long, slightly frizzy dark hair, big bones, large hands, high forehead, sharp features, and high cheekbones. She was taller than the man was. He had a small face and wore horn-rimmed glasses, but his hands were beautiful—elegant and veined but not muscular. That was the first time I realized that men could have such beautiful hands. It was as if I knew this couple intimately—knew their unhappiness, the bitterness between them. I kept trying not to stare, but I couldn't help it.

"After breakfast, I went for a long walk on the beach and picked up unbroken sea shells. Then, when I was good and tired, I sat in the sitting room reading *Madame Bovary*, which was too appropriate and too dull. It was almost impossible to keep my mind on my book; every two minutes I would look up hoping to see the silent couple until finally, towards evening, I dozed off. During dinner, the silent couple took their table while I sat at mine, trying not to stare but staring nonetheless while they ate in silence and left half their food on their plates.

"The next morning, they found the body of the big-boned woman on the beach. All the vacationers responded to the uproar, running out to see what was going on, crossing themselves nervously when they saw her inflated body clothed in wet tweed. The slight man with the glasses and elegant hands walked up and down the beach kicking pebbles. Mothers watched the man sadly and sent their children off to play. Men stared at the dead woman and then went off to have a drink. I wanted to speak to the man but thought we probably didn't speak the same language, so I wandered off to the village and bought a very expensive silk scarf that didn't go with any of my drab clothes. When I was in sight of the hotel, I removed the scarf since I kept thinking that everyone was staring at my neck.

"By the time I returned, someone had found a bottle with a note in it that read: 'The writer of this note died on March 7, 1937.' The policeman handed the bottle and the note over to the man, who put the note back into the bottle and walked towards the hotel. An hour later, I watched the man walking down the road towards the village with a travel bag in each hand. I wondered if the woman had hoped that her message would be carried overseas, or if she had wanted it to be washed up, like her body, onto the shores from which it had come.

"I left the next morning. There was the train ride between the sea and my father's house. In the compartment, there were three other people—a woman with her young niece and a salesman who kept looking at his watch. Every once in a while, the aunt coughed daintily, and every once in a while, the salesman cracked his knuckles, and every once in a while, the girl bounced up and down on her seat until the aunt told her, in some Slavic language, to stop. At night, we turned out the lights, and everyone slept except me. Every hour or so, the salesman woke up and lit a cigar. I had expected so much from the sea, but nothing had come of it. I was going back to my father's house, pregnant and alone. But where else could I go?"

"So the man at the sea was Karl?" Tommy interrupted.

"Karl? Oh no, that wasn't Karl. How could that have been Karl?"

"So who was he?"

"Just a man whose wife or lover had committed suicide. Remember, I already told you that Karl was the doctor. That's why I hate to tell the story out of order. Then you'll never remember it correctly."

"The doctor," Tommy said thoughtfully. "That's right, I don't know how I could have forgotten. It's not because you told the story wrong. Maybe it's the dementia setting in. I never forget what people tell me."

"It's not the dementia, Tommy. I'm afraid my story wanders more than necessary, but I cannot tell it any other way. You know, there are some people who never go through that phase."

"Ah! Are you telling me that I might be one of the lucky ones?"

"I didn't say anything about luck or the lack of it."

"I'm sorry. I didn't mean to be nasty. It just comes over me after all these years of practice. So when does Karl finally enter the picture?"

"I'm getting to that, but you must allow me to take my time or it will come out all wrong and you'll never understand."

"I want you to take your time. I want you to take all the time in the world. It's just that suspense is difficult for me. I used to find it so terribly attractive, but I don't have the patience for it anymore."

"I wasn't trying to make it suspenseful, but this is the only way to tell the story."

"I know. It's not you; it's me, so don't worry about my neuroses. Please, the last thing I want you to do is worry about my neuroses. They're so completely uninteresting. Please continue."

"Well, when I returned from Italy, my father was dying, although we didn't know he was dying then; we just thought he was sick. I walked in the door and there were half a dozen neighbor women and my two sisters in attendance. My father was the only one who was happy to see me. The rest of them said they had not expected me back so soon, as if they had all been hoping that I would never return. So I went to my room and waited until the neighbors went home and my sisters went to sleep, and then I sat with my father and held his hand while he came in and out of sleep. Every time he opened his eyes, he smiled, and he didn't ask me any questions.

"Karl was the young doctor who came to see my father every two or three days. And every time, he examined my father's heart and liver and pressed his abdomen and made him take deep breaths. And every time, he said there was nothing wrong with him. At first, he would try to convince my father he had rested enough, that it was time to get back to work. It was only after Mr. Kaufman, Senior of Kaufman and Kaufman came to our apartment to beg my father to return to work and after Kaufman and Kaufman was finally forced to hire another bookkeeper, a tall, thin, young man who could add a column of seventy figures in his head, that Karl decided my father was suffering from *melancholia*.

"But, you know, I think my father was at his happiest during his *melancholia.* He smiled like a child when we brought him his favorite food, and he told us about the junk man who used to let him ride in the back of his cart when he was a boy in Poland, and about how he would come home covered with dust and his mother would scold him gently and feed him a heavy stew dinner. Karl would shake his head and say, 'Your father is not an old man.' But I had always known him as an old man sitting in a frayed armchair, turning the pages of a newspaper with his fingers blue from ink.

"Then my father's mood changed. That was when he started talking about time, about how there wasn't that much time left. He asked for a clock, and he would stare at the clock for hours, holding it in his lap, his ear bent towards it so he could hear the ticking. Karl took this as a hopeful sign because he thought it meant he was afraid of dying. I tried to explain that perhaps it just meant he knew he was going to die and was waiting for it to happen.

"It was during this last stage that Karl started coming around every day, and I knew it wasn't because of my father. Sometimes I would catch him staring at my stomach, which was getting bigger and bigger. I could feel the baby kicking as I waited for Karl to say something, but he said nothing, so I would have to offer him a cup of coffee, anything to keep him from staring. After a while, I told him there was no need for him anymore, that my father was dying because he wanted to die, and there was nothing a doctor could do. But Karl kept up his doctorly visits— every day without fail. Sometimes we talked about books we had both read, and he told me about his patients. Once, while he told me about a boy, a very gifted young pianist who had died of scarlet fever, I noticed tears in his eyes. I didn't say anything, but I could tell I was helping him by listening.

"At night, I roamed the city thinking about telling the young doctor about my first husband and my soon-to-be-born child. And all night long my father lay in his bed, wide awake, watching his clock. Never once did my father call for a rabbi. Perhaps he knew what he would say: 'Go back to work; God did not make you to think so much. Thinking requires years and years of study and knowledge.' I walked along the outer districts of Vienna, staying away from the boulevards, from official buildings, and from the opera, where I had once waited for my mother night after night.

Strange how I can't even remember what she looks like now. I looked into dimly lit first-floor apartments and saw families eating together at heavy tables. I saw women knitting under the lights of floor lamps and men reading and smoking. In one room, I saw an old woman leafing through a photo album, and I wanted to rap on the window, go in and sit with her for a while, ask her about the people in the photographs. I never heard voices coming out of those apartments; only every now and then, there was the muffled sound of a radio playing opera or waltzes.

"Once, a drunk, fat man who had just come out of a wine cellar followed me all the way home, screaming for me to come into his arms, to warm his bed. I didn't run or even quicken my pace. I just kept walking slowly, never looking back, and I could tell he was afraid of me. He could have caught up so easily.

"My days consisted of sitting with my father and sisters, watching my sisters knit, watching my father stare. My sisters spoke to each other in hushed whispers so I couldn't hear and addressed me only to speak about budgeting. Every week, they worked out the expenses and were proud to be able to keep the four of us going on my father's savings and the neighbors' stingy charity. They bragged about their thrift, which I praised, wondering if they ever worried about what they would do when the savings ran out. Of course, I had already turned over what was left from my gloomy trip to the sea. Sometimes I wanted to kiss my sisters when I thought about how meaningless their lives would become if, all of a sudden, we had plenty of money. But they would have thought something was wrong if I had kissed them after all those years of distance.

"I always felt inspired after Karl left, even if he had only had time for a cup of coffee or to leave me another book. After his visits, I took long walks without looking into windows. I walked fast and was filled with a great desire to do something. I thought of him rushing from patient to patient, checking charts, giving orders to nurses, chatting a little with other doctors over a never-relaxed cup of coffee. I admired his eyes, which were ringed from too many night shifts. And I walked and walked the streets, dreaming of doing something but never able to figure out what I could do. I thought of the child that was coming and how it would keep me up at night and how I would have to feed it and carry it, but such activities didn't excite me. So I tried not to think of the child. I wanted to be tired, tired from work, physically exhausted and hungry. I wanted to be able to fall asleep as soon as my head hit the pillow. So I walked, walked until my fingers were swollen, walked until I could hardly climb the stairs from tiredness. But still I would lie awake at night, unable to sleep. Sometimes I put on my nicest dress and sat in a café waiting for someone to notice me, to sit down beside me and ask what I was reading, to ask me what I was doing, growing big, sitting alone in a café. But when someone did glance my way, I would jump up, pay my bill, and leave with my head bowed. I often passed my ex-husband's house and thought of ringing the doorbell, but I never did. I found myself thinking more and more about the doctor, wondering why he never asked me to go for a walk or to one of the operas he was always talking about.

"Sometimes I had horrible dreams. I dreamt that I was giving birth to a thin, naked, hairless, old man with brittle talons curving inward from his fingers and toes. I dreamt of smiling nurses handing me a long, wrinkled body that I would rock until it stopped crying, but then when I would try to wake it up, it was always dead. Many times I wanted to ask Karl if he could help me find someone who would perform an abortion. But I was afraid."

"When I told my mother that I was a homosexual, she said that she should have had an abortion," Tommy broke in. "They had never even told me that theirs was a shotgun wedding. They'd even lied about their wedding day and everyone went along with it."

"What did you say?"

"What could I say? I said nothing. I left the house and I've seen them perhaps twenty times in twenty years. Even those twenty times have been too much for them."

"Do they know you're sick?"

"No."

"Don't you think you should tell them? What if they go on for years thinking you're still alive?"

"That would give me great pleasure."

OLD PHOTOS AND A FRIEND

Summer 1995

I was thrilled my parents invited me to go to Spain with them. Usually, when they went on their trips, they left me with my grandparents. My parents always said that Morocco and Iran were not for children, and when I was really little I thought there were no children in those places—just adults. Our summer in Spain was my first trip abroad, and I don't think I had ever been so excited as the moment we boarded the plane at Kennedy Airport.

We were going to spend the summer in Madrid because my father was doing research on manuscripts he had found in the *Biblioteca Nacional*—some correspondence between Muslim and Jewish clerics from just before the Expulsion that demonstrated how well Jews and Muslims got along in those days. My father was extremely excited about the documents. It was as if he believed they contained some hidden secret, which, if he could only discover it, would put an end to the bitter war in the Middle East. My mother was excited too because she was going to roam through the hot, narrow streets of Madrid and work on her poetry late into the night. She had a poem of epic proportions in mind, something about a woman who kills her husband in bed like a modern-day Judith, hero of the Jews who was sent to seduce Holofernes, the general of the Assyrian army, so she could murder him in his sleep.

She read me lines from a leather-bound notebook on the airplane, but they were just lines—disjointed images, which I don't remember now except that the protagonist had a swan's neck, just like her. And I had plans, too. I had my cello with me, of course, and I was already enrolled in intensive Spanish classes.

We were renting the apartment of one of my father's colleagues, Professor Vásquez, who was an expert on the *judíos conversos* or the *marranos*, the term he preferred because he felt one should not underplay the disgust the Spanish Crown had felt for the Jews. Professor Vásquez claimed to be of *marrano* blood himself—I say *claimed* because apparently being of *marrano* extraction is very fashionable in Spain these days. He told us several times on the drive home from the airport how honored he was to have such an esteemed Jewish scholar *safeguarding* his apartment. Then, allowing us only fifteen minutes to deposit our bags and brush our teeth, he took us on a whirlwind tour of our new neighborhood's bars. My mother was in a great mood. She ate everything and announced to Mr. Vásquez that she was going to take a break from the dietary laws. Her fingers were sticky from peeling the skins off the grilled shrimp and she flung the skins on the floor happily, like a child throwing her food from her high chair. At the last bar, she insisted on ordering a plate of *jamón serrano*. After my first glass of beer, my father suggested that I have a soda or tea and Mr. Vásquez told him that he was being very American, very puritanical, which he isn't. On the contrary, he is always talking about how teenagers wouldn't end up drunk behind the wheel of a car if their parents introduced them to drinking at an early age, but he didn't explain all that to Mr. Vásquez. He just laughed and let him order me another beer. By seven o'clock we finally convinced him that we needed some rest, that we had been up all night, that we were jet-lagged, so he walked us back to the apartment and, once we were safely inside, disappeared back into the city. In the morning a taxi picked him up to take him to the airport. He was off to a summer in Thailand, where he spent all his summers, and we had the place to ourselves.

I loved our apartment. Even after everything that happened there, I still love it—the way you could feel the age in the stairs, the dormer windows and sloped ceilings, the walls that were cool no matter how blazing the sun, the bookshelves crammed with books, the smell of olive oil and sun at noon. I had my own room that faced the street, and my parents used Mr. Vásquez's bedroom because it had a double bed. After the first night, my mother suggested we switch bedrooms because she disliked the skylight in their bedroom; when she closed her eyes at night, she always felt as if someone were watching her from above like she was in a play. But, luckily, after a few days she stopped talking about it, and I was able to keep my room with the slanted ceilings and the window that looked out over the tile roofs and onto the street below.

The living room was like nothing I had ever seen before. It was furnished with gilded Thai couches and Persian rugs and on the walls were old maps of Madrid, also in gilded frames. My father, although he planned to spend most of his time in the library, had a study to work in too, complete with a computer, which he never touched. He encouraged my mother to use the study instead, but she announced that the cafés of Madrid would be better suited to her kind of work, and, sure enough, at lunchtime when I came home from my classes, I could always find her at the Barbieri, in the back next to the window, staring off into space, a half-drunk glass of sherry on her table, and I would stop in and we would talk for a while. I would drink lemonade and tell her about my class. She would help drill me on my irregular verbs, and then we would walk home together.

I was happiest in the apartment when I had it to myself. At first I didn't want to disturb anything and felt that even playing a CD was an invasion of the professor's privacy, but he had told us to use absolutely everything—to drink his wine, read his books, break his dishes—so slowly I grew braver. I would pour myself a glass of red wine and make a sandwich and put on some music. I really loved *Carmina Burana* that summer. Somehow it fit my mood—the tipsiness of drinking wine alone in the afternoon. I dozed a lot, thinking up melodies, which I jotted down in a music notebook I bought at a music store on the Gran Vía.

One day I discovered the professor's photo albums on the bottom shelf of a bookcase in his study with the art books. The first few times I looked at them, I flipped through them quickly, as if I expected the professor himself to walk in on me, catch me red-handed, but then they started pulling me in. It got so that I couldn't concentrate on my homework. Every afternoon after class I gobbled down my sandwich and took my glass of wine to the living room, got myself comfortable on the heavily carved Thai couch, and settled in with the photographs. The photos were in leather-bound albums with gold embossing indicating the dates and places where the pictures were taken—Morocco, 1959; Italy, 1967; Thailand, Thailand, Thailand. The albums smelled of new shoes and rain. There were no photos of the professor's childhood, no one resembling a mother or father, no spinster aunts or grandparents. Instead there was a small album, much thinner than the others, which contained portraits of people long dead—browned daguerreotypes mostly, of young men at the beach in those one-piece bathing suits that men wore in the early twentieth century, arms around each other, laughing or looking very seriously into the camera. There were men in those old caps like

London taxi drivers wear. Some of them had such long, beautiful fingers, like piano players have, only you could tell by their caps that they were neither artists nor wealthy. My favorite was of a burly, fully bearded man in his forties dressed up like Queen Victoria and a much younger man sporting a handlebar mustache standing side by side and holding hands very formally.

In one of the albums marked *Thailand* there was a shot of a much younger Professor Vásquez wearing a Hawaiian grass skirt and hoop earrings with an entourage of young Thai men in similar garb. They were all leaning on a veranda railing in front of the sea. Many photos were of naked men lying on beds, standing in windows, some smiling proudly, others somewhat shy. I tried not to look at those too much because they made me feel strange, distant somehow, as if I were a doctor examining a patient.

I liked the daguerreotypes better, so I concentrated on them one at a time, closing my eyes, trying to remember every detail, endowing the men with names, jobs, secrets. The man dressed up like Queen Victoria was William. He was a bank clerk with a tubercular wife and six children. His friend was a sailor who brought home exotic gifts like quivers with poison-tipped arrows from Borneo, which William kept in a hat box in a trunk containing his dead mother's wedding gown, her Bible, and her favorite linens.

Besides listening to Professor Vásquez's music and looking at his photo albums, my favorite after-class activity was meeting my mother at the Barbieri. For the first couple of weeks she always seemed happy to see me, glad to set aside her pencil, but slowly I started getting the impression that she wanted to be alone with her thoughts. I would look at her through the window and see her scribbling or staring off into space, watching the ceiling fan turn and turn and turn. Then, as much as I liked the clatter of the place with its sullen old waiters and pierced and tattooed Spaniards having loud, guttural arguments, I would move on. And if I didn't feel like going back to the apartment that day, I would start walking.

On one such day I walked down the Calle de Segovia and across the Manzanares to the Casa de Campo, where there was a small zoo. I always have found zoos depressing, even when I was really little. Amy's mother took us to Van Saun Park once and we had to go on a llama ride, which consisted of this guy leading the llamas with us on them round and round a small corral. I remember asking him if the llamas often spit at him, and he said they never did, which I didn't believe. That night I couldn't sleep because I kept thinking of those poor llamas spending their whole lives walking around in circles with kids on their backs. But somehow the zoo fit my mood that day. I spent a long time watching the gorillas imitating the visitors, who kept trying to get them to laugh. Then I sat in the shade and watched the couples rowing out on the lake. There were about twenty rowboats out there, each with a young couple in it, and in every single boat the guy was the one doing the rowing. I watched them for a long time to see if maybe any of them would switch off, but they never did.

That night my mother was in a rare, wonderful mood. She made a huge salad with olives and eggs and tuna and asparagus and we ate two loaves of bread between the three of us and drank two bottles of wine, and we sat at the table until well after eleven, practicing our Spanish. Then my mother set forth with her notebook under her arm. I could tell my father felt bad that she didn't want to work in the study near us so that he could sit in the living room reading with the knowledge that she was working in the other room. He would have liked that, after a nice long dinner, after the wine and a successful day at the library. But, of course, he didn't say anything.

We both went to sleep long before my mother returned, but I awoke abruptly in the middle of the night as if I had heard a shrill scream, thinking that my mother was about to kill my father in his bed like in the poem she was working on. I didn't know what to do, whether to keep very still and pretend I was still asleep, so that in the morning when I found my father's dead body and no trace of my mother I could tell the police that I had heard nothing, or whether to rush into their room before it was too late. Instead I snuck quietly down the hall to their room. The door was slightly ajar, which was unusual because my parents have always slept with their door closed and I have always known not to disturb them, not even to knock.

My mother was not there, and my father lay asleep in the middle of the bed, his arms and legs sprawled out recklessly as if he were resting in a meadow after a long hike in the mountains. It made me angry to see him there like that, as if he were happy to have some time to himself. I ended up standing watch at my dormer window until dawn when I finally saw her walking slowly down the street. Her lips were moving, but I couldn't tell if she was singing or talking.

That morning, as soon as I got outside into the hot sun, I decided that I was too sleep-deprived to go to class, but I couldn't go back upstairs to bed, so I started walking. I thought I might go to the Prado to study Hieronymous Bosch's *Seven Deadly Sins* more carefully since I had been thinking about composing some solo cello music, maybe something slightly atonal, based on it. I wanted to begin with gluttony. I started walking and found myself avoiding Lavapíes where the Barbieri was, even though I knew my mother couldn't possibly be there, that she was still at home sitting in the living room with my father. But then I realized I didn't really want to go to the Prado and be around all those people who had come from all over the world to look at paintings, so I went to the train station instead. I thought I could go to Toledo because my parents were always talking about how one of these days we were going to Toledo to see the synagogues, but I had the feeling that we were never going to make it. When I got to the station, I had just missed the train to Toledo and there wasn't another one for two hours, so I found a small bar to wait in.

"You're not English, are you?" a very tall man wearing a wine-red beret, a red ascot, and a blue suit with a handkerchief in the breast pocket asked. He sounded Irish.

"No." I didn't say I was American.

"Good. I'm tired of speaking to the English. They're so boring, always talking about their coin collections or the rain." He lit a cigarette and then apologized for not offering me one.

"I don't smoke, but thank you," I said and he raised his eyebrows as if not smoking were pure folly.

In front of him on the bar was quite an array of drinks—a cup of *café sólo* like mine, a brandy snifter full almost to the brim with a thick, clear liquid that he later informed me was his *beloved* (that was the word he used) Cointreau, and a glass of beer. He drank from each one, starting on the left with the Cointreau, then taking a gulp of beer, then the coffee.

"Aren't you having a drink?" he asked.

"It's still early," I said, looking at my watch. It was ten in the morning.

"Suit yourself," he replied and drank from each of his three drinks. "You're not Canadian, are you? Mind you, I have nothing at all against Canadians, but I don't feel up to them this morning."

"No, I'm not Canadian. I'm from the United States."

"Well, that's not your fault, is it now?" He chuckled.

"Have you been to the U.S.?" I asked, not having any idea what you're supposed to say to a fellow foreigner in a bar in a train station.

"I have, but I don't care to discuss it. Now, if we are going to have a conversation, we should introduce ourselves—George Liddy of Limerick," he said, holding out his hand.

I shook his hand and said, "Deborah Gelb of New Jersey."

George Liddy found my self-introduction very amusing and when he finished laughing he said, "So, what do you think we should discuss?"

I thought for a while. Everything that came to my mind seemed stupid—what he was doing in Madrid, what I was doing in Madrid, the Prado, where he was from.

"We could talk about the dog races. Do you enjoy the races?" he asked before I could think of a good topic.

"I've never been."

"Never been to a dog race? Not even in Alaska? I thought they had those wonderful dog sled races in America."

"They do, but I've never been to Alaska. It's very far."

"Far from where?"

"From where I live."

"I see. Well, I've never been to Alaska either. Alas." That got him giggling and then the giggling turned into coughing, so he drank from his three drinks. "Excuse me. I'm being quite silly."

"No, you're not."

"Well, there's nothing wrong with being silly. Now, where were we? Ah yes, the dog races. Frankly, I don't know the first thing about dog racing, so that probably wouldn't be a good thing to talk about now, would it?"

"Probably not," I said. "I'm going to Toledo."

"Ah, Toledo. A beautiful spot. I once had a friend in Toledo. Do you have a friend in Toledo?"

"No."

"That's a pity. There's nothing like a friend in Toledo."

"What happened to your friend?"

"Which friend? I have had so many." He sighed very noisily.

"Your friend in Toledo."

"Ah yes, my friend in Toledo. He developed an obsession for St. Teresa of Ávila and moved there to be closer to her. I never forgave him for it although perhaps I should now. It has been a very long time. Maybe tomorrow I shall go to Ávila to make amends. Would you like to accompany me?"

"I'm supposed to go to my Spanish class. As a matter of fact, I should be there right now."

"Well, there is such a marked difference between what one is supposed to do and what one actually does, don't you think?" He turned to look at me straight in the eyes. Up until that time he had been focusing upward towards the ceiling.

"What are you supposed to be doing right now?" I asked to avoid the subject of Ávila even though part of me was tempted to go with him. Still, I hadn't quite made up my mind.

"Me?" He laughed. "I'm not supposed to be doing anything except drinking here in this bar. That's the beauty of it, don't you think?"

"Well, then we could go to Ávila today. I can see Toledo some other time." I suddenly felt as if there was nothing I wanted more than to accompany him to Ávila to help him make up with his friend.

"Oh no, we couldn't go today. That would be ludicrous."

"Why?"

"Because you can't take a place like Ávila so lightly. You can't just hop on a train as if you were taking the Metro to the Corte Inglés or some other such horrible place. You have to be prepared for Ávila. The last time I was there I stayed for six weeks. You have to be prepared to stay on for the long haul. Why don't you have a drink with me instead?"

I looked at my watch. The train for Toledo was leaving in ten minutes.

"Don't tell me you're one of those people who doesn't drink before noon."

"No, I was just thinking about my train. I was going to Toledo."

"Well, suit yourself," he said and turned to the last of his three drinks.

"I guess I could always go to Toledo another time," I said.

"Well, if you're going to be so wistful about it, you'd better get going."

"I wasn't being wistful." I have always hated that word. It makes me think of pretty, stupid girls looking at flowers. "I'll have a beer. So why did you get so angry at your friend for moving to Ávila?" I ventured.

"Ah, that is a very long and complicated story, but I suppose if we are going to Ávila together, I will have to tell you."

"Then we are going?"

"Didn't I say I was going tomorrow?"

"Yes, but then I thought you'd changed your mind."

"What would have given you such a ludicrous idea as that now? I am a man of principle. I thought you had recognized me as such."

"I'm sorry, I just sensed you were reluctant."

"I am reluctant, but that doesn't mean that I will not go to Ávila. It really is time to go, and I never would have realized it if I hadn't met you and you hadn't been on your way to Toledo, where I once had a friend." His breathing was heavy as if he had just finished reciting a poem in one breath. "You know, although I love this bar dearly, I feel we should be moving on. I have learned over the years not to overstay my welcome." And before I could protest, he had settled our bill with the waiter and was heading for the door. He was not someone who could stand up and walk out of a bar without being noticed. His height alone made him conspicuous, and when this unlikely figure in a red beret with long Abraham Lincoln legs moved overly carefully across the room, all the patrons watched. They were waiting to see if he would fall, but he didn't. "I don't know what they're all looking at," he said when we were outside in the station. "They probably were wondering what an old sod like me was doing with a young woman like you. Now isn't that perfectly ludicrous?" I guess I thought it was a little weird at first, the way we kind of hooked up with each other, but George Liddy has a way of making you feel comfortable even in the most uncomfortable situations.

We made our way through the crowds of Atocha Station, or actually, I followed him, keeping his red beret always in sight. He did remarkably well given that he had had many more drinks than I had, and I was already feeling somewhat unsteady from my one beer on an empty stomach.

As soon as we got outside, I wished we were back inside again. Whatever glimmer of coolness had been lingering in the morning had now completely disappeared and I had to really concentrate to keep myself from lying down on the street right there and going to sleep. My new companion, despite the fact that he was wearing a full suit and a wool beret, seemed to be enjoying the outdoors. His walk became almost jaunty, and he started humming a Celtic-sounding melody.

Somehow I found myself walking into the Barbieri with my new friend. I tried to tell him that I didn't really want to go in, that I would prefer another place, the Barberillo where you can play chess, for example. I even asked him if he wanted to play chess.

"At a time like this?" he responded, completely baffled by my suggestion.

"I thought it would be nice."

"Actually I find chess unbearably tedious. My father used to torture me with it on Sundays after church while we were waiting for our dinner."

So we sat down at a nice table along the window. "I find this place terribly charming, don't you? You know it used to be where the communists gathered. I've always greatly admired communists in fascist countries, but, alas, both fascism and communism are dead now."

"Actually, my father was a communist," I blurted out without thinking. I'm not really a fan of telling lies, even to make the conversation more lively.

"Then he must be a very good person. I myself had neither the dedication nor the selflessness to join the Party, so I certainly admired those who did and can't quite get used to a world without them, although I'm not sure why. The Party never did take to people like me. But then, not very many people do, though that is changing now, too. It's quite difficult to keep up with it all, don't you think?"

The waiter came and my new friend ordered a *café sólo* and Cointreau. No beer this time. For me he ordered a pint of Guinness.

After he had taken a few sips of each of his drinks and lit a cigarette,

I asked him about his friend in Ávila. He promised to tell me about him when we were actually in Ávila, so I had to leave it at that. Instead, he went on and on about his mother's great aunt, who played tennis until the day she died at the age of eighty-something and about his favorite hotel in Istanbul and many other things, which I have since forgotten.

And then in walked my mother with a young woman who looked like she was in her mid-twenties. She wore a tight, sleeveless black shirt and her arms were delicately muscular. You could tell her arms were the part of her body she was most proud of. I didn't know what to do, whether to look down and hope my mother didn't notice me or whether to wave, but before I had time to make a decision, she and the woman had glided up to our table.

"Hi," she said as if I were a friend, not her daughter.

"Hi." I looked down. She introduced herself as Clara and her friend as Marisol, so I simply said I was Deborah. I had the feeling that's what my mother wanted. But my friend stuck to tradition. "I am George Liddy of Limerick," he said and shook their hands graciously.

Then my mother ordered a Jack Daniels, which George Liddy said was a horrible American concoction. I don't remember what Marisol drank, but George Liddy ordered me another pint of Guinness. They talked for a while the way I guess fellow foreigners are supposed to talk— about what they were doing in Spain, about where they were from. George Liddy told my mother that he had been spending his summers in Madrid for over thirty years. "The Spaniards have a much healthier attitude about the drink than we Irish do. They don't waste their time with guilt," he said.

I stopped paying attention to the conversation when my mother was hogging it. She and George Liddy were going on about poetry, but I didn't feel like talking about poetry. Marisol just sat there really straight with her legs crossed, smoking, listening really carefully but not making any attempts to join the conversation. At first I thought it was because she didn't understand English, but then I realized it was just that she was watching my mother so carefully as if she were trying to memorize her gestures and expressions so she could copy them later. I didn't really like her. It annoyed me the way her eyes so intensely focused on my mother.

At some point after my second Guinness, I just got up and walked out without saying anything. I guess I thought someone would come after me, but no one did, and once I was outside I couldn't go right back inside, so I took a walk. I walked up to the top of the Calle de Lavapíes and back down to the plaza and back up again and back down maybe ten times and then I went back to the Barbieri, but they weren't there anymore. I guess now that I look back on it, it was my fault for walking out like that, but they could have left a message with the bartender. I asked him, but he said they hadn't said a thing, so I started walking home.

THE CABARET AND THE OPERA

Since Tommy has come down with pneumonia, the doctors told me I shouldn't be visiting him—a person of my age runs a high risk of dying from pneumonia. Tommy's doctor was typically blunt about it, but I told him I wasn't that old and would take my chances, like I do every day on the stairs. I've been drinking a lot of fresh orange juice and even taking vitamins, protecting myself from Tommy's illness. It seems to be working. This is the strongest I've felt since Karl died.

"Are you sure you want me to continue the story?" was the first thing I asked Tommy today.

"I was afraid you weren't going to come. The doctors told me it wouldn't be good for you."

"Well, doctors aren't always right. I know. I lived with one for over fifty years. But maybe you're too tired for the story. Maybe you would prefer listening to music—Bach is always good when you're sick."

"No, your story is the only thing that keeps me from falling asleep, which is my biggest fear these days."

"Tommy?"

"Yes?"

"I hope you won't think I'm meddling, but I couldn't sleep last night thinking of your parents not knowing anything about this. It sounds silly, but they did bring you into the world. I could call them for you if you don't want to speak to them."

"Then they would want to visit."

"I could be here when they visit."

"Mrs. Mondschein, I don't want you to think I'm a cruel, horrible person, but not telling them is my only revenge. In the middle of the night, when I've worked myself into a terrible state of anxiety because of the pain and fear or because I've slept the whole day away, I just imagine my parents watching television on my birthday long after my death, wondering if they should, after all these years, pick up the phone and call me."

"Sometimes it is very difficult for parents to understand their children," I said.

"I didn't want them to understand—just a little kindness would have

57

been enough. When I was thirteen, I begged them to take me to the opera for my birthday. You know what they did instead? They sent me to my room. I spent my thirteenth birthday in my room, crying and hungry. The next day they acted like it had never happened. When I was fourteen, my father took all my books out to the backyard and burned them. Then they painted my room white and put up pictures of ducks. My mother took down everything I had had up—Oscar Wilde, Orson Welles, a reproduction of a Münch lithograph, the one with the young girl facing the sea. She threw everything out and put up ducks."

"Isn't it time to forgive them?" I asked.

"They don't deserve it. Their suffering will never make up for what they have done. They won't even feel the guilt. They don't even know what they did wrong. After all, they didn't create a faggot. I created him all by myself, to spite them for no reason at all except that I was born evil. They've taken to God. Once a year my mother sends me a pamphlet. *Homosexuality in God's World* or *Armageddon Is on its Way*." There were beads of perspiration forming in the little crevice between Tommy's upper lip and his nose, and he was out of breath.

"Maybe after you die, they will become true Christians."

"And what, Mrs. Mondschein, is a true Christian?"

"Like Jesus."

"Jesus was a crucified faggot. That's why they crucified him. Because he was an annoying little fag. Only a fag would have been content roaming around with a bunch of men, telling people to love each other and get rid of all their dumb rules."

"And he was a Jew, don't forget that."

We both laughed over that. Tommy laughed so hard that he started coughing, and then it seemed as if he was having trouble breathing, so I called the nurse, who said he needed his rest and shouldn't be riled up. That just made Tommy laugh even more.

"So, Mrs. Mondschein, tell me more about your doctor."

"My doctor. I suppose he was my doctor, though I don't like to think of him that way." I paused and imagined Karl in his green Loden coat and leather gloves, standing in the doorway, waiting for me to get ready. "Karl started taking me for walks," I began again. "He always wanted to head towards the center of town and end up in a clattering, well-lit café. In the evenings, we ate big bowls of spicy, unkosher goulash and went to the opera—standing room always. Karl knew the words to all the arias, both male and female, of every opera we saw. He was always talking about music. During the emotional finales to his favorite operas, he would take my hand and press it hard. He taught me everything he knew about music, and I developed a sweet ritual out of learning the names of all the composers. Sometimes melodies would stay with me for a few days after a concert or after the opera, and I would be surprised to find myself humming while I dressed in the mornings. I devoured all the books he gave me to read, pausing only to imagine him rushing around the hospital in a white coat healing people, arriving just in the nick of time to save a woman almost dead from self-inflicted wounds or taking the time to wipe the brow of a little boy with scarlet fever. I tried to think of making love to the doctor with music playing in the background, but I could never really get an image of it. I just heard music, and if I closed my eyes, all I could see was my tall first husband smirking at me.

"Karl brought me vitamins to strengthen the baby growing inside me, although we never mentioned my condition, and he brought my sisters candies. I think they were both a little bit in love with him, too. Sometimes, when we were not going out, he sat with them in the living room and told them stories about the rich children he had tutored and the luxurious dinners he had eaten in their houses. My sisters' mouths watered with delight as he described forbidden foods such as venison with sherry cream sauce and oysters. Afterwards, we would laugh at my sisters' fear of food while we ate pork *Wienerschnitzel* and drank wine in a little cellar restaurant frequented by students who talked drunkenly of communism.

"But every day my child became more visible, and it was like a barrier between us. We watched my stomach grow without either of us ever mentioning it. Instead we discussed music and medicine. He told me I was his only friend. He never once tried to kiss me; we never talked about the future, and I tried not to think about what would happen when the baby was born. Only my father talked incessantly about what was to come and about how there was so little time left. Now that I look back on it, my father's warnings were truly extraordinary. He never read the newspapers; he never listened to the radio. Sometimes Karl would tell me about the rising tide of fascism, but he was not that interested in politics.

He was concerned with saving lives and he loved music, and, for some reason, I was his friend.

"Then my water broke in the sixth month. We were sitting with my father, my sisters and I, not saying a word, my father staring at his clock, my sisters knitting, when I felt everything give inside me, and then I was sitting in a pool of water. My sisters panicked. They screamed and screamed while my father just kept staring. I tried to get up, but fell, and my sisters screamed even more. Finally, I had to order them to help me to the couch, to go out and find a taxi. I asked the driver to take me to Karl's hospital, praying—in those days I still prayed—that he would be there.

"When I awoke, I was in a clean, white room. A nun was sitting in a chair next to my bed, reading. She was very kind, asked me how I was feeling, smiled. I was afraid to ask about my baby, afraid that it was dead and afraid that it was alive, so I said nothing, just smiled and asked for water, which Karl brought me himself, rushing into the room in his white coat just as I had so often pictured him doing. He sat on the bed, took my hand, and started crying. 'I couldn't save her,' he said.

"'It was a girl?' I asked.

"'Yes.'

"'It's not your fault. She wasn't ready for life,' I said, feeling neither sadness nor relief.

"Karl had performed the Caesarean himself, and then he had sat up all night with my dying daughter. She lived for six hours. I had almost died too. They had to do a transfusion—there was so much hemorrhaging.

"'What did she look like?' I asked.

"'Tiny,' he said. 'She never opened her eyes. Like a little chick. That's what she was like—a little chick.'

"I was in the hospital for two weeks, and Karl was with me whenever he had a moment. He slept on a cot in my room, and he brought me a radio so I could listen to music. When it was time for me to go home, he took me back to my father's apartment. My sisters had not visited me once while I was away. They couldn't leave my father alone. It was understood. Neither of my sisters ever said a word about my child. They didn't say they were sorry, and my father said it was better this way since there was so little time left for all of us. I wasn't angry at any of them.

"Weeks went by, and I refused to get out of my bed. I felt as if the world were over for me. What was I to do? I had even lost the ambivalent feeling of waiting to give birth to an unwanted child. I lay in my bed and planned gruesome ways to kill my first husband—by fire, by dagger, by blows to his head. I could hear his skull cracking in my dreams. Karl still came to visit, but I refused to go out with him. He brought me flowers, and I let them die. Later, he told me he thought I was punishing him for killing my baby. I guess he was the only one who ever loved her, but we never talked about that then.

"My father and I both got weaker and weaker. The blankets were piling up on him while I could hardly spend more than a few hours a day with my eyes open. Karl started spending the night, sleeping fitfully on the living room couch. And then, one day he burst into my room and told me that I would never see him again unless I got out of bed immediately and joined the living. I had never seen him agitated before— crying, yes, agitated, no. He had always had that doctorly calm about him, so his behavior almost frightened me. He stood in the middle of the room with his arms crossed and waited. I had no choice but to get out of bed. 'Get dressed,' he ordered me, and I took off my nightgown and began dressing slowly with him standing in the middle of the room, watching angrily. When I was dressed, I said, 'And what, Doctor, am I to do now?' because I really could not think of a thing that I could do. My sisters were taking care of my father; my sisters were cooking and cleaning; my sisters were budgeting. I had absolutely no purpose, like my dead baby.

"'I have thought about what I am going to ask you long and hard,' he said. 'I can't offer you a normal life, but if you agree, I would like for us to be married.'

"I laughed. I will never forgive myself for that laugh, even though Karl told me hundreds, perhaps thousands, of times that he was not hurt by it.

"'You are right,' he said. 'It is an absurd proposal since I will never love you as a husband should love his wife.' And then I felt my stomach sink. For the first time I felt my stomach was empty, that there was no life inside it anymore, that life was dead."

"So you were in love with him," Tommy said, and there were tears in his eyes that I wanted to wipe away but didn't.

"Perhaps. Or perhaps I was in love with his kindness."

"Kindness! Proposing to a woman by saying he will never love her?"

"That is a form of kindness, which is so much more complicated than most people are willing to admit."

"So you agreed? You agreed to marry him?"

"I agreed, and I didn't even ask him why he couldn't love me. It was a question of faith, and I knew he would tell me when the time was right. If he had told me then, I would have had to refuse."

"Mrs. Mondschein, you are crazy."

"I would have died in that house, Tommy. I would have followed my father to my own grave."

"Did you have a wedding?"

"Wedding? Oh yes, there was a little ceremony at my father's house. My father laughed like a drunken gambler who had lost all his money. He thought it was odd that we were carrying on with things when the world was so close to its end."

"What year was it?"

"Thirty-seven still. We had not quite one year left."

"So when did he tell you that he was a fag?"

"You knew?"

Tommy laughed and started coughing.

"Did you know all along, right from the beginning?" I asked.

"Almost right from the beginning."

"What was it that gave him away?"

"Nothing specific. I can just tell these things. Never been wrong in my life, not since I was eleven and I first figured out there were two worlds—the straight one and the gay one." And then he looked up to the ceiling and said very dramatically, "I can feel myself falling in love with your husband."

"Ah, Tommy, even now you are making me jealous," I said only half-jokingly.

"Now Mrs. Mondschein, two people do not stay together all those years if there is no love."

"I have always observed the opposite: lovers become estranged, the others get too tired of looking for passion and grow old together."

"If I believed that, I wouldn't be sick."

"Now it's my turn to laugh. Do you really think that if you had found the right man, the two of you would be living happily ever after?"

"It's a nice thought—helps dull the pain."

"Does it really?"

"So when did he tell you?"

"He didn't tell me. He showed me. He took me to a cabaret, which was more beautiful than the opera. He knew everyone, and they all called him *Herr Doktor*. He introduced me as his wife, and no one tittered. They bought me drinks and taught me to dance the tango. Karl preferred to watch. He would sit very elegantly at our little round table, sipping cognac, smoking, following the dancers round and round the dance floor with his eyes, smiling at the master of ceremony's off-color jokes, nodding politely to acquaintances, clapping at the end of each cabaret number. He was very solicitous, always making sure I was comfortable, asking if I were tired. 'Are there any Jews here?' I remember asking him, and that was the only time he laughed at me.

"'This is the only place where counts, officers, Jews, Englishmen, and Hungarians share the same dance floor,' he said. When we went to the opera, we saw many of the same people. Some of us nodded quietly at each other, while some refused to nod at all; with others we exchanged a few words before settling into our separate worlds—Karl and I to the standing room section, the Count to his private box.

"Karl had a small one-room apartment with a tiny sitting room near the hospital in the Ninth District. He went about his work as a doctor while I tried to busy myself cooking French recipes and cleaning. But cleaning and cooking, I discovered, take much less time than most are willing to admit. I couldn't figure out how these tasks could fill my two sisters' days. But I didn't want to bother Karl about my boredom because he was busy and because he was kind and he brought me gifts—novels, a French grammar, Egyptian cigarettes. I visited my father dutifully and invited my sisters to visit me, but they never did. They were afraid to take the trolley alone, and when I offered to pick them up so we could go together, they said they couldn't leave my father.

"I lived for our outings to the opera and concerts and to the cabaret.

I practiced dancing in our dark little sitting room, and when Karl came home tired, with stories of dead children and the lack of hospital beds, I made him dance with me until he could no longer keep standing. He never refused."

"Were there women at the cabaret?" Tommy asked.

"Do you mean lesbians?"

"Yes, I just couldn't say the word." Tommy giggled.

"Yes, there was one I remember in particular—Lotte. She always sat alone in a corner and I always wanted to ask her to join us, but I never did."

"Did you ever think about women?"

"Frankly, I never knew quite what to say to them."

"Mrs. Mondschein, you have to remember that I am on my deathbed and dying men are allowed certain liberties, but, did you and Karl have sex?"

"Not at that time. But you are rushing me. I was enjoying the memory of my cabaret. I can practically taste the smell of French cigarettes and wet fur coats. There was a lot of snow that winter of 1937. Karl and I took long walks in the Jewish cemetery. He showed me his parents' graves jammed in like two unnecessary teeth with all the others. That's what those old Jewish cemeteries looked like—an old man's mouth."

"How could you stand it?" Tommy said.

"Stand it? It was the happiest I had ever been. I was free of my mother's memory and the dusty apartment and the incomprehensible prayers in a language I was not allowed to study and my father's torturous dying and the neighbors who whispered about how lucky it was the baby died."

"Did he have lovers?"

"You are rushing me again. All in good time."

"I'm jealous already."

"Jealous for me or jealous for yourself?"

"Ah, Mrs. Mondschein. Jealous for both of us."

ST. TERESA'S FINGER

I think my mother wouldn't agree with me, but Mercedes kind of looks like Marisol. The one time my mother met Mercedes was when Mercedes was early picking me up to go to Bergen Youth Orchestra practice. Usually I would be waiting and as soon as I saw her car, I would run out so my mother wouldn't see her because I knew she wouldn't be open-minded about the leather jacket and piercings. But one time Mercedes was early, so she rang the bell and my mother answered the door and told her to come in, and then we all had to stand around chit-chatting while my mother stared at her clothes, but I don't think Mercedes noticed my mother's staring. She doesn't really pay attention to that sort of thing since she's one of those people who knows what to say to everyone, even my mother.

Mercedes has Marisol's arms and is always wearing sleeveless T-shirts even in the winter, so everyone can see her arms. I wonder what would happen if I went up to my mother's room right now and asked her if she thought Mercedes looked like Marisol. I wonder if that would make things worse or if she might talk. I could just go up there and ask her if she remembers that day she walked into the Barbieri with Marisol and I was there with George Liddy and then they left without me. I guess I would talk to her about it if I thought it would make a difference, but I know it won't either way, so why bother. Maybe I should get all dressed up in my black concert dress, knock on her door, enter the room slowly so as not to startle her. Maybe all it would take is a nice dress to make her snap out of it, but I'm not in the mood for putting on a show. She, in my opinion, pays too much attention to clothes. I wouldn't care about it at all if she kept her obsessions to herself, but she has always tried to spark a similar interest in me and we've had screaming, door-banging arguments about clothes. It's so stupid, really; she has this thing about looking your best, but she won't accept my philosophy—that some people look their best unadorned. Of course, what makes the whole thing even more ridiculous is that she spends half her life lying around in a graying polyester nightgown and can't even get up enough energy to put on a pair of jeans. Whenever we have the clothes argument, I remind her of this and she tells me that it is unfair to bring her illness into the argument. I think my mother would have been happiest if I were really beautiful—strikingly beautiful like a Brazilian actress instead of just normal-looking without any distinguishing features, no long legs or craggy nose or violet-green eyes. My mother is always talking about how there is so much ugliness in the world that we should try to surround ourselves with beauty to counteract it. I think she almost believes that evil can be eradicated by beauty but if I told her I thought she believed that she would just laugh and go on about all the high-ranking Nazis who played Mozart on their gramophones all through the war. Still, there are all kinds of beauty. Some are just simpler than others. And what about all the beautiful things that are also horrifyingly ugly like Francis Bacon paintings and medieval icons of Christ on the cross? Not that I have any leanings towards Christianity, but so much of my favorite music was created as a devotion to Christ—to the passion on the cross, I guess. It's sickness and ugliness and suffering that seems to move people the most. Only today all these Christians don't want to harp so much on the blood and gore. These days Christ on the cross looks like he's sunbathing and kids like Jennifer Cameron smilingly make points about the power of prayer and Jesus' love in English class no matter what we're talking about, whether it be grammar or W. H. Auden. If only Jennifer Cameron and my mother bothered to really look at one of those paintings of Christ being taken down from the cross or listen to one of Bach's Passions. Stare Christ in the eye. Then maybe they could see it for what it really is instead of engaging in all this worshipping and demonizing, but people seem to have a need to believe in things.

Even Mercedes, who is pretty cynical about almost everything, has a little corner in her room with a shrine she made herself from stuff she bought at one of those *botanica* stores in New York. The shrine includes a plastic Black Virgin and some bottles with different-color oils, some flowers and I think I saw some chicken bones. She told me she lights a candle in front of it every night before she goes to bed. I wonder if my mother prays during her ceremonies. She has never told me that she does, nor has she ever told me to pray. She just always says we should concentrate on the suffering and the dying, try to transport ourselves back to those cold, smelly barracks where she was born. I used to be good at doing it, but I haven't really tried for a while now. I used to be able to smell the shit and the vomit and my fingers and toes and ears would get red and numb with cold, and I would start shivering so hard that sometimes my father put a blanket over me. When I was very young, I would lull myself to sleep pretending I was in the barracks, my stomach crying for food, my fingers cracked from cold.

When I was in seventh grade, I wrote a composition called "My Mother Was Born in a Concentration Camp." My teacher Mrs. Harris, an old woman who had some kind of condition that made the skin on her arms and neck scaly and bright red so she was always scratching herself, asked me to stay after school.

"This is very powerful," she said, and I said nothing. "Where did you come up with such an idea?"

"It's true," I replied simply.

"Now Deborah, you shouldn't mix fact with fiction."

"I'm not. My mother was born in Pribor on February 12, 1945, a month before the liberation."

Mrs. Harris didn't know what to say, so she gave me back my paper, which had a big A on it even though, as usual, I had made quite a few spelling errors. I've never paid much attention to spelling. After that, I wrote all my compositions about the Holocaust and I got an A on every paper. I don't know if that means that she finally believed me or if she just liked my writing, but Mrs. Harris never said another word about it.

By the time I got to high school, I was sick of writing about my mother and Pribor, so I decided not to tell anyone about it anymore. So now Amy is the only person I hang out with who knows because I've known her forever, but she has been sworn to secrecy. It's also not fair to go around telling people because it makes them nervous. What are they supposed to say, anyway? I wouldn't know what to say, so why should other people know how to respond? It's like when someone dies and you have to say something, so you say, "I'm sorry." I've actually become extremely quiet over the past two years. Only Amy and Josh get the benefit of my conversation, and Mercedes too, I guess, although I haven't talked to her much since her cousin moved here from Cuba.

In school I shut up almost completely. I answer if I'm called on, which doesn't happen very often because then I try to say something weird enough to make everyone uncomfortable, so the teachers pretty much leave me alone. Like just last week in English class we were discussing Thoreau, and I said that nature was overrated. The teacher didn't even bother to ask me what I meant, luckily, because I don't have a very good argument; it's just something I feel. Not that I don't like nature, but I don't get inspired by it like some people do, and I dislike art that depicts nature like those boring Dutch landscapes and poetry by Wordsworth. I prefer walking around a city, sitting on the fire escape of my grandmother's apartment, watching the Dominican men play dominoes. But I would never have said all that in class even if the teacher had bothered to ask me what I meant instead of just smiling and calling on someone else right away. I might have even explained it to Mercedes a couple weeks ago, but, as I said, we haven't talked much lately. I did notice that she smiled when I made that statement in class, though.

Mercedes has been busy with her cousin who just escaped from Cuba on one of those rafts. This cousin of hers is actually a very distant cousin who belongs to the only part of her family that stayed in Cuba after the revolution. His parents are communists, very tight with Castro even, and so Leon (he was named after Leon Trotsky) escaped all by himself on a homemade raft. He even had to spend a week in the hospital in Miami because of dehydration before they flew him up here to New Jersey.

Anyway, Mercedes is really into finding out all about this long-lost side of her family, so we haven't seen each other except at school. She keeps telling me that she wants me to meet Leon, but he's still feeling weak from *his ordeal*. That's what she calls it—*his ordeal*. It's not like we spend that much time together anyway. We were working on a flute and cello sonata, but that kind of fell by the wayside. I guess neither of us was really into it.

Mercedes hangs out with the theater people. She's been in all the productions and always gets an important part, especially in the musical theater productions, which most of the productions are because the drama teacher once had a supporting role in a Broadway play. I can't remember which one it was, but I really hate musicals, and I'm not much of an opera fan, either. Mercedes loves opera, and I think it kind of bugs her that, though she has a nice, steady voice, it's not anywhere near strong enough for opera. She doesn't really like musicals either, but she likes acting and hanging around the theater people who spend all of their lunch hours and free time in the drama room building sets and dressing up in costumes and being witty. At least she knows not to bug me about joining her. I'm only in the Bergen Youth Orchestra because Mrs. Abad-jian insists on it. She says that even if I were as good as Yo Yo Ma, there's no way I'll get into a conservatory if I haven't ever played in an orchestra. The Bergen Youth Orchestra is how I got to know Mercedes. Actually, I've known her for a long time—since middle school, but I had not really talked to her until she got a car. Then she asked me if I wanted her to give me a ride to the orchestra rehearsals since I often had to take the bus all the way to Hackensack if my father wasn't available. My mother never learned to drive. She's lived in the suburbs for half her life, but she still likes to act like a New Yorker who has no use for cars.

I'm not very good at talking to people my own age, so I was really nervous about having to spend forty minutes in the car with Mercedes with nothing to say. Usually I take my lunch to the park because I don't like to eat in the cafeteria where I might end up sitting with a bunch of people and feel obligated to converse with them. The problem is I never can think of anything worthwhile to add, so I just sit there racking my brains for something interesting to say. I don't have that problem with my parents' friends because they talk about a book or history or religion, but my classmates are always talking about other people—about teachers or something some other kid said, which I either find boring or none of my business. But with Mercedes it's a little different, largely because we try to talk to each other in Spanish, which is mainly for my benefit because, after all the progress I made last summer, I really want to prac-tice. She speaks Spanish with her parents, but she never talks to them, so that doesn't count.

At first the resemblance between Mercedes and Marisol didn't reg-ister, I guess because I hadn't really thought about Madrid in a while. When we first got back at the end of the summer, I couldn't bring myself back from there. If I was out riding my bicycle, I found myself blanking out, not knowing where I was, imagining that I was wandering around the streets of *La Latina*—looking up at the balconies, the tile rooftops, breathing in the smell of garlic and bread baking in the early morning. In school I found myself involuntarily conjugating Spanish verbs, muttering them, so kids started looking at me like I was crazy. One of my classmates asked me if I was meditating, and I told her that I have never even contemplated meditating in my entire life, which isn't exactly true, and then I could tell she felt bad because I know she's really into Buddhism and that kind of thing. Still, it scared me that she thought I would be interested in meditation. I felt it was almost a sign of sorts because I would be walking through the halls at school and all of a sudden one of the girls would look like St. Teresa—robes and all, with only the small oval of her stern face peeping out at me—and I would find myself laughing out loud. But all that died away by Thanksgiving, which was when my mother finally couldn't keep it together anymore and my father and I were too occupied with trying to coax her to the dinner table with special cheeses from Zabar's and heavy black Ukrainian bread. But, even if she did deign to come down for dinner, we would just end up watching her move the food around her plate and chewing with great effort like we had served her an overcooked mutton chop full of tendons and gristle.

It was just after Thanksgiving that Mercedes got her car and we started talking, but I've never talked to her about my mother's depressions or about Pribor or any of that. I think I was afraid she would think I was unstable. Maybe I thought she would think I was one of those *at risk* kids, one of those quiet, tortured types that murder their parents. Not that we ever talked about anything like that, plus she's the one with all the weird clothes that so many people think are a sure sign of extreme mental instability. I wonder whether my teachers would keep an eye on me if I brought in my concentration camp drawings for show and tell. But we don't have show and tell in high school. Maybe they should bring it back, though. They could call it something more mature like *sharing* and the teachers could encourage us to *reveal* things about our lives and families, and then afterwards the whole class could offer advice. Maybe Mercedes could show her nipple ring. Apparently she and a friend from music camp ditched school one day, met in the city, got drunk, and ended up getting their nipples pierced. When she told me about the pierced nipple, I could tell she wanted me to be shocked, but I wasn't. Instead I told her that when she's an old woman, she'll be covered with shriveled and faded tattoos and her nipples will hang down from the weight of the nipple ring, but she just laughed and said she wasn't planning on living to a ripe old age.

A lot of kids my age don't think about the future. Not that I am planning my life out career-wise or anything like that, but the future does concern me. I don't want to be sick when I'm old and it bothers me that I won't be around in a hundred years to know what's going on in the world—like whether China becomes the dominant power and whether people from different cultures are going to get along better because they'll be more similar or worse because they'll be more different, or whether things will always stay the same even though they change. I asked Mercedes if she insists on smoking like a chimney because she wants to make sure she'll die young, but she said that by the time she gets cancer, they'll have found the cure. Her smoking really gets on my nerves, especially since she's ruining her lungs, which are so essential to a flute player, but I never tell her not to smoke in my presence, even if it's in the car, which really makes me sick. She smokes about three cigarettes on the way to orchestra practice and by the time we get there I always have a headache. I should tell her that the smoke bothers me, though, because Mercedes is always telling me how she hates it when people don't speak up about things.

I often think about making an effort to communicate more of my thoughts, but I know people will just twist around everything I say, so that if I could get into their heads, I wouldn't even recognize my own ideas anymore by the time they had a chance to mull them over. I try to listen really carefully to what people say so I don't get it all screwed up, but I know that a lot of the time they're not telling me what they really think anyway or they're leaving out most of the important stuff, so I don't know why I bother.

I think that's why I enjoyed George Liddy's company so much— because half of what he said didn't make sense and the other half you could tell was just made-up stuff that he found amusing. Still, it took me a few days to forgive him for abandoning me for my mother and Marisol that afternoon at the Barbieri. And then once I did finally forgive him and sought him out at the bar in Atocha Station, it took me almost an hour to convince him not to be angry at me. He insisted that I was the one who had abandoned him, which I had to admit was true even though I had reason to be annoyed with him for showing my mother and Marisol way too much interest.

"I was just trying to be polite," he insisted. "How would it have seemed if I had been unconscionably rude to your mother and her friend? They would have thought me terribly uncivilized and we Irish must avoid that at all costs. You must remember we have a reputation for being terrorists."

"Polite is one thing, but you were laughing and reciting poetry and lighting Marisol's cigarettes."

"Was I supposed to make snide comments instead?"

"No, I'm sorry."

And that's really all he wanted to hear, so I let it go at that and we went to Ávila. George Liddy spent most of the train ride out there describing the bone-chilling winters of Ávila—the wind ripping over the plains and beating on the windows and how he was forced to spend days and nights on end without sleeping, sitting in front of a hearth (he loved to use words like that) drinking cognac at a very ancient bar under the walls of the city. He went on and on about eating bags and bags of *yemas*, a sickeningly sweet candy made of raw egg yolks that a young woman with whom he did not exchange even a word brought to him whenever he requested more. When we went to Ávila, it was unbearably hot and a dry wind ripped over the plains and the sun beat down on our heads as we walked from the train station, looking for that same bar under the walls, which we couldn't find, though we must have circled the city at least twice, hugging the walls that protected it. It seemed, also, that George Liddy was completely unaffected by the heat despite his usual attire—jacket, ascot, beret. After we had walked for over an hour, my scalp was scalded and my head ached from so much squinting, so I was the one who insisted we stop for a drink.

"I had been entertaining the thought of not taking a drink today," he said sadly as we entered a long slim bar with twelve paintings of St. Teresa running along the walls like the stations of the cross. "But I suppose it was a pipe dream," he laughed. "Yes, a mere pipe dream."

He wanted to sit at a table under one of the paintings, so we settled in and I went up and ordered his usual coffee and Cointreau and a beer for myself. The waiter brought our drinks and we sat silently getting used to the dark and quenching our thirst. I was sure he was about to tell me about his friend because you could tell he was thinking very seriously about something, like he was trying to figure out where to begin because it was a very long, complicated tale. I didn't want to push him because I knew if I did, he would give up on telling me altogether.

"I think we'd better go see the finger," he said, stroking his perfectly smooth chin. That was when I noticed that he didn't really have any facial hair even though he did have hair sticking out from under his beret, but there were none of the usual hair pores you can see on men's faces even right after they've shaved. His hands were completely smooth and hairless and there were no hairs peeking out from under the cuffs of his jacket, which is something that has always struck me as ridiculous, as if the hairs were surreptitiously trying to get a look at the world.

"What finger?"

"You shall see." He went up to the waiter and asked him in his Irish-accented Spanish how to get to the finger of St. Teresa, and the waiter gave his directions very nonchalantly, as if he were telling us how to get to a hotel or the train station, drawing a little map on a napkin for us as he spoke. George Liddy took the napkin and thanked him with a slight tip of his beret. Then we were back out in the sun.

We followed the waiter's directions exactly, but when we reached the end of them, when we should have been at the church that housed the finger, we were in front of a school. We walked up and down the street looking for the church, but there was nothing that even resembled a church, not even a chapel, so George Liddy decided it was a sign. Instead of asking someone else for directions, he insisted there was a reason we had been given the wrong directions, that we were not ready to be confronted with the finger, that perhaps our whole outing to Ávila was terribly misguided, that I should be in my Spanish class, that this was no way for a young lady to spend a day. He was extremely frazzled. His hands were trembling and I had to help him light his cigarette. I didn't know what to do with him, so I suggested we have a drink. This proposition seemed to cheer him up.

"Do you really believe in signs?" I asked once we were settled at the bar. I was disappointed that we weren't going to see the finger, and I was disappointed that he believed in signs. I hate it when people say things about fate and signs. The one that bugs me the most is when they say that something was *meant to happen*. Like if someone's mother dies, or someone's child is born with cerebral palsy, or someone gets hit by a drunk driver and ends up paralyzed, or someone loses her engagement ring, or whatever it is and they get that really fake peaceful look in their eyes and say, *It was meant to happen* or *The universe is trying to tell me something.*

"Do you believe in them?" George Liddy asked me.

"It depends what you mean by a sign. If someone is acting really crazy, crying all the time and not eating, that could be a sign they're depressed."

"You know and I know that we're not talking about that kind of sign."

"Do I think that our not being able to find the church is a sign? Is that what you mean?" I asked.

"Well, what else would I mean, then?"

"No, I don't believe in signs and neither do you. You're just being a coward." I don't know why I said that or why I knew that because I've never been very good at understanding people.

"Well, I suppose you're right. So now what are we going to do—two strangers in Ávila in the middle of the hot afternoon? Perhaps we should have some lunch," he said, his face lighting up.

So we had some lunch—a huge plate of *cocido*, a stew made with cabbage and something like thirteen types of meat including pork and veal and veal trotters and bacon and blood sausage and big hunks of fat. We were the only customers in the place, so the waiter kept coming up to us every few minutes to ask if everything was okay, bringing more bread and wine.

When we finally finished, I felt like all I wanted to do was sleep. I hate eating a big meal in the middle of the day because it makes me so tired and lethargic and I invariably end up dozing off, and then it's dark by the time I get up, and I feel like I've wasted a whole day like when you come out of an afternoon show at the movies, and you feel lazy and disoriented from the sudden darkness. Also, even though I'm a more practiced drinker than most teenagers, I was not used to keeping up with someone like George Liddy, so the beer and wine really had gone to my head. I'm sure we were quite a sight, George Liddy and I, walking arm in arm down the sun-baked streets of Ávila. We walked and walked with George Liddy leaning on me. My arm grew sore from trying to hold him up, and, once, he tripped over a protruding cobblestone, toppling us both to the ground.

"I must keep my eyes on my feet," he laughed, "but my mother always used to scold me about looking at the ground as I walked. She said people would think I was looking for money. My mother's main purpose in life was to make other people believe we were not poor. I gave her a grand funeral when she died. I hope she appreciated it, but somehow I doubt it. What do you think?"

"I think you should have cremated her."

"Well, I suppose I could have the body exhumed. Perhaps when I return to Ireland I shall do that. But we can't sit here in the middle of the street talking about cremation, now can we?" And up he stood, pulling me with him.

"Don't you think it's time to look for your friend?" I asked. I was sure I was getting heatstroke and figured that if there were no purpose to our wandering, we would wander forever because George Liddy seemed to have an inexhaustible supply of energy.

"Ah yes, my friend, the one who lives in Ávila. What does one call a person from Ávila, an *aviliano*? Perhaps we should stop in here for a moment and ask one of Ávila's own townspeople." And so we found ourselves in the courtyard of a very old apartment building. It was shady and cool and we could hear the noise of televisions coming from the apartments that overlooked the courtyard. I would have been happy to lie down right there and take a nap, but George Liddy had other plans. "Yoo-hoo," he called, cupping his hands around his mouth. "Yoo-hooooooooooooo."

No one answered.

"I don't think they can hear over their televisions," I said, hoping he would give up on his plan, but he just yoo-hooed even louder and longer until, finally, a woman leaned out of her window and asked us what we wanted. George Liddy proceeded to very gallantly remove his beret and then asked in his horrible Spanish if she would be so kind as to tell us what a person from Ávila was called.

"What?" the woman screamed.

He repeated his question in a slightly abbreviated form.

She still didn't understand what he was trying to say, so she told us to come up.

We ended up having to eat *yemas* and drink overly sugary coffee with the old lady, but I guess we couldn't just go all the way up to her apartment to ask her what people from Ávila were called and then simply say we had to run. We sat in the woman's apartment on a very hot brown velvet sofa with little doilies all over the arms and back while she made the coffee and arranged the *yemas* on a porcelain dish. I looked around the room. There were portraits of St. Teresa all over the walls, crammed into every possible inch of space.

"Are you a great admirer of St. Teresa?" George Liddy asked the woman when she had settled herself next to us on the sofa. I didn't understand why she wanted to sit so close to us, especially given the heat and the fact that there were three matching brown velvet armchairs crammed into her little sitting room.

"Please, take another *yema*," she said to me, holding the plate under my nose. I took one and she shook the plate to indicate that I should take another, which I did. If you have never eaten a *yema*, it is very difficult to understand how I felt sitting there, drunk and stuffed with *cocido*, sunstroked, squeezed between George Liddy and a rather plump, elderly *avilana* (which she later explained to us is the name for a person from Ávila) with a booming voice, forcing myself to eat the little, round, sugary sweets. I didn't know what was going to happen first—whether I would vomit, scream, or pass out. As it turned out, I did none of those things and was forced to sit politely for over an hour while George Liddy and the *avilana* discussed the wonder that was St. Teresa.

I didn't really pay attention to the whole St. Teresa conversation because I don't have much interest in saints. I know St. Teresa is admired by many women because she started a whole order on her own and ruled over it with an iron fist and wrote poetry and memoirs that scholars, to this day, can write volumes and volumes about, but for me she was still a saint, which means that she lived and died for religion. And that, frankly, is something I don't find all that enthralling. Later when I told my father that I had been to Ávila, he went on and on about how St. Teresa was actually from a Jewish family, which I don't think makes much of a difference if she wasn't a practicing Jew. People place way too much emphasis on blood. As far as I'm concerned, St. Teresa was a Catholic and I'm sure she would have agreed with me about that.

Finally, after what seemed like hours, George Liddy got up to leave. He kissed the woman's hand graciously and we were on our way. "Come back soon," she called after us as we descended the stairway. When we reached the bottom, George Liddy turned around and bowed.

"What a tedious woman. I absolutely despise St. Teresa and all the nuns of Christendom. They destroyed my childhood, but that's another story," he said when we were out in the street again.

"So why did we stay so long?"

"I just couldn't bear the idea of going back out into this sun."

"Don't you think we should ask around for your friend?"

"My friend? Ah yes, my friend. Well, Deborah, I will have to confess now because I'm too tired to continue this charade. There is no friend. I never had a friend either in Toledo or in Ávila, although I wish I did. I honestly wish I did."

"I knew it all along," I said and started walking more quickly.

"Well, why didn't you say something sooner? No one in his right mind visits Ávila in the summer."

"I was going to go to Toledo. You were the one who insisted on Ávila."

"So I did. Well, I must be a masochist."

And then we went back to Madrid after stopping for one last drink on the way to the train station. When we pulled into Atocha Station, it was past ten o'clock at night and my head ached from the sun and the alcohol and the cigarette smoke on the train, and all I wanted to do was go home to sleep. George Liddy and I parted on Atocha Street and he handed me a card—*Pensión Lugo, Plaza Tirso de Molina 3.* "You can always call for me there," he said. "I plan to stay for a very long time."

"I will," I said, but I wasn't sure if I would. I felt as if we had run out of things to say, but it didn't make me sad; on the contrary, I felt free and walked home almost happy despite the headache, looking forward to reading in my little room with the slanted ceiling.

When I got home, my father was sitting in the living room reading and I didn't ask where my mother was. I didn't really think to ask whether she was even home. My father and I said good night, and I fell asleep immediately and didn't wake up until the next morning. The apartment was empty. At that point, I had no idea that my mother hadn't come home the night before and that my father had gone out at about two looking for her. Still, I felt their absence because I wanted to talk to them, tell them about my adventure in Ávila—the meandering, the sickening *yemas*—because with experiences like that you can't really know if they actually happened until you start telling someone about them.

So I went out into the already hot day, hoping that I would find them in one of the bars on our street, drinking coffee, relaxing a little before my father went off to the library. I went to all the bars on our street. I asked the bartenders if they had seen them—two Americans, a man and a woman, husband and wife—but they hadn't seen any foreigners that morning. I went back to the apartment and grabbed a book to read at the Barbieri. At some point, I figured, my mother would show up there. I imagined her walking nonchalantly to where I was waiting for her, saving her preferred table.

"Where have you been?" she would ask and I would reply, "Where have you been?" And then we would laugh. That's how I pictured it. It was all very clear in my mind.

I wanted to tell Mercedes about my mother's disappearance when we were driving to orchestra practice the other night. I wanted to tell her about how I sat like an idiot at the Barbieri from eleven in the morning until five in the afternoon, trying to read, looking up every time someone walked in the door. She was telling me about her father's infidelities, about how her mother told her that it is a wife's duty to *support* (that's the word her mother used) her husband's weaknesses. She said, "My mother's a fucking idiot," and I blurted out that she shouldn't say things like that about her mother, and as soon as I said it, I knew it was a really stupid thing to say because why shouldn't she say whatever she feels like saying about her mother, especially when her mother was, in fact, being so completely idiotic. And of course Mercedes laughed, so I changed the subject.

"Did you know that when Hitler's army was stuck in the Soviet Union in the dead of winter, the soldiers' feet were so frozen solid that when they tried to run, their feet just broke off?" I asked.

I had just read an article about this on the Internet. I was supposed to be getting information about white supremacists for a project I was working on in history class, but I got sidetracked. I was tired of reading the same old nonsense about the Jewish plot to take over the world with the help of the "mud people." I don't know why I chose such a dumb topic because there's not much new to say about it, since what they believe is obviously so stupid and their ideas are obviously dangerous and sick, and how many times can you say that? I guess I could go on about how they have thousands of websites, but I don't in any way want to imply that censorship is the answer. If I were a hacker, I would download that little piece of information about the German soldiers' feet breaking off and put it on all of those websites, but they probably wouldn't get the irony. They probably would set up some huge memorial to the broken feet of the martyred German soldiers, and then I could chuckle about how they got their inspiration from the daughter of a Holocaust survivor.

I hadn't expected her to be too interested in the broken-footed soldiers, but she went on and on about how horrible it must have been to find yourself lying in the snow with your feet lost somewhere along the way.

"Do you think it hurt, or do you think they were beyond feeling at that point?" she asked seriously.

"I guess they were beyond feeling."

"Maybe they didn't even know that their feet had broken off. Maybe they kept trying to get up and walk and kept falling until they lost all their strength and died."

"Maybe." Then we both sat there feeling sorry for the Nazi soldiers. I wonder what those soldiers would have thought if they knew when they were lying there in the snow dying that fifty years later we would be sitting in a car in New Jersey wondering how they felt. I wonder if knowing such a thing would have made it worthwhile to them, not because of the Nazi cause or the Fatherland, but because two complete strangers on the other side of the world thought about them, immortalized them. Maybe I'll write a sonata for them, *The Sonata of the Broken-footed Soldiers*.

The rest of the way to orchestra practice we were silent. I was half thinking about my sonata, trying to come up with a theme—something arrhythmic, the beat of someone walking on stumps—and half thinking about what Mercedes was thinking about. I guess I could have asked her, but I always hate it when people ask me what I'm thinking about or when they say, *A penny for your thoughts*. I hate that expression.

THE WIZARD

"Mrs. Mondschein, you're looking very tired. Are you ill?" Tommy asked when I entered his room. Tommy's health, however, had improved immensely in the few days since I'd seen him. The nurses assured me that, as far as the pneumonia was concerned, he was out of danger, which was a great relief.

"No, I'm not sick," I replied, "but I couldn't sleep all night. My down-stairs neighbors had a terrible dispute. Jimmy, who is such a nice young man even though there always seems to be a different woman living with him, stabbed his most-recent girlfriend in the liver. They don't know if she's going to live. I awoke to terrible, hysterical screaming and, without thinking, put my bathrobe on and ran down my dangerous stairs. I didn't even think about the steps—can you imagine?"

"You didn't call the police first?"

"Police? No, they don't rush to get to our neighborhood. I should have awakened Mr. Claromundo, but honestly I didn't even think of it. I got to their apartment just as Jimmy was fleeing. There was blood every-where, and his poor girlfriend—she couldn't be more than twenty-two—was lying on the floor, bleeding and screaming like a cat. I've never seen so much blood before. I've seen many things, but not so much blood. But I was very cool, very rational, called 911—it rang twenty-three times—and explained everything very carefully. You know what they told me on the phone? You wouldn't believe it. They told me not to touch the blood, and I didn't, although I felt rather foolish standing in the middle of the room trying to calm the poor girl down, talking to her so she wouldn't go into shock, all without touching her. By that time, all the neighbors were crowded into the apartment, so I had to explain to everyone about not touching the blood. And I was actually afraid. Me, an old woman who spent almost every day of her life working around blood and sickness, afraid to touch the blood of a wounded woman."

"You did the right thing," Tommy said. "Do you want to die like this?"

"Death is never pretty."

"No, but you worry me. You could have been stabbed yourself. What-ever got into your head to handle such a scream on your own?"

"I'm more afraid of those stairs than of a man with a knife. Men with knives and much worse are familiar to me, but the stairs are always a mystery."

"What if this Jimmy guy comes after you?"

"I doubt I'll ever see him again. I'm sure he's far from New York by now. He was taking classes at City College. I wonder what happened."

"He sounds like a brute to me. A man with a weapon is always a brute; taking classes at City College has nothing to do with it. From your own experiences, you should know better than anyone. Weren't there officers at concentration camps who reclined on divans, listening to Bach while the prisoners carted away the dead bodies?"

"Yes, I have known a similar case, but it was more complicated than it seems. That, however, comes much later in my story."

"Should we listen to some Bach, Mrs. Mondschein?"

And so we listened to the *St. Matthew Passion* huddled close together. I could feel Tommy's frail, tubercular breath that smelled faintly of metal on my cheek, and the Bach was like a warm summer downpour on my brain.

"I want to hear about Karl's lovers."

"Why do you assume there were so many?"

"There weren't?"

"No."

"Did he always tell you everything?"

"What do you mean by *everything*?"

"Did he tell you about all his lovers?"

"There was only one."

"In his whole life, only one?"

"You are trying to get ahead of history again. His name was Bruno and he had lost an arm in World War I, but instead of making him look grotesque and already dead like most of the World War veterans whom you would see sitting forlornly on park benches in the Stadtpark, Bruno's missing arm made him distinguished, elegant. He always wore beautiful suits and pinned the left sleeve at his shoulder with a diamond. He had been Karl's teacher at the University of Vienna and was a specialist in skin grafting for burn victims. He performed operations with just one hand. They called him the Wizard.

"I didn't meet Bruno until two months after Karl and I were married because Bruno was on a lecture tour—Budapest, Berlin, Hamburg, Zagreb, Bucharest, Geneva, Paris. He brought Karl a leather-bound set of Proust. Karl told me all about Bruno and the nature of their relationship, showed me pictures, read me his letters."

"All of his letters?" Tommy asked.

"As far as I know. They weren't very romantic, just descriptions of museums and concerts, people and politics, and lists of his Jewish colleagues in Germany who had been asked to retire. They were very grim, his letters—fighting in the streets in Serbia, yellow stars in Berlin, tens of thousands of youths in uniforms singing patriotic songs at the tops of their lungs in Hamburg."

"He wasn't Jewish?"

"No."

"And you weren't jealous?"

"No, but I was worried about his return, worried that I would be in the way, that Bruno would hate me. The night before I was to meet him, I couldn't sleep because every time I closed my eyes, I saw the laughing face of my first husband. I almost ran back to my father's house for good, almost packed up my few things. But I remembered that I would not fit in there either and decided it was preferable to be in the way in my new life than to be in the old one."

"Had Karl warned Bruno that he had married?"

"We had written a letter together."

"And how did Bruno react?"

"He didn't. He never mentioned it. On the day of our first meeting, I didn't know what to wear, so I set his picture on the bureau to get a sense of his taste and tried on all my clothes—not that I had very many; still, I tried them all on, but the later it got, the plainer I felt. When Karl came home, I told him I thought it would be better if I didn't meet Bruno after all. There was no reason really. They were the friends, and I could stay quietly at home. Or I could visit my father. He could drop me off at my father's, and I could stay there overnight. In the morning he could call for me.

"But Karl insisted. He said that if we were truly to be companions, then Bruno had to know me and I had to know Bruno. We argued. It was the first time. 'Surely,' I said, 'Bruno would prefer never to set eyes on me.'

"'But why?' Karl asked.

"So in the end, I agreed. We met at a very expensive restaurant, where Karl and Bruno ordered champagne. Karl told him about my family—my melancholy father, my sisters—and how different I was from all of them. I held my breath, almost praying that Karl would say nothing about the baby, but I couldn't open my mouth to change the subject, to ask Bruno questions about the Iron Guard in Romania or whether he had actually seen Adolf Hitler. To this day, I am grateful that Karl never mentioned my pregnancy to Bruno in my presence because, although Bruno was perfectly nice, I didn't like him. He was too handsome, his voice too mellifluous, his eyes too blue. I kept imagining him sewing new skin onto a bloody, glistening body with one hand, stitching quickly yet carefully, his eyes intent on his task, laughing silently about something a friend had told him the night before. I couldn't help wondering if he had been faithful to Karl on his journeys. After dinner, he insisted we dance together, and he told me that I danced beautifully, to which I replied that I had learned at the cabaret. My reply made him chuckle.

"I spent a lot of time alone after Bruno returned. After that first meeting, Karl didn't insist on our all being friends, so the only time we really saw each other was at the cabaret, though sometimes all three of us would go to the opera. Bruno never set foot in our apartment. And why should he have? He had a very elegant apartment in the First District, complete with a view of the spires of the Stefansdom, with Ottoman furniture that he had bought on his travels. I never saw the apartment, but Karl described it to me in detail. I couldn't help asking about Bruno. It made Karl so happy to be able to talk about him, about his latest burn case—'the poor man's left eye had simply been melted down'—about his family's house in the country where Karl was often invited for the weekend. I was invited too, but never agreed to go and Karl got tired of pressing me. We both disliked arguments.

"I decided I wasn't going to be bored anymore. Bruno's return woke me up, pushed me out into the world. My days were spent exploring Vienna, the city in which I had lived all my life but had never really known. So strange how that can happen to a person living in what was considered one of the most exciting cities in all of Europe. A city can be so isolating, almost as if the more different types of people there are crammed together in a small area, the farther away they all are from each other. New York is the same way—a little island crisscrossed with thousands of invisible boundaries. Just a few years ago, Karl and I were walking towards New Jersey across the George Washington Bridge, as we often liked to do, when two youngsters from the Bronx stopped us to ask what was on the other side of the bridge. Can you imagine? Before I married Karl, that's how I was in Vienna—I had hardly heard of the Stefansdom, let alone set foot in the opera house or walked in the palace gardens or visited the museum.

"One day, I began browsing through the closet; it was one of those days when none of my clothes satisfied me, when I couldn't find the right match for my mood. Because Karl had not been home in a few days, I was out of sorts and vaguely thinking about how much more adventurous I could be if I were a man. As a woman, it was daring to go to the museum alone. But as a man, I could pack a little bag and go to Budapest. Not that I couldn't pack a bag and go to Budapest. I had been to Italy, after all. Yet I was tired of people watching me, wondering who I was, the pregnant, lonely woman in Italy, the solitary young woman examining the Bruegels in the Vienna Art Museum. And for whom was she waiting all afternoon in that cafe, smoking and reading a thin volume of verse? If I were a man, I could go to a bar and get drunk. I could go to a café by myself—sit at a corner table, drink cognac, watch. I could have a lover called the Wizard who made new skin grow like spring grass.

"It was that day that I started wearing Karl's suits. I found a pair of his old glasses, wore my hat tipped low over my eyes. My breasts didn't even need strapping; in fact, they were invisible under Karl's crisply starched shirts and wool suit jackets. I practiced walking in front of the mirror—long, confident strides, arms swinging jauntily. Karl's clothes felt especially warm and comfortable in the days of bone girdles and high, thin heels. I bought thick wool socks; two pairs were enough to allow my feet to fill Karl's wing-tipped shoes. In those shoes I could walk all day long. It is amazing how shoes can change your life."

"Did Karl know about this?" Tommy asked.

"I have never told anyone. You are the first."

"Do you still do it?"

"Now? Whatever for? No one bothers an old woman in New York."

"Maybe you should try it, just to see how you feel after all this time."

"Would you want to dress like a woman at this stage in your life?"

"Now that's an idea, a brilliant idea. When I die, they can lay me out in drag. You know, I don't think that in the end any of the scores of drag queens I have known over the years and who have died over the years were ever laid out in drag."

"You never told me you were a drag queen."

"I wasn't, but perhaps that was my mistake. Drag queens are always well-loved by all—couples drive in from New Jersey and Indiana to see drag shows. Everyone seems to adore a man dressed like a woman much more than a man dressed like a man who likes going to bed with other men. I could even invite my parents to the funeral; I'd hire a band like they have at weddings to play all their favorite tunes—Sinatra especially. They just love Sinatra."

"I think people love men who dress like women because they pity them. They have to pity a man who would want to be treated like a woman, wouldn't they?"

"And they would have to pity a man who would want to die as a woman—shriveled, covered with lesions, teeth rotting, thinner than death but wanting to be beautiful, soft, and loved."

"So you want people to pity you when you're dead?"

"No, I want to think of people pitying me when I'm dead. That way I can spend my last days pitying them for hating me while I'm alive."

"Will you have the energy to keep listening to my story with all that pitying you have to do?"

"That's what's so great about pity; it requires so little energy. So now, Mrs. Mondschein, I want to hear about your life as a man."

"I saw my first husband once. It was at Demel's, the finest café in Vienna. He kept looking at his watch nervously. He was my true test, and after my encounter with him, I knew I was safe. I watched for a while from my corner table and then approached him.

"'Herr Ohnmacht, what a pleasure,' I said. It was obvious he had no idea who I was, but he shook my hand politely and asked me to join him. I introduced myself as Herr Bernhardt and mentioned my affiliation to his political party.

"'Ah, of course. Herr Bernhardt. I'm afraid I'm a little bit preoccupied these days.'

"'Terribly sorry to disturb you. I was just on my way out.'

"'No, please, stay and have a cognac.'

"So we drank cognac together, my first husband and I. We talked about politics—the grim situation in Germany. I told him I had just returned from Berlin on business. He was fascinated by my accounts of the Nazi rallies and worried about Hitler's promise to annex Austria. I said perhaps it was for the best. After all, we had to pass through fascism before we could get to socialism. He said he'd rather have the Germans deal with that. 'And what about anti-Semitism?' I asked.

"'That is the least of our worries,' he replied and offered me a cigarette. I was just about to ask him about his Jewish lady friend when a gaudily dressed woman fluttered to the table. We were introduced; she smiled coquettishly. I kissed her hand in the Viennese fashion and left them to themselves.

"I got so confident in my new clothes that I almost went to visit my father as a man, but at the last minute, just when I was about to ring the bell, I panicked and ran away. I had planned to say I was a friend of Karl's, a specialist whom Karl had sent to see if perhaps there was something to be done after all. I had even brought a notepad on which to write down my findings.

"Being able to watch without being watched provided me with such a sense of pleasure and exhilaration that I very rarely thought of the adventures that could have been mine had I dared. I suppose I stayed away from my father's house because I was sure that there they would see through my disguise, smell me out as one of their own who had gone astray and given birth to a daughter too frail to survive. I also avoided the cabaret, where surely they would not have been fooled.

"Who knows if I would have eventually mustered the courage to take my new self into the depths of the city and abroad? Who knows if I might not have remarked over breakfast one morning that life had become so much simpler since I began dressing in men's clothes? Who knows if Karl would have laughed and suggested we go off for a stroll together one day, or if he would have felt guilty for leaving me out of his life? Karl was so easily prone to guilt. So often I thought of telling him about how I amused myself in his absence, but my secret became too precious. And then our German neighbors had other plans for us, and Herr Bernhardt, being much too sensitive for extremist politics, was forced into permanent exile.

"On February 26, 1938, my father died. On the eve of his death, he told his three daughters to go back to Poland before it was too late. He wrote down the names of all of our relatives in Lemberg and Warsaw, relatives I never knew we had. He told us to take his watch because it had been his father's and his father's father's before that, and he gave us old pictures of our mother when she was a child. There would be some old people who would remember her. We were instructed to say that she had died of scarlet fever.

"We gave my father a simple funeral. Karl paid for it though my father had set aside a small sum for this purpose. My father left a letter which he asked us to read to all those who came to pay their respects while we sat *shiva*. In his letter, he warned us all that the end was near, that within a month it would be too late, and that our only hope was Poland. How many times I must have read that letter during that long week of sitting dry-eyed in our living room with its yellowed curtains and the watermarked ceiling I stared at in between guests. My sisters cried and cried until a smell that was a combination of warm milk and dried beef emanated from them and filled the room. I had wanted to put the letter away after the first day, but Karl and my sisters insisted on complying with my father's request. And since my sisters could not bear to read it—they would begin to cry after the first sentence and fall wailing onto the sofa—the reading of the letter became my duty. Solemnly I read and reread it every time a new visitor arrived with a basket of baked chicken or fresh coffee cake. Some of the neighbors shook their heads and mumbled 'poor Herr Feinberg' as I read. And some of the neighbors laughed nervously when I finished and then began talking about the differences between Germany and Austria. And just a handful of neighbors—the old and feeble for the most part—blinked nervously and mentioned the names of distant relatives in America.

"I often wonder how many of them remembered my father's advice and, when the time came to abandon their homes, headed east for Poland.

And if they did, did they also curse his memory as the gas seeped into the chambers at Treblinka and at Auschwitz? But who besides my sisters would take the advice of my father, the tired bookkeeper who died of no illness at all just one month before the *Anschluss*? Only my sisters. Karl and I tried to convince them to go to London where one of Bruno's colleagues was helping refugees get work as live-in maids and cooks. Everything was arranged, but they wouldn't go because they had promised my father they would go to Poland. 'The Germans can never defeat England, but Poland, anyone can defeat Poland,' Karl told them, but they were going to Poland. 'Besides, there are hardly any Jews in England,' they said."

"And why didn't you go to England, then?" Tommy cut in. "How did you end up in Pribor?"

"I had a chance to go, but I didn't want to be a maid or a cook. The thought of being stuck in a kitchen or in a washing room all day long and then lying awake at night in a tiny bed in a tiny room in a big house made me want to die. Karl's situation was more difficult because they began arresting Jewish doctors and intellectuals immediately, and, though he thought about leaving, several of his colleagues had already been denied visas. It didn't take long to convince Karl to let me stay with him, and so we went into hiding.

"Bruno organized the whole thing. He had a friend—he seemed to have friends everywhere—who operated a small, very expensive insane asylum in the Austrian Alps. It was one of the few such places that survived the war, and its guests (for they truly lived like guests at a resort hotel) continued their mad lives safe from the front and the experiments of Auschwitz and Birkenau. Instead, they listened to the gramophone while dressed in ballroom attire. They waltzed through the war, happily or miserably out of their minds, depending on each one's particular case, but oblivious all the same. Bruno's friend, a Doctor Kiesslinger, prepared the basement of the South Wing for us. The South Wing was reserved for only the most serious cases. Day and night we listened to hooting, banging, singing out of tune, and grunting animal noises coming from above us. There was a man, the cousin of an important Nazi general, who thought he was a donkey. Many nights we would lie awake making up stories about our invisible upstairs neighbors: the woman who recited the names of hundreds of different flowers all night long at the top of her lungs was the abandoned mistress of the Count So-and-So's son and daughter of the Count's gardener; the man who brayed like a donkey had been flung from his stallion in the Serbian campaign during World War I; the man who cried out for food, especially eclairs, day and night in the high-pitched voice of a *castrati*, 'I'm hungry, I'm starving. Somebody help me!' was the homosexual son of a baron from Graz.

"We were only going to stay there until Bruno returned with false documents so we could leave together. We joked about our imminent *rebirth* as a young gentile couple—'the gentleman has a weak heart and is traveling to London to see a specialist.' Bruno was to get all the medical papers, too.

"And so we waited. One month, three months, six months, one year. Then I stopped waiting. Dr. Kiesslinger had a few contacts. He knew of people who would take us through the mountains into Switzerland. He even offered to pay for everything since he had no family, no one to worry about except his patients, who adored him even though sometimes they bit him or threw their food in his face like angry children. But Karl wouldn't leave. Just in case. How would Bruno find us if we left? When I told him I thought Bruno was either dead or had betrayed us, he flew into a rage, smashing books around our basement like our insane cohabitants. He wouldn't speak to me for days after that, looking at me with the eyes that an old rabbi uses on a fallen woman.

"Two years went by, and then it was too late. No one would risk the mountains. No one would risk false documents. And by that time, we were used to our seclusion and late suppers with Dr. Kiesslinger after the patients were locked in their rooms."

"So what happened? Did Bruno abandon you or was he dead?" Tommy asked.

"You must be patient. You will know when it is time."

"You want me to suffer as you did, don't you, Mrs. Mondschein? Isn't this enough suffering for you?"

"Would it help if I told you that your suffering is far greater than mine ever was?" I said, spontaneously taking Tommy's hand and kissing it like I had done in the café when I was introduced to my first husband's lady friend.

"Ah, Mrs. Mondschein, always the perfect gentleman," Tommy said, and we both laughed. "I'm tired, Mrs. Mondschein. I don't think I can stand any more of these terribly sad things today."

"I can stop any time you want."

"I don't want you to stop, just to wait until tomorrow. Tomorrow's always another day. Right?" he asked, as if he weren't quite convinced.

"Yes, of course it is."

THE TWINS

Sometimes when my mother is in a really bad state, my father gets into a cooking frenzy as if he thinks he can lure my mother out of her bed with the exotic smells of Moroccan *tagines* or orange duck. It doesn't work, and usually has the opposite effect—the sweet aromas and good cheer that food brings make her even more determined to stay in the safety of her sickly-smelling room, but he refuses to give it up because cooking helps him, and, for that reason only, I don't say anything. Last night we had rack of lamb with rosemary, lemon, and artichoke hearts, homemade spinach pasta, which he made with the pasta machine, endive and watercress salad, and, for dessert, an apricot-kiwi torte. All kosher of course. We actually keep a kosher home for my mother's sake.

I don't tell anyone at school, though, because I don't consider myself kosher and my parents never ask me what I eat outside the house. I'm sure they know I don't keep the dietary laws and I know my father doesn't. But my mother is very serious about the dietary laws. She likes having her rules and restrictions. I know my grandmother thinks that our kosherness is ludicrous because she really did grow up in an Orthodox home and is always telling me how lucky I am to be born late in the century and about how she would have ended up marrying a bearded shopkeeper with skin the color of a fish belly if she hadn't met my grandfather who, she says, is also responsible for my musical gift. He had wanted to be an opera singer when he was young and had a beautiful voice, but Jews didn't sing opera in those days—they played the violin. When they visited us on Sundays, my grandfather would excuse himself after we had our coffee and the napoleons that they always brought, and spent the rest of the afternoon glued to the radio in the living room, listening to the Sunday opera on WQXR, singing along in a slightly shaky tenor.

My grandmother told me once about the sense of freedom she felt when she first started eating pork—*Wienerschnitzel*, I think it was. My mother would never make *Wienerschnitzel*, even with veal, because of the cultural implications. I remember the first time I ate something nonkosher was at Debbie Muldoon's birthday party. Her mother took us all to McDonald's for lunch and I had strict orders from my mother only to eat salad, but I forgot. I was only six and my mother should have told Mrs. Muldoon about the salad, but she must have thought I would never forget something like that. I remembered right in the middle of my Big Mac, but I just kept eating because I didn't want Debbie to think I wasn't having a good time.

That night I kept waking up because I expected something bad to happen. I thought my mother would have a sense of my digression and would wake me up in the middle of the night to tell me she knew about what I had done, but nothing happened. I didn't get sick and neither my father nor my mother asked me anything about the birthday party. They didn't even ask me if I had had a good time. After that I just went along with being kosher around my parents, but didn't really worry about what I ate when they weren't around. I guess my father goes along with all of it because he doesn't really care what he eats. He always says that eating is a duty not a pleasure, although he does enjoy cooking his Middle Eastern specialties. Maybe eating isn't important to him because he's never starved before. Not that I've ever starved either, but when I was about eleven, I decided to find out what hunger was like.

It was when my parents were in Egypt and I practically gave the babysitter, who happened to be my father's star graduate student, a nervous breakdown. I kept trying to explain to her that I wanted to experience hunger since half the world was starving and since my mother and grandparents had experienced being on the brink of starvation. I imagine I thought I couldn't really feel alive unless I had experienced starvation. The graduate student tried everything to get me to eat—ice cream, pizza, McDonald's. She didn't realize that fast food probably wasn't the best way to tempt me. I lasted for five days. She was frantic and tried calling my parents every hour on the hour, but they were off in the desert somewhere. Unreachable. She made her boyfriend come over, and he tried talking to me, too. Finally, I just realized how ridiculous the whole escapade was. I was on my bed literally almost hallucinating when it dawned on me that I was lying on a Danish wooden bed, listening to music on my very own CD player, in a fucking four-bedroom house in New Jersey. I walked around feeling like an idiot for weeks after that, and it took me a long time not to be ashamed of eating. I suppose I'm lucky I didn't develop an eating disorder.

Tonight my father has a good excuse for creating a gourmet meal because his oldest friends, the twins, are arriving. Every winter their mother goes to Florida for six weeks and the twins come stay with us. "This is much better than Florida," they say. The twins aren't crazy about the sun and don't understand why so many people insist on running down to Florida for the winter. "We're not birds," they say. When they stay at our house, they sleep in the basement.

As far as I know, the twins have always looked absolutely exactly alike. Usually when twins get to be adults, they start looking really different because they have different lives and interests. I saw a talk show about it once at Amy's house. But Mordechai and Samuel are over fifty years old, and they look and dress exactly alike—black shoes, the kind Southerners in the movies wear to church, khakis with brown belts that wrap almost twice around their thin waists, plaid cotton button-down shirts, and brown cardigans. Then they both have horn-rimmed glasses and thick black hair parted on the side. They look a lot younger than fifty, but I know they're in their fifties because that's how old my father is, and they all went to school together. I bet those clothes are what they wore thirty-five or forty years ago when they were all going to the Yeshiva.

The twins are geniuses of sorts. In fact, the twins and my father were geniuses together at the Yeshiva; they could all argue even the oldest, wisest rabbi into a corner, and the rabbis had great hopes for all of them—the pride and joy of the Yeshiva University High School for Boys. I often think it would be cool to go to a Yeshiva (but not a girls' one, where they just study the basic laws and then learn all the wifely duties), to spend hours and hours poring over ancient texts and studying all those dead languages. My father and the twins used to sit up all night at some coffee shop on 181st Street discussing politics in Aramaic. I wonder what the subway workers on their way home from the nightshift thought of the three young guys with yarmulkes and glasses sitting in the back booth talking heatedly in some unrecognizable language. Or did they even notice?

Whenever I stayed with the twins in Queens, we always played Yeshiva. They actually taught me *Blatts*, pages from Talmud, and I got really good at finding all the possible interpretations, especially after they told me that we were all committing a sin together, that a woman is not supposed to study Talmud. We used to go out for huge, greasy breakfasts at a diner on 41st and 9th Avenue. The waitresses all knew and loved the twins, so they gave me free milkshakes and showed me around the kitchen. Then we would go for a ride on the Staten Island Ferry or walk all over the Lower East Side while they pointed out things like where their grandparents used to have an underwear store. On other days, we would go to Chinatown to watch the dancing chicken—you put a quarter in the slot and this live chicken starts dancing. And then, to top it all off, they would buy me mango ice cream. Or sometimes we walked across the Brooklyn Bridge, and I never tired of hearing about how all those people were trampled to death the day it opened because someone yelled that it was collapsing.

On Sundays, they took me with them to the Yeshiva where I got to sit in the library and look through the oldest books I could find while they helped bored Yeshiva boys research U.S. labor history or the Romans or laser surgery. The rabbis had allowed Mordechai and Samuel to build up the little library according to their interests. With their own hands, the twins built bookcases that reach all the way to the ceiling and require special ladders that can be slid along a rail to reach the top shelves. At first the boys were always trying to climb the ladders or slide each other around on them, so the twins had to make a rule that only they could climb to the library's heights. Up and down those ladders they would climb, like long, skinny monkeys, fetching books for the boys or me. "That one," I would say, "that old crumbly one about Celtic monsters." There was no subject matter that you could not look up in their little library at the Yeshiva University High School for Boys.

The twins are the best storytellers I have ever known. They told me stories about working at the Chrysler plant in Mahwah, New Jersey, when they were members of the Communist Party. They told me how they used to sit there during lunch with all the guys talking about things that they didn't know much about, waiting for an opportunity to bring up the workers' struggle and never finding the right moment. Not in four years. Every morning they took the bus out to Mahwah from the George Washington Bridge Bus Station, and they never told anyone at the plant that they didn't know how to drive. They still don't know how to drive.

Who needs a car in New York City? There was a guy at the plant who used to come to work drunk all the time, and then one day he pushed the wrong button on the machine that lifted the body of the car up onto the chassis, so instead of lifting it, he dropped the body on this young kid who was just out of high school. The kid died and the drunk killed himself the next day. The twins thought they would be able to talk about the workers' struggle after that, but, in fact, the accident made it even more difficult. So after four years of grease and sweat—they're actually really strong even though they're so skinny—they quit the Communist Party and started working at the library of their old school. The rabbis were glad to have them back even if they sometimes tried to talk to the boys about the Revolution. The twins cried when the Berlin Wall came down, not because it was the end of communism, but because communism had failed. Of course they always knew it would fail, rife as it was with logical fallacies that even I could detect at an early age. In fact, they taught me to find logical fallacies by using Marxist theories and the Talmud; then we would all laugh that the world had been fooled for so long.

I asked them once why they became communists if they knew the theory was unsound. They said it was because they needed to ease out of their religion gradually. After they had concluded that Judaism was based on a false assumption—the existence of a God who had chosen the Jews to carry out his laws on Earth—they needed to exhaust another system, find all its false assumptions, all its mistakes. They couldn't tear themselves away from the need to have a truth that easily, they said.

I used to think that the twins hated my mother because she took my father away from them, and then I thought maybe they were all in love with her, that my father was just the one she chose. Now I know they neither hated nor loved her. Still, the twins loved to talk about my parents' courtship. The three of us would walk aimlessly around and around Central Park, not knowing which direction we were pointing in or where we would end up, and they would talk and talk about my parents.

My mother was, according to the twins, the most striking woman at City College. They called her the Moor because of her thick, dark hair and Middle Eastern looks. She was as close as they could get to Sephardic in the cold Ashkenazic halls of City College. The twins were the ones who first told me that my mother used to write poetry, beautifully sad poetry with strange, surrealistic images—goats playing the cello and elephants eating their children. I used to believe the poem about the goat playing the cello was prophetic, but now I almost think that the twins made that up about the cello and the goats.

According to the twins, when my mother was at City College, she spoke to no one and hardly spoke in the literature seminar where the twins and my father first laid eyes on her. Only once in a blue moon would my mother offer a quiet analysis that no one else had even dreamed of. She especially loved Blake. "Blake knew that God was really the Devil and the Devil was really God," she reportedly said in class once.

When I was younger, I believed everything the twins told me about my mother, but now I can't help but think that only to my father and the twins was she such an extraordinary mystery. Not that you can't tell that she was an attractive woman. She still is attractive and her Moorish hair going partly gray is even more stunning than it was in the photographs. For days in a row, sometimes, my mother would not appear in class and my father and the twins were sure she had a secret rendezvous somewhere mysterious, in Harlem perhaps. Sometimes they imagined she smoked opium—her eyes were often so far away.

My mother was the one who sought out my father and the twins. She had heard that they were Talmudic scholars and was wondering if they wouldn't mind sharing their knowledge with a woman. But my mother had no head for Talmud. In fact, she was terribly disappointed in the sacred texts. What had she expected to find there? After a few months, she announced that she preferred Blake, and then it was summer. It was my father who ran into her at a concert and invited her out for a walk. They walked across the Brooklyn Bridge and along the Promenade in Brooklyn Heights.

What did she see in my father, a small man with rounded shoulders and a short torso? When I was little, I was always embarrassed to be seen in public with them together because my mother is a good three inches taller than my father. At the time of their first meeting, my father was renting a room in an old woman's apartment near City College. He was not allowed to have *lady visitors*, so he was often a guest at my grandparents'. On Sunday afternoons they listened to the opera on WQXR together and my grandfather talked of the great singers he had known and heard in Vienna. My father didn't particularly like or understand opera, but he liked being in their apartment, sitting on the couch next to my mother.

The twins didn't see as much of my father after that summer. No more late night sessions in all-night diners. No more Sundays on the Staten Island Ferry. No more long walks through Woodlawn Cemetery. The twins immersed themselves in U.S. labor history and my parents spent long afternoons in the New York Public Library, sifting through the Holocaust Collection. They were going to write a book—part poetry, part history, part philosophy. My father's little room in the old woman's apartment was cluttered with letters sent from Israel, South Africa, Australia, Chicago, Newark, Miami, Oklahoma, California—stories of dead relatives and little girls with numbers on their arms who had grown into middle-aged women with numbers on their arms. Once, when my parents were in Syracuse at a conference, I spent an entire weekend searching through my father's papers, trying to find those old letters. In those days I would never have doubted the twins, nor would I have asked my parents about such a personal project. All I know is that they never wrote the book and I never found the letters. When they graduated from City College, my father went on to Columbia to get his Ph.D. and my mother taught English at Stuyvesant High School. But that was all before I was born, before they moved out here to New Jersey to start a family.

Once, when we were walking to Riverdale along the El in Upper Manhattan, the twins told me that my parents first had sex in a parking lot near the 200th Street El stop. I don't think they meant to freak me out with this information. It just came into their heads because we were walking underneath the Elevated, but for months after that I was beleaguered by images of my parents, their clothes torn open, with the subway screeching by above them.

I'm sure a psychologist would have a field day with Mordechai and Samuel. But a psychologist would probably have a field day with me too. And the sad thing is that if I told a teacher or the social worker at school all the things the twins used to tell me when I was still in middle school, they would immediately be arrested for child abuse when all they were doing was trying to help me understand my parents. Isn't that something every child needs and craves? Even though after a weekend with the twins, roaming all over the underbelly of New York City, I would have weird dreams of my mother locked in a cage, naked, screaming for me to help her.

The minute I walked in the door this evening, my father said, without even saying hello, "She wants to see you." So, upstairs I went to see why she required my presence, but she didn't require it at all. I knocked and there was no answer, so I opened the door anyway. The room was totally dark, but I could tell she was awake by the stillness in the room. It was as if she were holding her breath. The smell was really strong—a vinegary sweetness that emanates from all her pores, and especially from her hair, when she is depressed. My father says it's because she doesn't eat and it's the toxins that are being released from her body. I tried not to gag too much, not to let her know that I could smell her.

"Is it very cold outside?" she asked.

"Not really," I said even though, according to the radio, it was in the teens.

I stood there for a while longer, but she didn't have anything else to say, so I left. She didn't say anything, not even "good night," and neither did I. That was it, so I went back downstairs.

In the living room, my father and the twins were in the middle of a heated discussion about whether or not, if a man falls out of a window and falls on top of a woman and accidentally *penetrates* her, it would be a rape according to Judaic law. My father and the twins can talk about something like that for hours. The consensus seemed to be that it is not a rape since there was no malicious intent, no sin involved, because sin cannot be unconscious. I wanted to say that the fact that he had a hard-on while he was falling might have had something to do with the fact that he saw this woman right below him and that it might not have been unmalicious at all, but I didn't say anything because I didn't feel like talking about sex with my father and the twins.

What I really would have liked was for all four of us to take a walk to the Tenafly Diner like we used to do. I would have liked for Samuel to set me up on his shoulders and run wildly through the quiet cold streets, screaming something crazy like *Eureka,* but they didn't notice when I got up and left the room. I went upstairs and tried to read, but I was hungry and it didn't seem like we were going to be eating dinner soon because no one was cooking, so I did something I never do. I called Mercedes up just to say *hi.* I thought maybe we could go get some pizza, but she wasn't home. Her mother said she was in New York with Leon, so I just lay on my bed in the dark, listening to my father and the twins laughing.

THE SANATORIUM

Tommy has pneumonia again and I have decided to stay here with him night and day until he's over it. They have set up a little cot for me in his room, which is quite comfortable since I'm not used to luxuries. Fruit and yogurt from the Korean grocery on the corner make up my breakfast and then a salad, which I can also buy from the Korean grocery, is sufficient for dinner. The doctors say that most AIDS patients don't survive pneumonia twice, that the second time is almost always the last time. But my story seems to have a healing effect on Tommy; he has said so himself, said that he would have died last week if it hadn't been for me and Karl. And yesterday I was so close to his letting me call his parents. Extremely close. But then he laughed and insisted it must be the morphine getting to him, that his parents had turned into mild-mannered Disney characters in his drugged-up brain and that I was taking advantage of him.

When he's sleeping, he looks dead already. His face looks like a pigeon's picked almost clean by vultures. He doesn't eat anymore, except for what they give him with the IV and the marzipan and chocolate I bring. Yesterday I brought back a wild assortment of goodies from the Bremen Haus and we had a feast, just the two of us. He ate a whole bar of Lindt and half a box of fruit-shaped marzipan.

"Every so often Dr. Kiesslinger would give us chocolates and marzipan that the rare guests would bring for an insane relative," I began my story once again while Tommy was still enjoying his marzipan fruits. "They always brought chocolate or marzipan for the men and flowers for the women. Dr. Kiesslinger would thank the guests for the gifts and promise to serve them with dinner, but he never did. Instead, we gorged ourselves on such delicacies late at night in our dark basement. It was all for the patients' good since sugar could set them off, cause violent displays, interfere with medication. They had to be very strict about dinner, very regimented. Like an army. Even towards the end of our stay, an old woman arrived dressed all in black, Dr. Kiesslinger told us, with a box of chocolates. How she got her hands on such luxuries, no one knew, but the patients' relations were all very well-placed, influential people. In fact, they were so important that, in order to stay in their good graces,

Dr. Kiesslinger hung out a big Nazi flag that billowed in the mountain breeze from the front porch. There was also a flag in the dining room and in the ballroom, where patients inclined to dancing waltzed clumsily and tirelessly night after night."

"Were you ever able to leave the basement?" Tommy asked.

"Sometimes when there was a full moon, we would climb out the window and walk around the woods. Karl collected little pieces of wood, which he carved into animals—wild boars, squirrels, birds. Our basement was full of them. I liked the wild boars the best. We would see them sometimes, though rarely, plunging in between the trees, tusks pointed at the ground. Towards the end, when food was especially scarce, Dr. Kiesslinger and Karl hunted them down in the night. Then we feasted on wild boar and potatoes for a week. But mostly we stayed inside. For four years. Four years of books and books and listening to insanity through the floorboards."

"I would have killed myself," Tommy said adamantly.

"It went by quickly. You wouldn't think that it would, but when I think back on those years, I don't remember being bored. We had so many books, and then Karl began teaching me everything he knew about medicine. If it hadn't been for the war, I would still be an uneducated skeptic from the Second District. There were anatomy lessons and chemistry lessons, and Dr. Kiesslinger brought us rats and birds to dissect. And then Natasha died. That wasn't her real name, but we called her Natasha for some reason. She was an industrialist's illegitimate daughter, and when she died, Dr. Kiesslinger carried her into the basement himself. We used vinegar to preserve the corpse; we cut Natasha up, examined her insides, and, when we were finished with her, sewed her back together. I was good with my hands, Karl said. I would have made a good surgeon. We cut open her hand so that I could see the tiny, delicate bones like in Rembrandt's painting *The Anatomy Lesson*. It was beautiful—all the little bones fanning out from the wrist. Karl tried experiments on her heart. He removed the valves and replaced them with wooden ones he carved himself. We cut her heart in half to see what was inside. We examined the brain. I remember Karl joking about how he wished he had a live body in order to do experiments on the brain. That was always his greatest interest. We laughed about that at the time, so far away was such a possibility from our minds, not knowing that at that very moment a doctor of the Third Reich might have been carrying out such a cruel experiment on my sisters or one of Karl's many cousins from Salzburg."

"And you and Karl?" Tommy asked.

"Karl and I?" Sometimes it seemed as if Tommy was only interested in the parts of my story that contained Karl.

"Yes, Mrs. Mondschein. Cooped up the way you were for four years, did something finally happen?"

I couldn't speak because of a bitter mixture of sadness and anger. My throat closed up, and I could feel tears forming in my eyes and rolling down my cheeks while Tommy held my hand and said, "I'm sorry, I was only asking." We sat that way a long time—tears falling from my eyes, Tommy holding my hand. He asked whether I wanted to listen to music, but I shook my head.

"It happened, didn't it? I'm sorry, Mrs. Mondschein, to bring it up so suddenly."

"Suddenly? No, that's where it fits in the story, and to think I almost got away with not mentioning it." I laughed a little and Tommy gave me a Kleenex to dry my eyes.

"Do you think he thought about Bruno every time?" Tommy asked.

"No. There are all kinds of love." And that made me start crying again. "Have you ever loved a woman, Tommy?" I asked.

"Loved, or made love?"

"Both."

"I love you, Mrs. Mondschein, ridiculous as it may sound. If I were healthy and you were young . . ."

"My father always used to say, 'If my grandmother had wheels, she would be a trolley car.'"

"So, you were imprisoned in the basement for four years. That brings us to 1942, right?" Tommy said, ignoring my comment.

"Yes, 1942. That was when they turned the place into a convalescence home for maimed soldiers. Well, for some it was a convalescence home and for others it was a place to die. Mostly they were pilots who had been shot down—burn victims, amputees, the paralyzed, the brain-damaged, the shell-shocked. There were a lot with shell shock. Dr. Kiesslinger needed help. He was a psychiatrist with only three nurses on staff, but the Reich could not provide him with more help—doctors and nurses were needed at the front.

"From the basement we heard the hysteria level rising—the doctor screaming orders at the nurses and the nurses screaming while trying to carry a paraplegic to the toilet. One night, Dr. Kiesslinger came down to the basement in tears because his patients were dying from infections and his beloved insane were afraid of the new residents. They all hovered in a corner watching while the wounded soldiers screamed obscenities at them all.

"After we had calmed Dr. Kiesslinger down and Karl had given him some advice about the infections and the paraplegics, Karl said that we had to figure out a way to help. Here we were, an experienced hospital doctor and a trained nurse (unorthodox as the training might have been) hiding away like rabbits while there were sick people who needed attention. I reminded Karl that they were Nazi soldiers, to which he replied that that was merely a twist of fate. So when Dr. Kiesslinger brought us our dinner the next night, Karl told him to go into the village and buy us new, countrified clothes. Our plan was to arrive the next morning, simply knock on the front door and say we had heard they were in need of a doctor and a nurse. And so we came, offering our services. I was actually wearing a *Dirndl*—you know, those Austrian dresses with aprons and silver buttons. Karl faked a limp and said that he himself had just returned to his native village from the front, where he had been hit by shrapnel and lost his leg. 'This is my wife,' he said, 'the beautiful Inge.' I could hardly keep from laughing every time someone called my new name."

"Wasn't it dangerous?" Tommy asked. "You didn't have papers, and what about when they brought more soldiers?"

"They always came on Wednesdays. Very orderly and on schedule to the end, they were. So on Wednesdays we disappeared, went to visit our elderly parents, we told the soldiers—the ones who could comprehend. But no one cared, really. The insane hardly noticed our existence and the soldiers were too tired."

"Didn't you feel like traitors, healing the enemy?"

"They didn't seem like the enemy," I said. "They seemed like wounded animals that we had rescued from a trap. And strangely enough, they never spoke of politics. No talk of the Führer or the Jews or the Reich. They talked about women they had slept with, Russian women mostly—soft, warm women who spoke words they could not understand, gave them vodka to drink, and asked for money.

"There was only one who talked of the horrors of war. He was a young, shell-shocked soldier who took to waltzing with the original patients, preferred to eat his meals with them in the kitchen, and was always trying to get me to show him my breasts. 'How would it hurt you to take off your shirt and just let me have one look? Just one look!' he would beg. Now I see I should have done it because how would it have hurt me? It was such a simple request, and it would have made him so happy.

"His name was Ignatz, and there was not much physically wrong with him. All he had suffered were bullet wounds in both thighs and both calves—self-inflicted wounds. They had sent him home since he was *incapable of coping with the circumstances of war*. His discharge papers said something to that effect. He used to hobble after me like I was his mother, holding clean bandages for me as I unraveled the old ones, pushing my supply cart. Karl used to laugh and call him my suitor. He followed me from bed to bed, telling me stories, horrible stories about trainloads of Jews being shipped from the ghettos to special camps. He told me about officers who used Jews for target practice. He told me about bodies piled high as the Stefansdom. He asked me if I had ever been to the top.

"The funny thing is that I thought he was an anti-Semite. He told me the stories, pulling on my dress, laughing. Only now I know he wasn't laughing, but crying. I don't know why I never recognized his laughter as the eerie weeping of the insane. I told Karl about Ignatz and his strange stories, and Dr. Kiesslinger transferred him to the South Wing. A week after his transfer, he was found hanging from the ceiling, the patients of the South Wing using him as a tether ball. There was a note pinned to his suit. 'I am not the one who is crazy,' it said."

"So you didn't know anything about what was going on?"

"Nothing. When we first went into hiding, Dr. Kiesslinger would bring us the newspaper, but all of us, including Dr. Kiesslinger, soon tired of Nazi propaganda and lies. And still we could not recognize the truth when it was staring us in the face. We knew that things were bad, that everyone was in jail, but we could never have imagined the truth. And then you must remember, I didn't want to leave. It was my time with Karl and his time with me. We wanted to prolong that. Both of us did, I think."

"So what happened? Who betrayed you?" Tommy asked.

"Betrayed us? That's much too dramatic a word for what happened. One day, after two hard years, some soldiers arrived with supplies. We didn't know they were coming, and there was no time to hide since we were in the middle of an appendectomy. One of the original patients had appendicitis, and I was assisting Karl with the operation. We had just finished, but before we could wash our hands, one of the soldiers, an especially diligent one, asked for our papers. We requested his permission to wash our hands first, which he very gallantly allowed us to do. He watched us scrub them clean, taking an especially long time, although I don't think either of us was thinking about how to get out of our situation. We just scrubbed. When we finished, we turned to him and said we had no papers.

"'Why?' he asked.

"'We are Jews,' we said, and he chuckled.

"I'll never forget that chuckle. It was as if he were laughing about a witticism he had heard at the theater. After the soldiers had finished unloading the supplies, we were taken away in their jeep. Dr. Kiesslinger tried to protest. 'How can I run this god-forsaken hospital without them?' he yelled. He had tears in his eyes. 'Do the best you can,' the soldier who had discovered us said and chuckled again in that same nonchalant way. 'The war is almost over.'

"We were taken to some kind of military offices where orders were given to send us to Pribor. Why Pribor, I will never know. Why not Auschwitz? Did they take pity on us, or was it a glitch in Nazi efficiency? Later, we found out that at that time—it was 1944—they were sending everyone to Auschwitz, so when we arrived at Pribor, there had been no new prisoners for months and our arrival was met with the excitement that a small village experiences when the traveling circus rolls into town. The prisoners leaned on their shovels watching us being led to the commanding officer's headquarters. I felt for a moment that I was a politician coming to give a speech to a starving people. I wanted to wave and say something hopeful."

"Weren't you scared?"

"No, not then. That would come later, after they separated me and Karl. First we had coffee with the commanding officer himself. We all sat at a table and a very thin young woman brought in coffee and little cakes."

"You had coffee with him?" Tommy asked, like I had said I had kissed him.

"Yes, he told us that most of the interesting people had died and there was no one left for him to talk to. We talked about medicine first. He was fascinated by Eastern medicine and philosophy and told us that he meditated for at least three hours a day. He said he could regulate his own heartbeat and that he had taught some of the male prisoners to do it, too. Apparently the survival rate of his *students* was much higher than that of the other prisoners. (Later I came to doubt he ever had the slightest interest in Eastern philosophy, that the thought of Eastern philosophy had just popped into his head and he thought it would be amusing to mention it.) Karl very calmly replied that the survival rate would improve much more if they provided the prisoners with enough food and warmth.

"'That is against our principles' was the commanding officer's calm response.

"'What principles?' Karl asked him.

"'We are trying to exterminate the Jewish race, not sustain it,' the commandant said simply.

"'Exterminate?' Karl said, and I could see the veins in his neck throbbing as they did whenever he was upset.

"'It was a pleasure talking to you, Dr. and Mrs. Mondschein. I'm sorry that we cannot continue our conversation,' the commandant said abruptly, and he kissed my hand, saying, 'Küss die Hand, gnädige Frau.' It was then that they separated us. Karl was taken to the men's barracks and I to the women's, but only after going through the usual procedure— my head was shaved, my clothes removed, my body disinfected, my arm tattooed, my body clothed in prisoner's garb. I was assigned a bunk and told that in the morning I had better be ready to work. 'Arbeit macht frei,' the prison guard told me and laughed. Of course I had no idea at the time that that was the slogan at every concentration camp.

"In the barracks, everyone was lying on bunk beds, too tired and too miserable to move or talk. I stupidly smiled and nodded a greeting as I passed each one on the way to my own little space in a middle bunk. My immediate neighbors stared, pressing their bodies against the wall as far away from me as possible. That night and for three nights after that, I couldn't sleep. I stayed awake, hoping to hear someone cry out in her sleep or moan or weep or toss about fitfully, but all I heard was an occasional weak cough."

"No one talked to you?" Tommy asked.

"No one talked to anyone. It was like living in a world of deaf mutes. They all stared straight ahead, and when our bread was brought, they devoured it like retarded children eating cake."

"Did you ever see Karl?"

"Every once in a while I would glimpse him from a distance while we were out working. On those days I was ecstatic, ready to jump up and down or waltz around with joy. Of course I didn't. It would have been the ultimate cruelty."

"Are you sure they didn't speak to each other? Maybe they hated you because you were still healthy."

"At first that's what I thought, but I watched them vigilantly. I was the first one up in the morning; I watched them with the regular efficiency of a scientist, and all I noted was that every once in a while, they would ask each other for help using a subtle movement of the hand or an almost imperceptible nod. At first I knocked myself out trying to chop as much wood as possible so that there would be less work for them. I soon realized our work was never finished. In the mornings, we had to carry the dead on carts to the crematorium. Our camp had once been a very efficient work camp, a rubber factory actually, and it still was, although it only operated on a small scale by that point. The Germans were running out of supplies and money. Only the strongest men worked in the rubber plant. Otherwise, the orders were to ship everyone to Auschwitz, to empty the camp as quickly and efficiently as possible. And the women were in charge of wheeling to the crematorium those who would not need to be shipped to Auschwitz. Everything you have heard about the smell of burning flesh is true.

"Then, at about mid-morning, when we were good and tired, they made us run races, the guards placing bets on us, screaming, 'Run, you little whores.' Sometimes they shot into the air to scare us into running faster, and sometimes they fired to kill. I never won a race because I didn't want to give them that satisfaction. I just made it a point to come in second or third. The slowest ones, the ones who could hardly stand up anymore, were weeded out and packed into the train that left each afternoon promptly at one o'clock—for Auschwitz."

"And during all this they never said a word?" Tommy asked yet again. "Not even to complain? Didn't you ever try to talk to them?"

"No, not a word. Talk to them? They wouldn't have understood."

"But you could have tried."

"They frightened me. I think I felt that if I could come to understand them and they could understand me, then I would become like them."

"When did you realize you were pregnant?"

"Now let's not get ahead of the story again."

"But don't talk about the prisoners anymore. Their muteness frightens me more than full-fledged, ranting and raving lunacy. If I get that, the dementia, will you still try to talk to me?"

"You're not going to get dementia."

"How do you know?" he asked.

"I just do."

"Mrs. Mondschein, the clairvoyant," Tommy said, then began to recite, affecting a high-pitched, exaggerated British accent: "Madame Sosostris, famous clairvoyante, had a bad cold."

"Clara used to love T. S. Eliot," I said.

"I still love Eliot, adolescent as that may be."

"Perhaps she still loves him, too."

"Perhaps. Promise me you will continue talking after I can no longer understand what you are saying. Promise you will not let me become mute."

"I promise, although I can't promise that you will be grateful. It would have been the ultimate act of cruelty to attempt drawing my fellow prisoners out of their silent world. In fact, I came to believe they were practicing a strange form of mysticism, a Buddhist escape from suffering. Our commanding officer would have been impressed."

111

"You mean that they had somehow escaped their bodies and entered into a spiritual state?"

"I mean that they had escaped both their bodies and their minds. Perhaps that's the purest form of spirituality."

"I've always despised meditation. I had a lover who used to bore me with talk about Buddhist monasteries in Tibet. He was always threatening to leave me to pursue his spiritual inclinations. In the end, he left me for a lawyer with a swimmer's body."

"And did he ever go to Tibet?"

"Not to my knowledge. He's probably dead or dying now. So, did you finally become like them?"

"Like them? Oh, no."

"Why not?"

"I think we should listen to some music now, or we could watch *Death in Venice* again. I'm tired, Tommy. I don't sleep very well here."

"You don't have to stay, you know. Why don't you go back to your apartment, get some rest. Remember, tomorrow's another day, even for a fag dying of AIDS."

"I wish you wouldn't be so flippant about your illness," I found myself saying.

"Was I being flippant? I'm sorry. But please, why don't you go home, make sure everything's okay up there in that war zone you live in."

"No, please, let's watch *Death in Venice* again."

"Don't you ever get sick of it?"

"No, are you sick of it? Do you hate it? You mustn't lie to me. If you don't like it, just tell me," I said, although I would have been devastated if he had confessed that he didn't really like it.

"I like it; I'm the one who wanted to see it again, but it's not the sort of movie you watch three days in a row."

"Then we won't watch it. We'll just listen to some music. I brought a recording of Sephardic music. Do you like Sephardic music? It's very soothing."

"I adore it."

"My granddaughter introduced me to it. She's a cellist."

"I remember. I'd like to meet her. Maybe there is something of Karl in her."

"Maybe. I have an idea. A wonderful idea. You call your parents and I'll introduce you to Deborah."

"That's not what I would call a wonderful idea. In fact, it's a terribly bad idea; moreover, it's very low of you to suggest it. And what about your not calling Clara in almost a week? What if they're all frantically looking for you?" Tommy said, almost raising his voice.

"They're not."

"And neither are my parents."

"But yours is an entirely different case. For you, your parents are the enemy while all I need is a little distance from my daughter as she does from me. It's healthy. We rub each other the wrong way; we think so differently. Sometimes we need a little vacation, especially since Karl's death. We both miss him terribly. It would have been better if I had died first."

"How can you say something like that? And where would I be, Mrs. Mondschein, if you had died first?"

"And where would I be, Tommy, without you? But I must make you understand."

"Make me understand what, Mrs. Mondschein?"

"You will have to figure that out yourself."

"Only if you give me the opportunity to do so."

"Then I will; I must continue my story. Should we wait until tomorrow?"

"I have decided not to sleep anymore. I can't bear the thought of sleeping through the last days of my life. I never have understood people who say they want to die in their sleep. Have you?"

"No."

"Can you stay awake with me? It won't be much longer."

"Don't you know that old people suffer from insomnia?"

"I thought that was a myth, like they say you get a burst of energy just before you're going to die."

"It's true. It happened to Karl. We sang along with the entire Sunday morning broadcast of *Carmen* the day before he died. His voice was steadier than it had been for years."

"Well, I feel incredibly tired right now, so I guess I must have some time left. You were telling me about your silent fellow prisoners."

"You know, I never even knew their names, nor did they know mine. I wanted to tell them sometimes, scream it out in the middle of the night: 'I am Ruth Mondschein, née Feinberg.' Sometimes I thought that all I had to do was make them say their names and they would come out of their trance, but I couldn't do it. So I suffered the silence. I worked in the cold. I ate only what was absolutely necessary and arbitrarily gave away what I could keep myself from devouring. No one ever thanked me, but no one ever refused either.

"I don't know how long I lived like that. Was it a week? Was it a month? The days and nights had no distinguishing features. But one day I was called for by the commandant. The guard woke me in the middle of the night; I was sure he was taking me outside like he had done with other women, who remained silent even during that. I begged him, I screamed, waking up the entire bunker. I knew I did because I could hear them turning in their beds, but no one said a word. He put his hand over my mouth and dragged me out through the snow in my bare feet. I screamed and screamed and then as we passed where the men slept, I was quiet for fear Karl would wake up and recognize my voice. I was silent after that and obeyed.

"When we got to the commandant's quarters, he berated the guard for not giving me a blanket to wear over my shoulders. The guard apologized mechanically and was dismissed. And then I was even more afraid than I had been with the guard. The commandant was not in uniform, which somehow made him even more frightening—bigger, stronger. I know that doesn't make sense, but I was used to uniforms. His woolen suit, however, reminded me of my first husband perhaps. He told me to sit down, and I sat. He offered me tea, and I accepted. He bent down to poke the fire and he moved my chair closer to the flames, but I could not stop shivering.

"He excused himself and returned almost immediately carrying a tray of cakes, which made my mouth water. I would have preferred meat, but I ate all the cakes. There were eight of them. He watched me eat them one by one without disturbing me while I tried not to reveal my hunger by devouring them too quickly. Later, my weakened stomach would rebel against those cakes, of course. When I finished eating, he sat down on a sofa on the other side of the room and crossed his legs. I noticed how large his feet were and how long his legs were. His feet frightened me more than anything, I think.

"'You are wondering, I am sure, why I have brought you here,' he said, and I nodded.

"'I am a selfish man—selfishness has always been my weakness, ever since childhood. I have been here for three years—three years with little conversation or companionship.' He stopped as if he expected me to comment, but I said nothing so he continued. 'I want to converse with you. It would be my greatest pleasure to converse with you.' I still had nothing to say, so I said nothing.

"'I know you would prefer another interlocutor, as would I, but I am all you have, and you are all I have. The others are too weak for conversation.' He waited for me to respond, but I said nothing. 'Perhaps you would like to choose our topic. The sky is the limit. It is entirely up to you.' Still I was silent.

"'Very well, I will choose,' he finally said. 'An icebreaker perhaps. I will tell you a story, a seemingly inconsequential story, but one I am fond of nonetheless. When I was eleven, I witnessed a very strange accident. It was on the school grounds during recess. There was a group of us that always stood as far away from the teachers as possible, telling off-color stories or practicing soccer moves. We were the athletes and the scholars—handsome, intelligent boys from wealthy families. We had no interest in our younger classmates or in anything but ourselves. It's the age, you know. But for some reason, I looked up just in time to see one of the younger boys throw a stone at another boy. The stone hit the boy's head, and the boy fell down immediately. Teachers and students ran to help him. I was the only one who remained where I was. The boy was dead—from a stone the size of a marble. The ambulance came and took the dead boy away. The boy who threw the stone never returned to school. His name was Hans—a thin, quiet child with glasses of whom I have often thought throughout the years. You see, I envied him. Imagine being so young and so tortured. I envied his suffering. I envied his nightmares. I envied the secret he would someday keep from his wife.'

"'And did you ever think about the boy who died?' I could not keep myself from asking him. He had a way about him, a certain charm, which I can't explain, just as a snake cannot explain why it dances every time his master plays the flute.

"'He died instantly. He never suffered,' the commandant said, leaning back in his chair as if he had just finished a delicious meal at an expensive restaurant.

"'I would like to go back to my bed,' I said. 'I have no desire to converse with you.'

"'But you can't. I'm sorry, but that is the way things are. I would let you go if I could, but I told you I am a selfish man.'

"'Then we must discuss something else,' I said forcefully.

"'Please, do you have any suggestions?'

"'No.'

"'Then I will continue where I left off. Are you in love with your husband?'

"'I don't even know if my husband is alive or dead.'

"'And do you want to know?' he asked, but I said nothing. 'I shall find out,' he said because he had to say something. 'Tomorrow I will tell you. Or perhaps you would like to know now. I can send someone right now if you so desire.'

"Did he think he was being kind or was this part of a cruel game? I couldn't tell. His eyes said nothing. 'No,' I said.

"'Are you afraid to know the truth?'

"'No.'

"'I see. Of course I understand that you do not want to be beholden to me. A wise woman. Very wise. So you will not answer my question. Very well. I will tell you about my wife. I don't love her. She is beautiful and intelligent. She plays the piano exquisitely, could have been a concert pianist if women were more respected in our world. She doesn't love me either. And do you know why? I will tell you. There is absolutely nothing romantic about our marriage at all. Nothing at all. We were not forced to marry by our families. Neither of us is in love with someone else. Shall I tell you then? Good, then I shall tell you.'

"'I have not agreed,' I said.

"'But I shall tell you anyway. We don't love each other because we are both too selfish. She is my perfect match and I hers. We never argue. Never. Everyone thinks we're the perfect couple. We dance beautifully together. We stroll arm in arm. We laugh at each other's jokes. People wonder why we have no children. Our one blemish. We smile and say we are too busy enjoying each other's company, and the old ladies shake their heads; the others are envious, although they would never admit it. We vacation in Italy. We attend the opera and the symphony. Of course all that has changed now because of the war. We haven't seen each other in three years. We never write letters. The German army is impressed with my dedication. They all think I'm terribly dedicated to the Third Reich.'"

"Why did you listen to this guy?" Tommy cut in angrily, in a way that I had never heard him speak before. I had heard him sarcastic and bitter too, but not angry.

"How could I not listen? I was facing him and he was facing me."

"You could have screamed."

"And who would have come running? Besides, he was only talking. I had expected so much worse. I won't tell you any more if you don't want to hear it."

"I have to hear it, Mrs. Mondschein. It's part of the story, isn't it?"

"There are many ways to tell a story."

"You better be telling me everything. I refuse to listen if you don't tell me everything."

"I'll do my best."

"Good," Tommy said and leaned back once again, waiting for me to begin. I took a deep breath, and I could hear the commandant's voice in my head as I spoke.

"'So here I am, my dear lady,' the commandant said. 'I try not to go out much. I have never liked the cold and have always been prone to depression. If I stay inside, things are easier. I have plenty of Sliwowitz, and my guards are quite dedicated to the Cause, so I know the work will get done.'

"And that was when I couldn't hold it in any longer, which, I realized later, was exactly what he was waiting for. 'Don't you know that people are starving to death here? Do you know that every night someone dies of hunger and cold? Do you know that every night another woman is raped? Do you know that your dedicated guards use us for target practice?'

"'Aah, so you have finally agreed to converse,' he said. 'I'm very pleased; however, I've had enough for tonight. We'll continue our conversation tomorrow.' And that was it. A guard appeared as if by magic and took me back to the bunker, where I was up all night paying the price for eating those eight delicate cakes.

"The next night it was the same thing. A guard came for me, only this time I wasn't as scared, which is not to say that I was completely without fear. It didn't take long to learn that the Nazis thrived on arbitrary and completely irrational cruelty. There was something about this commandant, however, that almost made me trust him, not trust him as a friend, but trust him as an enemy. In fact, I couldn't help thinking about our conversation the entire next day. It kept me busy, our little talk, so I didn't notice the cold so much or the hunger or even the silence.

"'How are you, my dear lady?' the commandant asked, and I decided to tell him the truth.

"'The cakes didn't agree with me, so I was a little sick. I'm feeling much better now. Thank you.'

"'Perhaps you would prefer some soup then?'

"'Soup would be lovely,' I said, not too eagerly. So he brought soup and bread from the kitchen and watched me as I ate.

"'Would you like to listen to some music?' he asked after a while.

"'Please,' I said and he put on Haydn. I remember it was *The Chicken Symphony*, and we laughed about the name.

"'Haydn is superior to Beethoven, don't you think?' he said and I had to agree.

"'I never really liked Beethoven,' I said, and he laughed.

"'I have some news for you. Your husband is doing very well. I told one of the guards to give him some extra bread, but he refused it. A brave man, your husband. A doctor, if I'm not mistaken?'

"'Yes,' I said.

"'When I was young, I often thought of studying medicine, but I've always been on the lazy side, so I never had any real intention of pursuing such a career. Will you tell me how it was that you and your husband managed to avoid the Gestapo for so long?'

"'No.'

"'I assure you that the information will not leave this room.'

"'I still will not tell you.'

"'So you are trying to protect someone. How noble of you.'

"'It's not a question of nobility but of common decency. But that is something you would never be able to understand,' I replied angrily.

"'You are wrong there, Mrs. Mondschein, although I realize it would be impossible to convince you of it at this point in our friendship.'

"'Nothing short of freeing us all would convince me.'

"'Free you so you can be captured again and sent to Auschwitz? That truly would be an act of mercy,' he said sarcastically.

"'You have a very limited concept of freedom, Herr Kommandant.'

"'Perhaps I do. Or perhaps you do. I am a prisoner too, you know. We are all prisoners of the Reich.'

"'Some of us more so than others.'

"'This I will certainly not dispute. But let's talk about something else, something more personal. I told you last night I was married. I lied. I often lie. It is one of my few entertainments. You see, I have never been married. In fact, I have very little interest in living in such close proximity to another human being. Do you have any children, Mrs. Mondschein?'

"'No, thank God.'

"'You don't like them?'

"'Are you living in a dream, sir? Anyone who is not thankful for having no children under these circumstances would be completely out of her mind.'

"'I suppose you're right. Forgive me. I wasn't thinking of our present circumstances.'

"'So you just ignore what's going on here? Is that your way of living with it?'

"'I am not a fool, Mrs. Mondschein, or a coward. Have you forgotten the little story I told you last night?'

"'About the boy who killed his friend?'

"'Did I say they were friends? One must be very careful not to change the facts of history.'

"'Are you saying that the event was less tragic since they were not friends?'

"'No, I am only trying to keep things accurate. Should I repeat the

119

story to make sure you have it straight?'

"'That won't be necessary, Herr Kommandant.'

"'Good. Do you remember that I told you I was greatly affected by that event, that, in fact, I envied the boy who threw the rock, envied his torment?'

"'I remember.'

"'You are an intelligent woman. I will let you interpret. You Jews are such talented psychologists, are you not?'

"'Are you referring to Freud?'

"'Don't be such a literalist. It doesn't become a woman of your intelligence.' He had a way of making absurd comments and then making me out to be the fool for pointing out their absurdity. And he loved it, grinning happily like a schoolboy prankster every time he managed to trick me.

"'So you want me to explain to you what this distant childhood event has to do with the way you are behaving in the present?' I asked disbelievingly.

"'Well put. But I don't want you to explain it to me, since I already know the answer. I simply want you to think about it.'

"Then he left me there to think, and didn't appear until morning. I tried to sleep since I had a comfortable couch in a warm room and perfect quiet—no coughing to keep me awake, no boots tap-tapping back and forth outside our bunker all night long. But I couldn't sleep. It was as if he had cast a spell on me, forcing me to envision the boy throwing the rock, and the other boy falling down dead, and the commandant watching from a distance, and all the boys gathering around the scene of the accident, and the shocked expression on the murderer's face, and the murderer as a young man drinking himself to death in some dive of a bar in Berlin, and his family begging him to see one of those Jewish psychiatrists. Or I saw a quiet man with glasses prone to depressions—a librarian perhaps, with a small family—living in a provincial capital. His wife is unfaithful to him, but he doesn't mind. It gives him time to himself. On Sundays after church, he takes the children out for cake. Or, I thought, perhaps he has become a real murderer, a particularly bestial camp guard, a rapist, wielding his guilt in the butt of his rifle. Perhaps the boy was the commandant himself, I was thinking the very moment the commandant appeared before me.

"'I see you are awake,' he said smiling. 'Do you have any theories?'

"'A few.'

"'Good. Now you must return to your quarters. Here,' he said, thrusting some bread and butter into my hands. I almost thought he was going to click his heels to dismiss me, but he just opened the door to the hallway, where a guard was waiting to take me back."

THE ECLAIR

The twins have a way of monopolizing my father's attention, which is one thing that really bothers me about them. I suppose I'm a little jealous because I think they liked me better as a child, when they could tell me their stories and I would believe them, drag me around to all their favorite weird places in New York and I would walk as fast as I could to keep up with them. Last night my father and the twins were up late, playing chess with a timer, so the clicking drove me crazy. I don't know why I didn't go downstairs and ask them to stop because they would have. The three of them just don't know when they're being annoying.

In the morning Samuel made *matzoh brei* even though it's not Passover. It's the only thing he knows how to cook and Mordechai can't cook at all. Everyone was quiet during breakfast except my father, who asked me what was going on at school these days, and the twins acted like they were really interested. They leaned forward on their chairs as if I were about to divulge some kind of big scientific secret, but I said, "Nothing interesting." I hate when people ask me what I did at school like I'm a fourth grader, especially since we never do anything at school worth discussing. I could have told them about the German soldiers' feet, but they probably know all about it already. The twins love that kind of information. Once they went on "Jeopardy" because they thought they would make tons of money. That was when they were still members of the Communist Party. They were going to give all their money to the Cause, but they were eliminated during the auditions because of, according to them, their limited knowledge of popular culture, but my father said that Mordechai blanked out completely, couldn't remember that Hera was Zeus' wife.

"Nothing interesting?" Mordechai laughed. "Public education is really going to pot, isn't it?"

And they all laughed and my father said maybe he should have sent me to the Yeshiva, maybe he should have dressed me up like a boy and sent me to study with the rabbis and they all looked at me as if they were trying to picture me dressed up like a boy, a yarmulke pinned jauntily on my head. Normally, I would have laughed with them, but this morning it just seemed like such a stupid thing to say, so I got up from the table without saying anything, grabbed my coat, and walked out of the house. And when I was out of the house, standing in the driveway in the cold, I felt like an idiot for getting so upset, imagining them shrugging their shoulders, saying, "Youths." My father loves to call teenagers "youths." Whenever we're driving through town and he sees some saggers with earrings and tattoos, he always says something like, "What charming youths."

That's what made me decide to ditch school and take the bus to New York. First, I wandered around the Village and almost got my hair shaved off at Astor Place. I thought maybe I needed a new look, something to attract attention, but then I decided my face is far too round to pull off a shaved head, so I went to the Strand Bookstore instead and spent a couple hours looking through the art and poetry books, but I didn't buy a book because I didn't feel like carrying anything. I went to Tower Records too and looked through their used CDs for a while and then I felt like being outside, so I started walking uptown and somehow I found myself on 72nd Street right in front of the Eclair. The Eclair is a Viennese restaurant run by Hungarians where you can get *Wienerschnitzel*, goulash, cucumber salad with sugar in the dressing like my grandmother makes it, mocha eclairs, and good dark coffee with real heavy cream. I guess I decided to go in because by the time I had reached 72nd Street, I was freezing and starving. All the customers were women, except for one tiny man with a gray wool suit and polished shoes sitting way in the back. I decided to sit in the back next to the lone man and felt the eyes of all those women—dressed for Sabbath even though it wasn't Sabbath—on me as I tried to slip nonchalantly into a chair across the way from the old man. The waiter brought me a huge *Wienerschnitzel* with boiled potatoes, boiled carrots, and cucumber salad. I kept glancing over towards the women, but they had gone back to their own conversations, which, I am sure, were more interesting than staring at me.

"I don't think I know you," the old man said from his corner. "I'm Saul Kaufman."

"Deborah Gelb," I said. "Pleased to meet you." I can't help but be polite, I guess.

"Any relation to Aaron Gelb, the upholsterer?"

"Not that I know of," I said and then added, "But we're not very close to my father's side of the family since my paternal grandparents died when I was young."

"I see. And your mother? What is her family?"

"Mondschein. My mother is Clara Mondschein, my grandmother is Ruth, and my grandfather—he died—was Karl."

"Karl Mondschein, the doctor?"

"Yes. Did you know him?"

"Yes, I knew him," he said sadly. "How is your grandmother?"

"She's fine, okay, I guess. Were you and my grandfather friends?"

"Yes, not good friends, but sometimes we saw each other at the opera and in the park. Do you like opera?"

"It's not my favorite musical genre. I prefer choral music when it comes to singing."

"Church music?"

"I suppose it is church music, but I don't look at it that way. I like it because it's melancholy even though it's not supposed to be. I guess it's supposed to be some kind of joyous praise, but it doesn't sound that way to me."

"Yes, a joyous praise for a Jew nailed to a cross. I don't find all that very interesting. Love, suicide, now that's life."

"That's exactly what I don't like about opera. It's so exaggerated. My grandfather used to take me all the time, though. I used to stare at the cellists. I'm a cellist."

"A cellist! A mournful instrument, but very beautiful. Now, how would a young girl like you know that opera was exaggerated? You must wait until you are my age and then you can say if it's exaggerated."

Usually I hate it when older people tell me I can't know something because I don't have enough experience, especially when they don't know a thing about my life. But I liked him and felt it must be hard to be one of the few men left in a world full of women, so I didn't say I thought opera was really tacky and that the exaggeratedness wouldn't really bother me if it weren't tacky. Instead I smiled and said I did like *Porgy and Bess*, which is true.

"Then there's still hope," he said, putting his hands together as if he had been about to clap and then decided not to. "But tell me about your grandmother," he said. "How is she doing?"

"Fine," I said. "She's fine, but I haven't seen her in a while."

"And your mother? How is she? I remember when she used to work at the clinic. She was very quiet."

"I would prefer not to talk about my mother" was my answer.

"Then we'll talk about something else. Would you like some *Mohnstrudel*? It's the only dessert I ever liked. When I was young, I thought I would die if I ate too much *Mohnstrudel* because opium is made out of poppy seeds or poppies; I never knew which."

He ordered two pieces of strudel and we ate our dessert in silence, giving the poppy seeds their proper respect. "How long were you married?" I asked him to break the silence.

"Fifty years. I seem to be one of the few men who has outlived his wife. She died eight years ago," he said in a way that made me feel his sadness.

"Did you love her?"

"Love her? What a strange question. Of course I loved my wife."

"Did you love others, too?" I said for some reason.

"Deborah, you should not ask an old man such questions."

"Why not? It's not like I would tell anyone."

"I'm afraid you wouldn't find my life very interesting," he said, shaking his head.

"More interesting than mine, I bet. You had to leave your home, figure out a strange new country, learn English."

"Ah, Deborah, history does not make a person interesting. I have made my life safe and comfortable, just like this place—a bowl of good, hot soup, a nice dessert, noodles."

"But you had to leave your home and didn't people in your family die? Don't you miss your wife?"

"They died and I have lived. Death is not unique either. And I do miss my wife, but millions of people miss their wives."

"What did you do for a living?" I asked to change the subject a little.

"I was a jeweler. I had a little shop on 84th Street. I sold watches and gold chains and wedding and engagement rings. I made a decent living. I have an apartment on West End Avenue."

"Were you bored?"

"Bored? No."

"You sound like you were bored, like you wish you had done something else."

"No, I am just trying to explain to you why I like opera."

"Because you had an undramatic life?"

"Exactly. And I have lived to tell the tale. I have lived to sit in the back of a Viennese restaurant in New York. I have outlived my wife."

"So, what are you trying to tell me?"

"Nothing. Are you looking for advice? Everyone these days is looking for advice. If you go to Barnes & Noble on Broadway, you will find a whole wall of books that offer advice about living with cancer, surviving divorce, grieving, loss, dieting, alcohol, abuse, sex."

"I wasn't looking for advice. I thought you were trying to explain something."

"Explain? There is nothing to explain."

We sat in silence again, but it was a pleasant silence because we had understood each other somehow. He ordered two more pieces of *Mohnstrudel.*

"This is a special occasion," he said. I ate my strudel and he insisted on paying for my dinner, too. I thanked him. We shook hands. I said that I had to get back to New Jersey. He said that he had enjoyed my company and that I could find him there every evening at the same time.

"Don't you ever get tired of eating the same food?" I asked.

"No, I guess I'm just a creature of habit," he said.

Then I walked all the way up to the George Washington Bridge Bus Terminal, even though it was dark and raining and freezing. I tried to walk really slowly, like I was just out for a jaunt, through the especially dark, scary parts around the Elevated at 125th Street and along the cemetery at 157th Street. It's so easy to get mugged or raped around those desolate parts. My parents would die if they knew I was walking around there in the dark. But I like being a little scared, listening carefully for footsteps behind me, wondering what could jump out at me from behind dark, empty warehouses surrounded by barbed wire. I prefer the danger to bright lights and blaring music and people rushing home carrying umbrellas.

My mother used to roam all over the city, day and night, east and west, up and down and through all the boroughs. That was when you could walk from one tip of Manhattan to another in the middle of the night and nothing would happen except maybe some drunk, bored, or lonely person would throw onions at you from a sixth-story window. That happened to my mother once. I think she even wrote a poem about it, but I'm not sure about the poem, only the incident. She told me about it when we were out on one of our walks. She told me it was important to understand what she called "the depth of human loneliness," and that's how she explained it. She told me the story about the onions and said that it illustrated, better than anything else, "the depth of human lone-liness." I was ten at the time, eleven tops. Did she think I knew what she was talking about, or did she think I'd remember later, like now, and finally understand?

Because it seemed to me as if I had been so far away—from one tip of Manhattan to the other—for a moment I had the feeling that I would come home to a house transformed, that my mother would be back to normal, that she and my father and the twins would be sitting around the table, drinking wine and eating my father's delicacies. But nothing was different at all except that my feet hurt, and I had that tiredness you get only from accomplishing something physical like shoveling the driveway, not like how you feel when you've finished reading a really long and hard book or even after spending six hours practicing the cello. That's a dif-ferent kind of tired, the kind of tired that keeps you awake for hours, tossing and turning with melodies repeating over and over in your brain.

But nothing had changed—nothing at all. My father had cooked couscous and he and the twins were dining late. "She's upstairs," my father answered when I asked where my mother was, obviously annoyed that I had entertained the thought that she had gone to the opera or out to a movie with one of her nonexistent friends.

Even though I tried, as I often have when my mother is lying upstairs and my father is carrying on with things, I couldn't get myself to feel angry with my father because what was he supposed to do? We both knew from experience that my mother's mood wouldn't change just because we dragged her downstairs and settled her in front of a piping hot plate of couscous. Still, we could have tried it once—dragged her, by the hair perhaps, so her head wouldn't hit the stairs. Standing there, in front of the table full of good food and in a room rich with discussion, my father sitting serenely, cupping his wine glass as if it were a hot mug of coffee, I finally understood that my playing the cello for her through those long nights had never made any difference at all, that it was just something my father made up so we both could feel better, that it was him, not my mother, that my music had helped.

"Would you like me to play some music?" I asked.

I would have played all night if he had asked, but he answered very quickly without giving it a thought. "Not now," my father said. "We're all tired tonight, aren't we?" He looked at Mordechai and Samuel, and they nodded.

I should have gone upstairs to sleep. I should have cried quietly into my pillow. I should have listened to some music or snuck a bottle of Jack Daniels up to my room and gotten smashed all by myself with the lights off and the music on low so as not to disturb anyone. But, without really thinking about it, I called Mercedes. This time she was home, and I told her I had to get out of the house or I was going to go crazy, and she said she was going crazy, too. Mercedes was at my house in fifteen minutes and I could tell by how loud she was talking that she had already had some drinks, but I decided not to say anything, not to worry about getting into her Volkswagen Jetta with her behind the wheel. I didn't really care and she didn't seem that drunk to me. Just loud.

She didn't tell me where we were going and didn't ask me what I felt like doing. We drove around for a long time—up and down side streets slowly, ponderously slowly. She had the heater blasting and the music was still really loud. It was Celia Cruz. I closed my eyes, trying to pretend I was far away—Havana in the 1940s, sitting on a veranda facing the ocean, just watching people. I could almost feel a warm, salty breeze on my face.

"Why are you closing your eyes?" Mercedes asked.

"I'm tired." I was embarrassed to tell her about Havana. "Where are we going?"

"I don't know." We drove around some more, but I kept my eyes open. "You can sleep if you feel like it," Mercedes said.

"That's okay. I'm not tired anymore."

We were still driving really slowly, so slowly that I thought the cops were going to stop us for driving erratically, but I didn't say anything. Mercedes headed up Clinton Avenue to 9W. She picked up speed a little, but not a lot. There was a line of cars behind us, but she didn't seem to notice. We drove to one of the lookouts my father takes all his visiting professor friends to see. We go on a Saturday or Sunday afternoon after a big lunch and I always end up sitting in the backseat, feeling sick. We haven't gone for a long time, though, or at least I haven't. When my mother isn't feeling well there are never any academic visitors.

Mercedes parked the car really close to the edge (a little too close for my taste) so we wouldn't have to get out to see the view. It was a clear night and we could see all the way down to the World Trade Center. She took out a bottle of rum and offered me a drink, which I accepted. "Warms you up, doesn't it?" she said.

"Actually alcohol lowers your body temperature."

"What about the St. Bernards and brandy?"

"They don't do that anymore."

"Well, we're not going to get stuck in a snowstorm, so drink up." Mercedes laughed and took a long swig. I tried not to think about how we were going to get home if we both got drunk and decided I would only pretend to take swigs so I could drive if I had to. But Mercedes caught me and then watched very carefully as I held the bottle to my lips. "That's better," she said. I decided to count how many swigs I took, but couldn't figure out how many would be okay. Three, I thought, or maybe four would be fine, but then I lost track. If worse came to worst, we could sleep in the car.

Then I thought we could drive to New York, go to the Eclair and eat *Wienerschnitzel,* and stay there until it closed. I thought Mercedes would like the atmosphere there even if it was quiet, and I almost suggested we go, but then we had some more rum and I got scared about driving all the way into the city in our condition. Now I wish we had gone and sat in a corner, ordered some wine, not coffee. It would have been nice to sit there like the old ladies.

"I have a friend who's an alcoholic," I said, immediately feeling guilty for choosing George Liddy's alcoholism as a way to introduce him. "He's not only an alcoholic, though. He's a poet, a prose poet."

"What school does he go to?" Mercedes asked, half-interested. It was the kind of question you could only ask if you really didn't care. What does it matter what school someone goes to anyway, even if they do go to school?

"He doesn't go to school," I said. I didn't feel like getting into it anymore because that would have been too long a story and Mercedes had other things on her mind.

"Leon wants me to go to Miami with him," she said, as if she were asking for my approval.

"Are you going to go?" I didn't want to give her my opinion because I didn't have enough information to formulate an opinion.

"He hates the cold." That didn't seem like a good enough reason to leave one place to go to another, so I waited for more, but there was nothing more.

"How about you? Do you hate the cold?"

"I don't really think about it," Mercedes said. And there I was once again, stuck because what else can be said about the cold? I thought about saying that I really like the cold, especially when you come inside after being out in it and your cheeks are burning and you have an engrossing book to get back to, but that was not what we were talking about. And then it occurred to me that they must have had a fight or Mercedes wouldn't have been sitting there with me, drinking rum and looking down onto the Hudson. She would be in a warm bed with Leon, not with me in a car. I saw them in her big double bed, or was it king-sized? Dark bodies on white sheets, long fingers resting on Leon's hairless chest. Or maybe it wasn't hairless; maybe he was hairy like Castro. I laughed and Mercedes asked me what was so funny. "Nothing," I said. "So where's Leon?" I couldn't not ask her that question as much as I would have liked to say nothing, to sit there in the car with Mercedes and drink rum until the bottle was empty.

"I don't know. He gave me a number in New York, in case I change my mind about Miami. He's leaving tomorrow."

"So why don't you want to go?"

"I do want to go, but what if . . . ?"

"What if what?"

"What if everything gets fucked up?"

"It won't."

"You really think so?"

"Yeah," I said.

Mercedes turned up the music and took a long, celebratory swig. "To Miami," she said and passed me the bottle.

"To Miami," I said as enthusiastically as possible because I knew my opinion was irrelevant. If she really wanted to go to Miami, she would go whether I thought it was a good idea or not, and I figured she might as well have a positive attitude about it from the start or things certainly would get all *fucked up*. At that moment I would have gone to Miami with them if Mercedes had offered, but of course she didn't. Maybe it wouldn't have been that bad. I could have spent all day walking on the beach or just exploring the city, and they could have done whatever they wanted to do without me bothering them. I could have gotten a job in one of the fancier hotels. I could have played the cello in the lobby or outside on the veranda, facing the ocean.

On the way home Mercedes drove really fast. I don't know which was worse—her slow driving or the speeding—but she floored it, and I thought for sure we were going to crash when she took the turn onto Engle Street. I was preparing myself for the worst, for the banal death of a late-twentieth-century teenager. As we raced down Engle Street, I was sure we were at least going to get stopped by the cops, and I even told her that if we got stopped, she definitely wasn't going to Miami. Maybe she had changed her mind and didn't want to go to Miami with Leon after all. Anyway, she kept on driving faster and faster, and then we were pulling into my driveway.

"Well, thanks," she said.

"You're welcome" was all I could think of saying. And then she leaned over and kissed me really hard on the lips, forcing her tongue way into my mouth. And I kissed her back. It wasn't a very long kiss, but it wasn't short either. I can't remember which one of us pulled away first.

"You have to get the fuck out of this town too, Deborah," Mercedes said, looking into my eyes, but, of course, she didn't ask me to come with her, and I'm glad she didn't because I probably would have gone.

At home I was faced with that nervous quiet that can only exist when you are not alone. It was a noxious silence, emanating like an odorless gas from my mother's bedroom. I could feel it seeping out from the thin crack at the bottom of her closed door. I stood outside her room, half-hoping to hear crying or screaming or head-banging on the wall. Then I could have rushed in. And then what?

The quiet made sleep impossible, so I closed the door to my room, took my cello carefully out of its case, rosining up the bow slowly, waiting to feel what piece I wanted to play, though I knew it would be Bach's Unaccompanied Cello Suite no. 2 in D Minor. The music welled up in me, moving slowly and sadly around my breasts, circling my nipples, rubbing me as I drew the bow back and forth, back and forth over the strings.

It doesn't always happen, not every time I play one of the Unaccompanied Cello Suites, but, when it does, I can't stop it, which scares me because I worry about losing control over my music, about sitting at orchestra practice, my eyes closed, the whole orchestra pounding around me and me crying out so that my voice carries above even the trumpets and timpani, so that everyone in the string section turns to look at me with my head back, screaming. I wonder if this happens to other musicians, too. Amy told me she had her first orgasm when she was riding her bicycle. She was nine, which is hard to believe, but she swears up and down it's true. She was riding down to the tennis courts for her tennis lesson. She's really bad at tennis, but she had a big crush on Jim Swenson, the tennis teacher. He is one of those tall, blond types with a square jaw and blond hair all over his legs. She loved Jim Swenson all the way through the seventh grade when he moved to Denver, and, as far as I know, that's the last time she played tennis. Sometimes I wish I were more like Amy. I wish I could tell people things like they were no big deal. I wonder if the breathy staccato of a flute has the same effect on Mercedes as the cello does on me, but I can't imagine that it does. There is something more distant about the flute. Maybe it's because it's metal. Anyway, Mercedes has Leon.

I kept playing, hoping someone would emerge from the bedroom, scream at me that it was the middle of the night and what was I thinking. The more I played, the quieter it seemed and I swear I could smell my mother's sickness in my room, though I know the odor wasn't there. It was like when you are sleeping in a strange bed and you get the feeling that the sheets aren't clean and you start imagining all kinds of unsavory odors. So I played and played because the last thing I wanted to do was lie in bed, imagining smells and trying to figure out why Mercedes kissed me and whether I should be angry about it, or just laugh because it was funny, thinking about Mercedes all freaked out in her room with the ceiling spinning, wondering why the hell she kissed me. And then I started thinking that maybe she wasn't going to Miami to be with Leon, maybe she was going just to take off, go somewhere completely different. Maybe she was too scared to leave on her own and thought I would come with her, but then she was afraid to ask me. But ultimately people do what they want. If all she wanted was to get out of New Jersey, she didn't need Leon or me, and if she had really wanted the kiss to mean something, it wouldn't have ended there. Still, I wish Mercedes hadn't kissed me because that just gave me one more thing that I couldn't get out of my mind. It was like the smell of early spring. At first you want to breathe it in deeply because it means the winter is over and things are starting anew, but then it makes you sick, all that sweetness, and the pastel colors hurt your eyes.

I almost wished that my mother were missing again like she had been in Madrid so that I would have an excuse to go out into the night looking for her. Instead of walking the crowded summer night streets of Madrid and pushing my way through people standing three rows deep in bars, faces wafting in and out of smoke, mouths busy shaping words or swallowing soft rings of squid, cold beer rushing down gullets dry from talk and a long day's work, I would have to search the empty well-lit parking lots of the Grand Union and CVS or behind the well-pruned bushes of our neighbors. I might find her sitting at the counter of the Tenafly Diner, talking to the all-night waitress, sipping a cup of weak coffee. Would she start walking towards the city, or would she take a bus to another suburban town that we know about only from signs—Northvale, Harrington Park? How would she know where to get off? Perhaps she would ride the same bus all day long, back and forth from Northvale to the George Washington Bridge Bus Terminal, and when the driver finally said it was over, would she be in New York or Northvale?

In Madrid my father and I searched for my mother for two days, eating only one cold meal at night, poring over maps as if by looking at them my mother's whereabouts would miraculously be revealed. Neither of us thought for even a moment that we would only find her when she was ready to be found, that otherwise Madrid's old and narrow streets would hide her from us forever.

At first we looked together. On the first day we set out early in the morning and combed Lavapíes. We went into every bar, every shop, asking if anyone had seen her. We even looked in all the dark corners of churches, thinking my mother might seek their cool shelter when she was tired from roaming. In the afternoon we made our way to the Puerta del Sol and covered each floor of the Corte Inglés department store, looking through every section equally carefully as if we thought my mother might have developed a sudden interest in towels and linens or electronic goods. We did not speak much while we were looking. We only spoke about our search—whether we should try another department store or move to cafés or museums or bookstores. By evening we were exhausted, but, though we no longer applied a systematic approach, we did not stop. We circled in and out of the same areas, passing the same bars and street corners over and over again. We no longer consulted the map and we talked even less, walking in a straight line until one of us felt the urge to turn. I think we thought that was what my mother was doing, walking in a dream of sorts, and that if we could imitate her mood and the randomness of her path, we would eventually find her.

After our small dinner, my father said he wanted to try looking in the underground parking garages near the Plaza Mayor. All of a sudden he was sure that was where she would be and I followed him, though I was equally sure that she would not. We had been driven through these garages a few times on our infrequent outings to the movies by taxi drivers, who use them as shortcuts to avoid the traffic around the Puerta del Sol and the Plaza Mayor. It is true, my mother was fascinated by the heroin addicts who lined the narrow ramps of these garages. She said she understood what would drive someone to become like that and my father said that she couldn't, that no one understood it, not even the addicts themselves. Some of the addicts in the garage were in the middle of shooting up while others were passed out, their arms and legs sticking out into the road so the taxi driver had to swerve to avoid hitting them. I walked with my father through that suffocating underground city. Every few steps a semi-lucid addict would lift himself up off the pavement just enough to ask us for money and at first my father was generous, handing out coins to all who asked, but after a while he ran out of change and then we walked by the addicts as quickly as possible. After we had been underground for over an hour, I started feeling dizzy from the exhaust and it was getting more and more difficult for me to make out anything in the dim light. I tried to convince my father to come up for air with me, promising that we could come back and look some more after we took a small break, had a cold drink and a bite to eat, but he would not leave the garage. He kept saying that he was sure she was there, that he could "feel her presence." Then he stopped and grabbed onto both of my hands and squeezed them tightly. "You go home," he said. Then he let go of my hands and walked away, leaving me standing there. Of course, I could have followed him, but I was tired and, just as he knew my mother was in the garage, I knew she wasn't, so I left him underground and ran as fast as I could until I was outside in the air again.

I didn't go home, though. I kept searching, walking up and down the streets of Lavapíes until I found myself slowly climbing the worn stairs to our apartment. I don't know when my father came home that night, but he woke me up at seven to tell me he was going out to look some more. I wanted to go with him, but I was too tired, so I told him that I would go out later and we made plans to meet at home around lunchtime. That night he went back to the garages and I went to the Barbieri. I thought that if my mother didn't show up there, maybe George Liddy would and then I could sit with him for a while and forget about everything. But neither my mother nor George Liddy appeared that evening and I was too tired to keep looking. At around ten o'clock, after sitting in the Barbieri for over three hours without reading or talking or writing, I went home.

My mother returned that night at around midnight. My father and I were sitting in the living room with the lights off when we heard the key in the door. We stayed very still and when she called for us, we did not answer. She walked into the living room and felt for the light switch. The light blinded my eyes because we had been sitting in the dark for quite a long time.

"What are you doing sitting in the dark?" she asked.

"Waiting for you," my father said.

She told us that she had been in Cuenca, which may or may not have been true. We didn't ask for proof, and she didn't volunteer much information about the place except that the houses were all built into the cliffs, which everyone knows about Cuenca anyway. My father and I listened to her talking about Cuenca, and when she was finished, he told her that he was glad she was back. That's when I left the room, said I was tired and was going to bed. But I couldn't sleep. I lay awake listening to them talking quietly in the living room, trying to get up the nerve to jump out of bed and storm in there and just scream at them until my voice was hoarse, but I never did, and finally, long after I heard them go to bed, I fell asleep.

After we found my mother, or rather, after my mother returned, I settled back into my old routine—class, then home for lunch, and then a movie or the Prado. I knew every painting in the Prado by heart by the end of that summer—even the ones I hated like the long, beefy El Greco Christs splayed on their crosses in ecstasy, lit up by a garish sky. I could spend an hour staring at Bosch's *Seven Deadly Sins* or Velázquez's *El bufón*. Yet Goya's *Pinturas negras* were my favorites, especially the one of Saturn eating his child. You can really see how he is suffering over having to kill him. In the modern world murderers don't have to feel their victims' bones breaking or taste their blood or even hear them howling—just a nice clean shot or a nice big oven and they're dead. If the Nazis had had to kill each of their victims with their own hands, bite off their heads like Saturn had to do, what happened might never have happened.

One of these days, I'm going to write music based on Goya's *Black Paintings*. Maybe I would call it *An Ode to Ugliness*. In general, I think people spend too much time on beauty. It seems to me that if we spent more time on ugliness, we wouldn't be so easily fooled into believing in God, and we would come to understand the arbitrariness of everything, that there is no explanation for the fact that I was born during times of peace in a prosperous country to a prosperous family, while at the very moment that I came onto this earth, someone else was born in a tiny village in Burundi, the entire population of which would, a few years down the line, be brutally massacred. Just as there is no explanation for the fact that once, on my way home from class in Madrid, a Doberman pinscher followed closely at my heels the whole way home only to jump on me from behind right in front of our building, straddling me like a child clinging to his mother's back in a flood. I felt its dog breath on my neck and was sure it was going to bite me, but I kept perfectly still and after a few seconds, it jumped off me and retreated. I watched it ambling placidly down the street as if this frenzy had been merely a figment of my imagination. But it wasn't. When I got upstairs, I found that my clothes were covered with the dog's menstrual blood. Now why did that dog choose me to follow and attack?

These days my mother would probably say the incident with the dog had been an omen. She started talking about omens in Madrid. Not that she ever actually used the word *omen*, but that's what she was saying. She was always describing strange people she saw on the streets, like an old man who was missing both ears whom she saw in different parts of the city one day as if he were following her. And she got very upset about a young heroin addict who wouldn't stop pounding on the door of the telephone booth my mother was making a call from. I think people have a tendency to mix up symbols with omens and then the next thing you know, the symbols become the reality. That doesn't make the symbols any less frightening, though. I still have dreams about that dog mixed up with images from my days at the Prado—large-headed dwarves and dancing witches and sinners burning in hell, their impaled bodies being raped by giant insects or lizards. I wonder if my mother dreams about the old, earless man. I think I saw him once too, but only once. It was at one of the bars on the Plaza de Tirso de Molina, which are favorite hangouts for old men who drink too much and live in boarding houses run by widows. I liked going to those bars because they had the greatest *tapas*— grilled pigs' ears, lamb intestines, gizzards, barnacles, blood sausages, all the weird stuff that I love despite, or perhaps because of, my ethnic background.

George Liddy liked those places, too, because he didn't stick out so much in them, the lone drunk at eleven in the morning. Tirso de Molina was his daytime haunt and, on my way home from the Prado, I often swung by there just to have some company. George Liddy was always happy to have it if he didn't have a young man in tow, which he usually didn't, especially at that time of the day. But if he did, I just stayed for one glass of beer and then I would leave him on his own. I never saw him with the same *companion* more than once. I didn't get it, though, why these young guys went with him, although I never asked him about how they arranged things, if money or gifts were involved. I'm sure he would have told me if I had asked because he wasn't at all embarrassed about what he called his *adventures*. In fact, he talked about them a lot more than I would have liked, including all the gory details. He probably thought he was freaking me out, but he wasn't. His tales neither disgusted nor excited me the way that Goya's paintings did.

One evening just when I was about to leave George Liddy to his own musings about how he would stop drinking and marry me the day Ireland became whole again, Marisol walked into the bar. I pretended that I had no idea who she was, but she came right over to us.

"What are you doing *here?*" she asked me as if I didn't belong there, when I was the one who had been spending practically every afternoon of that week standing at the exact same spot at the bar.

"Eating pigs' ears," I said, offering her a nice juicy one.

"I don't eat pork," she said and lit a cigarette.

"What are you, Jewish?" George Liddy asked, tittering into his Cointreau.

Marisol ignored the question. Instead she ordered a beer and squeezed in beside me. George Liddy turned the other way, laughing, but Marisol ignored him. She took a long gulp of beer while I tried to think of something to say to her, but all I could think about asking her was why she didn't eat pork, and I didn't want her to feel that I too was making fun of her.

"You look like your mother" was what she said when she finally decided to speak. I didn't respond because I don't think I look like my mother. My mother has black, black hair and dark brown eyes and a long elegant neck, and I'm what a Victorian novelist would have called *plain*. I don't really know how I ended up with almost blonde hair and blue eyes since both my parents and all my grandparents have pretty dark, typically Jewish complexions. The twins used to call me Isolde, like in the Wagner opera, but then they stopped. I wonder if my parents told them it wasn't funny.

George Liddy came to my rescue then. He had finished laughing about the pork. "It seems we've met," he said very gallantly.

"Perhaps," Marisol said, but she turned to me again. "I haven't seen your mother in days. Is she all right?"

"She's fine. She's working on a poem."

George Liddy turned to Marisol and said, "I once published a slim volume of verse. It got me a job at a mediocre university in Sheffield, of all places—world capital of cutlery. If it hadn't been for those few hundred lines, I would be at home now, wrapped in a cozy blanket by the fire. Perhaps a man not too much younger than I would be preparing a roast for us in the kitchen. I certainly wouldn't be here. That much I know for sure, not that I mind so terribly being here in your company, but it does get so very repetitious, I'm afraid."

"You don't write anymore?" Marisol asked.

"I have nothing to say except that there is nothing to say, which has been said before too many times."

"So your book was about having nothing to say?" I asked, trying to avoid further conversation with Marisol.

"When I was a young man, I was duped into believing that you could never say there was nothing to say too many times. It's quite overrated really, my slim volume, but since I don't plan on having any heirs, I needed something to leave behind. I suppose my thin volume of prose poems is neither inferior nor superior to any child I might have had. Children are just as overrated as art, I'm afraid. Do you know why I wrote poems in prose?" He laughed.

"Why?" I asked.

"Because there are fewer of them. How many prose poems have you ever read? How many are famous? The odds were better working in prose. Perhaps five hundred years from now my work will be read as an example of late-twentieth-century prose poetry. It's like having a dwarf for a child. People are more likely to notice a dwarf child than a regular one."

"But people don't admire dwarves. They gawk," I said.

"Gawk," he said very loudly so that the people at the table behind the bar turned to look. "What a wonderfully ugly word. I have always had a fondness for it and if I were still writing little poems in prose, I would write an ode to the word *gawk* and to dwarves. But, Deborah, don't you think there is any admiration in gawking? Don't you think people admire the trials and tribulations of a dwarf's life? As a matter of fact, sometimes I wish I were a dwarf myself, don't you?" He turned to Marisol.

"What is the theme of your mother's poetry?" Marisol asked very seriously, ignoring George Liddy's question.

"Theme?" I was disappointed that she didn't answer George Liddy's question about wanting to be a dwarf, and I tried to steer her back to the dwarves again, but she wasn't interested in discussing them. Instead, she asked me what the topic of my mother's poetry was and I remembered the few lines my mother had shown me about Judith and Holofernes. "She's writing an epic about Judith and Holofernes, but I don't know what the theme is. I think she likes the idea of a woman killing a military hero in his own bed."

"It's not such a great accomplishment, when you think about it," George Liddy said wistfully, as if he had briefly entertained a similar heroism.

"Your mother never said anything to me about writing poetry," Marisol said.

"She doesn't talk about it much. I just know she's working on it since she showed me the first few lines."

"Isn't the whole story about Judith and Holofernes apocryphal anyway?" George Liddy continued. "There's no actual proof that Judith even existed and what was much more likely was that the Jews lived under the yoke of the Assyrians (or was it the Babylonians?) for centuries. Wasn't that how it actually went?"

"I'm not sure," I said. The Bible is one of those books I have read and reread. I've even read the New Testament, and when I was younger, my father used to give me little quizzes on all the stories in the Bible. He is one of those people who thinks you can't be an educated person if you don't know the Bible inside out. But I can't ever seem to remember all those stories. I forget the most basic details about the most famous people like Naomi and Ruth and whether King Solomon lived before or after David. They just don't come alive for me, so I can't remember them. I can't picture them walking around the desert, eating and singing and going about their daily tasks. I can't picture their faces or their clothing. I've tried, but the Bible is kind of like *Leaves of Grass*—I want to feel it, want to feel each blade of grass growing and every hair on my body tingling from the smells of a meadow, but it's just a lot of overly long lines of poetry to me, just like the Bible is a bunch of stories that I can never keep straight.

"I'm quite sure of it," George Liddy said very emphatically. "The actual Bible doesn't allow for women killing men in their beds."

"It doesn't really matter, does it, whether it's apocryphal?" Marisol said, and that was the end of our conversation about my mother's poem, which I don't think she ever wrote, although I'll probably never know. Maybe she's still working on it. Maybe she's lying up there under the covers, spinning couplets in her head about some Jewish heroine who saved the world from the Assyrians. I guess someone must have defeated them finally since there are no Assyrians left today. The one thing I do remember about the Bible is that it's all about how the Jews are constantly avoiding obliteration. I wonder what will happen to us if the world starts leaving us alone. I suppose we'll die out then—stop passing on all those obsolete traditions. Somehow that doesn't scare me. We'd be like the Assyrians then with no claims to greatness—just a tribe of people whose men all had long beards (or was that the Babylonians?) who used to roam the earth fighting with its neighbors. Still, there's something almost comforting in thinking that maybe there was a long-forgotten Assyrian who composed the most heavenly music or had a voice sweeter than an entire boys' chorus. Maybe my mother is writing a poem more beautiful than *Leaves of Grass*. Maybe she has it all in her head like the memory of a long walk through Manhattan.

"No, I suppose it doesn't matter," George Liddy said, looking like he was going to cry, but instead he ordered us all a round of beer and a huge plate of little snails that you have to eat with a pin. "Do you eat snails?" he asked Marisol when they arrived.

"Yes, thank you. I adore snails," she said.

"Isn't that a little extreme?" he asked Marisol.

"Extreme?" she asked very seriously, as if she weren't sure he had meant to use that word.

"Are snails really worth adoring?" he explained.

"It's a manner of speaking," she said.

"I see."

Somehow the day has come and gone. I guess I slept most of it away. I feel refreshed. It's that feeling you get when a hangover finally lifts, when the sun is going down and the pressure of the day and activity weaken and you can settle into the quiet of the evening. My father came home before it got dark. He was twinless even though it's the dead of winter and their mother won't be coming home from Florida until March. I didn't ask him why they hadn't come back with him, why they had left all their stuff in the basement and not come back, because I didn't really care

"How's your mother?" he asked, and I told him I had no idea since she hadn't emerged from her room all day. He didn't ask me where I had gone last night or how I could know that she hadn't come out of her room if I had been in school all day.

"I didn't feel like going to school today," I said when he was already halfway up the stairs. I'm sure he heard me, but he didn't respond. I heard him knocking on their bedroom door and then I heard the door open and close again, really quietly. I dialed Mercedes' number, but luckily the machine answered, so I didn't have to talk to her. I didn't realize that I didn't really want to talk to her until I felt that relief when the machine answered and I knew I was off the hook.

When I was younger, I liked to keep the door to my bedroom open at night so I could hear my parents talking quietly as I fell asleep, but now I hate hearing their low whispers coming from their bedroom, my father's slightly high, gentle tones playing the melody to my mother's monosyllabic answers, so I closed the door, put on some music, and fell asleep only to be awakened by my father's furious typing. When I was young, I liked to listen to his typing, which sometimes lasted until dawn, but this was a different kind of typing, not steady and soothing, but clamorous and frantic without a single pause. It sounded as if my father were bashing out letters indiscriminately, without even hitting the space bar, just running words together the way the Romans did. He typed relentlessly, not stopping for a breath. "Stop!" I wanted to scream. I wanted to barge into my father's study, grab the stupid old Olympia typewriter from under his fingers and throw it out the window, watch it bounce down the driveway until it came to a mangled halt. But then I imagined my father sitting in his reading chair, his head in his hands, sobbing softly, mourning the death of his beloved typewriter, and all I could do was get the hell out of the house, which I did. I thought of calling Mercedes again just to see if she was going to Florida or not because if she wasn't, I thought maybe we could go somewhere together, someplace closer. But there's a big difference between thinking about doing something and actually doing it. Instead I found myself the only passenger on the last bus to New York, wondering what I was going to do when I got there.

INTERMISSION

WHAT SIMON GELB WAS WRITING
ON THE OLD OLYMPIA

My Dear Clara,

I thought, for some ridiculous reason, that if I sent the twins home, I could convince you to come out of your room or, if not something so drastic, to agree to sit up in bed, eat some toast or noodles with butter the way we used to after coming home from one of our all-night walks around the city. And why can't we take an all-night walk now? We are far from old. Our legs are good; our hearts are strong. If only it were about walking, I would strap you to my back and we would walk to Philadelphia. We have never been to Philadelphia. But I don't know if I would be up for such a long hike. There is something comforting almost, domestic in a nineteenth-century sort of way, about knowing that you are in the room across the hall, knowing that in the morning I will coax you into eating a soft-boiled egg, and you will drink some tea with honey and I will feel as though you are doing it for me. It could be much worse. You could be lost again, missing, walking aimlessly around these suburbs or, worse still, wandering through the most dangerous neighborhoods of the city or you might, at this very moment, be boarding the A train on your way to Far Rockaway. What on earth is in Far Rockaway? And then I would have to go out into the cold to look for you. I would not be able to settle into my armchair with a book and wait until you returned, or didn't return.

You were so angry that morning in Madrid when you finally came home after I had spent the whole night following you from bar to bar and made that awful scene in the end. I'm sorry for that. I suppose I was behaving horribly. It reminds me of the waitress we met in that beastly hot Moroccan town Beni Mellal. She had left her husband because he followed her everywhere. He was a retired bus driver and we both found that very meaningful. I can't remember why now, but we thought it was important, the fact that he was a bus driver. He followed her when she went to visit her mother three blocks away and when she went to visit her sister six blocks away. She had a heart condition, something she said would kill her eventually. They had met because she used to ride his bus to and from work. She had had a sewing job in one of those sweatshops where they pay by the piece. She said her eyes were shot from it. And she had married him because he was too old to want children and she dreaded being a mother—all that chastising and coaxing. She wanted a quiet life. He let her sit for hours on the roof of their house. She liked it up there because the noises from the street came to her, rose up to her like the smell of something good cooking, quietly surrounding her, letting her know that life was still going on down there while she sat in the shade.

He wasn't bad at all, she had said. Not too ugly for an old man, not too hairy. He enjoyed spending the afternoons and evenings in the café with his friends. Many of his friends were retired bus drivers. They stuck together, it seemed. But she couldn't stand being followed. Still, there must have been something else about him, or perhaps it was about her, that made her give up her quiet spot on the roof and move so far south to that horrible town Beni Mellal. Did she just pick it randomly on a map? Someplace very far away where no one would look for her? Or had someone told her there was an odd French spinster who was neither young nor old, neither fat nor thin, living in Beni Mellal, running a small, clean hotel? Did she think that perhaps such a woman would take pity on her and give her work and her own room with her own bidet?

You said there was something about that waitress's eyes you didn't like, something you couldn't put your finger on—not that you didn't trust her story. It wasn't that, although I suspect you couldn't quite believe it. Is it that you don't believe she would leave what, in Morocco for a woman of her position, was almost paradise, or is it that you could never trust someone who would sacrifice so much?

But really, I had not meant to follow you like a sleazy private eye out of some bad 1940s film. You will never believe me, but I was racked with worry. Can one say that—racked with worry? In any case, I was. There we were in a strange city and it was getting so late, past midnight and you never called. You hadn't left a note. So what was I to do if not take to the streets? I know, I should have announced myself when I found you. I should have said, "Where have you been? Don't you think it's time to come home?" I shouldn't have slunked around. (I don't know why all these expressions that I am not quite sure how to use are coming to my head.) I should have taken a seat next to you at the Juglar, ordered a cognac, and joined in on the conversation, but I didn't feel up to it. I was not in the mood for talking that night. And you looked so happy. You were talking, waving your hands around. I could tell you were practicing your Spanish because your mouth was making large Spanish vowels. It was as if you were pulling the world in through your mouth, embracing the room in your gesticulating arms. At first, I was intent on observing you being so animated. But then you paused, took a sip from your glass, your hands fell to your sides, you leaned over to your left, to hear better, I suppose, and only then did I realize that you had been engaged in conversation, that you had been talking to someone.

And in all those places you went to that night, you never spotted me, never even sensed my presence. Even at that last stop where you two ate tiny snails, digging them out of their shells with pins, with me only three people down from you at the very same bar. Even there.

So perhaps I shouldn't have said a word. I suppose it was quite unlike me to make a scene, to interrupt your conversation, to pull your arm and order you to come with me. And then to run out like that, leaving you there with everyone staring at you, although, remember, the bar was almost empty, that was especially horrible of me. Perhaps instead I should have snuck home through the dawn streets and gone to bed. Perhaps you would have tiptoed quietly through the house, taken off all your clothes and slipped in next to me. Perhaps you would have reached for me in the early light. But no, I had to sit up on that ugly gold and red Thai couch with my book, looking up every minute, my ears waiting for the sound of your key in the door. Did that make me seem stupid, buffoonish? And then you waltzed in, only you didn't waltz, nor did you stumble; you simply walked in, not weaving, not with your head bowed. You walked in as if you were coming home from work, only it was seven o'clock in the morning. You might as well have been whistling.

Still, don't you think my punishment for following you was a little stiff? You didn't have to leave us for two entire days, but perhaps it is presumptuous of me to think of your absence as a punishment. And Deborah? You didn't think about how she might feel in a foreign city with a missing mother and me, roaming through those underground parking lots where the heroin addicts shoot up, convinced that that was where you

were. I don't know why I was so sure you were lying in some oil spot surrounded by a crew of unsavory people. Yet you were the one who had said
just a few days earlier when we passed a young woman, her teeth rotten,
hipbones protruding, that you would try heroin if you were offered it, that
you wanted to know what it was all about. You had scoffed at my fear of
dirty needles.

We searched together for a while, Deborah and I, but then we went
our separate ways, I staying underground as much as possible. I have no
idea where she went, but somehow I wasn't worried about her. I suppose
I thought if she was looking for you, had a purpose of sorts, nothing
would happen to her. And nothing did happen. Nothing happened to
any of us. But why should I believe that you went to Cuenca, simply went
to the station and bought a ticket to Cuenca because someone had told
you how beautiful it was with its houses built right into the cliffs? Did you
wake up on those two mornings you were gone, wash your face with cold
water, and wander off through the still-cool narrow streets for a leisurely
coffee, sipping it slowly as you watched the good citizens of Cuenca go
about their morning business, buying bread, sharpening knives, hacking
up rabbits and chickens? Are you sure you were alone? But why shouldn't
I believe you? You are not the lying sort; on the contrary, you are always
too ready to tell the truth.

That last time we were in Morocco, on our second-to-last day when
we were relaxing in Casablanca, I had a little adventure, too. I never told
you about it because it didn't seem very important at the time, but I
imagine you would say that I didn't tell you about it because it was important. In any case, you weren't feeling well—the food always gets to you
more than me—and you insisted I go out and "amuse myself." Those
were the words you used. I would have been perfectly happy to sit in the
armchair and read by the open window. It was a beautiful night—the sea
breeze blowing the curtains ever so slightly. You could see tiny lights
speckling the sea. It must have been a good night for fishing. I stood
there looking out at the sea, imagining the fishermen on those lonely
boats, calmly expectant—a long quiet night ahead of them. They were
surely happy to be away from their homes full of children, and women,
and the smell of onions and lamb. But you urged me to leave. "Go on,"
you said. "I'll be fine."

I headed for the sea, down the hill from our window. I looked back a few times before turning the corner and saw that the light was still on. A young man called after me from the shadows of a doorway, but I didn't reply. "Monsieur, Monsieur," he called softly at first and then louder, "Monsieur, Monsieur." I didn't turn around, but I knew he was following me even though his shoes made no sound on the pavement. He walked next to me, asking me the usual: "Where are you going? Are you alone?" I didn't reply, but that never works. I don't know why I always think it will. I quickened my pace, then slowed down, and still he followed just a few steps behind me now, silently. We came to the end of the street, and I had to decide whether to turn left or right. The sea was straight ahead, but it was impossible to reach it without twisting and turning through the old streets.

"Where are you going?" he tried again, and this time I answered.

"To the sea," I said in Arabic.

"What business do you have at the sea at this time of night?" he asked in French.

"None," I said in Arabic.

"So why are you going there?" he asked, still in French.

I remained silent. He repeated his question. Again I was silent. I decided to turn right and he turned right with me. We walked for a while longer—he a few paces behind, I leading the way. At this point I had no idea what he looked like. I knew he was young by his voice. After a few minutes he said in Arabic, "If you wanted to go to the sea, you should have turned left."

"Why didn't you tell me?" I asked, turning around for the first time.

"You did not ask," he said. He was older than I had suspected—in his twenties—wearing the usual dress pants, T-shirt, and dress shoes. "My friends live just down this street."

"I see," I said, kicking myself for being so open to him. I should have yelled at him, shooed him away. It would have worked eventually. Then he would have laughed and said, "Comme vous voulez, Monsieur."

"Viens," he said and I followed him. I was not in the mood to get angry and knew that the sooner I resigned myself to his wishes, the easier it would be, for, in the end, I would find myself trotting off behind him anyway. I had let it go too far already, and Moroccans do not understand why one would want to be alone, especially in the dark by the sea, unless, of course, one were a fisherman or a truck driver or otherwise engaged in some kind of work that required one to be alone.

You would ask if I was afraid. I wasn't, although I probably should have been. We walked in silence, but all the while I kept trying to think of something to say to him, something innocuous and without implications, which is not so easy with people who seem to be able to communicate through implications alone. We came to a building. We had moved away from the sea now and were in the thick of the city again, and my companion opened the door without knocking. "Viens," he said again. At this point I could very easily have run off, darted down the narrow street. I don't think he would have tried to capture me since he did not seem too inclined to strenuous physical activity that evening. There was a lethargy about him that young people have in the summer. We came into a beautiful courtyard. Its walls were magnificently tiled three stories high. He led me to a windowless room off to the side although what I wanted was to sit in the courtyard and look up at the stars. I almost asked him for permission, but he was already telling me to sit down. The room was filled with other young men who were all wearing athletic warm-up suits.

"Did you just come from playing soccer?" I asked them in Arabic. They found my question extremely funny and laughed for a good minute over it before responding that they had not just come from playing soccer. It was the combination of the laughing and the athletic suits that made me uncomfortable. One or the other, I could have handled, but the combination gave them such an air of sleaziness that I was repulsed. Still, they did not seem particularly menacing. I kept looking at them for signs, but it was hard to tell what was going on inside their heads, especially since they weren't really paying any attention to me. At first I took this as a good sign, but after a while, I found it increasingly disconcerting, inhospitable. My *guide* was sitting on the other side of the room and wouldn't even look me in the eye. There were six men in all, none of them older than thirty. Instead of paying attention to their conversation, which was about a friend who had been cheated in a very complicated business deal (something about olive oil), I watched, turned off my hearing as one can do when one is not listening to one's native tongue.

They were all entwined in each other, holding hands, caressing each other's thighs and bare feet, arms drooped over shoulders, like a litter of kittens, I thought, although not so benign. None of them made any attempt to touch or talk to me. I began to think they had some plan for me later in the evening, when the *kif* they had started smoking right after my arrival had taken full effect. They offered me *kif* too and were not overly offended when I refused. They offered me tea, which I accepted, and one of them always made sure to refill my cup when it was empty.

I think they sensed that I do not really enjoy the company of men. But they were not as puzzled by my presence as I was. I kept trying to find a reason to stay or leave, but it was as if I were suffering from some strange paralysis like in that Buñuel movie *The Exterminating Angel*. As I sat there thinking that they probably thought I was the unfriendly one, that it would be so easy to move in closer to the huddle, make some joke, touch my neighbor's arm, I thought, why must they always be so close to one other? Don't they get claustrophobic?

I started feeling nauseated, sitting there enveloped in the sweet smell of *kif* smoke, male sweat, and cologne. I tried hard to find it all exotic or visceral or something to that effect, but I wanted nothing more than to be back in our room, with the window open and the smell of the sea wafting in and the sound of your light breathing in the background. I imagined they all were noisy sleepers who thrashed around and grunted and snored and woke up with rancid breath. Yet I envied them. The more repulsed I got, the more I wanted to be like them. Their talk had turned to women, sexual things that I do not find necessary to repeat. Their laughter grew lascivious and their hands stroked higher and higher on each other's thighs. I was careful not to allow my eyes to wander too close to their crotches. They no longer tried to include me and I found that I was getting more and more annoyed about being ignored. It was this annoyance that gave me the impetus to get up from the floor and walk out of the room, through that beautiful courtyard and out into the cool night. Somehow I found my way back to the hotel without any incidents. I passed a number of men in the streets, but almost miraculously, they said nothing, didn't even look at me. In the hotel, the young man behind the desk smiled at me as if he were in on a secret.

Do you remember that evening at all? For you it was most likely nothing more than a respite—your precious wallowing time. Once back in the hotel, our favorite, I tried to sit quietly in the chair by the window. I tried reading. I tried sitting without reading, but what I had thought I wanted more than anything else that evening was not what I wanted at all. I watched you for a long time, stood directly over you, and you didn't even flinch, but you should have. There you were so quietly sleeping, so happy to be alone in a pleasant room in a difficult country that you had no idea I was standing over you with terrible thoughts of ripping off your nightgown and much, much worse. I cannot bear to tell you the details.

You would ask if I have such thoughts often, and I am happy to say that they are not frequent at all, but they do occur and there is no way to stop them. I suspect that I have such thoughts far less often than most men do and that, I am sorry to say, is all I have to offer you.

The twins say that people fear homosexual men because they are the only ones who really get what they want. All they have to do is go into a bathroom or a park or a bar and in five minutes they can have what they want—no games, no dinners in restaurants, no flowers or tender conversations or poetry—while unhappy heterosexual men have to jump through thousands of hoops for such a simple thing. And women? I cannot begin to list what they must put up with for a tiny bit of affection. But I feel as if I have not failed you on those lines. Could I be horribly wrong about that, too? "Love is a female creation," the twins say, and perhaps they are right, but I have felt love myself, still feel it. I cannot speak for others, but I don't believe the twins to be an authority in this area either.

"Don't you ever get lonely?" I asked the twins once.

"Why should we be lonely?" they said. "We have each other." And I have you, Clara.

We have each other, which is not something to scoff at. Why do you think I spend hours and hours at your side, trying to convince you that Deborah needs you, that if you would only get out of bed, you would feel better? "Things don't change just because you get out of bed," you would say. I don't really agree with you about that, though. Fatalism has never been my preferred philosophy because I have seen the effects of action, both positive and negative, but effects nonetheless.

Maybe you have a better temperament for Morocco than I do. Maybe you wouldn't even notice you were depressed there. You could just lie on a couch watching television and you wouldn't think about how depressing it is to believe that nothing was in your hands. You would embrace it, and when one of your neighbors bade you goodbye after stopping for a cup of tea and sweets during the hottest part of the afternoon, you would say, "Come again soon," and she would say, "*Insha'allah*," and so would you. But what would be my purpose then if you no longer needed someone to keep you from jumping finally and irreversibly into the abyss? What would give me the energy to get up in the morning and read the newspaper, drink my coffee, arrange my notes on the importance of the dietary laws in Judaism and Islam? What would be the point of carrying on with endless ordinary days if you were not waiting for me and my embraces and tired words of encouragement? I would like to believe that if it were not for me, you would have given up long ago, but I know I should not give myself so much credit.

But really, what would happen if our little psychodrama were to come abruptly to an end? What if I started poisoning your coffee with antidepressants? Every morning I could slip the pills in and you would never know. They are tasteless, I am sure, like arsenic. Is arsenic really tasteless? Little by little you would spend more time away from your bed. You would hum in the shower, and then, without knowing why, you would be happy. Would you be happy? Do antidepressants make you happy or merely not depressed? So you wouldn't be happy, you would be undepressed, and you would go back to the store and we would have discussions at the dinner table and go to concerts and to the theater. In the spring you would plant tulips, or does one do that in the fall? You would plant something and read Virginia Woolf. We could go on a trip, somewhere completely different like Denmark or Chile.

Would they wear off after a while or would you figure out that something was not quite right? What if years and years went by and then, when we were in our eighties and living in one of those assisted-living places that your mother refuses to consider, I would tell you? What if we had thirty years of concerts and gardens and trips and books and discussions and minor ailments and dinners at our favorite restaurants under our belts? Would you be able to forgive me then?

Seriously, we could just try something different, couldn't we? After all, we should not be such old sticks-in-the-mud, refusing to even enter-tain the advancements of modern medicine. Because really, Clara, what is the alternative—Freud, Jung? What could be more absurd than psy-choanalysis? You yourself say that we are ninety percent water, pure chemical, so why not try a chemical solution? But perhaps you do not want a solution. Would you even be you without your moods?

I have reread what I have written and, really, I should tear up all this drivel because that is what it is. But I won't. I will save it as I have saved all my other undelivered letters to you. I will file it, under *Important Papers*. Then you will find it when I am dead because I know you will out-live me because you have always been the stronger one. What would you do if I did away with myself right now, smashed my head with this ridicu-lous typewriter, sliced my neck with a paper cutter? Would that change anything? I doubt it. I wonder if Deborah would take my place, but I don't think she would. She is already losing interest in us, and I don't blame her. On the contrary, I wish I could have sent her away long ago.

She has gone off somewhere. Gone off into the night. Slammed the door without saying goodbye. Did you hear it? Should I go out looking for her? But that would do none of us any good, and if she has learned any-thing from all this, she has learned to depend on herself. There is some-thing to be said for that. Perhaps she will be home by morning. Perhaps she will bring us breakfast in bed. Now I am really being ridiculous. It is because I am so tired. I'm sure a little sleep will do me good. Maybe it will snow tonight and when I wake up, the streets will be covered with snow and we can take a walk and afterwards drink hot chocolate with cognac.

S.

PART II

CELLO CONCERTO NO. 1
IN D MINOR

PRIBOR

When I turned to look at Tommy, he was sleeping. At first I was just going to try to get some sleep myself since it was after three in the morning, but then I remembered that he didn't want to sleep anymore, and I thought he would be upset if he woke up in the morning to find that I had allowed him to succumb. So I tried waking him up, but he wouldn't stir. He was breathing, though, that raspy, sickly breathing that he always has. "Tommy, Tommy," I kept saying, shaking him gently, but he wouldn't wake up. I felt his pulse. It was very slow. I called a nurse, and she said he was in a coma. "Call the doctor!" I screamed at her, and she was very patient, telling me that this was a hospice and no doctors were to be called.

At first I was almost angry at him for not letting me finish. Then I was angry at myself too for believing that listening to my story could keep him alive. What would have changed once I had finished it anyway? Maybe it just wasn't meant to be told after all. Perhaps, sad as it may be, it is necessary for some parts of history to die out.

But I remembered my promise to Tommy to continue my tale even if he couldn't understand anymore. It is said people in comas can actually hear what is going on around them and that talking to them and playing music can help to bring them back. I put Mahler's Fifth Symphony on very softly in the background, turned the lights down low, poured myself a glass of water. I thought maybe there was a chance that the music and my story would bring him back again for a short time, so we could at least say goodbye. I put on Mahler's Fifth because we both like it so much and because the Adagietto is the theme music to *Death in Venice*. I've never met anyone, not even Karl, who shares my taste in music as much as Tommy does.

When the symphony was finished, I began to speak. At first I felt a little silly speaking without being sure he could hear or understand me, but then I realized that that's the way it is most of the time when you tell someone about distant and complex matters.

"I was up the entire following night waiting for the guard to come for me, but he never did. In the morning, I was tired and angry at myself for waiting up, for wanting to continue our conversation, and I almost

159

decided to collapse mid-race during the Selection just to see if the commandant would intervene, keep them from putting me on the one o'clock train. I wanted to give him that choice, that dilemma, and I wanted to know if he would do it. Save me. But I didn't. And do you know why I didn't?" At this point I stopped and waited for Tommy to answer, to shrug, to make a comment, but he was perfectly still. His eyes stared straight ahead into the light. "Because I had no sense whatsoever of what he would do. Not a clue. It was not worth gambling with my life just to find out something more about a person whom I did not want to know anyway. And to this day, I think that gamble might have been the only way to really understand who he was and what he felt, only by playing such a very dangerous game.

"The more conversations I had with him, the more I was tempted to try my life-and-death experiment, but I never buckled, though there were days when I felt almost confident that he would choose my life over my death. Yet there were just as many times when I was sure he would choose, or simply allow, my death.

"He kept me waiting for two nights, and on the third night, when I was taken to his rooms, we were not alone. There were four almost-elderly gentlemen sitting on wooden chairs holding string instruments.

"'We have a little music tonight,' the commandant said as he introduced me as Mrs. Ruth Mondschein to the musicians, two Austrians and two Hungarians. They had all been professional chamber music performers in either Prague or Budapest—I can't remember which. As they tuned their instruments, the commandant and I sat waiting on the sofa. He sat as close to me as possible without actually touching me. He offered me a cigarette, which I refused, and he lit one for himself, inhaling deeply and then letting the smoke waft slowly out of his mouth. He requested Vivaldi, so they played Vivaldi. I remember it well because I was surprised that the commandant liked Vivaldi. I would have thought Brahms or Bach, something very serious and nothing as light as Vivaldi, and was vaguely disappointed with his choice. I asked him if Vivaldi was one of his favorites or if he had just been in a Vivaldi mood. He said he loved Vivaldi and all things Italian.

"'My favorite paintings are Italian, my favorite music, my favorite countryside. I suppose I'm not a very good German,' he said and laughed, putting his hand on my thigh and then removing it almost instanta-neously. He clapped then, very vehemently. 'Let the music begin,' he said.

"The musicians played for about twenty minutes. I was surprised at their strength because they had seemed so tired, so bored before they started playing, as if the physical act of running their bows across the strings of their instruments would require more energy than they could ever have. But they played well, not brilliantly, but beautifully and without making one single mistake.

"They finished playing and bowed. The commandant and I clapped.

"'And do you like Vivaldi, Mrs. Mondschein?' he asked very seri-ously.

"'I do, but he is not one of my favorites. I prefer more melancholy music.'

"'And you see, I don't. There is enough melancholy in the world as it is. Don't you agree, gentlemen?'

"'Yes,' they all said, nodding their heads agreeably as if he were asking them whether they wanted more dessert.

"'Thank you, gentlemen,' the commandant said. 'It has been a charming evening.' The musicians bowed deeply and a guard appeared to escort them back to their barracks. When they were gone, the comman-dant said, 'I often regret that I never studied music more seriously and have even contemplated asking those gentlemen to give me lessons, but I'm afraid this is not the place for pursuing hobbies.'

"'Have they been here long?'

"'The musicians? Yes, since '42. So far I have managed to hold on to them for my entertainment, but my orders are to increase the daily ship-ment numbers. Two hundred a day is what they are demanding now. We're losing the war, you know.'

"'I'm not exactly in a position to know such things,' I said.

"'No, you're not. Well, we are. Our armies are in retreat everywhere.'

"'You don't seem terribly upset,' I said, trying to get a sense of his feel-ings on this matter.

"'Not terribly. It will mean going home, though. I don't have much reason to go home. If I believed in God, I would pray that the war would last forever.'

"'If I believed in God, I would pray that the war would be over this minute.'

"'So you can return to your home?'

"'Perhaps.'

"'Nothing of what was will remain after this is over.'

"'And why do you assume that I would like things to be the same as before? You know nothing of my life before I came here.'

"'This is very true. I apologize. If you don't mind my asking you a question?'

"'I cannot say until you ask.'

"'Then I shall take that risk. Do you sometimes wish you believed in God?'

"'No. I come from a religious family and was once a good Jew. Do you know where my sisters went after the *Anschluss*?'

"'To Poland,' he said.

"'How did you know?'

"'So many of you went to Poland, as if Poland were the promised land.' He laughed.

"'They went to Poland because they believed in God,' I said. 'Those who didn't believe went to England or the United States or China—anywhere but Poland.'

"'And you and your husband stayed right where you were.'

"'Not exactly.'

"'Not exactly, but almost. Why didn't you leave?'

"'There were personal reasons which I cannot explain.'

"'Perhaps some night you will,' he said, shifting yet a little closer towards me so that now his leg was just barely touching mine.

"'No,' I said emphatically, shifting myself discreetly away from him as I spoke. The commandant smiled, but he did not move again to regain the territory he had lost.

"'So you believed in something else? What was it? I will die of curiosity.'

"'There are certain things you will never get me to explain.'

"'Nor should you. You are absolutely right. It would be unbecoming, and I would despise you for it.'

"'Then perhaps I will tell you after all,' I said and laughed.

"'A laugh. A miracle,' he said, laughing too."

I was staring at the shadows from passing headlights as they moved around the walls of Tommy's room like the ghosts of crowded boxcars perpetually on the way to Auschwitz. And that is when I thought I heard Tommy laugh. I responded without thinking, "Why are you laughing, Tommy?" But when I looked at him, he looked exactly the same—eyes open, staring ahead into nothingness, no sign of laughter on his lips. Still, I will swear to this day that he laughed. I only wish I knew why. Perhaps I should have stopped talking right then. Perhaps I should have held Tommy's hand in silence, but something was pushing me to the end of my story, even though I tried to stop myself from continuing my futile exercise. So, once again, I spoke.

"When the commandant finished laughing, he dismissed me, and part of me, I must admit, was disappointed."

I stopped briefly and watched Tommy for signs of life, but his eyes were as blank and frightening as a doll's. And when I spoke again, it was because I was afraid of the silence.

"One night we talked again about the young boy and the rock. He brought it up since he always directed our conversations. I asked him if he knew now, from personal experience, what it was like to be tormented by guilt like that young boy.

"'You will not believe me, but no one has ever been slain by these hands.'

"'And does that make a difference?'

"'You tell me.'

"'Those guards who use us for target practice are less guilty than you are,' I told him.

"'That is certainly something to think about, as is your frankness. Not that your answer is a revelation to me, obvious argument that it is. Have I told you that I appreciate your frankness? No one is ever frank with me here. Do you play backgammon?'

"'No.'

"'Then I shall teach you.' He took an inlaid backgammon board from a shelf. 'I bought this in Cairo, a very interesting city. You must go there if you have the chance ever—after the war, of course. There are some who think backgammon vastly inferior to chess, but I don't like games that rely completely on the powers of the mind. One must leave a little to chance, don't you think?'

"There were some nights after that when all we did was play backgammon. He insisted we take off our shoes and sit on the carpet with the backgammon board between us. He brought me a clean pair of wool socks each time we played, and he always watched me carefully as I took off my shoes and old socks and put on the new, clean ones. The commandant was always extremely pleased with himself when he won. Perhaps it was precisely because his victories were not entirely his own doing that he took such pleasure in them. We were a good match, though. I grew fond of the game too and got to be quite a backgammon master, priding myself on my speed, which could surely have impressed even the champions of Cairo's cafés. I haven't played since, although I have often thought of challenging one of those overconfident Washington Square Park players. But they probably cheat. That's one thing about the commandant; he never cheated. A man of honor, he would say."

I feel as if I'm racing against time. How long can an AIDS patient stay in a coma? How long before all the bacteria and viruses and infections in the world throw their last New Year's bash in the withered flesh that is Tommy's body? Try as I might to speed up my story by skipping less relevant details, it only seems to get longer and longer. I find that I'm repeating myself, getting confused in my effort to tell it exactly as it was. Is that what happens when a story remains untold for so long? Does it get long-winded and full of unnecessary details that would otherwise have been purged over the years of telling and retelling? Or is it truer than it would have been after years of practice and embellishments and tiny stretchings of the truth?

"Funny how I wish I had kept that photograph the commandant had taken of the two of us together," I resumed. "I would like to know if I remember him correctly. I promised to keep it, but I knew he knew I wouldn't. 'We all do what we think we have to do,' he was so fond of saying. There were all those years when I tried so hard to forget his face, his eyes, his hands, his feet. And now that I realize I was successful in forgetting, I feel something is lost—the fear, the anger, sadness. I can describe him with words, quite accurately I think, but I have no complete image of him, just the pieces—green eyes, large feet, glasses, long legs, hair that was neither blond nor brown. If I could draw, I would try to sketch one of those police composites to see if it would come out looking familiar. Then I would tape it to the wall directly ahead of you. Can you see the wall? Do you see light, or is everything dark?

"If only I weren't so tired, then I wouldn't feel this great urgency, but I'm afraid to sleep, afraid that if I sleep for just a few minutes, close my eyes just to regain my strength, if I stop talking just to sigh or listen to the cars swooshing by in the rain, you wouldn't have the patience to hold on.

"What I'm going to tell you now is the most difficult part. It would be so much easier if you would help me, ask me your questions, make your snide remarks. It would make it so much easier.

"One night, about a month after I had arrived, he offered me some cognac. I was afraid to drink it since I ate so little; even with his offerings I was undernourished. I had sores in my mouth. I was afraid the cognac would make me faint or vomit, but he insisted. 'We have to discuss something very serious,' he said. 'Cognac is in order.' He poured two glasses from a crystal decanter and brought them over to the couch where I was sitting. He sat down close to me and looked into my eyes. I did not avert my gaze because I felt that he was expecting me to do just that. 'A toast,' he said and raised his glass. I raised my glass, but did not say a word.

"I sipped very slowly, and the taste reminded me of the cabaret in Vienna, which made me want to tell the commandant about my life before the war. As always, these yearnings to tell the commandant true things made me angry at myself for this sign of weakness, and I had to struggle against a strong desire to throw the glass at his head or pounce on him and scratch his face.

"'Why do you agree to converse with me whenever you are called for?' he asked.

"'Agree?' I said. 'I don't have a choice.'

"'I see. Perhaps that is true, perhaps it isn't, but I'm not in the mood to discuss metaphysical matters. What I am going to ask you now will be your choice entirely. Is that clear?'

"'You are asking a favor?'

"'You could call it that. I like the term. Yes, a favor.'

"'Well?' I said.

"'You understand that you can refuse or agree. Your decision will not affect your safety or your husband's.'

"'I understand.'

"'I want you to have my child.'

"Now it was my turn to laugh, but I didn't. I didn't even smile because I knew he was being serious, and I was afraid my laughter would turn his mood, though I had always seen him in the same slightly detached, slightly amused condition.

"'You don't have to answer now. Sleep on it. Take as long as you like.'

"'I want to know why,' I said, leading him on. For I believed that now my turn to play with his emotions had come.

"'Why?' he repeated.

"'Is it such an odd question?'

"'No, but I'm afraid I can't answer. But you have my word that if you agree, you will know. I promise.'

"'You are asking me to believe in you,' I said.

"'Believe in me? I would never ask that of anyone, not even myself.'

"'Why would you want to bring a child into this world? It would be like knowingly giving birth to an orphan.'

"'You are asking me the same question with different words. After all this time, do you take me for an idiot?' he said, showing anger for the first time.

"'No, I am asking myself these questions. Why would I want to bring the child of my enemy into this world?'

"'Am I really your enemy? I thought we were friends of sorts, strange friends, but still friends. And since my boyhood, I have shied away from friendship.' His face was as close to mine as it had ever been. His breath smelled of cognac and cigarettes. I did not move away from him this time. I looked right into his eyes and breathed in his breath.

"'Perhaps, then, you have forgotten what it means.'

"'On the contrary. Only deprivation gives one an understanding of the value of what is missing.'

"'Then we Jews must be the wisest people in the world.'

"'There have been many persecuted peoples and there will be many more. And over and over there will be times when the persecuted will become the persecutors. Valuing what one does not have has nothing to do with wisdom. On the contrary, deprivation leads to cruelty and self-ishness.'

"Later, when Karl and I visited Israel, I remembered his words, and it made me seethe with anger to realize that he had predicted what I saw and I wanted to stand on a street corner and tell the world that the commandant was surely laughing in his grave because he was right, because we have turned out no better than he did.

"The commandant insisted that I sleep on his proposal, though I told him I didn't even have to think for a second to arrive at my answer. But he insisted. He stood up, opened the door, called for the guard and I was dismissed. 'Good night,' I said as I walked out.

"'Good night, Ruth,' he said. It was the only time he ever called me by my name.

"When I went back to the barracks that night, I came up with a plan—I would kill him in his bed. I would kill him and take his gun and kill the guards, pounce on them all when they least expected it, when they were enjoying a cigarette. Then I would liberate the camp, so the world could see us—emaciated mutes wandering the countryside—and someone would give us shelter. But as I lay awake fantasizing, it was almost as if I could feel him laughing about my heroic little plan—sipping his cognac and laughing. Sometimes I think he was a soothsayer of sorts, that he knew I was pregnant, could smell it, could see the child growing inside my thinning frame. But how could he possibly have known when I myself had not even begun to suspect, and would not until my fourth month when I felt my belly becoming heavier despite my starvation diet? How different this second time was from the first, when I was overcome with that voracious hunger. How odd the human body and mind, that when I was practically starving, I had very little desire to eat.

"When he called for me, I was shaking because I thought for sure my answer to his request would anger him, that something terrible would happen. I thought for sure he had been planning all along to rape me, that all this had been a perverse prelude for him and that in the end he would have his way. But that is not how it turned out. He just laughed and said, 'I suppose that brings an end to our little friendship.' Then he called the guards, and I was taken away. After that, I used to wonder if he had found someone else to entertain him on those long, cold nights.

The only thing more I know about our commandant is that he committed suicide, put a gun in his mouth and pulled the trigger while the Russians were liberating us. At least that's what they said. The Russian soldiers hung his body from the flagpole and, as I watched it swinging in the sun, I was sure that he—not my endurance, not fate—was the reason Clara had survived. What would Clara do if I called her up right this moment and told her that she owes her life to the commandant of Pribor? Would she say I should have killed her at birth rather than let him triumph over us?"

That was when Tommy woke up. It was the middle of the night. The music had stopped. First his body was taken over by convulsions—his arms flailed, his legs shook, his head threw itself back and forth with such strength that I thought his neck would break. I tried to hold his hand, but instead I was jerked to the ground. I thought for sure this was the end—his last violent struggle with death. And this time I didn't call the nurse. I spoke to him softly. "Tommy, it's me, Ruth Mondschein. Please get a hold of yourself." Why I said that, I cannot explain. It sounds absurd in retrospect, but it must have worked. After about two minutes, his body relaxed and his eyes looked at me, not the wall.

"Who are you? Are you the devil? Have you finally come to take me home?" he said and laughed, so I thought he was teasing me.

"Tommy, you've been in a coma; this is no time for jokes."

"Jokes? Ha. I love a good joke. What better time than now? Will you tell me one? I like dirty ones. Do you know any dirty ones?"

"Tommy, please."

"I know an especially dirty one. Would you like to hear the story? It's a little long. Am I sick? What is this place? Mint-green walls? I would never agree to mint-green walls, which leads me to believe that I am in a hospital, and you must be a nurse or a nun. Are you a nun? But you probably wouldn't tell me if you were. Nuns are so sneaky these days. They should never have abandoned those uniforms—I liked the ones with white, winged headpieces. What order were they from? But you wouldn't tell me that, either. Not if you're the devil and not if you're a nun. You're not allowed to give yourself away, are you?"

"Tommy, don't you remember me? I'm Ruth Mondschein. This is the Christopher Street AIDS Hospice. I was telling you a story. Don't you remember?"

"A story? I've heard so many stories. AIDS hospice. What are we aiding? Why are you lying to me? I can tell a hospital when I see one!"

"It is a hospital. You have AIDS. It's a disease. Don't you remember?"

"Frankly, I don't and, frankly, I don't care. Am I very sick? I don't feel any pain. No! Don't tell me! I don't want to know."

"You are very sick, Tommy. You were in a coma."

"I told you not to tell me."

Then I burst out crying. I couldn't help it.

"Are you crying because I am dying or because of something else?" he asked me.

"Both."

"Well, it's good to see you crying after all these years."

"Tommy, we've only known each other for a couple weeks."

"Actually, Mother, we don't know each other at all."

"Mother?"

"I know you would prefer Mom, Mother, but you have always been just Mother to me."

"Tommy, don't you remember? I brought you music; I've been telling you about Vienna and Karl and Pribor."

"Music? You wouldn't know what kind of music to bring me. You'd bring some horrible musical or Glenn Miller. Not all fags love musicals, you know. But you could never get that through your head."

And then for some reason I found myself saying, "I'm sorry, Tommy, I'm no expert on music. I did my best. You never told me you hated musicals."

"Never told you! Remember that time you took me to see *Oliver!* and I got so angry and said that Dickens would be outraged to see his work turned into such garbage? Don't you remember that?"

"I thought you enjoyed *Oliver!*"

"Enjoyed it? No, you were the one who enjoyed it, not me. I never enjoyed anything."

"Nothing?"

Tommy looked away from me and only then did I realize what I was doing. I don't even know how I let it go so far.

"Tommy." I put my hand on his shoulder. "I am not your mother. You must believe me."

He turned towards me and squinted as if I were very far away. "Are you sure?"

"Yes."

"Then who are you?"

"A friend."

He was still squinting, trying so hard to remember who I was. "I'm afraid I don't know you," he said sadly.

"It doesn't matter," I said. "Let me put on some music. How about the *St. Matthew Passion*?"

"You know the *St. Matthew Passion*?" he asked, his face lighting up.

"Yes, I think it's Bach's greatest masterpiece."

I put on the *St. Matthew Passion* and we listened to the entire mass without speaking. When it came to the last chorus, Tommy conducted while I sang along softly. I had not known that I knew the words so well.

DOMESTIC ANXIETY

George Liddy, Marisol, and I ended up spending the whole night in Tirso de Molina square, and we finished off the night having hot chocolate as thick as porridge and *churros* in a little place where, according to Marisol, they had been making *churros* for three centuries. It was just before dawn when Marisol and I left George Liddy outside the *churrería*, which was getting so crowded there were people waiting outside to get in. I remember seeing the tip of his cigarette glowing when he turned to wave goodbye. He was tottering in his usual tall way down one of the hills of Lavapiés and his cigarette was glowing in the dark street. Marisol and I were quite a ways ahead of him, but he wasn't calling for us to walk more slowly or to wait. He just let us disappear into the night, and the next thing I knew I was climbing the stairs to Marisol's apartment, and George Liddy wasn't following close behind and I wasn't even thinking about where he was or if he was okay, tottering back to his room in the *pensión* operated by the unmarried brother and sister from Galicia. The sister had an unfixed harelip, which George Liddy said gave her a *corpselike* beauty, while the brother is what George Liddy calls *brutally handsome*. Apparently the brother used to be a sailor and that's how he saved enough money to open up the *pensión* in Madrid. They didn't talk much, except to discuss the damp grayness of Galicia.

George Liddy loves to talk about rain and grayness and the Celtic soul and attributes all the macabre greatness of Spanish culture to the Celtic influence. I wonder if the sister would say that she sometimes wishes she were a dwarf. I wonder if a harelip is one of those deformities that isn't quite bad enough to make people gawk or feel sorry for you. I wonder if she would rather be a dwarf or if a harelip is enough to make her miserable. Maybe that's why she doesn't get it operated on. No one would really want to be a dwarf when it came down to it. If the choice were a real possibility, no one would choose dwarfdom except someone who was even more deformed or disabled than a dwarf, like a paraplegic or someone who was dying of cancer. Marisol, on the other hand, is one of those people you notice, not because she has any obvious deformity, but because of her beauty. Maybe beauty is a type of deformity. If George Liddy were here right now, I would ask him what he thought. He would have something to say about it for sure even if it wasn't really what he believed. That's what I like about him; if you ask him his opinion, he always comes up with something.

Marisol led me to an attic apartment very similar to the one we were living in, only instead of being filled with books and artifacts from all over the world and red and gold textiles, her place was hardly furnished at all. There was one big room with a kitchenette that looked like it had never been used, and a hallway, a rather long one with a closed door at the end of it. In the large room with the attached kitchenette was a non-descript bed. There were no books anywhere in sight and no adornments on the white walls. It was freezing in the apartment due to the noisy labors of an oversized air conditioner, which Marisol told me she kept going twenty-four hours a day, whether she was home or not. She had no tolerance for the heat. We had to raise our voices to hear each other over the air conditioner, which drowned out the usual urban sounds. It was strange being without Madrid's noises after having them around almost constantly even in the middle of the night—leather shoes on the side-walk, people walking home from the bars, stopping to discuss one last thing, to have one last cigarette underneath my window. But in Marisol's apartment you couldn't hear any of that. All you could hear was the droning of the air conditioner.

I didn't know what to say to her in all that quiet, so I said nothing while Marisol went to the kitchen to get us water. She brought a tray with a pitcher of water and two glasses and told me to sit on the floor. We sat on the floor drinking our water slowly as if we were drinking wine. It seemed as if it took us almost an hour of silence to finish drinking it. I kept trying to focus on a thought, on something to say to Marisol, some-thing about my mother or Madrid or George Liddy, but there were just a bunch of disjointed words knocking about in my head. And she looked perfectly calm—as if she were meditating.

After a while, when I was just getting up my nerve to tell her I was leaving, she started laughing, so I had to ask her what was so funny. I could have not asked her anything; I could have stood up and told her I had to get going, but normally when someone starts laughing and you have no idea why, you ask them what they're laughing about. But she never told me what was funny. Instead she stopped abruptly and asked me how old I was. Now it was my turn to laugh; after all that sitting and water drinking and being uncomfortable, all she could ask me was how old I was.

"Sixteen," I said.

"And your mother?" she asked.

I wanted to tell her it was none of her business, but at least we were talking, so I answered. "Fifty."

"That means she was thirty-four when you were born."

"Yes," I said. I should have asked her how old she was, just to finish up the conversation.

"I don't want children," she said sadly as if she wished she really did want them, but just couldn't bring herself to go ahead with it.

"My mother didn't either, but in those days abortion wasn't really an option." I hadn't planned to say anything like that, but what's said is said, so I had to stick to the story.

"She told you that?" Marisol asked.

I nodded because I felt nodding wasn't exactly lying. "I think she's relieved now. It's much easier to have a child than to write poetry."

"What happened?"

"Nothing really. That's what happened. Anyway, why are you so interested in my mother?"

"I wanted to do some portraits of her, but she refused. Usually people are flattered, no matter what they look like. The ugliest ones are the most cooperative."

"Why do you want to paint my mother?"

"Do I have to have a reason?"

"No, but I'm sure you do. Otherwise you wouldn't care whether she agreed to it or not. You would just go out and find someone else, someone ugly."

Marisol ignored my question and asked, "Why do you think she refuses?"

I ignored her question because I didn't want to tell her that my mother was probably jealous of Marisol, especially if she were any good at painting. Either that or she thought Marisol's art was garbage. My mother has very strong opinions about art—she's not one of these people who believes in art as therapy. Maybe that's why she stopped writing poetry. She either had to be a Yeats or nothing. So I asked Marisol if I could see her work.

Marisol led me down the long hallway to the closed door at the end. She pushed the door open as if she were expecting to find a dead body, very slowly, almost holding her breath. She turned on the lights, which were so blindingly strong I felt as if I had entered a movie set or an interrogation room. The floor was splattered with paint and so were the walls, as if Marisol periodically got furious and threw paint all over the room. Otherwise, the room was bare—there were no works-in-progress in the room, no unframed canvases pinned to the walls. Marisol opened the door to a walk-in closet and began pulling out canvases.

I liked the paintings. The predominant color in all of them was a kind of uriney yellow-brownish color, and I almost asked her if she actually painted with urine, but when you got up close to the paintings, there was a thickness to the strokes that made it obvious she had used paint. Most of them were portraits of women doing domestic chores—Castillian-looking, old Madrid types hanging out the laundry, sewing, peeling potatoes. The backdrops were very old-fashioned—widows in black leaning on balconies, old courtyards, overstuffed furniture. But the figures were scary and seemed as if they were made of wax that had melted. Some of them were naked, some were wearing layers and layers of lace, some of the women's faces were too young for their bodies and activities, while others had really young bodies, like those of thirteen-year-old girls, and old faces, not really old like an old woman's, but middle-aged, I guess, like my mother's.

"Well, what do you think?" Marisol was standing right behind me. She smelled of smoke.

"They're cool," I said. I don't really like to go on and on analyzing stuff like art and music.

She didn't reply. She asked me if I had finished looking, and I said I had, so she turned off the lights and went back down the hallway to the living room.

"Did my mother like your work?" I asked.

"She said she did. What do you think? Do you think she liked it?"

I tried to imagine my mother standing in that room with all that light, straining her neck the way she does at concerts, as if it were her neck, not her ears, that was listening. My mother has always been more focused on music and literature than the visual arts. We used to go to the Met a lot when I was younger, but she seemed to enjoy the Greek vases and Egyptian stuff more than the paintings. And then we had to spend practically an hour in front of every stupid rug. I remember always being whisked through the paintings. Actually, I didn't really know much about painting at all until we went to Madrid and I spent all that time at the Prado. But I told Marisol that my mother probably really liked her paintings because she is not the sort to say she likes something when she doesn't. That seemed to satisfy Marisol. Then I added, "My mother doesn't like to encourage images of the human form. She feels they can too easily become graven images," which isn't true, especially since we always use my drawings for our ceremonies.

Marisol didn't doubt my explanation. Apparently my mother had presented quite an orthodox image of herself to Marisol, but she started a theological argument with me as if I too were a believer in the sinful nature of graven images. "But my art is not meant to depict God or anything sacred. On the contrary, my paintings' sole purpose is to illustrate the mundane."

"But the mundane is also God's creation," I played along.

"I suppose," but that's all she said. As we sat there some more, I wondered why Marisol didn't ask me to model for one of her paintings. I was starting to get annoyed, sitting there wondering that, wondering why she didn't find me interesting enough to paint yet worried that she just hadn't gotten around to asking me yet. What would I do if she suggested such a thing? How would I be able to stand her staring right into me? And what would she see that would end up captured on canvas?

"So why did you want my mother to model for you so much?" I asked.

"I didn't want her to model for me so much. I just thought she would make an interesting subject."

"Can't you work from memory? I never understood why artists have to have models. Beethoven didn't even need to hear to compose music."

"Well. We're not all Beethovens, are we?" she said triumphantly, although I don't know what the triumph in admitting one isn't as good as Beethoven is.

And that was the end of that discussion. Somehow we couldn't fall into a conversation and pursue it, let it run loose, see where it took us like the way I talked with George Liddy, but I guess that's partly because he does all the talking. Marisol didn't seem to be nervous at all. She just sat there as if she were meditating again, looking straight ahead, but not really at me. It was as if she were using me to imagine my mother. I felt as if Marisol would have happily sold her soul to be able to paint my mother because what painter wouldn't jump at the opportunity to paint the face of the Holocaust? I wanted to ask Marisol if my mother had told her all about her birth, but I didn't know how to ask that question. That's always my problem; everything I want to say or think of saying seems so stupid in my head, so not worth saying at all. Once, in English class, when we were studying public speaking, one of the Korean kids in our class, a very shy girl who still used a pencil box in which she kept colored pens, White-Out, erasers, and paper clips, raised her hand and asked the teacher to explain some techniques for interrupting, for getting a word in when two or more people were talking and you had something you thought was worth saying to say. She was one of the few Korean kids in our school who was actually Korean, not just of Korean descent. At that time, she had only been in the United States for two years. A lot of the kids in the class tittered, but the teacher answered her very seriously— explained how you had to physically move in on the conversation and then just start talking. If one talked forcefully enough and smiled, for some reason she emphasized the smiling, people would listen. I remember thinking that I would have liked to ask the teacher how to find something worth saying, or how to interrupt silence. I envied my classmate's dilemma. It seemed so solvable at the time, although I know that our teacher's earnest pointers really did nothing to alleviate the girl's agonizing. I wonder if it only got worse for her after that, after she knew theoretically what she could do, but still found herself unable to act.

And then just when I was thinking about telling Marisol about my concentration camp sketches as a way to begin talking about my mother's birth, she got up slowly from the floor and embraced me from behind. I felt her arms on my breasts and her breath on my neck and the next thing I knew she was removing my shirt and I wasn't stopping her. Everything was done in silence only it wasn't an unpleasant silence anymore. In the beginning, I kept thinking that I was supposed to say something or make some kind of sounds, but then I stopped worrying about it.

After it happened, Marisol took me out for coffee and then walked me home. At the door to our building she gave me a long kiss, then turned around and walked away without saying a word. I didn't say anything either because I was still whirling from what had happened, from the smell of her and what it felt like to touch her. Then I got so incredibly tired, as if I had been swimming for hours and then lain down in the midday sun. So I mounted the stairs slowly, dreading having to explain my overnight absence to my parents, but I was lucky—I came home to an empty apartment and was able to fall into bed, let myself be taken over by a dreamless sleep.

I woke up in the late afternoon. My mouth was parched, the sheets were wet with sweat, and the first thing I thought of when I came to consciousness was the feeling of her tongue on my nipples. I closed my eyes again, trying to remain a while longer in that half-sleeping, half-waking state, but sounds from the kitchen forced me to complete consciousness. Putting on my clothes made me gag—the smell of cigarette smoke from the bar in them was so strong—but I didn't feel I had the right to clean clothes or to a shower. Also, I thought that if I were especially quiet and didn't wash up, I could slip out of the apartment unnoticed.

And thus I found myself in the blazing late afternoon sun, smelling of sweat and cigarettes. I could hardly feel my legs or arms, but my head throbbed and my mouth and throat felt as if they were stuffed with dead moths. Since I had no idea what to do or where to go, I went looking for George Liddy, knowing he was always happy to have some companionship and that it would not be too difficult to find him at this time of day.

He was at the Barberillo drinking a giant glass of fresh juice, his usual snifter of Cointreau ready on the table. "Can I invite you to some vitamins?" he said. "They have a wonderful selection here—coconut, orange and banana, peach and orange, pear, peach and raspberry. The sky's the limit." He raised his juice glass up in the air as a priest raises the chalice of wine before dispensing the Eucharist. "Take this juice and drink it," George Liddy said and proceeded to down his juice in one gulp. He set the glass down with a thump and immediately finished off the Cointreau. "I'm a great believer in vitamins, Deborah, for I certainly would have been long dead without them."

The next thing I knew there was a similar huge glass of thick orangish liquid in front of me, which I drank dutifully, feeling it ooze its way into my bowels. "I've decided to forgive you, Deborah, although last night I certainly did not appreciate being left to find my own miserable way home while you waltzed off with that amazon. I almost ended up in a terrible scrape, you know."

"What happened?" I had visions of poor, tall George Liddy being chased by youths in tight pants.

"You see me before you in one piece, without even a scratch on my body, so there is no point in repeating what might have happened when nothing, in fact, happened at all, which, I am sure, is not what happened to you." He pushed back his seat like a satisfied diner after finishing a hearty winter meal.

"No, I didn't almost end up in a terrible scrape," I said, knowing full well what he was implying.

"Well, that's a big relief now, isn't it? Almost getting into a terrible scrape can leave one quite shaken up."

"I don't know. I've never been in a life-threatening situation, have you?"

"If you must put it so dramatically, I suppose I haven't. Well, we should have a drink to that; let's count our lucky stars, shall we, Deborah? It's as good a cause as any, don't you think?"

However, the thought of alcohol mixing in my juice-filled stomach was too much to bear, so I declined, much to George Liddy's disappointment. He wasn't disappointed for long since he was used to drinking by himself. As he sat there drinking another Cointreau, it dawned on me that, because he was an alcoholic, he was in a life-threatening situation right at that moment, but I didn't let him in on my thoughts because being an alcoholic doesn't mean you're an idiot. We talked about insignificant things like how his landlady spends all afternoon in front of the television and how her laughing combined with the screeching of the television makes it impossible for George Liddy to spend a quiet day in his room reading.

"Why don't you find another place to live?" I asked and he said it would be too much trouble. I kept half-hoping he would bring up Marisol again, but I guess he was respecting my privacy. George Liddy was a great believer in minding one's own business. I was getting so hungry that I wasn't even thinking about Marisol anymore and so we ordered crêpes, which was the only food they served at the Barberillo. What I really wanted was a huge *calamares* sandwich, but George Liddy refused to leave the Barberillo. "One can't let one's stomach make one's decisions for one," he said and asked for the crêpe menu. I didn't protest because one thing I knew about him by then was that if he felt entrenched in a place, comfortable like a cat in a sunny spot, he wouldn't move. So we had soggy crêpes; well, I had soggy crêpes. George Liddy took about three bites of his, which was ham and spinach sautéed in olive oil, and pushed his plate away. "I've never liked crêpes," he said.

So I ended up eating his lunch plus two other equally soggy and salty crêpes, but it didn't really matter since I was so hungry. After I finished my lunch, that horrible mothiness in my mouth was replaced by a subtle taste of garlic, but my head was still throbbing right behind the eyes. If I had had another kind of companion, I might have suggested a walk in the park or another excursion, to the mountains, perhaps, where it would have been cooler. But George Liddy was ensconced for the day. That was evident. There he sat in the corner underneath a photograph of Simone de Beauvoir, his red beret resting jauntily on his head, long legs crossed, yellowed fingers scratching his chin as if he were very seriously contemplating why he didn't like crêpes.

"What happened with that vixen last night?" he asked. I guess he had been pondering whether or not to ask me about Marisol.

I decided to completely ignore his choice of the word "vixen." "She doesn't talk much," I said.

"Now that's a bad sign. Never trust someone who doesn't talk."

"I don't talk."

"You don't talk to people to whom you have nothing to say. There's a difference."

"Maybe she didn't have anything to say to me."

"It is more that you had nothing to say to her, I am sure."

"Don't you like Marisol?" I asked.

"No. She's melodramatic, and I loathe melodramatic women. And do *you* like her?" he asked.

"Why do men have a right to be melodramatic while women don't?"

I wasn't ready to decide whether or not I liked Marisol.

"I said absolutely nothing of the sort. As far as I'm concerned, no one has the right to be melodramatic, and the world would be a better place if there were an international edict prohibiting such behavior. I also happen to avoid melodramatic men, although, given my predilections and given other favorable characteristics, I have been forced to tolerate melodramatic behavior in men on occasion."

"I wouldn't call Marisol exactly melodramatic." I guess I had made up my mind to defend her and my connection to her.

"Long silences, eyes that never blink, black attire, tight blouse, smoke wafting out of her mouth, the pallor, the thin fingers. Please."

"You're thin."

"I am. Thin and yellow." He held his hands up to the light. "I've been noticing it more and more lately. It certainly is not attractive, the beginnings of cirrhosis. Perhaps I should start using powder. What do you think, Deborah, a little powder on my hands and cheeks? I could start a fashion—the eighteenth-century look. It's not that ludicrous really."

I suggested we go to a wig place I had seen on the Calle de Hortaleza, but it was two-thirty and the store was closed. That's one of the things that drove me crazy about Madrid—just when you got up the energy to do something, it was siesta time and all you could do was eat, drink, or go to the big department stores. Not that George Liddy would have gotten up to walk in the hot sun to a wig store. It was just an idea, something to do that might have broken the monotony, taken my mind off Marisol—because she had started weighing heavily on my mind.

"Do you think I should go see her?" I asked.

"See whom?"

"Marisol."

"Oh." George Liddy knew I was being serious, so he thought for a while before he answered. "How do you think you will be received?"

"I'm not sure," I said, because I didn't know whether what happened the night before was some kind of spontaneous fluke or whether she had planned it out beforehand.

"Well, then you certainly should not. We should try to avoid setting ourselves up for rejection. I have learned as much, and, frankly, I can't imagine that her intentions were good."

"Why is that?"

"No one's are. That's the sad truth of the matter. I shall tell you a parable. Mind you, I am only telling it to you as a parable. If for any instant you feel pity for me about what I am telling you, I will fly into a rage."

"How will you know what I am feeling?"

"It will be evident. Now, let me also remind you that I have told this story to very few people, not because it is a shameful story, but because there are very few people who have the capacity to understand its significance."

"I hope I don't disappoint you," I said very solemnly.

"You won't. I know how to choose my audience."

"Thank you."

"Now don't start getting obsequious on me. You have my word that being chosen for my audience is a dubious honor, very dubious."

"Then I am even more honored," I said very seriously.

"Enough, lest I change my mind."

I said nothing and waited for him to begin. "Not so long ago, when I could still consider myself middle-aged, I cultivated the friendship of a small group of young men with literary aspirations. I chose this select group from among my students—handsome, intelligent young men who were passionate about the giants of Irish literature. Irish literature is very popular with the English these days. We met often, our little group, at a local pub where they would drink Guinness. (Irish I may be, but I have my loyalties to Cointreau, as you are well aware.) They brought their works in progress and earnestly solicited my advice. Our evenings almost always ended with a recitation; usually it was Yeats, by yours truly. They would take turns sitting next to me, as if it were a special honor. I looked forward to our outings with exaggerated anticipation and had myself convinced that they did too. And it is possible that they did. It is certainly possible that they had not meant to put an end to our soirées by what they did. But that, in fact, is what happened. Not only did it put an end to our charming little encounters, it put an end to a lot more, which I do not care to discuss at the moment.

"We left the pub at about eleven-thirty since I felt that if I stayed any longer, I would not be able to hold my head up straight and tall. I always made an effort not to get into too miserable a state around my young literati. That night, perhaps, I had indulged a little more than usual, but was perfectly capable of booming out *Innisfree* without getting confused or maudlin. We were all in great cheer as we left the pub, especially since it was such a beautiful spring night, the kind I love the most—a soft drizzle, an almost summer warmth, the smell of damp earth and leaves. There was no trace of that flowery sweetness that can make one sick on a spring night. I invited them to my apartment, thinking we would all have one last drink together; we could have a fire, and some melancholy music in the background, something Irish. It made a lovely picture—six young men in sweaters lounging in my living room. I remember my favorite, a quiet West Indian lad with green eyes, was sprawled out on the carpet. But one drink led to another drink and to yet another. There were two who had been friends since childhood, who were most keen on prolonging the party. My West Indian lad neither drank nor spoke and concentrated on kneading the carpet with his beautiful hands, flautist's hands—nimble, strong, and wide at the ends. Well, you can imagine the scene—nymphs in the salon of an aging gentleman.

"The last thing I remember is being carried to my bedroom. I remember the West Indian looking at me from the doorway and the others all gathered around me as if I were their distant old father on his deathbed and they had come to make their petitions or their peace. It was not a completely unpleasant feeling, and I am still not able to reconcile this charming death-of-a-patriarch scene with what met me when I awoke in the morning, stark naked on the floor. That is how I found myself—on the floor, naked, my body marked out in black like those horrible pictures you see at butcher shops, with all the cuts and chops and ribs and loins labeled. The labels, written in regular uppercase letters with a fine marker, were the worst of it all."

What are you supposed to say to a story like that? It's like when someone dies. What would George Liddy have said if I had told him what I was thinking, that his story made me want to see Marisol even more, that I was just like him, coming to consciousness on the floor of his room among all his familiar things—his favorite books, the alabaster bust of Samuel Beckett, Persian rugs. Would he have been disappointed or delighted?

George Liddy broke the silence. "I think we have outworn our welcome in this charming little corner."

"Let's go on a trip." The idea occurred to me as I was speaking. "We could go to Granada or Barcelona."

"I'm afraid my traveling days are over, Deborah. That trip to Ávila nearly did me in. All that walking in the sun—mad dogs and Englishmen behavior. I'm really too old for that sort of thing. I've decided to spend my time indoors."

"We could go on a train ride, just go to Barcelona and come right back on the next train. You would hardly have to go out at all. Don't you like trains?"

"I do. They are my preferred means of transportation, but I prefer not to transport myself anywhere."

"But you wouldn't be really. We'd just go and come back."

"Then why go in the first place? I'm no Huckleberry Finn, you know. You can't get me to go on the train just for the fun of it because I wouldn't find it fun at all."

"But you said you don't feel comfortable here anymore."

"This is true. I need a larger room—*Lebensraum*." He stood up and started stretching his arms, demonstrating how small our little corner was, and then he took three or four Lincolnesque steps and was out the door. I followed him because I had nothing else to do.

We ended up at the Barbieri because George Liddy couldn't walk any farther than that, and it certainly was more open, larger than any other place in the neighborhood that we could think of. George Liddy chose a table right in the middle of the café, stretched his arms out to see if he had enough room, and started moving them up and down like when you make angels in the snow. Luckily the Barbieri wasn't crowded at all and most of the people there were alone, reading newspapers or books, and were seated along the edges of the room.

"That's better, don't you think?" he said, finally sitting down.

There was no point in arguing with him about it and even less reason to tell him I was worried that Marisol might turn up here, so I tried to convince myself that it was a good exercise for me, to sit there and make myself not nervous about seeing Marisol. The only thing was that I didn't expect that I would be faced with Marisol and my mother together. We had only just ordered our drinks—I had decided to stick to soda water—when they walked in.

I felt bad for my mother right away because she was the only one who wasn't uncomfortable. She seemed pathetic to me, like a child happy to be on an outing with her parents, oblivious to the fact that her parents despise each other. She actually seemed glad to see George Liddy and me and sat down at our table without even doing the usual standing and talking that you do when you bump into someone but aren't sure if you are interrupting. That's the sort of thing that usually annoys me about my mother, that she can't even imagine there might be people in the world who would not want her to sit down at their table, that maybe they had things to talk about that didn't include her.

Although the table was round, we ended up sitting in two distinct camps—George Liddy and I on one side and my mother and Marisol on the other. George Liddy graciously or not so graciously, I'm not sure, broke the ice by turning to my mother and saying, "Deborah tells me you're a poet."

"She does?" was her only reply.

"Yes, she mentioned you were working on something about Judith and Holofernes. Have you ever seen Goya's Judith? She's absolutely marvelous, lascivious, bosom exposed, red cheeks."

Marisol offered my mother a cigarette, which, to my surprise, she accepted and masterfully breathed in deeply as Marisol held a match to it. This was the first time I had seen my mother smoke and I tried my best to look nonchalant about it. My mother exhaled slowly and replied that she hadn't seen Goya's Judith, to which George Liddy said, "But you must. It is a tragedy to die without seeing all of his later paintings, don't you think?" This time the question was directed at Marisol, who merely shrugged, to which George Liddy responded by very dramatically lighting up one of his Lucky Strikes.

"Don't you find the summers here unbearably hot?" my mother, very comfortably and charmingly, asked.

"Actually, no. I thrive in this heat. It gives me an excuse to be languorous, which I much prefer to being industrious. Don't you?"

I wondered whether George Liddy would consider my mother's depressions languor or whether he might think of them as the complete opposite of languor, as a great expenditure of effort. During this conversation, Marisol was smoking, looking around the Barbieri as if she were hoping to spot someone she knew to save her from our company. I concentrated on being really attentive to my mother and George Liddy's conversation because I didn't want to have to try to talk to Marisol.

My mother went on to say something platitudinous about the necessity of balance.

"Balance?" George Liddy laughed. "Balance, like happiness, is overrated." George Liddy is really good at terminating stupid conversations, which I could tell this was going to be. What is balance, anyway?

"Are you a Catholic, then?" my mother asked, turning to George Liddy as if she were asking him if he were an early or late riser. "I believe Catholics are not particularly concerned with happiness or balance."

"Now that would depend on your definition of *Catholic* and *happiness* and *balance*, I suppose, but as a rule I suppose you're right. We certainly don't thrive around too much happiness. Imagine what the Irish would do with peace. We certainly would kill ourselves with happiness, which brings me to the answer to your question. I am a Catholic in spirit although I have absolutely no patience for such things as the Resurrection and the Virgin Birth. And Salvation, what a preposterous notion!"

"Then you're not really a Catholic," my mother said.

"And you? Do you believe in God?"

"Yes, I do," my mother said very quietly, as if she really didn't want anyone to know. And that's how we reacted, as if she had told us something embarrassing. That was the first I heard about my mother's belief in God, and I realized I didn't even know if it was a new belief or one that she had always held because we never talked about God in our house. God was taboo. Like true Jews, my parents were afraid of the power of the word. If we had been alone, sitting at a corner table away from everyone, I might have asked her if she had had some kind of revelation or if this is what she had always believed and just never told us. But we weren't alone. There was Marisol fidgeting with her earrings, watching the ceiling fan go round and round and round, and George Liddy sitting tall over us with the trace of a smile on his lips. I wanted to grab my mother and take her away from them. I would have given anything if, at that moment, the Barbieri were magically transformed into a concert hall and all the patrons reading political columns in the paper or talking and talking and talking and all the waiters in their smudged white jackets and ornery expressions disappeared, to be replaced by a full symphony—men in black tails and women in long black gowns, waiting attentively as the conductor raised his baton.

But George Liddy rescued us all by saying he had always followed the flipside to Pascal's principle: that if there were a God, one would have to ignore Him and live as if there weren't.

For some reason my mother found this funny, although her laughter sounded exaggerated, like she didn't quite understand the joke. Marisol laughed too. I didn't really understand what was so funny, anyway. I guess George Liddy just has a way of making serious things seem funny.

After that, George Liddy got carried away and invited us all to come visit him in Ireland for Christmas. He described the Christmas dinner he would prepare for us in great detail—duck with red currants—and said he would have to consider suicide if we refused his invitation, so we all promised we would come even though we knew we wouldn't.

Finally, after what seemed like forever but was really only as long as it took George Liddy to drink one Cointreau and coffee, Marisol and my mother left. Apparently my mother had agreed to model for her after all. I wanted to ask them if she would be modeling clothed or nude, but I didn't.

Just as they were leaving, my mother suggested that it would be nice to have me play for them while Marisol painted and my mother sat or stood or whatever it was that Marisol would have her do—iron or peel onions. "It would be calming, don't you think?" my mother said and Marisol said she didn't want her to be calm, that the whole point was to capture what she referred to as *domestic anxiety*. That's when I realized that my mother knew even less about Marisol than I did, and I wanted to warn her but didn't know how, short of telling her what had happened, blurting it all out right there with everyone listening.

"Well, perhaps another time then," my mother said. "The cello really is the king, or should I say queen, of instruments and Deborah is a master. You must play for Marisol, Deborah." She turned to Marisol and added, "No one plays Vivaldi better than she does!"

I hate it when my mother brags about me. She doesn't do it often, largely because there really are very few people around to brag to. Still, my mother is not the bragging sort, so it always throws me off guard when she does.

"Maybe some other time," I said, knowing there would be no other time.

"Yes," Marisol said, looking at my mother, not at me. Then she turned and headed towards the exit with my mother following behind her.

"You've never offered to play for me," George Liddy said as soon as the door closed behind them.

"You've never asked."

"I try not to ask for favors anymore. They always come with strings attached, no pun intended."

"I'd love to play for you, no strings attached. I promise."

"I hope my Gallegos don't mind. I'm not supposed to entertain visitors, you know. We might have to invite them to listen too if they aren't watching some terribly important television show. You wouldn't mind playing for them too, would you?"

"Of course not."

"Good. You still have my card, don't you?" And so it was decided I would get my cello and meet him at the pensión.

George Liddy's place was tucked away on a small street behind Tirso de Molina. I rang the bell downstairs and someone buzzed me in without asking who I was. The pensión was on the fourth floor and, as I climbed the well-worn stairs with my cello, I thought of George Liddy ascending to his little room in the early hours of the morning. Does the timed light go out before he makes it to the top, or does he use his last burst of energy to dart up the stairs?

Pilar, the sister, opened the door for me. Her harelip was worse than I had expected—the split went all the way up into her nose—and I couldn't help staring at it. I tried to look into her eyes instead, but couldn't. She didn't seem to mind, though. I guess she was used to people staring at her that way. They had set up a little area in the living room—a chair for me to sit on and three other chairs in a neat row facing mine. Pilar introduced me to her brother Manolo, who was already sitting in the middle chair, waiting. He had a thick red mustache and beard and his forearms were covered with tattoos of the Virgin Mary and ships. I asked him if he sometimes got a hankering to go back to sea, but he said he didn't at all. That was the end of our conversation. He was not a very talkative man. Manolo watched me unpack my cello, tune it, rosin the bow. When I was ready, we sat face to face staring at each other. After a while, I asked him if George Liddy and Pilar were getting ready and he called to Pilar, who came running into the room with her hands wet.

"We're ready," he said. "Tell the Señor."

Pilar hurried off down a hallway and returned with George Liddy. He had changed into a linen summer suit—something very Italian-looking—and had showered for the occasion. Pilar took off her apron and sat down, too. She crossed her legs and stared straight ahead. They all stared right at me and sat stiffly in their chairs as if I were a teacher about to give them a very stern lecture. And that's how they stayed the whole time—whether I played Dvořák or Schubert or Bach or Vivaldi, they maintained their postures. So I stared back at them and found myself playing incredibly well because I had stopped trying to please my strange trio of an audience and instead played for the sake of playing, as if I were alone in my room or alone on top of a mountain.

When I stopped between pieces, they remained motionless, waiting patiently, and when I finally had had enough, I was drenched in sweat and my thighs hurt from pressing hard on my cello. Two hours had passed. I stood up to let them know I was finished, and they all applauded furiously; they clapped so hard their hands must have stung and Pilar yelled, "Bravo! Bravo! Bravo!" over and over and over again until her brother told her to be quiet.

"I hope I didn't bore you," I said, not out of false modesty but because two hours of straight solo cello music is hard to take.

"Not at all," George Liddy said. "It was absolutely mesmerizing."

Then Pilar started crying, not just a few quiet tears because she was moved by the music, but giant sobs befitting a truly tragic occasion. Manolo completely ignored her as if he were used to this type of outburst, but George Liddy and I couldn't just pretend that nothing was happening, so we each took one of her hands and tried to console her, which only made her cry harder. Since she was crying so hard and trying to speak at the same time, it seemed as if she were about to choke, so we stopped asking her what was wrong and just let her cry without letting go of her hands. I was standing on one side of her and George Liddy was on the other side. We must have looked odd—like an unlikely family posing for a portrait. After a while, Manolo got up and left the room without saying a word.

We stood like that until Pilar calmed down. It happened quite suddenly. One minute she was still sobbing and the next minute she was offering us something to drink. While she was in the kitchen getting us some special homemade drink from her village, George Liddy explained that he had heard her crying several times before when she was watching something on television.

"Isn't it weird for the guests?" I asked.

George Liddy agreed that it did make him uncomfortable but that the guests didn't spend much time in their rooms. They were mainly young backpackers and newly arrived Moroccan workers.

Pilar returned with the special drink called *orujo*, which turned out to be a very strong spirit made from grape resin. She did not drink with us, but made sure that we were drinking ours. Apparently it had medicinal qualities, although she didn't name them specifically. I could tell that George Liddy was really upset about drinking it since he firmly believed that sticking to one drink was the only thing keeping him from total alcoholic collapse and because from experience he knew that once he got started on something as potent as *orujo*, he couldn't stop until he passed out. Pilar and I carried him to his room ourselves. That's how light he was.

THE UKRAINIAN

The *St. Matthew Passion* came to an end and Tommy fell asleep again. I thought he had fallen into a coma, but the nurses assured me it was nothing more than sleep. I tried to rest too, but I was sure he would slip away from me during the night. "When will he wake up?" I kept asking the nurses, who patted me on the shoulder and said pneumonia is very, very tiring, so I should let him sleep. "But he doesn't want to sleep," I said in his defense. "It is what he needs" was their reply, and I was afraid to disobey them, afraid to bring him back to consciousness, afraid he would awaken in the same state and that never again would he remember who I was. So I let him sleep, sleep way into the next day. I denied myself rest, though the nurses admonished me about how important it was for me to maintain my strength and my health for Tommy's sake.

At three in the afternoon he stirred, asked me for a glass of water, which I brought him, and then fell back asleep. At six he opened his eyes and spoke. "Ah, Mrs. Mondschein. I dreamt that you and my mother were having coffee and éclairs on the top of a mountain. You sat at a table set with a perfectly white tablecloth and silver cutlery. You were both wearing hats with feathers and white dresses, and the wind blew your hair and you said it was a little chilly despite the sun, and my mother lent you her shawl."

"And then?"

"Nothing. You drank coffee and ate your éclairs. It took a very long time and I thought you would never finish. The éclairs didn't seem to be getting any smaller and no matter how many times you lifted the coffee cups to your mouths to sip, there was always something there."

"Did we talk?"

"No, or maybe I just couldn't hear because you were so far away on top of the mountain."

"And where were you?"

"I'm not sure, too far away to hear you talking."

"Do you know that you were in a coma?" I asked.

"A coma?"

I explained to him that I had kept talking because I had promised to do so and because they say patients in comas can see and hear everything that goes on around them. "What is the last thing you remember from my story?" I asked. He remembered everything about the commandant's proposition; he even remembered the Vivaldi and the cognac. I didn't ask him whether he remembered laughing or that he had been awake and could not recognize me.

"What a pleasure it would be to die in one of those Magic Mountain-type sanatoriums in Switzerland. Imagine spending the warm afternoon sitting in the mountain sun all wrapped up in a Scottish blanket, listening to the birds. Then we could drink coffee and eat éclairs, too."

"I would prefer something harsher," I said, not because I had ever thought I would prefer to die a violent death but because the thought of coffee and éclairs in Switzerland reminded me too much of my first husband.

"Well, it seems incredibly civilized to me, quiet and civilized and mundane. I think it must be nice to die doing something perfectly mundane, but not sleeping. That's too neutral."

"I don't see what's so civilized about drinking coffee and eating pastry."

"It's civilized because there's nothing spiritual or hopeful or philosophical or meaningful about it."

"Then why does it have to be on top of a mountain?" I asked.

"It doesn't have to be on top of a mountain, but it should be someplace beautiful. I would prefer to die someplace beautiful, but, alas, that is not my fate."

"Nor mine," I said and we both laughed.

"Mrs. Mondschein, could you prop me up on these pillows? I feel the need to be upright." It was easy to move him because he was so light and the distance was not at all far. Then, there he sat, upright. "Now, Mrs. Mondschein, let's continue with your story before I fall into another coma."

"I think we have finally come to Clara's birth. The last three days of my pregnancy I did not leave my bunk. I decided that since I had come that far, it was my duty to protect the baby. I had not expected to be able to carry her to the end and during those last couple months, I waited for something to happen. I would awaken in the middle of the night, my heart beating violently and I would feel for blood, but my hands always were dry and then I would feel her kicking softly as if to remind me that she was still there, still planning on going through with it. The other prisoners brought me food and water and the guards ignored my absence from work. I am sure they had orders from the commandant because they were very efficient about keeping track of us, recording the deaths in a leather-bound ledger and counting and recounting us throughout the day.

"The night of Clara's birth it snowed and the usual sound of the guards marching back and forth outside the barracks was muffled by fresh snow. I concentrated on those muffled footsteps through the long night of labor. The other prisoners stood around my bed as if they thought they could create a human wall to protect Clara and me from harm. They did not touch me, nor did they speak, but they stood three rows deep around my bunk. When a woman grew tired, another would replace her. It got closer and closer to dawn and I knew that if I did not deliver before the guards woke us to begin our long day, we would both be lost, so I pushed and pushed, biting my own hand to keep myself from screaming.

"When Clara emerged, the women washed her as well as they could, and one of them—she had red hair and for some reason I thought that it was because she had red hair that she was chosen—bit the umbilical cord in half with her front teeth. After that I slept and when I woke in the morning, Clara was sleeping on my breast. Outside, the camp was covered with snow and I watched the prisoners cutting wood and shoveling, working slowly, like sleepwalkers. In the evening the prisoners brought bread and, since my body was too undernourished to produce milk, I chewed the stale bread and spit it directly into Clara's little mouth. The next day, though I was afraid to leave Clara alone in the bunker, I went back to work because I was more afraid that my reprieve could be withdrawn at any moment and that the guards would come for both of us.

"And then, not even a week after Clara was born, the Russians arrived. We had no idea they were coming, no idea that we were so close to the end because even I had come to believe that there would be no end, that this would be our lives and then, sooner rather than later, we would die.

"Everyone was afraid of the Russian soldiers. The women hid under their thin blankets, refusing to meet their liberators face to face. Some of them had to be dragged out into the sunlight, kicking but not screaming because they were still mute. It took over a week for them to begin talking again, slowly and simply at first like small children, uttering only nouns like *bread* or *soap* or *tree* and then adding more words each day as if they were rediscovering the world. They took their bowls of soup from the Russian soldiers with trembling hands and huddled in faraway corners, eating as fast as possible in order to be prepared for the Russian attack, which they had no doubt would come when they least expected it.

"Karl and I were the lucky ones again—the only surviving couple at Pribor. When the Russians had secured the camp, they opened the gates of the men's compound first, and the men stumbled across the snow-covered field that separated us from them. We watched them walking from behind our barbed-wire fence. They spread out along the field as if they were trying to free themselves of each other. Some of them were too weak to make it through the snow and they collapsed in the field and the Russian soldiers carried them back to their bunkers. Karl was ahead of the others. He was stronger and, though he did not walk quickly, he walked steadily. Every few steps, he looked back to see how the others were doing and he paused a few times as if he were thinking about going back to help them, but then he would begin walking again. When Karl had almost reached the end of the field, the Russians opened the gates to the women's compound and we flowed out, like an oil spill, seeping through the gates and then bobbing at the edge of the snowy field, looking for familiar faces, waiting. Karl saw me then and he lifted his arm to let me know he had seen me and I lifted Clara as high as I could and stood there, holding her high in the air until he reached us. Then I handed Clara to him and she looked so small in his arms even though he was so thin a summer breeze could have toppled him.

"It was almost too much for the other prisoners—our intactness, Clara. They avoided us and we avoided them, yet sometimes I noticed women furtively glancing at Clara as they walked by us slowly, heads down. The soldiers were afraid of all of us, afraid of the way you could see the outlines of our skulls in our shaved heads and the way we munched our bread, hunched over like small rodents. On the first day of our liber-

ation the soldiers made us a huge meal—real soup with meat and potatoes and lots of good black bread—and they made us drink vodka with
them. Karl warned us all to stick to one bowl of soup and to avoid the
vodka. 'Thank you,' he said to the soldiers. 'Why don't you drink for us.'
He tried his best, but many of the prisoners could not stop themselves.
They had one bowl and then another and then another, and they stuffed
themselves with bread. 'Please.' Karl pulled on the young soldiers'
sleeves. 'Don't give them any more to eat.' But they thought he wanted
more and they brought us more bread and they took long swigs of vodka
and they sang mournful Russian tunes into the night. The prisoners sat
and watched the Russians silently as if they were a movie.

"And then at around midnight their shriveled stomachs began
exploding; the vomiting started and the gasping for breath and the
writhing on the ground and clutching. The soldiers, all of whom were
drunk, dashed from prisoner to prisoner, pulling them up onto their feet,
slapping them on their backs. One soldier turned a woman upside down
and shook her, mouth to the ground as if he thought all the poison would
flow out of her like blood flowing from the neck of a butchered lamb.
Sixteen of us died that first night, and in the morning the hungover soldiers wept when they saw what they had done. Karl told them that it
wasn't their fault, but they didn't understand what he was saying.

"That first week more of us died, mostly of diarrhea. You cannot
imagine the smell. We dragged the bodies over to the edge of the running
field and left them there because no one had the energy to dig graves.
And after a week, the Russians told us they had to move on. They were
heading north to Poland. 'Who is going to Poland?' they asked. 'We can
take you.' But no one wanted to go to Poland, so they gave us bread and
water and pointed us west, and those of us who were strong enough
started walking west. The rest stayed behind, waiting for the strength to
leave. I wonder how many of them ever found it.

"We started out together, but Karl and I were able to walk faster and
longer than the rest, so we kept having to stop to wait for them to catch
up. Karl tried carrying some of the weakest ones, but they screamed with
pain when he picked them up, complaining that they could feel their
organs swishing around inside them like a balloon filled with bile as he
walked. 'Not so fast,' they yelled until he was hardly moving at all."

"So they felt that, too," Tommy said.

"You can feel your organs?" I asked, surprised because I suppose I had not believed them. I had thought they were just too tired to move.

"Even when I shift from lying on my right side to lying on my left side, I can feel them all shifting with me, piling over to the other side. And they make a horrible *glug-glug* noise, which is much worse than hearing your own heart beat. That's why I can only lie on my back now."

"I'm sorry."

"Sorry for what?" Tommy asked.

"For not believing them."

"I wouldn't have believed them, either," he said.

"We kept with them all day and we slept near them, but not among them, that night. They all huddled together as if they weren't ready to give up the overcrowded barracks we had suffered in for so long. Karl thought we should sleep among them so as not to set ourselves apart, but I couldn't. 'I don't want to disturb them in the night if Clara needs something,' I said, but we both knew it had nothing to do with Clara.

"We were up at the crack of dawn, anxious to get as far away as we could from Pribor, but it was impossible to rouse the others. We poked at them and sprinkled water on their faces, but they just looked up at us for a few brief moments like opium addicts. We shouted, clapped our hands, but they refused to budge, so we left them there under the trees. Sometimes I dream I return to that place and find their skeletons picked white by birds, and I gather all their bones and put them in a burlap sack and sling the sack over my shoulder and start walking down the road towards the west. Then I wake up thinking that we should just have buried them right there. It was a beautiful spot.

"After having walked at a very brisk pace for only two hours, we came upon a village but were afraid to enter it, so we hid behind some trees until it had been dark for a very, very long time. Then we tiptoed slowly and very quietly through the town. The stone buildings seemed to move towards us as if they were inviting us inside. There was a smell of somewhat distant manure and wood burning that made me want to run up to one of those thick doors and bang and bang until an old peasant woman let us in and asked us to sit around a table near a fire and fed us thick slabs of black bread and poured us glasses of *sliwowitz*. But we were still afraid of food and trusted no one. I imagined the three of us tucked in under an eiderdown comforter, falling asleep as soon as our heads hit the pillows and then waking up in the middle of the night clutching at our stomachs, choking on bloody vomit, and then seeing the old peasant woman washing the sheets in a cast-iron cauldron full of boiling water while her sons dug our graves. So we walked on until we spotted a horse-drawn cart in the distance coming our way.

"I think we walked like this for three or four days and then we had neither food nor water left. If it had been just Karl and me, we could have walked longer, but we couldn't keep on starving Clara and decided that at the next village we would have to ask for help. We chose a very modest house towards the end of a little lane. It appealed to us because, unlike the other houses in the village, this one was not decorated with little painted flower pots waiting for spring flowers. I don't know what we thought the lack of flower pots symbolized—perhaps that the house belonged to someone very old and crazy. Perhaps we thought the war might have passed the occupant by as he sat in a chair by the fire.

"You can imagine my surprise when a young, beautiful woman opened the door. She neither smiled nor frowned when she saw us, although I imagine we were quite a frightening little group. She spoke but, of course, we didn't understand Czech, so we smiled and made cups of our hands, asking for water. She kept talking in a soft, toneless voice as if she were reciting a prayer out of habit rather than out of faith. We made cups of our hands again, and I held Clara up for her to see because I wasn't sure she had noticed that we had a baby with us. I pulled back the thin blanket from Clara's face. The woman recoiled from Clara, so I covered her face quietly and held her to my breast. Up until that moment I hadn't thought about what she looked like, and if you had asked me to draw her, I wouldn't have been able to render a likeness. Perhaps it was a kind of defense mechanism that my brain had conjured up so that I would not be frightened of my own creation. She looked like one of my favorite Vermeers at the Met—a portrait of an embryonic young woman with a very high forehead and skin so translucent it has a greenish hue. Have you ever seen it? It doesn't have any objects or cloths or windows or maps in it—just the head of a woman, her big round eyes staring right out at you."

"I'm sure I've seen it, although I can't seem to find the image. I just see that woman with the jug," Tommy said, staring up at the ceiling as if he were trying to see the young girl up there.

"From that day on, I could see the blue veins at her temples and the gray-green puffiness around her eyes, and my love for her took a leap, from being catlike, with me instinctively picking her up by the neck and removing her from danger, to human. It was as if I could sense Clara's sadness and I wanted more than anything else to protect her from it, yet at the same time I wanted to hold on to it because Karl and I were too tired to feel sadness ourselves and would have walked and walked without stopping, without eating, until we came to a place where the people made us stop. Whether they put us in another camp, shot us in the back, or offered us éclairs and hot chocolate, we wouldn't really have noticed a difference. Only Clara kept us from walking off the edge of the earth.

"So we followed the young woman into her house, and we sat on wooden benches by a fire, only there were no thick slices of black bread. 'The Russians,' she said and opened up all of her cupboards so we could see that there was nothing inside. Then she said some more things we could not understand and we all laughed about not being able to understand, and then she went to the kitchen and brought back a huge bowl filled to overflowing with robust wild mushrooms. She set the bowl down in front of us so we could examine them, and then she took the bowl away. After about ten minutes, she came back with the same bowl only now, after being cooked, the mushrooms looked meager and sickly. The woman gave us two spoons and watched silently as we ate, turning away when I fed Clara the already chewed mushrooms from my own mouth. We ate slowly, one limp piece at a time, not only because there was so little but because it tasted so good.

"'What if they're poisonous?' Karl asked when he had finished half his mushrooms.

"'Then we will die,' I said, and we both laughed because it seemed so ridiculous to have survived everything and then to die from eating mushrooms.

"We left a small portion and offered it to the woman, but she declined, which made us suspicious again, but we finished them all anyway. After our meal the woman made up a pallet of eiderdowns and pillows for us on the floor near the fire, gave us a bundle of old but clean clothes, and boiled water for our baths. We took off the layers of rags in which Clara was swaddled. Her little body was covered with yellowish blisters and Karl punctured them all with a sterilized knife, and then we washed out the wounds and wrapped her in a clean towel. Even then she neither cried nor flinched; she just lay quietly while Karl worked and the woman watched us without speaking. Karl and I took our baths in private.

"Taking that first bath was one of the most frightening experiences of my life. I hadn't seen myself in all that time and expected the worst, expected my skin to be bored through by parasites and my flesh to be filled with tiny eggs. I thought if we were starving to death, we could eat those eggs and they would burst open in our mouths like caviar. But there were no eggs, no insects, just dirt and a scaly red rash that lingered for months and only started itching that day I took my first bath and discovered it. Karl had it too and said it was from the cold and malnutrition and that it would go away, which it did, eventually."

"You know, I haven't had a bath since I've been in the hospice. Do you think I should request one?" Tommy wondered dreamily as if he had said he hadn't been to the beach in a long time.

"You could get pneumonia again."

"That didn't stop you and Karl."

"No, it didn't, but your case is different," I said feeling immediately bad about using the word *case*.

"You're right. I sometimes forget that I am not like you, but like your fellow prisoners, and now I have interrupted you again. So were the mushrooms poisonous?" he asked as if he hoped they had been, but knew they hadn't.

"No, they weren't poisonous, although I couldn't sleep that night and was aware of every strange pang and rumble in my stomach. Once I was sure I couldn't breathe and woke Karl up to tell him. 'It's just the weight of all these covers,' he said and fell back asleep. And in the morning we weren't dead at all.

"We had planned to leave in the morning, but when we opened our eyes, we were not alone. About fifteen villagers, women and old men, were standing in their coats at the edge of our pallet, staring down at us.

"'What do you want?' Karl yelled and they backed up slowly, as if we were dangerous animals that needed to be subdued. Then they started whispering to each other, and we lay there, immobile, while they whispered. Finally, one of them stepped forward. He was an older man and he took off his hat and asked us in very bad German where the Russians were. We told them we didn't know. Then the old man went back to the huddle of villagers and told them what we had said, and they whispered some more until finally our hostess led them out of our room so we could make ourselves ready for the day. As we put on our new old clothes and washed Clara's wounds, we could hear them in the kitchen. Their voices had turned from whispers to yelling.

"I was sure they were planning our deaths and envisioned us hanging from a tree, but Karl insisted they had no reason to kill us.

"'As if that has ever made a difference,' I replied. 'Maybe they want to do their patriotic duties, one last hurrah before the Russians come.'

"'Can't you feel their fear?' Karl asked.

"'No,' I said because it was impossible for me to feel any fear but my own.

"'Let's try to talk to them,' he said calmly, and we went out to join the villagers in the kitchen. The old man told us about what had happened when the Russians came through their village. They had taken more than food and he nodded sadly at the women. It was time to leave, they told Karl. They had packed a cart with the few things that remained. They wanted to know whether we were heading west and, if so, whether we could be their guides.

"'Your guides?' I said laughing, and they lowered their heads.

"'The Russians will not hurt us if you are with us,' the old man said.

"'So you know who we are?' I asked.

"'Yes,' he said, but he bowed his head again and did not elaborate.

"'There is strength in numbers,' Karl said, and the old man looked up at us.

"'Thank you,' he said and then went to tell the rest of the villagers our answer.

"At first they insisted we ride in the wagon, which the men pulled— the horses had been slaughtered by the Russians. But they pulled so slowly—as if they were dragging their dead relatives to the churchyard. We couldn't bear it, sitting atop all their worldly possessions like a royal family fleeing, abdicating the throne. Karl volunteered to help them pull, but they said they did not want the Russians to see us working.

"We didn't run into the Russians, though. We ran into the Germans—bedraggled troops heading reluctantly towards home and, accompanying them, lines and lines of civilians with wagons piled high with bundles and farm equipment, heading west away from the Russians. The old and sickly took turns riding in the backs of the German trucks and, because of Clara, the German soldiers encouraged us to accept a ride, but we preferred walking. It made us feel stronger and I had visions of a once fat and red-cheeked sergeant throwing her gleefully from the truck.

"We tried hanging back to distance ourselves from the German troops and their co-travelers, but it was impossible to lose them because the line of refugees went on behind us as long as the eye could see and much farther. After we joined the Germans, our villagers ignored us, except when it came time to distribute food and drink. They handed us our provisions with bowed heads and always looked away if Clara's face was uncovered. We didn't try to engage them because there was no point. We simply received our rations as they all did, quietly and humbly. We wondered what happened to our original hostess and if there was some reason why she had stayed behind. But there probably was no real reason except that she was the sort who preferred to stay home, the type who is more afraid of what she does not know than of what she knows."

"And you, Mrs. Mondschein, which are you more afraid of?" Tommy asked.

"The known," I said. "There is always hope in the unknown."

"Hope is what scares me the most because it will come to nothing and then you are just back to the known."

"I don't think it comes to nothing," I said, not really sure if I believed what I was saying, but saying it nonetheless. "If nothing else, it comes to something else than what you had before, which is at least a change, something you have to figure out, something to keep you engaged for a while longer."

"What do you think happened to that woman?"

"She probably had children. Women almost always have children."

"So you don't think she was killed by the Russians?"

"No."

"Why are you so sure?"

"I'm not sure. I just don't think she was. I think she had children and worked hard and was cold in the winter and looked forward to the summer."

"I bet she stayed behind because she was waiting for her husband to come home."

"Maybe, but if she had a husband, he probably didn't come home."

"Probably not," Tommy said, sinking back into his pillow. "Do you think she ever regretted not going along?"

"Yes, and if she had come with us, she would have regretted that. She would have spent years in a dingy house in Cleveland, dreaming of her village and complaining about how the bread in the United States could never be the same as the bread that came out of her three-hundred-year-old oven in her three-hundred-year-old house back in her village in Czechoslovakia, and her grandchildren would raise their eyebrows every time she started talking about bread. At least we were spared that."

"Spared what?"

"The nostalgia."

"You never miss Vienna? Not even during those moments just before you fall asleep at night, when your mind wanders to places you don't usually let it wander to? You don't sometimes think, *wouldn't it be nice to spend a rainy afternoon in a café, drinking coffee and savoring some overly sweet and creamy pastry?*"

"No. Sometimes I think of my sisters' heavy arms mixing dough with wooden spoons, and then I have to get up and listen to the radio until I can no longer see the little beads of sweat that formed on their forearms as they mixed and mixed and mixed in that quiet apartment with its yellowing curtains and Passover silver."

"Well, then in some way you are lucky because in the summer I still wake up yearning for the sounds of lawnmowers and the Good Humor Man and my mother vacuuming that horrible orange shag carpeting she was so proud of and that feeling of summer, knowing I had the whole day to myself, knowing that my father was on his way to work, sitting on the train reading his stupid paper, and, best of all, knowing there was no school with bullies that made fun of the way I walked or held my pencil or threw a ball. It was just me and the hot, long day. Don't you have any memories like that at all?"

"No. Do you feel like some music?" I asked. He lay very still, looking up at the ceiling, as if he were trying to imagine the long line of people moving like one wounded mass towards the west. His eyes strained up toward the ceiling, as if he saw an actual image on the ceiling and was straining to get it into focus.

"What?" he asked.

"Do you want to listen to some music?"

He sat up then, fighting to get himself upright, pushing me away when I tried to help him, his breath rattling in his chest. "Doesn't certain music remind you of Karl, of your first year together, before the war, before your father's death?"

"No, when I listen to music, I think of nothing at all."

"How could that be?"

"I have trained myself. It's the only reprieve I get from my thoughts."

"I've never wanted a reprieve from my thoughts, no matter how terrible they may be." Tommy tried to raise himself up even higher, but he was too weak.

"We all have our weaknesses," I said, smiling, but Tommy remained utterly serious.

"And Karl, did music have the same effect on him?"

"I don't know, but I doubt it. It takes quite a bit of practice to empty your mind so completely."

"Did he know that's what you do?"

"No, we never discussed it."

"So, when you used to go to concerts together, he had no idea?"

"No idea," I said.

"Hmm. Maybe he knew and just didn't let on."

"Maybe, but I don't think he did. Did you know? You and I have listened to a lot of music together."

"No, but Karl had a way of knowing things."

"Yes, but he was better at knowing things about strangers than about me."

"That's because you kept secrets from him."

"Yes, and he kept secrets from me."

"How do you know?"

"I just do."

"Still, I wouldn't have kept anything from him," Tommy said with the utmost seriousness, but then his seriousness embarrassed him, so he chuckled and asked, "So, how did you train yourself to be thoughtless?"

"I started with Bach because it's the purest of all music. The *Brandenberg Concerti* worked the best because the harpsichord is so crisp, just short, finished notes that don't linger in the air like pain the way organ or even piano music does. With the harpsichord you can concentrate on each individual note separately as if it were a section of an even, black line separating you from your thoughts, from everything. After you learn to separate each note, you can let them flow back towards each other without any interference and then all you know is the music."

"Do we have the *Brandenberg Concerti* here?"

"Yes, should I put it on?"

"No, I feel like something more emotional. Maybe some crying will do me good. Let's put on the Mahler Adagietto again." And when it was over, he asked me to play it again and then again and then again. Finally, after four times he cried out in a high-pitched, hoarse yelp, "Enough! I guess I'm just not up for crying today. Let's go back to your line of pathetic refugees."

"Fine. We shuffled on, stopping as little as possible, especially as we got closer and closer to Germany. The Germans kept a steady pace too, as if they were eager to hand in their weapons and go home, as if they expected everything to be the way it had been when they left. Just outside Regensburg we met up with American troops, who ordered the German soldiers to give up their weapons and then led them away. They didn't meet with any resistance at all. I don't know where they took the soldiers, but they piled us into trucks and took us to the Displaced Persons camp that was to be our home for almost two years.

"The camp was a former army base with rows of simple wooden barracks covered with tin roofs. When it rained, we lay awake listening to a strange drumming that was half cacophonous and half soothing, like crows cawing at dusk. At first we shared our barracks with some Ukrainians. How they had made it west before us, we never knew. We kept to ourselves and so did they, all of us tiptoeing on the wooden floors as if we were sharing the room with a dying celebrity. They prayed before each meal. After about a week, they left. I don't know where they went, but they were replaced by Polish Jews, all young men who tried to speak to us in Yiddish. We pretended we understood less than we did, so they left us alone too, spending most of their time in the canteen drinking cup after cup of weak coffee and smoking American cigarettes. After a few weeks, they left for Palestine, so we got new barrack mates, who also left for Palestine, as did the next set and the next.

"At the camp there were rabbis, whom Karl and I avoided, and there were the Zionists to whom we half-listened with polite expressions on our faces but who scared us even more than the rabbis. It was amazing how quickly our fellow prisoners grasped at Israel. How our fellow sur-vivors cried when young American Zionists spoke of sinking their hands elbow-deep into the soil of the Promised Land, their eyes brimming over for the grapes and wheat and oranges they would pick, and the sheep blood they would spill with their own hands. These were people who had never even planted a flower nor thought of keeping a potted plant in their dark apartments, people who had always covered every inch of their bodies and avoided sunlight whenever possible. It was as if centuries and centuries of a repressed longing for nature rose to the surface. Men and women alike woke up at the crack of dawn, even though they had nothing but time on their hands, to do their exercises, prepare their bodies for the hard work of turning desert into farmland. In the evenings they sang songs and practiced speaking to each other in Hebrew, turning pages and pages of memorized *Blatts* into talk about children and clothes and their favorite foods.

"But we studied English. We followed the relief workers around, asking them silly questions in our horrible accents just for the practice, and, when they were not too busy with important things like making sure everyone was taking parasite medicine, we invited them for coffee and we asked them about their families in broken English, carefully writing down our new vocabulary in little notebooks that we carried with us everywhere. They were always very polite and thanked us for the coffee and gave us chewing gum, which we graciously took and hoarded in our small box of belongings along with our tin plates and enamel coffee cups. We gave all those things to Clara on her eighteenth birthday. She had been begging us to give them to her for years and finally we relented. We should have just left everything in the camp, but people grow attached to material objects and to memories.

"We had a special place for those memories in our apartment in the buffet behind the Scotch and brandy and gin Karl's patients gave him, which we never drank from except on rare occasions when we had guests. I can count the guests who came to our apartment on two hands and that's including Simon when he and Clara were dating as well as the one or two school friends Clara invited over the years. We had no time for guests and preferred to stick to ourselves, spending the free time we did have at concerts. We didn't go to the opera much. It had lost its appeal, but we took comfort in the neat austerity of chamber music. Once when Clara was still very young, we took her to the symphony. It was Mozart, the Thirty-ninth. Clara held her hands over her ears the whole time and afterwards told us she could feel the music pounding in her stomach. But she didn't cry. She just sat stiffly, her hands over her ears, doing everything in her power to keep from screaming.

"Clara never cried as a child. She would only stiffen. It was her version of crying, a carryover from her first days, when she instinctively knew that crying would be the end. For the first few weeks after Karl and I were reunited, she stiffened every time Karl tried to pick her up and that stiffening was worse than the most piercing scream. And then it just stopped. One morning she looked up at Karl and smiled, only it wasn't really a smile, more of a half-smile. And after that morning she almost preferred Karl to everyone else, including me, even to the sweet-smelling UNRO nurses who brought her chocolate milk and played with her toes.

"Gradually it became Karl who would wake up in the middle of the night to feed her. It became Karl who sat with her in the warm afternoon sun, pointing out things he found amusing—'There goes the future Miss Israel,' he would say more loudly than was polite, pointing at a youngish woman with frizzy red hair and thick calves. When we first arrived at the refugee camp, Clara was the only baby among us, but when we left almost two years later the place was swarming with babies. Every time a baby was born, there was a party, and we were all expected to attend, drink thin coffee, eat bad American chocolate, and then cry tears of joy because the world would be a better place now. They were all convinced of that, so they made new babies to replace the dead ones and Clara was the mascot of all the new babies, the first, the prototype. Wherever she went, women would smother her with kisses and cry if she so much as looked at them. Karl indulged people their fantasies. He would parade Clara around, taking her for a sip of tea here, a few kisses there. Up and down the camp they wandered and Karl would cheerfully tip his hat at them all.

"But then Karl began helping the overworked medical staff, and I was the one who spent the long days with her, changing her diapers, walking round and round the periphery of the camp, trying to stick as close to the edge as possible. I could have walked on the other side of the fence too. Nothing kept us locked in. There was a gate and a road, and surrounding the camp were fields, and in the distance you could see the rooftops of a village, but we never left the camp. Not once, although sometimes I stood at the gate looking out for hours.

"'Ruth,' Karl used to say to me after I had come home from one of my long walks, 'we will look back on this time as the freest period of our lives.' And perhaps it was, but everyone has a different definition of freedom. I cannot blame him for enjoying our little island of safety. But I couldn't relax, despite the fact that we had all the diapers we needed and all the bad white bread we could eat. I kept trying to imagine what our lives would be like in New York, because we were going to New York; that much was sure. We just didn't know when. Every morning I went to the mailbox hoping for our visas, and every morning when I came back empty-handed, Karl would smile and say, 'Patience is the mother of all virtues.'

"'You only say that because you don't have to be patient, because all you do is work, save lives, save minds,' I would say, and he would just shake his head and say that it was not so simple anymore. I waited for him to ask me to help him with his work, but, in all fairness, I don't think he knew I wanted to help and I didn't ask him, so maybe I didn't really want to work at curing then. Maybe I thought it was hopeless to patch people up and send them on their way. Maybe I thought it would have been better to die from gangrene or hepatitis. But Karl they needed. The doctors had gone home, exhausted from the war. They had gone home to houses with cars and garages and bathrooms and to children with ear infections and the mumps. They didn't need another attentive woman because there was an overabundance of nurses. Maybe if they had really needed me, it would have made more sense to me to inoculate and sterilize and bandage and wash and soothe than to walk around and around in the gray air. Then I might have been able to leave Clara with one of the many groups of female knitters who sat in circles near heaters, knitting blankets and socks and sweaters for all the new babies. They could have used Clara as a model. But there were all those nurses, all those young women afraid to return to prewar fiancés and widowed mothers and future children, clamoring for peanut butter and jelly sandwiches and dogs.

"'Enjoy this time with Clara,' he said, 'because when we get to New York, we will have to struggle.' And I tried to enjoy my time with Clara, but how can you enjoy walking round and round and round a refugee camp all day long until your feet hurt?

"'There are plenty of books in the library,' Karl would tell me, but I couldn't concentrate on books. 'And why don't you try to make some friends?' But I had no interest in friends, so I walked and walked and Karl worried that Clara would catch cold when it rained or snowed, but she was never sick. I think Karl would have stayed there forever or at least until the last DP had been placed. All he had to do was work and the rest was taken care of. He could work twenty hours a day if he felt like it.

"*Herr Doktor*, all the nurses called him, and he would call them *gnädiges Fräulein*, and they would titter and blush. I'm sure every last one of them lay in their cots at night wishing they could go home to a man like Karl, a man who called them *gnädiges Fräulein* and looked straight into their eyes. I'm sure they wondered what horrors those eyes had seen and wept when they tried to imagine them.

"One of Karl's patients was a middle-aged Ukrainian man who complained that the devil resided in his brain. All night long the devil would tell him pornographic jokes, so he could not sleep. If he tried to tune them out, the devil would bang on the inside of his skull until he agreed to listen. The devil only needed about two hours of sleep a day and preferred to take his rest in the late morning. That was the only time the devil left him alone. Throughout the day the devil would command the man to do strange and sometimes terrible things like walk around the camp naked holding his penis, or eat his own excrement, or whisper obscenities at the female refugees.

"One day he tried to bite off a cat's leg, but the cat lashed out at him and he and the cat were brought to the infirmary a bloody mess. It took four large men to keep the Ukrainian from banging his head against the wall and smashing his skull. 'Doctor,' he begged Karl, 'take the devil out of my head! Take the devil out of my head!' So Karl, with the help of the *gnädigen Fräulein*, performed a devil-removing operation. They gave him a full anesthesia and made a small incision in his scalp and then sewed it right up again. When the man awoke, the devil was gone and he kissed Karl's hands and he kissed the nurses' hands and they brought him chicken broth and then he slept again. They kept him in the hospital for three days and made a big to-do about dressing his wound, and then they released him.

"After his release, the Ukrainian visited Karl at our bunker regularly. He would sit in a chair facing Karl, smiling, and Karl smiled back at him. They talked a little but not much because they didn't have a common language. If I came into the room when he was there, he would start humming and tapping his foot nervously, so I always left them alone. He loved Clara, though. Karl would let him hold Clara on his lap and play horse and rider with her, and Clara would bob up and down, expression-less. 'It's good for him to be around children,' Karl would say, but it made me nervous. He was a fleshy man whose name I never knew, not because it was kept from me, but because I never asked. Karl always referred to him as *my Ukrainian*. When he held Clara on his lap, she looked even tinier than she was—his large, red hands covered most of her body. I asked Karl once not to let him hold her and he got angry with me. 'Don't be so selfish. Clara calms him, helps him laugh,' he said.

"'But he makes her nervous. I can feel it.'

"'He makes you nervous' was Karl's reply and he refused to say any more. Sometimes he and Karl would talk in low voices so I couldn't hear them, but when I asked Karl what they talked about, he said, 'About food and things like that.'

"'What do you mean by *things like that?*'

"'Insignificant things. He teaches me how to say *chicken* and *cabbage* and such things in Ukrainian and I teach him the same words in German, and then we talk a little bit about chicken and cabbage.' Still, I always had the feeling there was more to it than that."

"More between him and Karl?" Tommy asked.

"Not in that way, Tommy."

"How do you know? Things between men can happen so easily."

"He was crazy, psychotic. He was capable of doing terrible things."

"I just have a feeling. I don't mean to upset you, but I have that feeling, which is rarely wrong."

"It doesn't upset me, but it would have been cruel of Karl to use him in that way. Karl wouldn't do that."

"Why do you call it using? Maybe that's what he needed more than anything else. Human contact. He used Clara, didn't he, used her to help the Ukrainian?"

"That was different."

"Why? The Ukrainian must have gotten attached to her too. How did he feel when you left or when he left? He would have come to think of Clara as his daughter or perhaps his niece."

"In the end, he was sent away. The devil kept coming back. Karl had to operate more and more often, making deeper and deeper incisions, but then the Ukrainian started believing that instead of extracting the devil, Karl was adding a new devil every time he operated. One day it would be the devil from India that spoke to him and the next it was the devil from China and then the devil from Russia and the devil from France. Every country had a devil and sometimes they would fight on top of his brain, and then he felt as if he were going to explode and he would hit himself on the head with a rock until he passed out. So they had to put him in an insane asylum in Regensburg."

"You see. He was in love with Karl," Tommy said.

"He was psychotic, Tommy. He was incapable of love."

"How do you know such a thing?"

"You didn't know him, didn't see the way he sat in that chair with Clara on his lap smiling stupidly, no, not stupidly, but smiling without feeling. If you had seen him, you would agree."

"Don't feel bad about Karl, Mrs. Mondschein. He was trying to help. Even after all he had been through, he thought he could help. There are not many people like that in the world."

"He just made things worse, Tommy."

"Maybe not. Maybe while the Ukrainian was staring out of the window of the Regensburg insane asylum on a beautiful sunny day or on a dismal winter day, he would think of Karl and of Clara's tiny hands and he would smile, and maybe it would be a real smile."

"And what about the devil? Would the devil ever let him think such thoughts?"

"Even the devil rested for two hours every day."

"Yes, but not after the other devils joined him."

"Still, even with the devils, he could remember other things, better times in his life, like chicken and cabbage and Karl."

"Do you really think . . .?"

"Yes."

"But he was monstrous, Tommy. His hands were so big. They were the kind of hands that could snap your neck in two."

"Men crave that kind of strength," Tommy said.

"I see."

"Maybe we should listen to the *Brandenberg Concerti* now," Tommy said.

So I put on the CD and I could tell Tommy was trying very hard not to think of anything, trying to separate the notes and then string them back together again, but he couldn't do it. He stared straight ahead, concentrating with all his might on not focusing, but I knew what he was seeing—Karl and his large Ukrainian. I knew that's what he was seeing because that's what I saw—his pink, flabby stomach pressing on Karl's slight frame. Only I didn't try not to see it. On the contrary, as the harpsichord plucked away its melody, crisp like a sunny October day, I watched Karl and the Ukrainian until they were both tired and the Ukrainian lay peacefully on Karl's chest as Karl stroked his thinning hair. And then I saw him in the insane asylum in Regensburg, looking out the window with a vague memory of Karl buried deep in his brain as the devils from all around the world did battle in his head.

And Tommy slowly let himself be taken in by Karl and his Ukrainian. His expression was no longer vacant but was as if he himself were looking into the Ukrainian's watery green eyes. What did he see there? How could he even bear to look?

"Tommy," I said softly so as not to startle him.

He did not respond.

"Tommy," I repeated more forcefully. Still no answer, so I sat very still, completely oblivious to the *Brandenberg Concerti*, focusing only on Tommy, waiting for him to return.

He didn't return. His hand fumbled for his crotch and he pulled. Faster and faster, and I didn't leave the room. When it was over, he slumped back on his pillows, wiped his sticky hand on the sheets, closed his eyes, and slept. Then I continued my story because I did not want to leave him and I had no book to read, no crossword puzzle to solve. Perhaps I should have waited, listened to some music, stretched out on the plastic couch in the waiting room, but I was compelled to go on and I believed that, if nothing else, the sound of my voice would soothe Tommy's restless body that gasped for air and flailed and flinched until dawn.

THE DENTIST OF 148TH STREET

The bus pulled into the George Washington Bridge Bus Terminal and I had no idea what I should do. I thought of going to the Village, but it was getting late and I didn't feel like being around a lot of people, so I sat in the plastic orange chairs at the terminal for a while, trying to decide where to go. A drunk sat down in the seat next to me and then asked me, "Do you mind if I sit down?"

"You've already sat down," I said.

"Oh," he said, but he didn't make any move to get up. He just sat there staring straight ahead as if he were watching a ballgame. I decided, just as another not-so-steady character was heading towards me, that a walk would be good, so I headed downtown, passing the Museum of the American Indian on 157th Street where my grandparents used to take me when I stayed with them. We must have gone there at least thirty times, but I don't remember much about the exhibits. There were lots of dimly lit dioramas with Indian families canoeing and grinding corn, that much I can picture, but I don't remember the individual scenes the way I can picture whole rooms in the Met. We used to go to the Museum of the American Indian in the winter and it was always really hot inside and my grandparents made me carry my own coat, so sometimes I kept it on and I would get sweaty and tired. Maybe that's why I don't remember much about it. I remember trying to seem more interested than I was and feeling bad that I didn't really like the place. And I was slightly embarrassed because my grandfather always carried my grandmother's pocketbook. I feel stupid for feeling embarrassed about that. It's actually touching that he never cared what other people would think. Maybe that's one of the things that happens when you get old—you can carry your wife's pocketbook. After the museum we usually picked up pastries and went back to their apartment to have coffee and dessert instead of dinner—napoleons, éclairs, cream puffs, marble cake, cheesecake. I've never been a really big fan of sweets, but there was something exciting about eating pastries for dinner. They told me not to tell my parents, which I never did.

Afterward my grandfather quizzed me on anatomy. He had three categories of questions—function, location, size and shape—and if I got all

213

of them right, I got to have one more napoleon before I went to bed even though I was usually full, but I would eat it with relish anyway while he watched. When I was really little, I thought they ate dessert every night for dinner, that they survived on pastries, but later I realized it was their way of doing something special.

It was really hard to sleep at their apartment. In the summer, it was both muggy and noisy; my grandparents didn't even have a fan. In the winter, the radiators hissed out way too much heat, and I would wake up in the middle of the night to banging pipes and a throat so dry I could hardly swallow.

Before sixth grade my grandparents used to come out to New Jersey every Sunday afternoon because Sunday was the only day they didn't work. They worked more than full-time until I was in sixth grade, and then they had to retire because the building where my grandfather had his office burned down. I think towards the end of his career, he was as busy as ever because word got out that he only charged five dollars per visit or whatever you could afford, so he would have throngs of people lined up every day. The kitchen cabinets are still filled with bottles of liquor that their patients brought as payment. I don't think my grandparents ever opened even one bottle. Over time they had lost most of the older patients they had started out with—Jewish people who had hung onto their apartments on the Grand Concourse. As the patients died or moved to nursing homes, my grandparents began treating the new inhabitants of the Grand Concourse—Puerto Ricans, Dominicans, and Cubans, but mainly Puerto Ricans. My grandmother took Spanish classes at City College in order to be able to talk to their new clientele. Once when I was in fourth or fifth grade, they got held up at gunpoint and my parents tried to convince them to close up shop, retire, but they said you couldn't judge a neighborhood based on two young hoodlums, so they kept on going, six days a week, and then on Sundays they came out to New Jersey. They came on the two o'clock bus and left on the five o'clock bus, and never stayed for dinner. Before sixth grade I used to spend the weekends there every few months or so when my parents were out of town, but after they had to retire, they stopped coming every Sunday and my parents only had me stay over there a couple times a year. We would all go there to dinner sometimes and my grandmother would make chicken soup with potatoes, carrots, and parsley, and cucumber salad, and they always had Wild's black bread.

I guess they just got really slowed down after they had to close the practice. They stopped going to concerts and the theater, but they said they were working on rereading all their favorite books and didn't have time to go out. From what I could tell, though, they spent most of their time listening to music, not reading. There were never really any books lying around that looked like they were being read. They listened to records on an old Panasonic record player and sometimes they took a trip downtown to buy CDs, which they played on a state-of-the-art CD player my parents bought for them. Then my grandfather had a heart attack in his sleep and died. Everyone said it was best that he died pain-lessly in his sleep, that he didn't suffer, but I don't want to die in my sleep. I want to know that my consciousness is about to be extinguished. I want to feel that fear because I know it is fear, not peace, that the dying experience. Unless they are robbed of it like my grandfather was. At the funeral the rabbi kept talking about how, after having come so close to dying a horrible death at a young age, my grandfather was blessed with a peaceful death at an old age, but rabbis just say things like that to make everyone feel better, only it makes it worse. I think maybe my mother is right after all—maybe that moment in the gas chamber when people realized they were being massacred was the most intense experience a human being can ever have.

Since my grandfather died a year ago, we have seen even less of my grandmother than before. I think the last time was in the summer. She came out to New Jersey during a heat wave, but my parents couldn't con-vince her to stay overnight in our air-conditioned house even though the outside temperature was something like one-hundred-four degrees with ninety-eight percent humidity. She said she couldn't stand the quiet whirring sound of the air conditioner and that it was good to sweat, that it gets all the toxins out.

Passing the Museum of the American Indian gave me the idea to visit her. It was a good solution because I wasn't about to spend all night wandering around the city like a teenage runaway, nor could I return home to my mother's stink and my father's anxiety and the quiet of cars passing by in the night.

The door to her building was open as usual because the neighborhood kids are always breaking the lock. I climbed the stairs in the dark. Someone must have smashed all the light bulbs. I held onto the banister really tightly and tried out each step before putting my weight on it because lots of them are broken. My grandmother's apartment is on the top floor, which makes it quieter, but it's hard for her to carry her groceries up that many flights.

I rang the doorbell over and over and no one answered. (You have to ring the bell a lot, and when you call, you have to let the phone ring at least ten times because sometimes it takes her a while to make it to the phone or door.) Every once in a while someone came up the stairs, and I would say hello and ask if they'd seen my grandmother recently, but no one had. "Not in a few days," they said.

After I had been waiting for almost an hour, Mr. Claromundo, her next-door neighbor, came home and said he hadn't seen her in a while, either. Then he told me about how their downstairs neighbor, this guy Jimmy, stabbed his girlfriend about a week ago and how my grandmother had seen Jimmy with the knife and had called 911. He said he was worried that maybe this Jimmy had come back for her, although he said Jimmy was a really nice guy and he and my grandmother had always been friendly. Then he started going on about how he only had two more years until he retired from the United States Post Office. That's what he kept saying—*United States Post Office*. When he retired, he told me, he was moving back to the Dominican Republic for good. "Up to here, I have it with this city," he kept saying, holding his hand up over his head.

When he got tired of talking about what he was going to do when he retired from the *United States Post Office*, he suggested I could easily get into my grandmother's apartment if I climbed out his kitchen window and stretched my leg over to the ledge of my grandmother's kitchen window. "Easy. No problem for a young person like you," he said. So I agreed to have a look to see how easy it really was. Sure enough, it didn't look like it would be too difficult, and my grandmother's window was open just a crack because she was a big believer in fresh air even in the winter. All I would have to do was step from his ledge to hers, open the window a little wider, and slip in. The only problem was that she lives on the sixth floor. Mr. Claromundo then suggested I might find it easier if I had "just one little glass of rum" first. So we sat down in his living room and drank a glass of rum. Mr. Claromundo used to be a dentist in the Dominican Republic but never got his license here, so now he just does a little dentistry on the side. His living room operates as his dentist's office, and it has a very old-fashioned dentist's chair, a little sink, and a table with all the instruments on top of it, ready to go.

"You want your teeth cleaned?" he asked. "I'll do it for free since you're Mrs. Mondschein's granddaughter."

"No thanks, I just had them cleaned a month ago."

"Let me see," he said, and before I could protest, he was looking into my mouth.

"Looking good. Very nice teeth. Clean and straight."

"Thanks."

"You want more rum?" he asked.

"No, thank you. I think I'd like to try the window now."

We both went into the kitchen and he opened up his window and said, "Be careful now." Now that I think of it, I must have been completely out of my mind, especially after having the rum, but I did it without being too scared. I moved really fast so there was no time to think too much.

My grandmother's apartment looked just the way it always did—immaculately clean and orderly. Everything had its place—the kitchen towels were hanging from their little hooks, the old copies of the *New York Times* were in the box near the door, ready to go out when she accumulated enough. The glass doors into the living room and bedroom were locked as they always are whenever she leaves the house.

Mr. Claromundo rapped on the apartment door. "Hey, do you see anything?" he asked.

"Not really," I said.

"Aren't you going to let me in?" he asked, and though I didn't want to, I unlocked the door for him. I made him put out his cigarette before he came in. My grandmother would have had a fit if anyone ever smoked in her apartment My grandfather had been a smoker, but he quit years before I was born. The story is that he used to smoke four packs a day, and then one morning he woke up and decided it was stupid to smoke, so he quit. Never smoked a cigarette again in his life. Mr. Claromundo stamped out his butt on the floor right in front of my grandmother's door, which is another thing that would drive her crazy, but I didn't say anything. He was carrying the bottle of rum.

Since the doors to the living room and bedroom were locked, we sat down at the kitchen table, which was covered with an old Pennsylvania Dutch-style oilcloth. I got two glasses and Mr. Claromundo poured us each a shot four fingers high. Under different circumstances some rum in a nice warm apartment in the middle of the winter would have been just the right thing. Mr. Claromundo smiled and made that *aaahhh* sound that people make after taking a nice big gulp of a strong drink. He leaned way back in his chair, getting himself nicely settled in, and told me that my grandmother was "a great lady."

I didn't dislike Mr. Claromundo and knew he was happy to be having this spontaneous little get-together, but he was the kind of man who liked to talk and didn't really care if you were listening or not. He told me all about how Dominicans don't take care of their teeth and about how you could tell a Cuban from a Dominican by their teeth because no matter how poor a Cuban was, he always took care of his teeth. If I had been sitting with George Liddy, I would have asked him if that meant that Cubans were more vain than Dominicans, but I didn't think Mr. Claromundo would find that question amusing.

"What about Puerto Ricans?" I asked.

"What about them?"

"Do they take care of their teeth?"

"Some do and some don't" was his answer.

"How about Colombians?" I asked.

"Colombians?" But he had lost track of the conversation.

Then, luckily for me, his cell phone rang. It must have been a date because he was really happy when he got off the phone, did a little jig-like dance and was out the door. "Don't worry about your grandma," he said as he was leaving. Until he said that I wasn't worried about her, but after he left me alone, I realized it was almost midnight. As far as I knew, ever since my grandfather's death, she never came home after dark unless my parents had taken to a concert or dinner, which didn't happen very often. My mother made her promise never to come home after dark like she was some kind of kid, but she's not a night person and has always gotten up really early and gone to bed really early. This promise was only made after my mother agreed to stop trying to get my grandmother to move into one of those retirement homes. Right after my grandfather died, my mother got it into her head that my grandmother would be better off in one of those places. My father tried to pretend that we were really driving around to look at the leaves, but you would have to be crazy to spend every Saturday for two months looking at leaves. One of those Saturdays I very nonchalantly said that I felt like staying home and practicing and my mother nearly had a fit about how this was a family issue and how we all had to be involved. When we found a place my mother liked, my mother would make my grandmother come with us the next Saturday to check it out, but she was just humoring my mother. There is no way my grandmother is ever going to leave her apartment.

I turned on the radio and made myself a cup of tea. I didn't even have a book with me, so I practiced writing down the notes for the music I was listening to, but I couldn't concentrate because they had their music on really loud in the apartment below me, so loud I could feel the thumping in my thighs. I guess it's good all my grandmother has to do to stop the noise is take out her hearing aid because I don't know how she would be able to stand it otherwise. She only likes classical music. I was getting tired of sitting in the kitchen with nothing to do but was stuck since leaving so late would have been dangerous. The bass thumping got louder and louder. It was almost two a.m. *Why doesn't she call?* I thought and then remembered that she had no idea I was sitting at her kitchen table drinking my sixth cup of tea with her little mint-green radio turned up in a futile effort to drown out the noise.

I thought of calling my parents, telling them where I was, crying, making them drive all the way to New York to pick me up, but I didn't want to worry them. Should I call the police? I rang Mr. Claromundo's bell, hoping he might be back, but no one answered, and then I was relieved because Mr. Claromundo was not the person I wanted to talk to.

The person I really wanted to talk to was halfway across the world in Ireland, probably lying in bed by himself, the ceiling spinning and rain pouring down outside his window. It would have been nice to sit in my grandmother's overly heated kitchen with George Liddy. I think he would like her apartment, the sparseness of it and the old stove that you have to light with matches. He might have even agreed to a teeth-cleaning by Mr. Claromundo. I could just hear him say, "I certainly have been neglecting my teeth and don't suppose a little cleaning would hurt, do you, Deborah?" And then we would ring Mr. Claromundo's bell and he would come to the door in a silk robe, but he would be so happy to have a customer that he would leave whomever it was in his bedroom with the door closed and set to work on George Liddy's teeth.

I tried to sleep, putting my head down on the kitchen table like they make you do in elementary school, but I never slept then either. I wonder if anyone does. The music from downstairs pounded through the table and straight into my ears. I tried to block it out, tried hard to think of something else like running or riding my bicycle down Clinton Avenue really fast. I wish I weren't such a light sleeper, but I can't sleep if there is the slightest unusual noise like a dripping faucet or someone breathing softly. I need to work on that, practice falling asleep with lots of noise all around me because when you travel a lot, you have to be able to sleep no matter where you are or what is going on around you.

If I really had the guts, I'd buy a plane ticket to Ireland and go to Limerick. Wouldn't George Liddy be surprised to see me on his doorstep? Would he be glad to see me, or would he just start talking a blue streak? When we were together, I often had the feeling that he would have been just as happy or unhappy to talk with Pilar as with me because, let's face it, he did most of the talking anyway. But deep down I knew that he really did like talking to me, that we were close. Well, maybe *close* isn't the right word to use about George Liddy, but it was something close to close.

When we parted, George Liddy told me that he was unable to write letters because they always sounded like bad prose poems to him. For that same reason, he never kept a diary even though he liked the idea of people reading all the sordid details of his life after he was dead. I wrote him a couple letters anyway, thinking he would break his habit and write back, but he didn't. For all I know, he could be dead. I asked our health teacher Mr. Herr what the average life expectancy of an alcoholic was, and, without even thinking for a second, he said forty-three. (He's the kind of person who has a statistic handy for every occasion. Ask him about teenage pregnancy in Norway and he'll have an answer.) We were in the middle of discussing the high rate of diabetes among Native Americans. He had worked on a reservation in New Mexico or Arizona when he got out of college, so he was always trying to tie Native Americans into whatever it was he was teaching. I wonder what it is about New Mexico and Arizona that seems to attract my teachers. Actually, Mr. Herr was kind of obsessed with diabetes and we had already heard all about the problems Native Americans had with the disease, so I figured someone should change the subject, so I asked him about the life-expectancy of alcoholics.

"Forty-three," he said without blinking. "And what, may I ask, are you implying with that question?"

"Implying?" I had no idea what he was talking about and was about to tell him that I had a friend in his sixties who was an alcoholic and I was worried he didn't have much time left, but I didn't want anyone to ask me about it afterwards. I could just picture him sending me to talk to the guidance counselor because a high school girl who has befriended an elderly alcoholic must certainly be off-kilter, to say the least, and might even be leaning towards suicide.

"Yes, implying." His voiced was raised now, almost to a screech. The class was quiet and he was staring at me.

"I'm sorry. I didn't mean to change the subject," I said.

"I'll see you after class then," he said, getting his composure back. He changed the subject too and started talking about self-love and how you can't love anyone else unless you love yourself. Then he made us all stand up and put our arms around ourselves, reach back, and give ourselves big hugs like you do when you are trying to warm yourself up. "Tighter, tighter!" he shrieked at us and we all complied. Then he started doing it too, rubbing his hands up and down his shoulders and back. "Do that for at least ten minutes every day and your life will be filled with sunshine," he said as we were leaving. I tried to slip out the door with everyone else, wondering how many kids in the class would actually go home and follow his advice. I could just see them holding themselves more and more tightly, feeling the self-love surging up inside them.

"Where are you going, young lady?" He was calling me.

"Oh, I forgot," I said.

"Forgot? Well, have a seat." I sat down at one of the desks in the front row and he pulled up a desk and sat on it. Looking down at me from his perch, he said, "You know, not all Indians are alcoholics." There were tears in his eyes.

I didn't know how to respond to his statement. All that came to mind was what George Liddy would say—"But the best of them are, I'm sure." I said nothing.

"Have you ever even met a Native American?" he asked.

I hadn't. It seemed ridiculous, but it was true. "No, actually I haven't."

"So how can you pass judgment?"

I tried to tell him that I had never really considered the drinking habits of Native Americans, that I had been thinking about a friend (I didn't tell him he was Irish because that would have led to a whole other issue) when I asked the question, that I hadn't really been paying attention in class and my question popped into my head, so I had asked it. I promised to think first before speaking in the future. I wanted to tell him that I knew so little about Native Americans that I didn't even know they had the reputation of being alcoholics, but I kept my mouth shut.

Then he started lecturing me about the hereditary nature of alcoholism and the next thing I knew I had been assigned a twenty-page research paper on the subject. He gave me the title: "Alcoholism, Genetic or Psychological?"

"What if it's both?" I asked, knowing that I would never write it.

But our little session was over. He got up and started packing up his papers, putting them very neatly into a hand-tooled leather briefcase.

I was starting to get sleepy, but I didn't want to fall asleep until I knew my grandmother was safe, so I started walking around the apartment. What would it be like living here with my grandmother, washing out my clothes in the bathtub, hanging my used paper towels to dry along the edge of the sink? We could get up early together and drink our coffees, looking out at the river. I could go down for the *New York Times*, save her the trouble. She would give me my mother's old room, the room with the photo of all of us—the one with me on the donkey when I was two, my father on one side of me, my mother on the other. I asked her once whether it wasn't time to put up something more recent and she said that's how she thought of me, as a little girl on a donkey flanked by my parents. She said it made her feel I was safe. I don't remember that day, though, or the donkey. In the room, on the same desk, next to the picture of me and my family, is a photo of my grandfather when he was young, before the war. His hair almost covers his eyes, longer on one side than the other. Even though it's a black-and-white photo, you can tell his eyes are black. When he was really sick just before he died, his eyes shone like sea glass. When I was little, I always wanted to touch them and had the feeling they would be soft and smooth, not squooshy and wet like eyes really are. His hands were like that too, worn smooth like the wood on the banister in Mark Twain's house in Hartford, Connecticut.

My grandparents took me up to Hartford to see the Twain house one fall Sunday when I was in fifth grade. We took a bus to Hartford and then a taxi. The taxi driver didn't know where Mark Twain's house was, so my grandmother had to show him on the map. I don't remember much about the house itself except that the banister was really smooth and that the guide said Mark Twain had smoked at least twenty cigars a day. She said that on a really humid day you could still smell them, but it wasn't humid that day. I remember there was a room with a really fancy pool table, and the guide told us that Mark Twain used to go in there and play when he was thinking about his writing. When we got back from Hartford, my grandparents presented me with a hardcover copy of *The Adventures of Huckleberry Finn*, which I read over and over again, always imagining Mark Twain playing pool with a cigar hanging from his mouth, thinking about Huck and Jim riding down the hot river, and I would imagine my grandfather shooting pool with Mark Twain, closing one blue eye as he took aim.

On the bus on the way back, a little girl just about my age vomited and her mother scolded her. "Why did you have to go and ruin your new dress?" she said.

"I didn't mean to," the girl answered.

"That's what you always say: I didn't mean to, I didn't mean to, I didn't mean to." The mother's voice got higher and higher and each time she said, "I didn't mean to," she slapped the girl on the face. My grandfather had to stop my grandmother from going over to the mother and telling her that was no way to treat a young child. "She probably beats her," my grandmother said loudly and my grandfather put his smooth finger to his lips. "Please," he whispered. The three of us were quiet for the rest of the trip as if silence would cover up the girl's sobs better than chatter.

I could almost feel my grandparents in the room now, walking in slippers, getting things ready for dinner, my grandfather setting out the silverware, my grandmother carrying the soup into the dining room on a bamboo tray. Everything had to come in on a tray—there was a small one for silverware and napkins and salt and pepper and larger, sturdier ones for dishes and platters. I was happiest when we had chicken roasted with apples, prunes, and carrots. My grandparents always let me have the wings, both of them all to myself—at home I had to split them with my mother. I could almost smell the chicken and feel the warmth from the oven on my face.

I tried to convince myself that my grandmother had gone to visit a friend, and it had gotten late and dark and cold and her friend had made up the couch for her. I heard both of them snoring, the door to my grandmother's friend's room slightly ajar, the sounds of their sleeping bumping into each other in the dark.

But, as far as I knew, my grandparents didn't have friends, not even Dr. Müller, the ophthalmologist who gave us our yearly eye examinations. He and my grandfather shared office space in the Bronx. Maybe my grandmother had made some since my grandfather's death. Maybe they had always had friends, but didn't want us to know. Or maybe they just didn't have much to say to other people. But that was when they still had each other.

Any minute now, I thought, and the key would turn in the lock and there she would be, carrying the *New York Times* in a net bag, her pocketbook slung over her chest like ammunition. Then I imagined her lying face down between two parked cars, blood in the corners of her mouth. Would my mother come out of her room for the funeral?

I really wished she hadn't locked the doors to her room because then I could have stretched out and slept, and in the morning I would awaken to the sound of her key in the lock. Would she be happy to see me? I decided that if she wasn't back by noon, I was going to Ireland. What if I got to Limerick and George Liddy was dead, buried in the corner of the churchyard next to his parents with his favorite lines from Yeats on an overly shiny marble tombstone at his head? Then there was always Florida. How difficult would it have been to pick up the phone and say, "Hey Mercedes, I was thinking, maybe if things don't work out with you and Leon, maybe I could go with you to Florida." Or "I've been thinking about what you said about getting out of Tenafly and I thought maybe the two of us could go to Miami together, that is, if you and Leon aren't going together because I don't want to be a burden, I just thought . . ." Going to Ireland would have been simpler. It might not have seemed so then, but things with George Liddy are simple. He would probably hate it if I said so, but it's true.

NEW YORK

I stopped talking for a while, walked slowly down the hall to the water fountain for a drink, returned to Tommy's room, closed my eyes a little, but I couldn't sleep. It's impossible to sleep if you are waiting for someone to wake up, so I went back to my tale. "There have been times when I wished we had chosen Israel—picking grapefruit by day and sitting around a campfire singing newly composed patriotic songs by night. Maybe there Clara would have skinned her knee on sacred pebbles and learned to cry. Maybe she would have been blown up in a bus. Then we all would have had something to cry about.

"But we chose New York. It was winter when we arrived, and our room on 106th Street, which we rented from an aging widow, smelled faintly of Vienna—mothballs and warm milk. Except for the nail polish. Our landlady was very proud of her long fingernails. Once a week she went to the movies, but otherwise she was always home, listening to the radio and reading movie magazines; and every evening she painted her fingernails the same color—bright red. We were polite and so was she, but we avoided each other; her domain was the kitchen, and we stayed in our room with the door shut, playing our own radio, drowning out Frank Sinatra. Our little room on the second floor looked out on the airshaft and in the mornings I stuck my head out the window to look up at the sky to see whether it was sunny or not. It usually wasn't. Our landlady told us it was an unusually cold winter, but we were not cold. At first I thought I would never want to leave our room thick with heat from our sputtering radiator because it was the first time we were truly warm in years. But we woke up in the middle of the night sweating, the covers in a heap on the floor, and had to stand by the open window, naked, letting the cold winter air bring our bodies back to life, standing there until our flesh was cold and we could sleep again. Our landlady merely shook her head and smiled when we asked about turning off the radiator. It was as if we were asking her not to paint her nails.

"For a few extra dollars a week, our landlady watched Clara while Karl and I attended English classes. The classes were taught by an overly exuberant elementary school teacher who clapped her hands whenever we were able to spit out a few intelligible words. She clapped her hands when the words were unintelligible too. She wore very high heels and I wondered if she wore them during the day also or just for our benefit. I tried to imagine her running after a classroom full of small children, clapping her hands, bursting into song when her charges performed especially well or wrote an especially symmetrical line of Fs or Qs. Our teacher was very fond of tongue twisters and spent more time than necessary making us repeat them in unison. *Betty Botter bought some butter, but, she thought, this butter's bitter. If I put it in my batter, it would make my batter bitter. But a bit of better butter, that would make my batter better. So 'twas Betty Botter bought a bit of better butter.* Still, we didn't dare miss one class, eager as we were to gobble up every bit of English that came our way.

"When we came home from our class, the landlady always reported that Clara was such a charming, easy child. 'Not a peep from her all night,' she would say, but we hated leaving Clara with her because it would usually take at least an hour to unstiffen her little body when we got home, and we wondered why the landlady didn't think it strange that Clara could spend two hours sitting in the armchair, her legs sticking straight out, her tiny nails digging into the cushions, not moving, without making a *peep*. Maybe the landlady thought Clara couldn't speak yet because she was such a small child, stunted from her early trauma. But we had to go to our classes and we knew no one else to ask, and Clara never formally protested having to stay behind with the landlady. She never mentioned it at all, and when we asked her what she did while we were away, she said, 'I was thinking.'

"'What were you thinking about?' we would ask.

"'Things.'

"'What kind of things?'

"'Words.'

"'Which words?'

"'Words like *book* and *table* and *chair*.'

"We figured there was nothing wrong with leaving Clara behind to think about words, especially when we were in class thinking about words too, although she didn't pick up much English until the spring when we started taking her to the park to play with other children. We thought English would confuse her as it confused us, but she never mixed languages. From the very beginning, she instinctively kept German and

English separate and always knew, even before someone opened his mouth, which language to use. At the time we thought her language abilities were nothing less than miraculous. The funny thing is that she doesn't remember anything from that period except the smell of nail polish. She doesn't remember our little room or sitting in that chair being *watched* by the landlady. She doesn't remember the refugee camp either, not the nurses or all that bad chocolate, not even the Ukrainian. What she remembers, or claims to remember, is lying still, wrapped in a dirty blanket in the concentration camp. She remembers the cold, the stench, the silence, the bony bodies that held her, trying to keep her warm.

"I would like to tell you that we had a very difficult time when we came to this country, but that would not be true. Although my first job was tedious, it was not burdensome. I worked for a year as a token seller at the 110th Street IRT stop. From four in the afternoon to midnight, I slid tokens through the little window to passengers who paid absolutely no attention to me. I saw only their hands—fat hands, thin hands, gloved hands, black hands, white hands, old and young hands, cold red hands. I liked not having to look people in the eye, and there were times when I thought I could recognize my customers by their hands, but I never tested myself because I didn't really want to recognize anyone. The hands seemed innocent to me, angerless, devoid of malice. Of course I knew the hands were capable of terrible things, but I imagined them as disembodied creatures who felt like taking a ride on the subway. They weren't going to work; they weren't going to meet lovers or friends; they weren't going to the movies. I saw them sitting properly, one hand crossed over the other, or swinging their fingers off the edge of their seats like children.

"By that time we already had our apartment and could not rely on the landlady for babysitting, so Karl and I took turns watching Clara. I worked the evening shift so I could spend the days watching Clara while Karl went to the library to study for his Medical Boards. On Sundays we went to the park. In a year Karl passed his boards and, through the *Aufbau* newspaper, found another doctor who wanted to set up a small practice. They opened an office in the Bronx and I came to work for them. And, since people are always sick, we always had plenty of patients, and we worked hard—six days a week. We were efficient, and we charged little. Our only real hardship in New York had been the smell of nail polish.

"People did not look at us strangely when we walked into a store; in fact, they didn't look at us at all. It was as if we were invisible or as if we had been coming into their stores all their lives. I kept expecting someone, a cashier or a bus driver or the woman at the post office, to look up as we asked for something in our bad English. 'Six stamps, please.' We always made a point of saying 'please.' But the woman at the post office just handed us our six stamps and took our money. Sometimes when we thanked her, she said, 'You're welcome,' and sometimes she didn't. But I always expected her to look up and see me for what I was. I expected her to hold my hand, look into my eyes and say she was terribly, terribly sorry for what had happened. Of course, I realized even then that that was too much to ask. They were civil to us, which is all we needed, and we ate well and had our own apartment with a river view, and we went to the park on Sundays, and we went to concerts, and most of our patients had minor illnesses, which we cured or, most commonly, which cured themselves.

"Still, I suppose deep down we expected them not only to care about our suffering, which perhaps they did in a theoretical, general way, but to acknowledge it. But they had their lives and they let us slip into their city, their streets, their shops, their subway, concert halls, schools. It took me years to learn to love the privacy of New York, the solitude that is possible only here. Of course, now I realize that they would have crushed us with kindness if they had decided to be kind. We would have buckled under the pressure, felt indebted, moved, sentimental. What if our land-lady had baked us cookies or pressed secondhand sweaters into our hands? What if, instead of letting Clara sit for hours in a chair, our land-lady had taken her to Radio City Music Hall or read her bedtime stories? Where would we have gone to hide then? What if the ladies from the United Jewish Federation, from whom we received monthly checks for the first year, had shown up at our apartment laden with toys and smiles? What if they had held our hands and said, 'You have suffered enough.' Would we have asked them in for tea?"

"Tea?" Tommy's eyes popped open suddenly. "I would love some tea, Mrs. Mondschein." He looked me straight in the eye without a trace of embarrassment. Did he remember how he had fallen asleep last night? Did it matter? I made chamomile tea in the waiting room microwave and we sipped our tea out of Styrofoam cups.

"I dreamt I remembered my own birth, so if you think your story is having no effect on me, you're absolutely wrong."

"I didn't think that," I said because I wouldn't have kept on going through all the details if it were having no effect whatsoever.

"I remembered my mother's screams and somehow knew I was the cause of them, and there was an awful lot of blood and excrement. The world smelled of blood and excrement. And then there was a horrible total silence when I was placed in my mother's arms. She didn't say a word. She just stared into my eyes, and those eyes frightened me. Finally, she fell asleep and I lay there looking at the pores along the sides of her nose. What if it really was like that? What if my memory is being jagged somehow, now that I am slipping away from the world? That would be the ultimate act of cruelty towards oneself, to force oneself to remember such a thing." Tommy paused and looked into his Styrofoam cup without drinking. "But it was just a dream because I know I can't remember anything before the age of four. That's when the Scottos moved in next door, and Mrs. Scotto used to invite me over for hot chocolate and to play in the sandbox with Jimmy Scotto, who always wanted me to bury him right up to his chin in sand. I remember wondering what it would be like to be nothing more than a head that your mother could carry around with her, put in her pocketbook or set on the table. How can Clara remember so far back? Is that even possible? I had a boyfriend who was always trying to get me to go to a hypnotist to do some kind of *rebirthing*, but thank God he dumped me before I actually agreed to do it. The things I used to do for love."

"Clara is the one who claims she remembers her own birth, being pushed out of a warm, wet place into the cold stench of the bunker, but I don't believe it. She only *thinks* she remembers, and I have told her that time and time again, but she just shakes her head sadly as if I were the one who believed in something impossible. You see, we told her about it so many times. Every night almost she would say, 'Tell me about how I was born,' and we would tell her. Every night since the first night we sat by her bed and told her about Pribor."

"How old was she when you first told her?"

"Three. It was the night of her third birthday."

"Mrs. Mondschein, I don't mean to criticize, but wasn't that a little strange, to tell a three-year-old such a bedtime story?"

"It didn't seem strange at the time. We tried to make it into a fairy tale, viscerally frightening yet heroic like 'Hansel and Gretel.' You know how frightening 'Hansel and Gretel' is."

"But your story was reality, and children know when you tell them a fairy tale that it's a fairy tale, both too horrible and too beautiful to be real."

"I realize that now, but perhaps we were trying to make a fairy tale out of reality. Perhaps that was our biggest mistake. We made such an effort to tell it beautifully, using that almost hypnotic rhythm that fairy tales have, repeating key phrases and images over and over and over again."

"Tell it to me," Tommy said, pulling the covers up to his bone-thin cheeks.

"No. I don't think I could remember it properly," I told him, though as I spoke I heard myself whispering in my storytelling mode—'And the women chewed their stale crusts of bread until they were soft and warm in their mouths, and Clara opened her tiny mouth like a little bird and Mother fed her, touching her lips to Clara's lips as the warm mush passed gently from one mouth to the other.'" Tommy knew I was lying and I knew he knew, but I could not say those words out loud, not because I knew I should never have spoken them—I am still not convinced that it was wrong of us to try to explain and even to immortalize our experience—but because the words were sentimental, like a prayer. There was no horror in them and perhaps that was our biggest mistake.

"It's not your fault." Tommy put his hand on mine. It was freezing cold.

"Are you cold?" I asked.

"I'm always cold, Mrs. Mondschein."

"Then let me get you more blankets." I started to get up.

"Mrs. Mondschein, it's not that kind of cold. You know, just because you told her that story so many times doesn't mean she doesn't remember. What is memory anyway except a feeling? She can feel the cold, feel the darkness, the fear, all those things you told her about. How can you know she doesn't remember?"

"I know," I said.

"And why are you so sure? And even if she doesn't really remember, don't you think that if I finally do get delirious and start thinking that the SS is coming to get me or that Jesus Christ is really Hitler or whatever crazy thing it is, that all those things will be true on some level?"

"On some level, they will be true, but that's the point—only on some level. You yourself just said that you know your dream was a dream and not a memory of your birth. False memories might be true, but they won't be *The Truth*."

"Well, I'm not sure I believe in the distinction," Tommy said and flung his arms down hard on his thighs. "I just wanted to see if I could still feel them. My legs, that is."

"Can you?" I asked.

"I'm not sure. I'm afraid it might only be a memory of feeling that I am feeling."

"Please, Tommy," I said.

"Please what?"

"Please don't joke at a time like this."

"And what kind of time is it, Mrs. Mondschein?"

"You know what kind of time it is," I said and I found that I was crying.

"Mrs. Mondschein?" Tommy whispered.

"Yes?"

"I'm so very, very cold, Mrs. Mondschein."

I pulled the covers up around him as tightly as I could so that all I saw of him was his small, thin head sweating on the white pillow. I could feel the heat emanating from his forehead and cheeks as I tucked him in, so I called for a nurse, who brought a cool wet cloth, which I placed gently on his forehead.

"Why is it so cold?" Tommy asked. His eyes looked as if they were about to jump out of their sockets, as if they were going to make a run for it and escape while there was still time, but, after a few minutes, his eyes retreated as if they were afraid to venture out into the world, and a few moments later Tommy closed his eyes.

Tommy slept rather peacefully for about four hours. I stayed with him, flipping through magazines, listening to him breathe. His breathing became more relaxed, steadier, and his body lay quietly without flinching or twitching. Every once in a while, he coughed in his sleep. And then towards morning, he stopped breathing. One second he was breathing and the next second he wasn't. There was no death rattle. He took one breath and then he didn't take the next breath. I must admit that the first thing I thought when I realized he was dead was that I hadn't finished my story, that there was still so much more to tell, that there were still years and years left until Karl died, until today, and then I burst into tears because I didn't know what to do with myself now that he was gone and there were still so many things left untold, which made me feel horribly selfish. And then I let myself succumb to that selfishness, and I resumed my story. We could have made it without interruption until the early morning rounds, yet it was different now, as if his ears were walls rather than windows.

"Mrs. Mondschein," I imagined him saying, "enough is enough." And so I stopped talking, and only then did I realize I was crying because I would really miss him, and that meant we had been friends, which meant I had lost a friend. It occurred to me that until now I had never really had a friend except for Karl, and I wondered whether Tommy and Karl would have been friends, and, if they had been friends, whether I would have been left out. Then I thought I should play some Mozart before I called the nurse, so I put on the Piano Concerto no. 20 in D Minor. I don't know why I had never played it for Tommy before because it is one of my favorites. I guess I thought we still had time.

"Sorry," I said. "Do you know Mozart's Piano Concerto no. 20, the one that opens up with the cellos playing the melody that sounds like massive iron ships sailing heavily yet gracefully across a neither stormy nor calm sea?"

"What are they carrying?" he would have asked.

"I don't know," I would have said. "Maybe nothing, maybe nothing at all."

At six a.m. the nurse came in to take his blood pressure. His eyes were still open, his palms, facing limply upwards, were cold. "Mrs. Mond-schein," the nurse said very gravely, "he is deceased." Then came a flurry

234

of activity in which I was neither given a part nor asked to leave. It was as if I no longer existed too or as if Tommy's death had made me invisible.

Yet it wasn't time for me to leave, not because Tommy needed my assistance but because being on the street on a crisp, sunny winter Saturday morning was something I wasn't quite ready to face. There would be happy, rested couples off to a hearty brunch, and quiet office clerks, newspapers in hand, ambling to their favorite cafés, where they would distractedly read the paper, looking up hopefully every few lines so as not to miss the woman or man of their dreams, who might walk through the door because this Saturday might be the Saturday that would change their lives forever.

The staff must have contacted Tommy's parents because towards noon they arrived. I tried to feel angry with Tommy for having turned them into villains and I tried being angry with them for not being villains at all. But there was no anger in me, just sadness as I watched them approach the bed. I had imagined they would be large people, but they were small, Italian-small with dark hair gone gray. Tommy's mother took one look at her son and started screaming hysterically, covering her eyes with her hands. At one point I thought she would rip out her hair, but instead she banged her open palms against her temples. Tommy's father stood at the side of the bed very quietly, letting the tears slip out of his eyes and run slowly down his face. At one point I thought he was too weak to stand because his legs were trembling, so I brought him a chair and pushed him gently into it. He sat in the chair crying softly while his wife screamed and banged her head with her open palms. I went back to my chair by the wall where I wouldn't bother them. Then the nurses and the doctor and the social worker arrived and led Tommy's mother and father away to another room.

I stayed to watch the orderlies remove Tommy's body and then slipped out, past the nurses' station. Waiting for the elevator, I half dreaded, half hoped someone would pat me on the shoulder and say, "Mrs. Mondschein, please don't go," but no one witnessed my departure. Then the elevator opened and I stepped in, and then, before I knew it, I was out in the winter sun.

JUDITH AND HOLOFERNES

Once Marisol managed to convince my mother to model for her paintings, they were always together. I avoided going into the Barbieri because it was where they would go to take a break from their work. I saw them walking across the Plaza de Lavapíes one afternoon. They were talking and laughing and Marisol's black shirt and jeans were splattered with yellow and red paint. After that afternoon, I went out of my way to avoid Lavapíes altogether. I spent more time in the apartment practicing the cello and reading. My father was making up for lost time with his research, so he rarely came home until eight or nine at night. Sometimes my mother would join my father and me for a late dinner, but usually she didn't come home until midnight or even later. My father didn't seem to mind that she was never around and neither did I. He didn't have that much time left to finish his research and I was happy to be practicing seriously again. In the evenings I still walked over to Tirso de Molina to hang out with George Liddy. It was nice to be out in the cool night air and to be around people and talking after spending most of the day inside.

Late one afternoon, about a week after my mother started modeling for Marisol, I found that I was not in the mood for practicing or reading. I tried to sleep, but I was restless, so I walked over to Tirso de Molina, hoping to find George Liddy. After checking all the bars on the square, I headed down the hill towards Lavapíes, forgetting that Lavapíes was dangerous territory. The next thing I knew, I was standing right in front of the Barbieri. It was like something was pulling me towards it like some kind of siren-like magnet, half singing sweetly, half pulling violently. I went inside. My mother and Marisol were at their usual table, Marisol wearing her paint-splattered clothes, my mother smoking again, the smoke seeping out of her slightly open mouth like wholesome breath on a crisp winter day. I pulled up a chair and sat down.

"How's the modeling going?" I asked, feeling completely comfortable, chatty, like George Liddy after three maybe four drinks.

"It's very difficult to sit still," my mother said, laughing girlishly.

"What's the painting about?" I asked Marisol, avoiding my mother's giggly eyes.

"It's not finished yet," she answered.

"I'm not allowed to look at it until it's finished," my mother said as if this were the most incredible thing in the world.

This time I wasn't afraid to ask. "Are you posing clothed or unclothed?"

"Clothed," Marisol answered and my mother almost giggled again, but she bit her lip. I saw her bite her lip.

"Why can't you paint from memory?" I asked once again. I guess I wanted to prove she wasn't a good painter even though I knew she was.

"I can, but I don't choose to," she said, full of her usual self-confidence. "I like the communication between the model and the painter. If you paint only from memory, your subjects have no thoughts of their own, they are only you, but if someone is sitting right in front of you, thinking, restless, that gets into the painting."

That's what I hated about Marisol: she wasn't stupid. I would have liked to talk to her more about such things, but I knew that if I had the opportunity to talk to her seriously, I wouldn't know what to say. I wanted to tell her that maybe it was kind of like the difference between playing the cello for an audience and playing it alone, just for oneself. Instead I raised my eyebrows as if what she had said was really pretentious, which in a way it was, and she and my mother laughed.

"Do you paint with music or without?" I asked to change the subject, though I already knew the answer.

"I prefer silence."

"Except for the sound of the air conditioner," I said, looking at my mother to see if she'd notice, but she was looking up at the ceiling as if she were watching a spider making its way across the room.

"I don't even hear it," Marisol said, but I didn't believe her. I wonder if her paintings would be different if she opened up the windows and let the street noises and the oven-blast heat in. I wonder if instead of yellows and browns and reds, she would paint in purples and blues and greens.

Some woman whom Marisol knew came up to the table to say hello. She looked a lot like Marisol—thin, short dark hair, white, white skin, somewhere around thirty, but maybe younger. I'm really bad at ages. They talked for a while about a mutual friend who had just come back from Scotland, and my mother kept staring at the ceiling, so I got up and walked out the door without saying goodbye. I knew both of them saw me leaving, but they didn't say anything, so I didn't feel the need to say anything either.

Again I found myself with no place to go, so I decided to see if George Liddy was at his *pensión*. I practically ran all the way there, so anxious was I to see him.

"Just in time for some *flan*," Pilar said the second she opened the door.

"Is George Liddy home?" I asked, out of breath, ignoring her offer.

"Not yet. Please, come have some *flan*. It's my grandmother's recipe, with orange peel. My grandmother was a very imaginative woman. She was always putting strange things into food, but it always tasted delicious. Everyone said she was crazy, but I don't remember because she died when I was only ten, and when you're ten, you can't really tell who is crazy and who isn't."

"I don't like *flan*," I said and immediately regretted it because I have nothing against *flan*.

"I'm sorry," Pilar said.

"Sorry for what?"

"That I made *flan*." She was on the brink of tears. "My brother hates our grandmother's *flan*, so I rarely make it."

"Well, maybe I'll like this kind of *flan* since it's so different." Her face brightened up. She brought the *flan* to me on a little porcelain tea saucer with pink flowers on it and watched me eat every bite. "Mmm," I said enthusiastically. "It's completely different from any other *flan* I've ever tried before."

"You like it then?" she asked, full of hope.

"It's delicious."

"Do you want some more?" And I had to have more as a punishment for my previous insensitivity.

"Where's your brother?" I asked to stop her from watching me eat so closely.

"He went to his meeting," she said like it was something really, really stupid.

"What kind of meeting?"

"Oh, I don't know, but he never misses one of his meetings." Then I became really intrigued with Manolo's meetings and kept asking Pilar all sorts of questions. I guess I just needed to talk and that's what there was to talk about. "Are they political? Religious? Is it some kind of club or professional organization?" But she just laughed and said she had learned at an early age not to be too curious about Manolo.

"Why?" I wanted to know.

"Because he's a pathological liar."

"Does he lie about everything?" I asked.

"Not everything, but sometimes it's hard to tell. Just yesterday he told me he was going out to buy fish for lunch, but then he changed his mind and bought chicken instead, but I knew he was lying, that he was planning on buying chicken right from the beginning."

"How do you know that's a lie?" I asked, wondering why anyone would lie about something so insignificant, thinking that was probably the trick, to make up really boring lies, catch people unaware so you could slip in some really unlikely ones, too.

"Because we had fish yesterday," Pilar said.

"Maybe he liked it so much he thought he wanted it again but changed his mind when he was at the market and saw the chicken," I offered.

"Maybe," Pilar said, but she was just humoring me.

At that point the door opened and Manolo himself walked in. He was wearing his usual training outfit and his pants went *ft, fttt, ftt* as he walked across the room. "How was your meeting?" Pilar asked him.

"What meeting?" he said and she winked at me. "What meeting?" he said again.

And she said, "Your *meeting*."

"Oh," he said, "my *meeting*. It was fine."

It was as if the meeting were some kind of cue because Manolo walked over to the CD player and put on this very strange Gallego folk music. It was a song with about one hundred bagpipes and a large chorus of what sounded like very old women—very old women on their deathbeds. I had an image of a large ward packed with hardly any space between the rusty hospital beds, the women propped up on graying pillows, singing at the tops of their lungs. Pilar and Manolo started dancing a slow-motion folk dance that was kind of like the *Hora*, but much slower, like they were dancing in a pool. The song went on and on, repeating itself, coming to what seemed to be a climax, but not ending like Beethoven. They danced opposite to the music: when it got faster and seemed as if it were drawing to a close, they danced more slowly, and when the music slowed down, they danced faster. Their eyes never made contact with mine even though they were looking straight at me the whole time.

For a while I thought they were trying to hypnotize me, that they were just waiting for me to fall into a deep sleep and then they would steal my money or worse, but I didn't feel at all tired or entranced. I tried really hard to sit still and just watch, relax, get into the music, but my stomach and neck muscles were too tense. Then I thought I should join their dance, but that would have been too weird.

When they finally stopped, sweat was running down their faces and they were breathing heavily. Obviously the dance required incredible physical effort despite the slowness. Perhaps dancing so slowly, holding back, made it more difficult. They sat down on the sofa in front of me and grinned. Pilar wiped the sweat from Manolo's brow with a handkerchief.

"That was a very beautiful dance," I said.

"It was not meant to be beautiful," Manolo said, his voice filled with sadness.

It seemed especially quiet in the room after the dance was over and the music had stopped, but no one said a word and, after about five minutes, Pilar got up and put the television on. It was some kind of game show. The contestants were blindfolded and had to figure out what certain food items like octopus and melon and fish and strawberries were just by touching them. Pilar and Manolo thought it was really funny and I watched along with them for about fifteen minutes to be polite, and then I thanked them for the *flan* and the dance and told them I had to get home. I was surprised to find both my parents at home. They were sitting together on the couch having a predinner glass of wine while they were waiting for the trout to bake—my father was cooking trout with fresh figs and apple. Perhaps it was because I had not expected to find my mother at home, and I was even more surprised to find a special dinner cooking and wine being drunk, but I certainly had no idea I was going to sit down in the chair across from them, look my mother straight in the eye, and ask my mother if she had fucked Marisol.

Maybe it was because my mother smiled at me in what seemed to me a patronizing way, like she knew everything about me, and my father was making his wine glass sing, licking his finger, passing it slowly around the rim of the glass, so I felt as if I were in some kind of sick play, like they had just murdered a small child and shoved her under the Thai couch and were trying to act very calm and wise and happy.

My father kept running his finger around the rim of the glass, but there was no moisture left, so it didn't make a sound. My mother looked at me and chuckled. "Don't be absurd, Deborah," she said very calmly.

"Well, I did. I fucked her and she fucked me," I said.

"That's enough," my father said. "That's enough," he said again as he walked to the kitchen to check on the trout. Neither my mother nor I moved from our seats or said a word until my father brought in the food and said, "Mesdames sont servies." Then we all moved silently to the dining room table. We ate as fast as we could, as if we hadn't eaten in days, and my mother and I kept saying that this was the best trout we had ever eaten. My mother's hand trembled ever so slightly as she pushed the fish away from the bone, but it was hardly noticeable. She was sitting up really straight and she brought her fork the distance from the plate to her mouth without bending at all. And then I knew that nothing had happened between them because she wouldn't have been able to lie about something like that. I wondered whether she was trembling because she had wanted something to happen and it hadn't, or because she believed me, knew that I wasn't lying about me and Marisol, or because the thought of all of it, of her with Marisol, of me with Marisol, made her want to vomit. I don't think it did, though, because if she had felt like retching, she wouldn't have been able to sit there so tall, eating one bite of fish after another until all that was left on her plate was a fish skeleton.

And that's what happened. After dinner, I went back to my room and fell asleep, and in the morning my mother was on the couch, and in the afternoon she was still there, and in the evening too, and after a few days she started to smell, and no matter what my father cooked you could always smell her underneath everything. My father kept his usual watch, leaving her side only for necessities the first few days, then slowly, when he knew it made no difference whether he stayed or didn't, he went back to the library for a few hours each afternoon. At least that's where he said he went. I certainly didn't have the energy to follow him around.

She wore the same clothes until my father changed her right there on the couch like they do in hospitals. I wonder if she gets bedsores. Maybe that's part of the smell—erupting bedsores. He handed me the pile of dirty clothes and told me to wash them, which I did, using almost half a bottle of Woolite so it took hundreds of rinses to get the soap out. Still, they smelled funny when they were dry, like wet dog, so I washed them again, but they still smelled. I don't think my father notices the smell, or maybe he loves it like he loves everything about my mother, maybe it's like loving someone who is really ugly, but the ugliness becomes beauty when you're in love. I wonder if that really happens or if it's just another one of those things people say, that people try to convince themselves of but feel guilty about if they can't really pull it off.

My mother's eyes bloated to the size of oranges, like tumors—her eyes were like infected tumors, yellow and red like Marisol's paintings. In fact, I should have invited Marisol up to paint a portrait of my mother. She could have focused on her arms, which lay by her sides so limp and weak it seemed as if one little pull would have detached them from my mother's body, as if they were sewn on to her with dried-out rubber bands. I would have painted her with one arm swinging from its socket, just about to pull loose.

I tried to apologize, but my apology only made things worse. My mother's sobs grew louder and louder the more I spoke, and she covered her eyes as I tried to approach the bed. Once, I stood in the doorway watching her and I could tell she knew I was there, but she wouldn't look at me. So I apologized to my father for swearing, and I got a very cursory and distracted acceptance. My parents believe foul language is used only by people with too small a vocabulary and imagination to use real words. That was only the second time in my life I had used such language in front of them. The first time was when I was thirteen. I had been invited to a bat mitzvah and my mother had bought this ugly plastic purse for me to give the girl for her bat mitzvah present. "It looks like a piece of shit," I had said and my mother had looked at me as if she had just seen me slit the throat of an innocent kitten. For days afterwards I couldn't look her in the eye, and I gave the girl the ugly purse without any further protests.

This time, though, I didn't feel bad about using such harsh words because they were the most appropriate words to describe what had happened. In fact, there are times when it would exhibit a lack of imagination not to use such expressions. I guess I expected them to help me in some way. Maybe I expected my mother to march over to Marisol's studio and slash all her paintings, tell her she was a jerk, which she was, but not because of what happened. We were both jerks. They could have said something. They could have said that, according to the Old Testament, what I did was wrong, but, of course, none of us believe that. And I had wanted to ask my mother so many things, about what she had felt standing for hours while Marisol looked deep inside of her.

I saw the paintings. At first Marisol didn't want me to see them, and I thought it was because they would reveal something she didn't want me to see, but now I think it was because she didn't want to be alone with me again, because it had been just as weird for her as it had for me, even though she had seemed so calm, surrounding us in all that silence. There were two very large canvases, maybe eight feet high by five feet wide, which took up a whole wall from floor to ceiling. She told me that instead of working on the floor like most painters do when they are working on large canvases, she nailed the canvas to the ceiling and painted from a ladder. "Like Michaelangelo painting the Sistine Chapel," she said. I tried to imagine her high up on her ladder, the blood rushing to her head and my mother below, standing very still. Had Marisol had her holding a decapitated head like in the painting? It was Judith and Holofernes. I recognized them right away, only Holofernes looked like a Latin pop singer—handsome in a dark and boring way. The head wasn't bloody at all. It was as if Judith had just finished a laser surgery and was holding up her work for all to see, only the setting for the scene was an old-fashioned milliner's shop, not an operating room. In the background were shelves lined with women's hats and those old, round hatboxes you see in movies. There were red velvet hats with black veils and black flowers, yellowish Easter bonnets, and pillbox hats in all the possible shades of brown, yellow, and red. Judith, my mother, wearing a doctor's smock with a surgical mask dangling around her neck, was holding up Holofernes's head as if she were showing it to a customer.

The other canvas depicted my mother, bare-breasted. (They had told me my mother had modeled clothed. I should have asked Marisol whether she had used her imagination to paint my mother's bare breasts or whether that had been a lie.) My mother was sitting up in a big four-poster bed, reading a book; the rest of her was covered by a white sheet. The room was filled with birds, crows mainly and some vultures and yellow and blue canaries. They were perched on all four bedposts and on the headboard and the chandelier that hung directly over her head, and they were all over the floor and on the sheet about where my mother's stomach would have been. My mother, the reading woman, didn't seem to notice the birds at all, but she also didn't appear to be engrossed in her book. Her eyes were somewhere else, neither in the room nor in the story contained in the book. It was as if Marisol had seen my mother's decline coming on, seen it in her eyes and in the flesh around her nipples.

I liked the paintings. I didn't want to like them, but they were the kind of paintings you could look at for hours and keep seeing something new. Marisol told me she had a solo show opening in Amsterdam in the fall and she wished my mother would model some more because you can't make a show out of two paintings; she had wanted to get at least eight large canvases out of my mother.

"Why doesn't she want to do it anymore?" I asked innocently.

"She says she's bored, but . . . just look at that." She pointed to my mother holding up Holofernes's head. "Does that look like a bored woman?"

I had to agree. She was anything but bored. *Triumphant* is the word that comes to mind.

And then I almost told her that my mother had sunk into one of her depressions, that she was extremely ill. But I stopped myself. "She's weird," I said. "Sometimes she walks out of concerts in the middle of a piece. She just gets up and slides out of the row and runs out of the hall. She says sometimes it's too much for her."

"Then perhaps I should be honored," Marisol said.

"Perhaps," I said. There was no need to have a long discussion about it. If she wanted to feel honored, let her; let her think that her paintings were just so deep that my mother couldn't stand being inside of them.

"Tell her I would be forever indebted to her if she would come back."

"I'll tell her," I said, but of course I didn't. If she really needed my mother so much, she would have called her up, told her herself.

"How about going out for a drink?" she asked.

"I've decided to stop drinking for a while," I said because I didn't feel like having a drink with her.

"How American of you," she said. I just let it go because I didn't want to get into an argument about something I had just made up anyway.

I wanted to know if Marisol had come onto my mother, although that term didn't seem quite right. *Propositioned* might be more appropriate, but that too didn't really fit. There was no point in asking, though, because she would not have told me the truth. I wonder if Marisol misses my mother. Maybe she doesn't even think about her at all. I wonder if she is standing right now in her cold apartment, gazing out at a brilliant winter sun, thinking she missed her chance, that my mother missed her chance. They could have been happy—the artist and the model. In the morning that same cold sunlight would warm their naked bodies. Nights they would spend in cozy corners of warm bars drinking red wine, eating thick rings of squid, planning a trip to Bucharest for Marisol's next opening. But my vision is different; it is of my mother, naked, lying on a mattress in the corner of Marisol's bare room, her skin yellowish from a sickly winter sun, her smell seeping into the unfinished canvases that hang upside down from the ceiling like sides of beef. And Marisol? Where is she in my vision? I'm not sure, but she is not sitting next to my mother, holding her hand, whispering about how if she would only get up and go outside, she would see what a beautiful, crisp day it was.

It wasn't easy walking out of Marisol's apartment, not having a drink with her, not touching her, not letting her touch me. We didn't even exchange the usual friendly Spanish cheek kisses. We waved at each other in the doorway, and then I turned around and fled. It was fleeing. There is no other way to describe it—my heart was beating fast, like I had narrowly escaped being hit by a car.

When we first got back from Spain, I used to have dreams in which I found myself throwing things at her—usually living things like plants or mice. Once it was chickens—raw chickens with their heads chopped off. She laughed when I threw the chickens at her, and I woke up crying.

In one dream my mother and I were throwing rocks at Marisol as if she were Mary Magdalene. There were other people throwing rocks too, but I didn't recognize them. In a way, I wish I hadn't gone to see the paintings because now when I think of my mother, I picture her holding up that head like a hat or lying on the bed with all those crows around her. It's like after you've seen the video for a song and then every time you hear the song those video images run through your brain and you can't make up your own images for the music no matter how hard you try. If I could paint, I would try a simple portrait of my mother standing in the Magic Carpet, surrounded by rugs in deep red.

We left Madrid as if we didn't know anyone there at all, as if we had just been tourists on a brief vacation. It was very early in the morning, still dark, when the taxi called for us. My father got my mother all cleaned up—dressed her in her travel slacks, washed and pinned up her hair so it wouldn't be in her face. It made her eyes look really old. On the plane I kept thinking that everyone could smell her, but it was probably just my imagination. Still, I kept looking around to see if people were holding their hands over their noses. No one was, but I kept looking anyway, sure that as soon as I turned around, they pulled their hands away.

Have my mother and Marisol exchanged letters? Perhaps they have called each other. Did Marisol manage to pull off some more pieces for the Amsterdam show? Maybe she sent my mother the reviews—"stark images of feminine rage." What if I sent Marisol a notebook full of sketches: *My Mother Lying in Bed I, My Mother Lying in Bed II, My Mother Lying in Bed III* . . .

THE TYPEWRITER IS SILENT

Walking up the stairs to her apartment, Mrs. Mondschein realizes just how tired she is after staying up all night. She walks slowly, stopping at each landing to catch her breath. An adolescent boy with huge feet bounds past her, taking the steps three at a time. "Be careful," she wants to call after him, but doesn't have the energy for it. As she unlocks the three locks on her apartment door, starting from the top and working her way down, her mind settles on a nice hot cup of coffee and oatmeal. Yes, oatmeal. It would be good for her stomach. She would sit at her little kitchen table and drink coffee and eat oatmeal, and then she would take a long, hot bath, and then she would sleep. More than anything she wanted to sleep.

From the bathroom, Deborah hears her grandmother unlocking the door, then taking off her winter gear and hanging it on the rack. She imagines her sitting on the little bench in the entryway removing her street shoes, setting them neatly underneath the bench, and slipping on her house shoes. Down the long hallway she comes. Deborah hears each slow step. She dries her face and hangs the towel, which smells of Ivory soap and old magazines, back on its proper hook. Should she come out to greet her? Now Deborah hears her in the kitchen, running water, opening the refrigerator. A bag rustles, a pot clanks. Deborah tiptoes towards the kitchen, trying not to make the floorboards creak, but the more softly she treads, the more they creak. Now she is in the kitchen doorway peeking in at her grandmother, who is still oblivious to her presence. She watches Mrs. Mondschein pour boiling water from a kettle into her old percolator. *How long can I stand here before she notices?* she thinks, wondering if it wouldn't be better to slip out of the apartment now, walk back up to the bus terminal, get on the 14K.

"Hi," Deborah says.

Mrs. Mondschein turns to the doorway. "Deborah," she says. There is very little surprise in her voice.

"I came in through the kitchen window from Mr. Claromundo's apartment. I waited for a long time, but you didn't come home."

"How long have you been here?"

"Almost twenty-four hours. I thought something terrible had happened to you."

"I was with a friend. He was very sick, but now he's much better. I haven't slept all night. It's been years since I've been up all night."

"You should rest then," Deborah says.

"Yes, I'll just have a little bite to eat first. I was going to take a bath, but I think I'll wait. Come, have some coffee. Do you like oatmeal? It will settle your stomach. But your stomach is probably not unsettled."

"I like oatmeal."

"Good." They sit down and have some oatmeal.

Mrs. Mondschein eats her breakfast very slowly, giving her stomach a chance to receive each mouthful. *I don't want my bowels exploding*, she thinks.

Deborah eats slowly too; there is something hypnotizing about her grandmother's movements that makes her try to lift the spoon at the same time, raise it to her mouth, chew, swallow at the same time. When they are finished, Deborah says she will clean up and Mrs. Mondschein hesitates for a moment. "I'll take . . . Thank you, Deborah. I'll excuse myself then."

And then Deborah hears her grandmother close the door to her bedroom. There is just a slight rustling after that—the newspaper being folded properly, the shades being lowered, and then it is quiet. All Deborah can hear is the eternally thumping bass through the floorboards, and she sits at the kitchen table for a while, listening for a change in the rhythm, but it doesn't change, so she washes the dishes, has another cup of coffee, and decides to go to the museum, the Metropolitan Museum, not the Museum of the American Indian, which is far too close. Her grandmother needs at least eight hours of rest—a woman of her age needs her sleep even though Deborah read somewhere that old people have a hard time sleeping. It must be terrible, she thinks, having all that time on your hands, sitting in a chair all day long, just waiting for bedtime and then not being able to sleep. But her grandmother is different. Mrs. Mondschein has never been the type to sit around in a chair, nodding off in front of the television. She is the type of old person who will sit up all night with a very ill friend.

But Mrs. Mondschein is unable to sleep. She wants more than anything else to sleep, but all she can think about is how small Tommy's father's hands are. They seemed familiar somehow and she wonders if maybe he bought a token from her years and years ago. She feels like going right back down to the hospice, asking Tommy's father if he used to take the subway at 110th Street fifty years ago.

"I recognize your hands," she could say to him as he stands in front of his dead son, crying so softly, and he would look at her in his small way, and his wife would ask them what they are talking about and they would answer that they are talking about buying subway tokens at the 110th Street station fifty years ago. They wouldn't say they are discussing his hands.

"Oh," she would say.

Now she wishes Deborah had not gone out. She heard the front door open and close and lay in the bed thinking that now that she was alone, she would be able to sleep, but apparently Deborah's presence wasn't the problem. Mrs. Mondschein rereads the Op-Ed Page of the *New York Times* she bought a few days ago but can't concentrate. "I don't even know what's going on in the world," she says out loud and laughs. Yet realistically, how much could happen in a few days? A lot. A lot could happen in a few days, but if something important had transpired, she would know about it—one of the nurses would have said something.

Normally when Mrs. Mondschein feels like this, she goes to a matinee. She has been lucky so far and does not suffer from insomnia. The nights have been kind to her; it has been the days that, on occasion, have proved insufferable. Yet today, she is tired. "Dead tired," she says aloud. The thought of descending the stairs, walking to the subway station, waiting for a train, sitting up in a dark movie theater that smells of old lady perfume makes her so incredibly tired that she should be able to fall asleep, but it is not a sleeping kind of tired she is experiencing. She feels like a patient suffering from a concussion who is being kept awake to avoid the risk of slipping into a coma. Karl had such a patient once, a young girl who had fallen off a seesaw right onto her head. He had instructed the mother to stay up with her all night, to walk around and around their tiny apartment, to sing, to play games—paddy whack, Monopoly—but under no circumstances to let her daughter fall asleep. But the mother was so tired; she worked six days a week as a maid. She had varicose veins. She fell asleep and the little girl fell asleep in her arms, and when the mother woke up with a jolt—it had only been fifteen minutes—the girl was unwakeable. "I was so tired," the mother repeated over and over and over again. Mrs. Mondschein wonders whatever happened to that little girl. She could be alive today, out on her lunch break eating a sandwich at a counter somewhere in Midtown, or she could be alive today, still lying in the hospital, her breath even and steady. Or she could be dead. If Karl were alive, he would be sitting at the table reading—he always preferred to read at the table—and she could ask him, "Whatever happened to that little girl who fell off the seesaw and whose mother let her fall asleep?" But if she doesn't know, he wouldn't know either. They had lost track of the case—the hospital had taken over. That is what had happened. Still, she likes to think that Karl had gone to visit the girl, that he had gone every week and then every month, and then whenever he got a chance, just to see how she was. But he would have told her. They would have gone together to visit the little girl. Why hadn't they ever gone to visit her?

After a while Mrs. Mondschein stops thinking about the girl with the concussion. She tries listening to music but isn't able to blank out her mind in the usual fashion. Mozart makes her think of Tommy as does Bach and even Mendelssohn, although they had never listened to Mendelssohn together. He isn't one of her favorites; there is something insignificant about Mendelssohn. She tries some stretching exercises she learned from the Health section of the *New York Times* about a year ago. For a while she was very disciplined about her stretching exercises, but in the last weeks she has forgotten all about them. Maybe they will tire her out, she thinks. Then she will be able to sleep. But after doing ten bends to the right and ten to the left, she is restless, bored. She laughs. I am not the type to feel boredom. Perhaps I am finally getting old.

Somehow the light has shifted in the apartment—shifted to semi-obscurity. She would not be able to read in this light, but she doesn't feel like reading, so the lights are left off. Maybe she will doze. Maybe Deborah will return soon and they will fix a bite to eat.

Deborah has decided to take the bus back uptown. After a long day on her feet at the museum, shuffling slowly from one wing to another, the prospect of walking all the way uptown is tremendous, even for the die-hard walker she is. She has decided on the bus despite its excruciating slowness. She tries not to watch the blocks as they ooze by. You could declaim an entire medium-length Emily Dickinson poem in the time it takes the bus to lurch away from the curb, gather speed, and make it to the next corner just as the light is turning red. She does that, recites the three medium-length Emily Dickinson poems she knows by heart— "Because I could not stop for Death," "Success is counted sweetest," and "I heard a fly buzz when I died."

Finally, the bus creeps to the curbside at 148th Street. There is no light on in her grandmother's window, but Deborah cannot think of any- place else to go. She climbs the stairs slowly as if that short time would give her grandmother a chance to wake up, splash some water on her face. Loud music and laughter are coming from Mr. Claromundo's apart- ment and, just as she is turning the key in the last lock, Mr. Claromundo's door opens.

"Deborah!" he shouts effusively. "Come in, I'm having a party!"

"Thank you, but my grandmother is expecting me."

"So she came back?" he asks laughing.

Deborah wants to ask him what is so funny about her grandmother's return, but she simply answers, "Yes."

"Well, I'm glad to hear it. Come over if you get bored. Your granny goes to sleep early." He winks.

"Maybe some other time," Deborah finds herself saying.

"Is that you, Deborah?" Mrs. Mondschein calls out of the darkness at the end of the hallway.

"It's me."

"Come sit down," Mrs. Mondschein tells her granddaughter.

"Should I turn on the light?"

"Please. I didn't feel like getting up, but there's no reason to sit in the dark, is there?"

"I guess not."

"In the morning we will have to make a trip to New Jersey," Mrs. Mondschein announces as Deborah sits down after turning on the light.

"I was hoping you would let me stay with you for a while," Deborah says. "I won't be any trouble."

"I wouldn't expect you to be any trouble."

"Then I can stay?"

"We must see your mother first. Are things very bad?"

"You can't help her, you know."

"Yes, but it's been a long time since I've seen her. It's time I paid a visit."

"Why do I have to go?"

"Because we must all discuss things properly. If you are going to stay with me, we must discuss everything properly. All of us."

"She won't be up for discussions. She'll just lie there in her stupid bed. You'll be lucky if she turns to look at you."

"We can talk to your father then," Mrs. Mondschein insists.

"He won't care."

"Deborah, we must make an effort."

"Well, I guess I have to get my cello."

So it is decided; they will go to New Jersey in the morning. They stay up a little longer, chatting about music.

"I have always wondered what it is like to experience the world with a musician's mind. When you listen to music, are you aware of the names of all the notes and chords? Do you see D sharps and B flats in your mind's eye?"

Deborah pauses to think about it because no one has ever asked her such a question before. "I do in a way. It's like seeing colors. You always recognize blue when you see it or red and colors made with blue like purple and green and you notice dark and light colors, soft and harsh colors, but you don't say to yourself every time you see something blue, 'Oh, that's blue.' It just is blue and your mind registers it. That's what I do with music."

"It must be wonderful," Mrs. Mondschein says.

The next morning is gray and bone-chillingly cold. From the window, they watch people on their way to work—huddled into their coats, scarves around their mouths to protect them from the wind whipping off the Hudson River.

"It's too cold for snow," Mrs. Mondschein says.

"Maybe we should wait until tomorrow," Deborah says.

"Tomorrow it might snow, and then we would have to spend the night in New Jersey. I don't think I'm up for that. Snow in New Jersey is too clean."

Mrs. Mondschein and her granddaughter sit in the fifth row on the left so they can see the New York skyline from the bridge. They have not removed their coats even though the bus is heated. Overheated. Mrs. Mondschein is sitting next to the window. Her granddaughter is in the aisle seat. They both crane their necks, trying to pick out Riverside Church from the general grayness.

"Your grandfather and I used to go to concerts at Riverside Church," Mrs. Mondschein says. "But you can't see it today."

"If it warms up a little, it is going to snow," Deborah says.

"We can't turn back now," Mrs. Mondschein says, and Deborah doesn't disagree even though it would be so easy to get off in Fort Lee, take the overpass across the highway, and wait for the next bus back to New York. They wouldn't have to wait for more than five minutes.

The bus pulls away and they stand directly across from the house, waiting to cross the street. There are no lights on in the house, but it is still morning—ten o'clock—so there is no reason for lights to be on. They have crossed the street and are walking slowly, somewhat reluctantly yet with determination, up the driveway, up the three little flagstone steps. Deborah puts her ear to the door.

"Do you hear anything?" Mrs. Mondschein asks.

"No, the typing has stopped."

"What typing?"

"My father was typing when I left. Should we ring the bell, or should I unlock the door?"

"What do you think?"

"Let's ring first."

"Yes, let's ring first," Mrs. Mondschein says and pushes the doorbell hard as if it were difficult to press. Deborah puts her ear to the door, but hears no steps. They wait a while, and this time Deborah presses the bell. Still no answer, so Deborah unlocks the door after all.

"Hello," Deborah calls. No answer.

"Hello," Mrs. Mondschein calls. No answer.

In their coats they walk around the downstairs, quietly, as if they were expecting to come upon a secret. They walk up the stairs slowly.

The door to the bedroom is open. A shaft of sunlight slices the wooden floor by the bed. They are sleeping, her father's face nestled in the nape of her mother's neck, his arm wrapped around his wife's middle. At first Deborah thinks they might be dead, but it is only a thought. The smell is still there, as strong as ever, and Deborah covers her nose with her hand. *Strange*, she thinks, *that they left the door open.* She thinks maybe it is because they are waiting for her to come home. But then she thinks that maybe they only keep the door closed when she is home, that maybe whenever she is gone, they fling everything open. Maybe they dance.

Mrs. Mondschein is having her own thoughts, wondering whether Clara would laugh if she woke up now and saw the two of them standing there in their winter coats, watching. Would she think it was a dream? Perhaps later, when they were sitting in the living room drinking coffee, Clara would say, "I dreamt you were standing in the bedroom doorway wearing your winter coat, watching me."

"They must be very tired," Mrs. Mondschein whispers.

"Yes," Deborah says even though she can't imagine what they would be tired about. "I guess we should let them sleep then."

"Yes, we can have some tea."

They descend the stairs, remove their coats, hang them up in the closet.

"Should I turn the heat up?" Deborah asks.

"That would be nice," Mrs. Mondschein says.

They sit at the dining room table drinking tea without speaking.

"Should I get my cello?" Deborah asks. "It might be hours before they wake up."

"Do they often sleep so late?"

"My mother hasn't left her bed in days."

"There's a difference between sleeping and lying in bed," Mrs. Mondschein says. "My father wouldn't leave his bed the last year of his life, but I don't think he slept for even one hour during that final time. I think sleeping is a good sign."

"Your father? I thought he died in Auschwitz."

"That was my sisters, my two sisters. My father died just before the *Anschluss*. Did your mother tell you he died in Auschwitz?"

"She said everyone died in Auschwitz. She never mentioned anyone in particular. All she says is that everyone except you and my grandfather died in Auschwitz."

"I never told your mother anything about my father's death, but for years we ran a classified ad in the *Aufbau* looking for my sisters. Your mother must remember the ads. She must have always wondered why we didn't mention my father. Maybe she never really thought about it. Sometimes I told your mother about my sisters, as a lesson of sorts. I didn't want her to be like them. When your mother was a child, she always preferred staying in the apartment. She never was one for walks in the park or hopscotch. I used to worry she would turn out like my sisters."

"What was wrong with them?"

"Nothing. They were neither happy nor sad. They liked to cook and eat and avoided the outdoors."

"And your father?"

"He was a bookkeeper, and one day he fell ill. *Melancholia* was your grandfather's diagnosis. That's how I met your grandfather. He was the doctor who diagnosed my father's illness."

"And he died of it? How can you die from it?"

"I don't know, but there was nothing else wrong with him."

"*Melancholia*. It sounds like a piece of music, like a slow movement."

"I don't even have a photo of my father," Mrs. Mondschein says. "I have one of my sisters. Remind me and I'll show it to you, but my father always refused to have his photo taken. He was extremely Orthodox. One day, not too long before the *Anschluss*, Karl and I took my sisters to the *Prater*, and we had our pictures taken, all four of us together. My sisters aren't smiling in the photo because they were worried about leaving my father alone."

"What did your father look like?"

"He was small and thin and balding, but I can't really picture him. I probably wouldn't be able to picture my sisters either without that photo. His fingers were blue from ink and he wore glasses. He looked much older than he was."

"Like my father?"

"No, much, much older-looking than Simon."

"Do you think my mother will die from *melancholia* too?" Deborah asks, thinking about what it would be like to find her mother dead, lying in the same position, but dead.

"No."

"How do you know?"

"I just know. Come," she says, "let's see if they're awake."

"Don't you think we should let them rest just a little more?" Deborah asks.

"No. They've slept enough."

Together they mount the stairs, taking each step very slowly, very deliberately. At the top of the stairs they listen for voices coming from the bedroom. There are no voices, no sounds at all, so they proceed to the doorway. They pause and watch for a while, waiting for some movement, hoping perhaps that Simon and Clara will sense someone watching them and wake up on their own. In the end, Deborah has to knock on the door.

"Come in," Simon whispers, so they do.

ACKNOWLEDGMENTS

I would like to thank the following people who, in one way or another, led to the creation and completion of this novel:

Marc and Lillian Raeff, my parents, for being my first guides through literature and history;

Josephine and Irving Gottesman, my maternal grandparents, for their stories;

Victoria Raeff, my paternal grandmother, for her support of me and my writing and for her one hundred years of strength;

Catherine Raeff, my sister, for her companionship and for being my first reader;

Lori Ostlund, my partner, for her encouragement and her (at times brutal) honesty, and without whose support this book would never have been possible;

Anika Streitfeld, my editor, for her enthusiasm and intelligent scrutiny of my manuscript.